D1268338

OPERATION MEDUSA

BOOK SIX

OF THE CASTLE FEDERATION SERIES

OPERATION MEDUSA

BOOK SIX
OF THE CASTLE FEDERATION SERIES

GLYNN STEWART

Operation Medusa © 2017 Glynn Stewart

All rights reserved. For information about permission to reproduce selections from this book, contact the publisher at info@faolanspen.com or Faolan's Pen Publishing Inc., 22 King St. S, Suite 300, Waterloo, Ontario N2J 1N8, Canada.

This is a work of fiction. All the characters and events portrayed in this book are fictional, and any resemblance to any persons living or dead is purely coincidental.

This edition published in 2018 by:

Faolan's Pen Publishing Inc.

22 King St. S, Suite 300

Waterloo, Ontario

N2J 1N8 Canada

ISBN-13: 978-1-988035-54-3 (print)

A record of this book is available from Library and Archives Canada.

Printed in the United States of America

1 2 3 4 5 6 7 8 9 10

First edition

First printing: December 2017

Illustration © 2017 Tom Edwards

TomEdwardsDesign.com

Read more books from Glynn Stewart at faolanspen.com

1

Midori System
06:00 August 1, 2737 Earth Standard Meridian Date/Time
DSC-062 *Normandy*

"ALERT, alert, all hands to battle stations, all hands to battle stations. System Command has identified multiple Alcubierre emergences.

"All hands to battle stations!"

Vice Commodore Russell Rokos spared approximately three-quarters of a second to look despairingly at the freshly warmed-up homemade scone sitting on his desk, a gift from his currently almost fifty-light-years-away wife.

Getting homemade baked treats to one of Castle Federation's carriers deployed on the front took a minor miracle and a *lot* of determination, but his wife had somehow made it happen. Being a senior police officer on the capital planet probably helped, but it wasn't *easy*.

So, of course, the Terran Commonwealth would choose this particular moment to attack, forcing him to waste a full quarter of her gift.

The broad-shouldered starfighter officer, however, was a professional and ran through that entire thought process in moments. Then he tore a chunk of the scone off and stuffed it in his mouth as he rose and began to run toward *Normandy*'s flight deck.

The one hundred and ninety-two starfighters aboard were his responsibility now. The almost six hundred crew who flew those ships were far more important than his ruined snack.

As he ran, he linked his neural implant up to the carrier's main tactical feed, downloading the update that Midori System command was feeding the ships of Task Force Midori.

He swallowed his piece of scone in horror.

Midori had been the scene of no less than four battles so far in the seesawing war between the Castle Federation and her allies and the Terran Commonwealth. Most of those battles had been relatively even, with attempts by the Terran commander, Marshal James Calvin Walkingstick, to force the Alliance to defend the refueling infrastructure in Midori and allow him to destroy ships.

Ships the Commonwealth could replace far more easily than the Alliance could. Over twenty Alcubierre-drive starships, an entire star system's GDP's worth of warships, had died defending this system, a slow grind that weakened the Alliance more than Walkingstick's fleet.

This was *not* that kind of attack.

"CAG," the mental voice of Captain Karl Herrera cut into Russell's thoughts. "Are you ready to launch?"

"Twenty seconds from flight deck," he responded crisply. "Two squadrons of Alpha Flight Group are already out as the CSP; two more are in the tubes with crews aboard.

"None of the bombers are up and everything is going to take at least three minutes to man," he reeled off. "Standard launch cycle; we'll be live and in space in five minutes, no more."

"Even the bombers?" Herrera asked.

One of Russell's four forty-eight-ship wings had been swapped from starfighters to bombers barely two months before. The Vulture-type ships and their new torpedoes were a boost to his fighter group's capability, but few of his compatriots trusted them yet.

"Even the bombers," Russell confirmed. "We'll be ready."

He felt Herrera shake his head over the mental channel.

"It won't be enough," the Captain told him, the channel through their neural implants utterly secure and with no chance of eavesdroppers. "I can fight this battle in my head. I just don't see a way out."

Russell said nothing.

Task Force Midori had eight ships from three of the Alliance's major powers, a force that made the "Task Force" designation a severe underestimation.

The Terran fleet was being led by eight battleships—and another ten carriers and cruisers came behind them.

Midori was doomed.

THEY HAD TIME. Not a lot of it, but time. The massive Terran fleet was only accelerating in from the outer system at two hundred gravities, which gave the Alliance fleet several hours to put together their response.

Like the rest of the starfighter CAGs, Russell's place in that conversation was aboard his starfighter. The speed and power of the neural implants all of the Alliance military personnel were equipped with meant that he might as well have been in a room with the starship Captains and flag officers, though.

"They brought their A game," Vice Admiral the Elector Parth Rothenberg noted to his subordinates. The dark-skinned man was an Elector of the Coraline Imperium, part of their pseudo-military aristocracy, and the man in command of Task Force Midori.

"All eight battleships are *Saint*-class," he continued. "That's more *Saint*s than we thought Walkingstick had left after his losses—it's easily half of the Commonwealth's surviving strength of the class until their next wave of new construction finishes.

"The rest is no better. Four *Hercules*-class battlecruisers of the same vintage, four *Volcano*-class carriers and two *Lexington*s."

Everything except the *Lexington*s were relatively new units, built in the last ten years and easily the equal of a *Victory*-class carrier like *Normandy*.

"We're out-numbered two to one. The cubage disadvantage is

about as severe: we have *Summerlands* and *Genghis Khan,* but most of our ships are smaller."

The two ships he had named were the heavyweights of the Task Force, modern, top-of-the-line Castle Federation warships bigger than anything the Commonwealth had yet built. Alongside *Normandy,* the Federation had sent three ships to Midori.

Not to be outdone, the Coraline Imperium had also sent three: one modern carrier, *Righteous Fire,* and two *Rameses*-class battlecruisers.

A single modern battlecruiser from the Star Kingdom of Phoenix and a Renaissance Trade Factor–built carrier belonging to the Midori Self-Defense Force made up the rest of Rothenberg's fleet.

"They haven't summoned us to surrender. They know we won't," Rothenberg concluded dryly. "We have no choice but to assume they have bombers as well, so our Vultures won't be a surprise."

"What about the fixed defenses?" Colonel Jenaveve LaCroix, the CAG aboard the Phoenix warship *Dauntless,* asked. "The MSDF has another thousand fighters to back up our strength."

"And I intend to use them," Rothenberg replied, his virtual avatar glancing at the still-silent form of Admiral Paris Kennedy, the woman in charge of the MSDF. This was her system, after all, even if Rothenberg commanded the Alliance Task Force. "But they aren't enough to turn the tide against *eight battleships.*"

Kennedy finally stirred.

"No, they're not," she concluded. "Admiral, do you honestly expect to be able to save Midori?"

The mental conference was silent for several long seconds.

"No." The words were tombstones. "But I see no other option but to take a leaf from the Fox's book—a head-on assault with everything we have. Target the battleships; the Commonwealth commander is almost certainly aboard one of them."

Russell kept his laugh out of the channel. The Stellar Fox, his old Captain, had once taken a single carrier against a Commonwealth battle group. Of course, he'd emerged from FTL *inside* the battle group's formation, accidentally rammed a battleship, and *lost* his carrier in the end...but he'd won.

"But regardless of whether the Terran admiral dies in your strike, they will complete their mission plan," Kennedy said softly. "This Task Force will be destroyed. Midori will fall."

No one had the courage to confirm what she'd said.

"That's what I thought," she continued. "Ladies, gentlemen, officers. Under Section Seven of the Alliance Treaty of Mutual Defense, I am assuming command of all forces in this system."

As the ranking officer of the local government, she had that authority, though the Midorians had generally been willing to let Alliance officers lead the defense.

"I have only one order," Kennedy continued into the silence. "You will withdraw. *Midori's Hope* will withdraw with you; I will have the President transferred aboard immediately."

Kennedy herself was aboard a station in orbit. For some reason, Russell didn't expect her to be leaving aboard the carrier she was sending away.

"Ma'am, I served with the Fox," he found himself objecting. "We all know what he said when he went to Tranquility in a shattered carrier: there may yet come a day when the Federation must break its word to its allies from necessity. Today is *not* that day!"

The woman who spoke for Midori chuckled sadly and shook her head.

"No, it is not," she agreed. "I am *ordering* you to withdraw, Vice Commodore Rokos. We cannot win this battle—and your warships will better serve my world defeating the Commonwealth tomorrow than dying pointlessly today!"

There was a long silence. It probably wasn't more than ten seconds, but given the speed a neural implant conference usually moved at, it may as well have lasted an hour.

Then Admiral Rothenberg bowed his aristocratic head in agreement.

"You have that authority," he told her. "We will acquiesce." He smiled grimly. "I will *not,* however, withdraw from this system without bleeding the Commonwealth first. Request permission to launch a long-range bomber strike?

"We won't need the MSDF fighters for that," he continued. "Between my *Righteous Fire* and the Federation carriers, we have three wings of Vultures. One hundred and thirty-six bombers."

Kennedy nodded once.

"I will have no vain hopes launched on our account," she told the assembled officers. "No grand sacrifices. Bleed the Terrans, yes. But not yourselves. I insist."

"This will be our first major battle where both sides have bombers," Commodore Viktors Ozolinsh, the senior Federation CAG, noted. "They'll know what our attack pattern means if we keep the range open."

"Let them," Rothenberg said grimly. "They'll send their fighters out to intercept and we'll lose people—but less than if we go head-on and throw the entire fighter strike into the teeth of their formation.

"One million kilometers, CAGs," he ordered. "You won't be in range of your starfighter missiles, so use them to defend the bombers.

"And let me be clear," Rothenberg concluded. "Any pilot who closes within a million kilometers of the Terrans and isn't blown to pieces by them will be busted back to ground crew. Am I clear?"

"Yes, sir," Russell chorused with the rest of the pilots. Orders like that were why, if Rothenberg had given the command, every starfighter in his command would have gone straight down the Commonwealth fleet's throat.

"We will deploy our starfighters as well," Kennedy informed them. "They will close for a standard strike before rendezvousing with your fleet."

"We will take as many of them with us as we can fit aboard," the Imperial Admiral promised.

Russell shivered. The Midori Self-Defense Force flew an upgraded version of the Federation's last-generation Cobra starfighter. The Alliance ships could easily take on the three thousand or so crew aboard those ships, but stacking another thousand starfighters on their decks would be hell.

Unfortunately…if the MSDF starfighters pressed a close attack on the Commonwealth formation, there wouldn't be very many of them left to cram aboard the Alliance ships.

RUSSELL BLINKED his attention away from the meeting to the immediate task. A *Victory*-class carrier carried four fighter wings of six squadrons apiece, a total of one hundred and ninety-two starfighters and five hundred and seventy-five other lives dependent on him.

"All right, people," he snapped over the fighter group channel. "Orders from on high. Starships are going to make a run for it, we've got the geometry and the Terrans can't catch them."

"We're just *leaving*?"

"We are leaving," Russell confirmed. "Orders from the Midorians themselves. We can't hold and the locals have forbidden us to be stupid.

"That said, we're not going to let the Terrans just waltz in and take over," he told his people. "Form up on the Vultures; we're making a one mega-klick pass and dumping every torpedo this Task Force has down their throat."

"Wing Commander Reyes, are your people ready to serve me some fried battleship?"

"Hell yes, Vice Commodore!" his bomber commander replied instantly. "Would you like them over easy?"

Russell chuckled.

"I'll settle for 'in pieces', Wing Com," he told her. "Coordinate with the other bomber wings. We're going to get one shot at medium range and then we are going to run like scared rabbits who saw the hound; you get me?"

"I get you, sir."

"And the rest of you." Russell turned his digital attention to his other three Wing Commanders, eighteen Flight Commanders, and five hundred starfighter pilots, gunners and engineers.

"The Terrans aren't stupid," he reminded them, "and they have bombers of their own."

In fact, they'd had them *first*, but the Alliance had stolen the plans.

They'd done a better job of rolling them out than the Terrans had, too, completely destroying any advantage the Commonwealth would have received from the deadly little ships.

"We don't know who's in charge over there, but Walkingstick isn't going to roll out sixteen of his most modern toys under command of an idiot!

"They're going to realize what we're doing as soon as they run our vectors, which means we are going to have every starfighter an entire *fleet* carries coming our way. We're not closing to our range of the enemy capital ships, which means our job is to cover the bombers.

"With the MSDF along for the ride, we have *more* fighters than they do. Let's demonstrate why that was a bad plan on their part, shall we?"

2

Midori System
10:00 August 1, 2737 Earth Standard Meridian Date/Time
Task Force Midori Fighter Strike

"HERE THEY COME," Russell's gunner, Jan Hu, observed softly as the tactical feed showed the Commonwealth fleet finally separating into multiple visible components.

It had taken the Terrans a surprisingly long time to move their starfighters out, though the Vice Commodore supposed it wasn't going to make too much difference. Checking the vectors, the Terran ships would still intercept the Alliance formation two million kilometers clear of their starships—and launch missiles several minutes before that.

"Let's make things more confusing for them," he observed. "Commodore Ozolinsh, I recommend the Spartacus Protocol."

Russell wasn't entirely certain of the source of the name. His understanding was that it was one of the VR dramas that the Commodore liked—Ozolinsh being a fan of the Tau Ceti Silver Road era, when the twenty-third-century VR producers in Tau Ceti had spent much of their time remaking the twentieth century's classic movies.

For, oh, the ninth time.

"I agree," the Commodore replied instantly. "Make it happen, Rokos."

Russell pinged the op plan in the datanet linking the two thousand-plus starfighters, feeding the instructions that most of them had been briefed on.

The final build of the Vulture *looked* different from the Terran Longbow Russell had helped steal the plans for, but its core design and function were very similar. What it had that the Longbow lacked, however, was the same electronic warfare suite that had made the Castle Federation's Falcon starfighter the terror of the Commonwealth Navy.

The Arrow-B type fighters, an upgrade from the Imperium's original seventh-generation starfighter, had a functionally identical electronic warfare suite installed, as did the Star Kingdom of Phoenix's Templars.

The Midorian King Cobra-type fighters weren't as capable, but their EW was easily a match of that of the Terran's seventh-generation Katana-type starfighter.

Which meant that when Task Force Midori's starfighters activated the Spartacus Protocol, the starfighter strike went from being roughly ten percent bombers to appearing to be *all* bombers. And, in Rokos's own contribution—learned from the Stellar Fox—all of their *bombers* were pretending to be starfighters.

Starfighters that were pretending to be bombers.

"I only make it nine hundred Katanas," Hu noted. "Shouldn't they have over a thousand starfighters?"

"They should," Russell confirmed to his gunner. "That means the *other* hundred and fifty are Longbows and they're holding them back."

For the Alliance, the bombers were the key to this strike. For the Terrans, they were entirely unnecessary.

"Thirty-six minutes to fighter-missile range," Hu reported. "Forty-two to positron-lance range. Fifty-one to closest approach to the Terran starships."

"Make sure the tactical net is running cleanly and in random-swap mode," Russell ordered. "And if our Terran friends have had an unexpected moment of incompetence and *aren't* running in random-swap mode, feel free to designate their command ships for everyone else."

Hu laughed bitterly.

"Not a chance," he replied. "These guys know their business."

Russell nodded.

Like Admiral Rothenberg had said, the Commonwealth had sent their A game. Terran biases meant they hadn't brought enough starfighters, and they were going to pay for that mistake, but there was no way the Alliance could hold Midori.

All they could do was *hurt* Walkingstick's people.

THE HUMAN BRAIN interacted with neural implants in odd ways. Some people interpreted the data from the implant faster or more easily than others. Some simply processed more data at once. Some could process less data simultaneously, but did so faster than others.

All of that capacity was lumped under the generic term of "bandwidth"—and to be a starfighter pilot, gunner, or flight engineer, a recruit had to be in the top half-percentile of the human race for it.

Vice Commodore Russell Rokos was in the top half of the people who could fly starfighters, but as the two forces rushed together, even *his* ability to process the data his Falcon-C command ship was throwing at him was strained.

He was tracking the vectors and targeting lines of nine hundred Terran starfighters, watching to see if there was any change in their pattern that suggested they'd identified the bombers.

He was tracking the vectors and lines of fire of all almost two hundred of his own starfighters, plus surveying the electronic-warfare efforts being coordinated by his subordinates.

On top of that, he was flying his own starfighter, keeping it constantly evading in three dimensions as he accelerated toward a point one million kilometers away from the Terran starships at five hundred gravities.

His own starfighter's contribution to the electronic warfare chorus singing across the Alliance formation was being handled by his gunner, even as Hu was also making sure the Falcon's missiles were being constantly updated with potential targets and the lance was ready to go the moment they were in range.

All of the data flowed from sensors and computers in the Falcon's computers, run through the artificial intelligences that interfaced with human minds, and presented itself to his brain in ways he could understand.

Which meant his reaction time was far beyond human normal. Their computers could fight the vessel without him…but the humans in the loop increased its survivability and lethality a hundredfold.

The *instant* the two forces crossed the line in space where the geometry meant their missiles could reach other, space lit up with thousands of tiny fireflies. Of the almost three thousand starfighters in space, two thirds launched four missiles apiece.

The Midorian King Cobras and the Phoenix's Templars only launched three each, undermining the illusion that they were bombers —and the bombers and the Coraline Arrows held back two missiles each, since those ships carried six launchers.

There were still over ten thousand missiles in space, their antimatter drives filling the area around the two fighter groups with radiation, light and drives.

Under the cover of that distraction, the Alliance force split in two. The MSDF fighters continued their charge, holding the rest of their missiles back to launch into the teeth of the Terran fleet.

The Alliance fighters turned away, their engines now straining to begin the long, arcing turn that would eventually intercept their motherships. Their launchers continued to cycle, emptying the three-round magazines in under thirty seconds.

Lasers and positron lances lit up around Russell as he danced his starfighter through the chaotic environment. By now, the Terrans had probably identified the bombers, but their formation was still wide, the missile salvo spread out.

It wasn't a great strategy for taking out the bombers, but it would make sure they killed at least *some* of the Alliance ships.

Missiles began to explode. First in handfuls, as lucky extreme-range shots from the defensive lasers hit them, then in dozens.

Then in hundreds. It was becoming harder and harder to see anything clearly, but Russell watched the range and the status of his own people. There wasn't much he could do at this point other than fly his fighter and make sure none of his crews strayed too far from the flight group's defensive umbrella.

The cascade of fire swept toward them, reaching out for his people —but nine hundred starfighters could put only so many missiles into space against the defensive firepower of two thousand. Only a handful of missiles punched through the Alliance defenses.

It was enough. Each missile that made it through killed a starfighter, and that tiny fraction of the original salvo was enough to kill over a hundred of Russell's comrades by the time they reached lance range of the incoming starfighters.

The subtle shift in formation had hopefully been missed by the Terrans, but it put the Star Kingdom of Phoenix's Templar starfighters in front of the bombers. Their heavy sixty-kiloton-a-second positron lances were the only ones in the Alliance force that could match the Katanas for range.

Three hundred of the Katanas survived to smash into LaCroix's Templars, and the Star Kingdom's pilots held their attention for those precious few seconds where no one else could engage.

They got and held the Terrans' attention—and paid for it. Dozens more Alliance starfighters died, but the Katanas' heavier lances could have shredded the Falcons and Arrows.

Now the Arrows and Vultures salvoed their last missiles into the Commonwealth's teeth, followed by the massed positron lances of the rest of the flight group. Beams of pure antimatter ripped across the stars, and Russell focused his attention on staying alive.

Then they were through, a scattered handful of Terran starfighters fleeing behind them. Their course would keep them well clear of any of the starships or defenses in the system, but they'd done enough.

Russell could see the numbers in his head. A third of their bombers and a quarter of their fighters were gone—barely a single squadron of *Dauntless*'s Templars remained. The MSDF had gone mostly unscathed, something the Terrans would regret, but there was no way the Alliance fighter strike could take out the prepared formation waiting for them.

"We hold to the plan," Ozolinsh ordered grimly. "All bombers, salvo torpedoes at the designated point. All Alliance fighters…get ready to turn for home."

Russell waited, watching, as they rushed towards their closest approach. A hundred and five surviving bombers lit up the stars in the middle of their formation, each of them firing four massive torpedoes at the Terran fleet.

"Turn and burn," Ozolinsh barked. "Break for the barn. Our part in this is over."

THE SKY LIT UP with fire as the torpedoes charged in, the MSDF starfighters hot on their heels. The Gemblade torps were no faster than the lighter missiles the starfighters had been flinging at each other minutes before, but they burned longer and harder and came in at a higher velocity—and had more powerful electronic warfare suites as well.

The *Saint*-class battleships had been built to stand off massed starfighter salvoes, however, and so had the *Volcano* carriers and *Hercules* battlecruisers. Missile defense lasers lit up the void, and defensive positron lances tore into both missiles and the closing fighters.

Russell watched in silence, his own course carrying him farther away from the firestorm lighting up the Midori System behind him with each passing second.

"Sir," Hu said quietly. "We're detecting missile launches from the starships."

"Aimed at the Midorians?"

"Negative. At us," his gunner confirmed. "Three hundred and fifty-plus missiles. Apparently, the Midorians aren't a high-enough priority."

Russell shook his head. It was a rare commander with the nerve to assess an incoming fighter strike, calculate that he could handle it with his ships' defensive positron lances, and then launch missiles at the retreating enemy.

He wasn't entirely surprised that this fleet had one.

"Still no sign of their bombers?" he asked.

"Negative."

The Vice Commodore grunted. The Terrans were probably holding them in reserve for the defensive platforms in orbit of the Midorians' planet.

"Any chance we're just going to leave them behind?" he asked. They did have a pretty significant velocity away from the Terran fleet, after all.

"It's going to take them a while to catch us," Hu replied. "But they're going to. Probably…two hours."

That was pushing the endurance envelope for even capital-ship missiles…but it was still endurance the things had.

"Make sure everyone knows," Russell ordered. "Keep the EW up. If they've fired one salvo, they'll fire more."

"And the Midorians?"

Russell shook his head, his attention focusing back on the suicide charge of the Midori Self-Defense Force.

"We'll wait for any of the starfighters that survive, but there's nothing we can do for them now," he admitted.

"I meant the planet," Hu said, his voice grim.

"There is even less we can do for them."

THE TERRANS LAUNCHED over three thousand missiles at the fleeing starfighters, ten salvos chasing the Alliance formation through space.

For the first few minutes, Russell ignored them completely, watching the explosions lighting up the star system around him. Hundreds of quantum-entanglement-com-equipped probes were positioned around Midori, providing the Alliance fleet with a real-time view of everything going on.

Right now, that view was depressing.

As Task Force Midori withdrew toward the other side of the star system from the Terran fleet, they left behind the massive fleet base and refueling infrastructure the Alliance had spent the inter-war years building and upgrading.

That infrastructure and those supplies couldn't be left for the Commonwealth. Once the fleet was clear, pre-positioned missile warheads began to detonate, a sequence of one-gigaton explosions marching their way through forty years of construction and several trillion Federation stellars of investment.

Brutal as that view was, the feed of the Terran fleet itself was worse. A thousand King Cobra starfighters had flung themselves into the teeth of the Commonwealth formation, behind a wall of torpedoes and fighter missiles.

Even with the Q-probes, it was hard to see what happened, but the Terrans had been confident enough to spend their missiles flinging them after Russell's formation.

It turned out that hadn't been the smartest idea they'd had today.

The torpedoes struck first, most dying before they reached their targets but enough making it through that several of the battleships began to lurch out of formation, their engines and mass manipulators flickering from near-fatal hits.

The starfighter missiles were more numerous but less capable, dying in their hundreds as they approached. None of them made it through the defensive fire, but every beam that fired at the missiles didn't target a starfighter.

The final clash could only ever last seconds, with positron lance ranges measured in tens of thousands of kilometers and the closing velocity measured in fractions of lightspeed. The starfighters flashed into range and opened fire, beams of pure antimatter linking ships together.

The starfighters got the worse of the exchange, dying like moths to a flame as they tore through the Terran formation—but they didn't die alone. Both damaged battleships disappeared, and one of their undamaged sisters joined them.

A *Volcano* lurched out of formation and then came apart.

A battlecruiser twisted, damaged but still fighting.

And then it was over, the scattered survivors of the fighter strike fleeing into the outer system, their courses already adjusting as they twisted to try and meet the Alliance task force.

If they couldn't meet up with Task Force Midori before the starships left, their only hope would be surrender.

"That was better than I was afraid of," Hu murmured.

"I wasn't allowing myself to hope they'd get anyone," Russell agreed. His attention turned to the missiles coming after them in the long stern chase.

"Start scanning those missiles," he ordered. "We've got a lot of time to dial them in; this is about as clean a shot as we'll ever get at incoming fire.

"I refuse to lose anybody else today."

3

Castle System
18:00 August 1, 2737 Earth Standard Meridian
Date/Time
New Cardiff

"What was the final count?" Rear Admiral Kyle Roberts, commanding officer of the Alliance's Joint Strategic Options Command, asked his aide grimly.

"We've confirmed three of the *Saints* and one of the *Volcanos* taken out by the fighter strike. Another *Saint* badly damaged and a *Hercules* mission-killed by the orbital defenses. Just over eight hundred Katanas destroyed and seventy Longbows."

Senior Fleet Commander Archie Sterling reeled off the numbers quickly. Six months working for the still-freshly-minted Rear Admiral had given the portly bald reservist a new confidence in his ability to wrangle officers both senior and junior to him in the service of the Alliance.

His massive red-haired boss nodded, looking out the window

across New Cardiff, one of Castle's largest cities—and home to Castle Federation High Command.

"We've confirmed they only launched a hundred bombers in the final strike?" he asked.

"As much as we can," Sterling said cautiously. "Admiral Rothenberg detonated the Q-probes as he withdrew. We're running off what information Midori System Command sent us before they went dark. There's no switchboard station in the system; they used our net and the Imperials'."

A quantum entanglement communicator was inherently a two-point system: the particles talked to each other. Nothing else. The solution had been obvious to engineers, if not necessarily the scientists who'd built the first q-coms: one part of every entangled pair was kept in a single place, allowing everyone to link in to the switchboard and be connected.

Those "switchboard stations" talked to each other and were kept in orbit to minimize interference. They were also expensive and heavily defended, so a smaller system like Midori rarely had one of their own.

"Has EW Command locked down those pairs?" he asked. Access into the Alliance's military q-com network would be a huge bonus to an already devastating victory for the Commonwealth.

"All q-com blocks known to be in Midori have been quarantined," Sterling confirmed.

Kyle nodded again, sighing and studying the city as he braced himself for the next question.

"How bad is it, Archie?" he asked.

"Phoenix lost almost the entirety of *Dauntless*'s wing," Sterling told him. "The Imperials got off lightly, but we lost over seventy Vultures and three hundred Falcons. No chance to retrieve life pods; anyone who ejected…"

"…is now a Commonwealth prisoner," Kyle agreed. There were worse fates, at least. The Commonwealth Navy's atrocities were grander things, the results of moments of passion in people who held the firepower to devastate worlds, not the slow cruelty of prisoner abuse.

"And the rest?"

"Task Force Midori picked up one hundred and seventeen King Cobra starfighters on their way out of the system. That…wasn't even enough to refill *Midori's Hope*'s fighter decks. They're falling back to join Seventh Fleet."

Without replacement starfighters, TF Midori was well under capacity now. Seventh Fleet could use the extra ships, especially if some of what JSOC had been working on came to fruition.

"We owe Kennedy," Kyle admitted. "Rothenberg would have stood and fought—would have been *right* to stand and fight—but he would have lost. And we didn't need to lose another nine starships."

He rose, his implant linking into the screen over the window and darkening it to display the data he was asking for.

The man the media called the Stellar Fox had spent six months stuck in this office, handed an impossible mission: find a way to win the war against the Terran Commonwealth.

The display overlaid over the view of New Cardiff told the dark truth behind that. On one side, the holographic presentation of ships and starfighters lost by the Alliance. On the other, the estimated losses for the Commonwealth.

Six months.

In six months, the Alliance had lost twenty-six capital ships. Each of those ships represented between five and ten thousand lives, five percent of a star system's GDP, and four years of construction time. Combined, those losses brought the Alliance's total ship strength down to barely two hundred and fifty starships.

Including today's losses, the Commonwealth had spent thirty-three capital ships to inflict those losses. Roughly a fifth of the strength assigned to Marshal Walkingstick, leaving the Terran commander with an estimated one hundred and twenty capital ships.

Except that the Terran Commonwealth was building twenty-four capital ships a year and the Alliance produced ten. At that, the Alliance was at a full war footing, pressing every sinew of its member systems' industry to produce starships and starfighters.

The Commonwealth…wasn't. The Terrans were fighting a two-front war and dealing with half a dozen minor revolts or resistance movements and winning—on what was still basically a peacetime production schedule.

For whatever reason, they'd focused their efforts over the last year on the Stellar League, the third party the Alliance had dragged into war with the Commonwealth, but they could change that on a dime. If half of the fleet deployed against the League was redeployed against the Alliance, it was over.

"What do we do, sir?" Sterling asked. He was looking at the display and had to be running through the same analysis Kyle was. Gods knew they'd gone over it in private and in meetings and conferences enough.

"In four hours, I walk into a conference with the political and military leaders of the Alliance and tell them we can't win this war the way we've been fighting it." Kyle smiled sadly at the city behind the disheartening display.

"And then I tell them all of the horrifying ways we might be able to win anyway."

KYLE AND STERLING stepped into the auditorium being prepared for the presentation, the Federation Marines standing guard checking their implant IDs without even needing to break their step.

The auditorium space was buried seventy-six stories underground. To even reach this floor, the two Federation officers had passed through fourteen different layers of security—and yet if their implant IDs hadn't been cleared for this room, the power-armored Marines would have detained them immediately.

The room wasn't large enough to hold every member of the meeting, but holoprojectors covered every available surface. Once active, the room would artificially expand to hold the dozens of senior flag officers and heads of state that Kyle was going to be presenting to.

It was large enough to hold all forty-odd members of the Joint Strategic Options Command, a collection of the most off-the-wall tacticians, mavericks, and generally effective pains in the ass that the Alliance had to its name: commanded by Kyle himself.

Those officers weren't going to be saying much today, but they'd drafted the four options that Kyle had to present.

Two non-JSOC officers were also waiting in the room, and Kyle saluted crisply as he realized he was the last to arrive of the three flag officers who would be physically present.

"Are you ready?" Admiral Mohammed Kane, chief of personnel for the Castle Federation Space Navy, asked him. Kane was a tall man, skin pale from years of indoor and spaceborne work assembling the edifice of living bodies that kept the Federation in the war, clad in a black Navy uniform and matching turban.

"What's to be ready for?" Kyle asked with a bright grin. "All I have to do is convince the leaders of over a dozen star nations and their top flag officers that my own brand of calculated hyperaggression is the only way we're going to win this war.

"It'll be easy!"

The third flag officer chuckled and shook her graying head repressively at him. Fleet Admiral Meredith Blake was the Federation's Chief of Naval Operations and the head of the Alliance Joint Chiefs. No single person was more responsible for the prosecution of the war against the Terran Commonwealth than she, and it had aged her decades in years.

"You, Admiral Roberts, can fool your minions," she told him. "You can fool your fellows. You can even, Stars hoping, fool the Senate and our allies. But you have *never* fooled me."

Kyle inclined his head in acknowledgement of her point.

"None of our options are good," he admitted. "But if Walkingstick has taken Midori, he's already begun his next offensive. We don't know where he'll strike next, but he's already demonstrated that this time, he's prepared to go head on at our largest concentrations.

"We need to get ahead of the curve, make the Commonwealth dance to our tune, or it's all over, bar the dying."

Blake nodded her agreement.

"I think I liked it better when he was being cheerful," Kane told the CNO. "Are we sure we can sell the Senate on any of this?"

Even if Kyle sold the rest of the Alliance on his plans, the thirteen-person executive of the Castle Federation would decide if the Federation Navy was involved in carrying them out—and without the CFSN, none of the possible operations would work.

"We've run the numbers," Kyle told the two flag officers, pitching his voice so none of the surrounding junior officers could hear him. "Eighteen more months. Plus or minus six."

The head of the Joint Department of Personnel winced.

"How *do* you manage to be cheerful?" he asked.

"Practice," Kyle told him, the bright grin returning to his face as he controlled his fear. "Lots and lots of practice."

He checked the time in his implant.

"We're on."

4

Castle System
22:00 August 1, 2737 Earth Standard Meridian Date/Time
New Cardiff

As the projectors came online and the virtual conference room expanded around Kyle, he buried the last of anything resembling stage fright as he mentally cataloged his audience. Every major leader and their top flag officers were there, linked in by the near-instantaneous connections of the q-com networks.

His own implants interfaced with the system, the virtual conference as much in his head as it was in the holograms around him, highlighting individuals he looked at and making sure he knew who they were. A faux pas today could cause all kinds of trouble.

"Closest" to him were the thirteen men and women of the Castle Federation Senate, a co-equal executive that controlled the seventeen star systems of his own home nation. Central in their ranks was the mask-like face of Senator Joseph Randall, the Senator for Castle and unchallenged first among equals of the Senate.

He was also a man who had repeatedly tried to have Kyle killed and, relatedly, whose son remained in a Federation penitentiary for treason.

Next was the pale and dark-haired Imperator of the Coraline Imperium, John von Coral. Still looking surprisingly young for his authority, von Coral was the unquestioned ruler of the Imperium and single-handedly directed the might of the Alliance's second-most powerful nation. In many ways, von Coral was the man Kyle needed to convince the most. Fortunately, they'd met, and he trusted the younger man's judgment.

Sky Marshal Octavian von Stenger sat carefully next to his Imperator, the bald leader of the Imperium's military looking like he'd swallowed a raw lemon. Like the rest of the Alliance Chiefs of Staff, he'd been briefed on what JSOC was here to present—and like JSOC themselves, he didn't like it.

The list of names of import went on and on. Queen Victoria II of the Star Kingdom of Phoenix and her Prime Minister. Hanne Kovachev, the pudgy transhuman Chairman of the Renaissance Trade Factor Board. Two dozen heads of smaller, single-system governments.

The Alliance of Free Stars was made up of sixty-five star systems collected into thirty-two nations. With the fall of Midori, six of those nations and seven of those star systems were now occupied by the Terran Commonwealth.

Every unoccupied nation was represented here. Their leaders gathered to hear what Rear Admiral Kyle Roberts's research group had pulled together. As he'd told Kane, however, he'd put a lot of practice into not merely projecting a bright cheer in any circumstances but in actually *being* cheerful in the face of almost any challenge.

"Ladies, gentlemen, officers and representatives," Admiral Blake greeted the gathering crowd. "My systems show that we have everyone present that was invited…except the President of Midori."

There was a rumble of concern.

"Thatcher was successfully evacuated aboard *Midori's Hope* and is in transit with the rest of Task Force to join Seventh Fleet," Blake continued. "While we could probably loop him in, he is understandably exhausted. We'll provide him and his government-in-exile a recording of Admiral Roberts's presentation later, but he will not be joining us tonight."

The rumble died down, but Kyle knew the undercurrent remained. A year earlier, a series of offensives had reclaimed all of the captured systems and enabled follow-through operations that had struck into Commonwealth space.

Now, over the last six months, seven systems had been lost. Different systems from before. The Alliance's morale was wavering, and everyone in this room was expecting JSOC to provide a miracle.

"You have all been briefed on the mandate of the Joint Strategic Options Command," the Admiral noted. "We have provided them with complete access to all of our intelligence across the board—I think Admiral Roberts knows more of what's going on right now than I do! —and their task was to find a way to win this war.

"To present their conclusions, I yield the floor to Rear Admiral Kyle Roberts—the Stellar Fox."

Kyle smiled and bowed his head to his boss. He might have grown used to the nickname, but that didn't mean he liked it.

"Officers, representatives," he greeted them as he stepped into the center of the auditorium. "We all know who the others are, so I think I will get directly to the point."

A thought through his implant triggered a simplified version of the chart in his office, showing losses across the last six months.

"Let me begin with what has to be said, what we must all understand for this presentation to be relevant, and what I know everyone in this room suspects even if few of us have dared to say it out loud:

"The Alliance is losing this war."

KYLE WAITED out the mix of angry, surprised and disappointed responses, judging the hubbub carefully before raising his hands and cutting everyone off.

"Everyone in this meeting has been fully briefed on our situation," he reminded them. "We started this war with two hundred and ninety active-duty ships and eighty ships in reserves.

"We have barely two hundred and fifty ships left—and over two years, we've commissioned sixteen new warships. Over one hundred and thirty starships have been lost in action. *Twenty thousand* starfighters. Eighty-seven manned defensive platforms."

He let the numbers sink in.

"Putting aside the Kematian Massacre, we have lost over two hundred thousand spacers and soldiers in the space of two years."

He hated the fact that that number was the least important. The Federation alone had over forty billion citizens. Even with barely eight percent of the population qualifying to be starship crew and less than one percent qualifying for starfighter service, the Alliance could replace its personnel losses easily.

What they could not do was magically increase the production of the massive exotic-matter coils required for Alcubierre-Stetson FTL drives.

"We are accelerating our construction dramatically," he noted. Ten ships this year. Fifteen next year. He knew the numbers by heart now.

"We have reached the point where we are crippling our production of civilian shipping to provide A-S for warships. Part of JSOC's job was to run the economic numbers, so we did."

Another mental command opened a map of Alliance space, with a number of bright green markers.

"Each of these markers is an exotic-matter production facility of sufficient scale to produce A-S coils," he said quietly. "In the entire Alliance, there are only thirty-four such facilities. Each is capable of growing four starship-grade exotic matter coils a year."

Enough for one civilian ship or two-thirds of a warship's needs.

"We will have no new facilities of this scale for at least three years," Kyle warned them all. "That means that even if we completely shut down civilian starship construction, we cannot build more than twenty-two ships a year."

"The Commonwealth has taken their own losses," Senator Randall objected. "Worse losses!"

"Yes," Kyle agreed with the Senator, despite the fact that the audience wasn't supposed to be heckling him yet.

"The Commonwealth initially equipped Marshal Walkingstick with a fleet of one hundred and ten capital ships, plus fifteen Q-ships. To all intents and purposes, that fleet has been destroyed.

"He has been reinforced continuously throughout this war, leaving him with a current estimated strength of approximately one hundred and twenty warships. He has *lost* roughly equal numbers of ships to the Alliance, representing basically one hundred percent losses from his original fleet.

"Prior to the beginning of the war with the Stellar League, he was slated to be reinforced with a single lump of an additional one hundred and twenty warships, concentrating thirty percent of the Commonwealth's fleet into his Rimward Marches command and allowing him to simply…run right over us."

Almost a year later, Kyle still had twinges of guilt over dragging the League into the war. The Commonwealth's determination to reunify humanity had meant war between them and the League was inevitable, but the false flag operation that had triggered it still sat poorly with him.

"Instead, the Commonwealth now finds itself in a two-front war. Their own internal politics mean a minimum of fifty percent of their fleet is locked down in either defensive or suppressive formations inside their own borders.

"That leaves them with a *mere* three hundred starships for deployable strength, and an annual production of twenty-four starships."

Kyle grimaced.

"That, to be clear, is still a functionally peacetime production schedule," he reminded his audience. "An equivalent effort to our current projects would double that. An all-out war industry in the Commonwealth could easily produce sixty starships a year.

"A starship is a three-year project, so it would take them *time* to ramp up to that…time the existing six hundred warships of the Terran Commonwealth Navy would easily buy them if they were truly threatened."

He shook his head.

"You all know this," he reminded them again. "We have whispered it in back hallways and thought it in the quiet of our minds, but we must confront the reality:

"So far, we have a fought a conventional war against the Commonwealth and held our own, but we cannot win a conventional war."

With a wave of his hand, he disappeared the displays and faced his audience.

"Confront that," he told them. "Accept that. We at JSOC had to do that months ago. You asked us to do the impossible: find a way to win this war."

"You just said we couldn't!" someone objected. Kyle could have learned who, but he didn't need to.

He smiled toothily.

"I said we cannot win a *conventional* war," he echoed. "But that, officers and representatives, is why you gave me all of your worst mavericks and most unconventional tacticians. It was JSOC's job to find a way to end the war.

"After six months, we have four options. Which one the Alliance will act on is a political decision...but I warn you now: we *must* act."

He waited for the audience to quiet. There were a lot of important people in the room, but it didn't take as long as he'd feared. They were all aware just how many *other* important people's time they were wasting.

"I'd ask that you refrain from questions or comments until I have listed all four possible options," Kyle told them. "All of them will be controversial, and this is not a decision I would expect to make in a few minutes, or even a few hours."

He paused, giving them a moment to raise any preliminary questions, and then squared his shoulders and faced the cameras and his audience as steadily as he could.

"The first option is the one we all hate," he told them. "While we are reasonably certain that we cannot win the war, we remain in a position to inflict massive damage and casualties on the Commonwealth, not to mention the costs to ourselves to continue prosecuting the war.

"We represent the third-largest grouping of human worlds in existence—and the largest is at war with the second-largest as well!

"If we request a cease-fire to negotiate the terms of our absorption into the Commonwealth, it will be granted," he said softly. "Peaceful annexation would inevitably include the transfer of our ships, potentially with crews intact, to the Commonwealth.

"If we surrender," he used the word with careful intent, "we doom the Stellar League as well. The Unificationists in the Commonwealth claim that the course of history is inevitable, that all of mankind will be unified.

"If we join the Commonwealth, that becomes inarguable. The League would go from outnumbered two to one to three to one, and *that* war would be over within months. Combined, the new Commonwealth birthed from our concession would represent sixty-two percent of human-occupied space and seventy-six percent of known human populations."

Despite his request to wait to comment, there were shouts and questions. He ignored them, but he let them die down before he continued.

"On the other hand," he told them, "we are at a point where we can negotiate extremely favorable terms for our member worlds. The surrender of our fleets would be bought with cash and technological subsidies the like of which have never been seen before. While our multi-stellar governments would be dissolved, our worlds and our *people* would be far better off than if they were forcefully annexed."

Much as he hated to even think it, Kyle had run the numbers. Even purely from the perspective of the Alliance worlds, surrendering to the Commonwealth had the biggest upsides. From a cold-blooded "greatest good for the greatest number of people" perspective, their concession would benefit them, the Commonwealth—and even the Stellar League, which would trade a long, grinding war for a swift, crushing defeat.

"We would represent just over twenty-five percent of the Commonwealth's population after annexation," he said quietly. "A political and economic bloc that could not be disrespected.

"But. The nations everyone in this room is sworn to serve and defend would cease to exist. The *people* we swore to serve and defend would survive, but only at the price of our sovereignty, nationhood, and unique identities."

Kyle smiled.

"But that is a way to *end* the war," he noted. "And you charged me and my fellows to *win* the war. Towards that objective, we have designed three operations plans that we believe can win the war in under a year.

"*None* of these plans are clean," he warned, the last of his customary cheer fading. "If we sign off on any of them, there will be more blood on our hands than any Alliance leadership before us. Some of these ops plans will make the Kematian Massacre look like a tea party and will render us galactic pariahs.

"But they *will* win us the war. If we are prepared to pay the price."

NOW KYLE HAD everyone's attention. JSOC had been made up of… problem cases. Mavericks. Officers who no one liked being in command of but who got results. They were the type of officers whose commanders believed they could see an unconventional end to the war.

"The three operations plans are designated Dragon, Hydra and Medusa," he told them. "The names don't tell you much, but I must make clear that we only have the resources to execute one of them. Each will require us to take immense risks in exchange for potential immense reward.

"Operation Dragon is…total war," Kyle noted first. He brought up a strategic display of the Commonwealth's core and highlighted Sol.

"Analysis of the Commonwealth's old worlds based on several classified covert operations suggests that they are not as well defended as we are used to thinking," he told them. "The starfighter complements are modern, but the defensive forces are otherwise equipped with older gear. Most of the fixed defenses are, frankly, garbage, and the starship commands do not expect an attack.

"While they are well defended, they are not invulnerable," Kyle concluded. "Operation Dragon calls for us to assemble a force of approximately one hundred capital ships and punch directly for Sol. Secondary forces, totaling another sixty to eighty ships, will accompany the main fleet to carry out harassing strikes on the other older worlds, keeping the Commonwealth Navy off-balance."

He paused to let the sheer audacity of the concept sink in.

"The fleets will need to steal Commonwealth supplies along the way," he noted, highlighting four systems. "These four systems are major rear-area supply depots. Two are otherwise uninhabited; none are heavily defended. A single carrier should be able to seize each system and neutralize communications before the main force moves in.

"That will allow us to reach Sol with the advantage of surprise. The Dragon fleet will then secure the Sol System and take control of Earth's upper orbitals, at which point they will demand the surrender of the Commonwealth."

His audience was silent.

"What must be understood before embarking on Operation Dragon is that the Commonwealth Senate will almost certainly *not* surrender simply because we have occupied Sol. The fleet *must* be authorized to carry out demonstration nuclear and antimatter strikes on civilian targets and sent out with the understanding that those strikes *will* be done.

"We assess the likelihood that it will be necessary to functionally destroy Earth at over sixty percent," Kyle noted very, very quietly.

Earth had a population of roughly fourteen billion. If his superiors signed off on Operation Dragon, Kyle was probably going to have to resign. He had the sneaking suspicion most of JSOC would follow him. They might have drafted up the plans for Operation Dragon, but they'd be *damned* if they'd carry them out.

Kyle didn't even believe in Hell, but he suspected he'd end up somewhere equivalent regardless if he was the architect of the destruction of humanity's homeworld.

But there was a *reason* he'd started with Dragon, and the shocked silence on the virtual conference told him he'd made his point. Dragon was the least complex and least risky of the plans from an immediate perspective, though it carried massive long-term risks—Kyle doubted the rest of the galaxy would allow even demonstration bombardments of Earth to go without retaliation.

"Operation Hydra," he finally continued, "is closest to the conventional war we have been fighting. With, of course, a level of strategic aggression they've rarely seen from us so far."

Hydra wasn't necessarily the best choice, but the op plan was near and dear to Kyle's heart. It had every hallmark of the over-the-top calculated aggression that marked his own career and tactics, drawn on a strategic scale.

"The combined fleets of the Alliance outnumber Marshal Walkingstick's forces two to one," he told them. "He has a far larger reserve of reinforcements, but those hundreds of starships aren't on the frontier with us."

The map around him changed from the inner systems of the Commonwealth to the front with the Alliance.

"Hydra calls for us to strip our systems of *all* mobile defenses and deploy the entirety of our starship strength forward into a single offensive, built around three striking forces," he explained. "These six systems"—the systems in question flashed red on the hologram around him—"are key components of Walkingstick's logistics pipeline.

"Without them, he only has the resources at his main fleet base in the Niagara System to sustain active operations for a few weeks at most. Taking out these systems would also involve the destruction of thirty to forty of his capital ships, clearing the decks for an all-out assault on the Niagara fleet base.

"With the capture of Niagara, the defeat or destruction of Marshal Walkingstick's fleet, and the capture or destruction of the Commonwealth Navy's rimward frontier logistics infrastructure, we will be in a position to either carry out deeper offensives or negotiate a peace in place."

A peace in place would only buy the Alliance time. The previous Imperator had told them all that at the end of the last war—and history had proven him right.

"Hydra is risky," he warned them. "It leaves much of the Alliance almost unprotected for a single strike at Walkingstick's strongest point. If Walkingstick launches his *own* offensive at the same time, Hydra will doom the Alliance.

"A successful Operation Hydra does not guarantee the end of the war, but it will unquestionably seize the strategic momentum—*if* we have enough ships left after it to prosecute the war further," Kyle noted.

"The last option my team and I have put together is Operation Medusa," he continued again after a moment. The map of the frontier between the Alliance and the Commonwealth moved and expanded, until he stood in the middle of a rotating display of stars that showed the entire Terran Commonwealth.

"Operation Medusa is an attempted one-punch knockout. Like Hydra, it calls for us to strip our defenses bare and move forward with a single do-or-die strike. Unlike Hydra, a successful Operation Medusa *will* win the war."

Kyle smiled. *That* got everyone's attention.

Bright red dots now speckled the display rotating around him, highlighting star systems.

"Operation Medusa will strike at the very fundamentals not only of the Commonwealth's day-to-day operations but of the belief structure of the Unificationists.

"That fundamental belief is simple: that instantaneous communications via the q-com network require the consolidation of the human race into a single nation." He smiled grimly. He could, if he twisted his brain just right, see their point.

He just didn't *agree* with it—and certainly didn't agree with their right to impose that consolidation at the point of a sword.

"Those instantaneous communications require the manufacture of entangled quantum blocks and the maintenance of q-com switchboards to allow point-to-point FTL communications," Kyle continued. "Like most of us, the Commonwealth combines the manufacturing facilities and the switchboards aboard single-purpose communications space stations to minimize gravitational interference in either process.

"The Commonwealth has twelve general purpose q-com switchboard stations, two government-reserved switchboard stations, two military-reserved switchboard stations, and a top-secret reserve facility that most of their military officers don't even realize they're carrying entangled particle blocks for."

He let the toothy Cheshire Cat grin return to his face.

"For those of you whose implants aren't keeping up"—which was absolutely nobody in this audience—"that is seventeen stations." He gestured to the red highlights. "Three, including the one no one is supposed to know exists, are in Sol.

"The other fourteen are in various systems throughout the Commonwealth.

"Medusa calls for us to destroy them all in a time-synchronized assault hitting every station across the Commonwealth in one strike."

Kyle paused to let that sink in.

"The opening moves of Operation Medusa are quite similar to Hydra," he told them. "We will assemble a midsize strike force to target systems across the frontier in what we will make look like an attempt to undermine Walkingstick's logistic support.

"The purpose of this part of the operation is to hold Walkingstick's attention while we send fifteen assault forces totaling over two hundred capital ships on a deep-strike operation into Commonwealth space."

Icons lit up the map as he spoke, showing the path of the assaults.

"We will use our own q-com networks to guarantee a simultaneous attack. Some of the switchboard stations are in relatively unfortified systems; others are in the very heart of the Commonwealth.

"As with Dragon, we may need to raid supply depots on the way in, a potential risk to any chance of surprise, but we will be sending ships clear across the Commonwealth, nearly to the border with the Stellar League."

A coordinated strike with the League would have made any of the ops easier, but while the Commonwealth might not be entirely certain it had been lured into launching a punitive expedition against the League, the League knew perfectly well *they* hadn't raided Tau Ceti.

They were understandably unwilling to work with the Alliance.

"The destruction of the Commonwealth's FTL communications network is a threat they have few plans or structures in place to handle," he continued. "The idea of someone striking at the connections that bind humanity together is anathema to the Unificationists—Gods, the thought makes *my* skin crawl.

"What plans they have are purely theoretical, with few exercises carried out at anything above a single-station scale.

"Loss of communications will paralyze their military, political, and economic structures. Without tactical FTL communication, even Walkingstick will be *incapable* of prosecuting a war against us, and the internal fracture lines where star systems were annexed by force will be drastically aggravated.

"None of these systems are easily or quickly replaced. We estimate a minimum of two years to get even a single switchboard station online on an emergency basis, and more like twenty to thirty to completely reconstruct the system.

"Not least," he concluded with a cold smile, "because they will feel the need to build a more secure, more fortified and more redundant system.

"Medusa will buy us a generation. More importantly, though, Medusa will stop *all* Commonwealth expansion for a generation. The destruction of their communication network will force an internal focus they haven't had for over a century.

"Our sociologists suggest a sixty-three percent likelihood that such an extended period of inward focus will severely undermine the Unificationists' current dominant cultural position. Given that we would be able to provide FTL communication and humanitarian assistance to factions we want to support, we could use direct and indirect social-engineering projects to assist that changeover.

"Dragon or Hydra might end the war. Medusa has a chance of ending the Commonwealth's aggressive expansion…permanently."

THE OPTIONS PRESENTED, Kyle stepped aside to let the leaders of the Alliance argue. He and JSOC were only present at this point to answer questions, but most of the flag officers had been briefed well enough in advance to provide at least the first layer of answers.

It took almost forty-five minutes of argument before Joseph Randall turned his glare back on Kyle and asked the question he'd been waiting for since the beginning.

"You drafted these plans, Admiral Roberts," he said bluntly. "You swore an oath to serve the Federation and have fought the Commonwealth for this entire war. Many say you fired its first shots. You're the 'hero' everyone looks to."

Randall couldn't quite keep his snide distaste out of his voice, even as he was trying to use Kyle as a hammer against the rest of the Alliance.

"What would *you* suggest?"

For one brilliant moment of amusement, Kyle wondered what the reaction from this assembly would be if he recommended surrender. So far, Randall had been the loudest advocate of Dragon, and while none of the major powers had spoken in favor of surrender, several of the single-system nations had.

But as Randall pointed out, Kyle Roberts had sworn an oath to defend the Federation. Recommending his nation surrender would fail in that oath.

"I think Medusa is our best option, Senator," he said calmly. "Dragon would make us galactic pariahs. We might defeat the Commonwealth today, but if we bombarded Earth, we would never know peace.

"Hydra is less ambitious but requires almost the same level of risk as Dragon. If we're going to gamble *everything* on one throw of the dice, I suggest we gamble *for* everything as well."

"That sounds like your reputation, Admiral," Randall snapped. "And what command would you take, Roberts? The strike at Sol, the greatest glory?"

Kyle chuckled.

"I am a mere Rear Admiral, Senator Randall," he pointed out. "The strike at Sol will require a full Admiral to command it. I will serve where the Alliance needs me. I've had enough of glory for one lifetime."

The Senator coughed, but to Kyle's surprise, he nodded his understanding.

"I don't believe," Randall told the gathered conference, "that this is a decision we can make in an hour without consultation.

"Admiral Blake, there were briefing documents prepared, I presume?" he asked.

"There were," she confirmed.

"Please have JSOC distribute them to everyone," Randall said politely. "I remind *everyone* that all of this is classified at the highest levels. A leak of these plans…could doom us all.

"Review them. Discuss them with the necessary members of your administrations. We shall reconvene in forty-eight hours—and then, I believe, we must make a choice."

"I hope," Imperator von Coral interjected, his voice a smoothly trained instrument, "that we make the right choice. The leadership of this Alliance has already gone down in history once for our mistakes. I would not wish to become like my father, an ignored voice of reason."

Randall chuckled.

"I think that is unlikely, my lord," he acknowledged. "Whatever happens, we aren't going to let the Commonwealth get back up this time!"

5

Castle System
07:00 August 3, 2737 Earth Standard Meridian Date/Time
New Cardiff

KYLE ROBERTS WAS LESS than enthused with many aspects of working a desk job on the Federation's homeworld. After two years of serving on the front lines, though, he'd accepted that he *needed* the time away from the psychological crush of war.

The fact that he woke up most mornings next to Captain Mira Solace was definitely an additional selling point, though. His fiancée had been assigned to the homeworld for psych evaluation after having her command battered to pieces around her.

She'd promptly been scooped up by the same immense analysis, design and support machine that had dragged Kyle into JSOC, and assigned to the team designing the Alliance's latest generation of battlecruisers.

Like JSOC's mission, that project was now complete. They'd both be getting new assignments soon, and the big redheaded Admiral slipped an arm around the elegantly tall black woman in his bed, holding her close for a long moment as she yawned awake.

Both of them were entirely capable of snapping awake instantly, but that was rarely required here. Once they were back in the field, they'd need that skill again, but for now, they could wake up lazily holding each other.

"What's on your docket today?" he asked softly, kissing her hair.

"More virtual wargames," Mira told him, shifting to lean against him. "We think we've locked down most of the designs for the Armada ship classes, but I know Admiral Vong wanted the battle-cruiser team to run Op Force for some more tests for the carrier design."

She didn't ask about his day. Kyle was cleared for Project Armada, the design project for the next generation of Alliance capital ships, but Mira wasn't cleared to know more about JSOC than that it existed.

"So, I'll have *Drake*- and *Istomin*-class ships for my next fleet?" he asked.

His lover chuckled.

"Three-year construction timeline. You know that."

"I know," he agreed, concealing a moment of fear beneath his usual cheer. Unless their plans worked out perfectly, the starships designed by Project Armada would never see service. One way or another, the war would be over before ships being laid down in September 2737 would ever see active duty.

He was checking the time and was about to suggest a productive use of the minutes before they had to get heading to work when his implant buzzed with an incoming call.

He checked the code and sighed.

While Sterling would understand him taking a minute or so to respond at this time of morning, there was no way his aide would have commed him at this time at all unless it was important.

"Duty calls, my love," he told Mira.

"I know the siren song," she replied with a soft smile. "Get going, Admiral."

Kyle stepped out of the single bedroom in their apartment and took the call in the living room. Running the communication through his implant, there was at least no need for him to get dressed or for Sterling to even know that he wasn't dressed yet.

"Oh, thank the Stars," his aide said as soon as he answered. "I was worried you were asleep."

"You do have a priority alert that will wake me up," Kyle observed.

"And we all hate that thing," Sterling confirmed. "I was about to use it anyway. You have Admiral Blake and three Senators scheduled to be in your office in sixty-three minutes."

His implants allowed him to control the spike of adrenaline *that* news delivered, and he considered the situation. Even though he and Mira had acquired an apartment together, both currently worked at the Fleet HQ and they hadn't purchased a vehicle. They used New Cardiff's network of self-driving transit pods, which ran a pathing algorithm to match passengers with destinations and get everyone where they needed to go as quickly as possible.

On a good day, he was twenty minutes from his office. In rush hour, he could easily be forty—and he needed to shower and dress.

"Can you get an aircar to the apartment?" he asked.

"I coordinated with your security detail while I was waiting for you to answer," Sterling confirmed. "Vehicle will be on your building's roof in twenty-four minutes."

Barring some kind of incident, then, the military aircraft should get him to work in under ten minutes.

"All right, Archie. Hold down the fort."

His aide laughed.

"Sir, what in the Void gives you the impression that *I've* made it to the office or even into uniform yet?"

Relegating Marines to taxi-driver status always felt silly, but Kyle had to admit that he'd never found a more reliable transportation service than a Castle Federation Marine Corps armored aircar with a Marine pilot.

The aircar delivered him to the landing pad on Castle Federation High Command's highest tower, where Archie Sterling was waiting for him with a reserved elevator.

In the end, he reached his office with enough time to spare to inhale a cup of coffee and was waiting, appearing perfectly calm despite the unexpected rush to be ready, before his visitors arrived.

When the Marines escorted Admiral Blake and her guests into his office, he rose with a salute and a cheerful grin.

"Good morning, Admiral, Senators," he greeted them. "Can I get you something to drink? Coffee? Tea? Beer?"

"Your beer fridge has a reputation," Senator Maria O'Connell noted. The petite redheaded Senator for the planet Tuatha smiled. "That said, I'll take a coffee. It's a bit early in the morning, even for me."

"Coffee," Blake grumped. "As big a cup as you have."

Senator Madhur Nagarkar of New Bombay took tea and Senator Joseph Randall took nothing. The blue-eyed man with the silver hair propped up the office wall in silence as the others sat. The first time Kyle had met Randall, he'd been a fading blond, but no hint of gold remained in his hair now.

Despite their disagreements and a not-insignificant number of assassins, even Kyle had to admit that Randall had stepped up as a wartime leader in an impressive manner. He'd managed to line the Federation's merchant houses, First Families, and industrial cartels up in a row that was churning out warships, starfighters, and missiles with phenomenal efficiency.

It had taken its toll.

"To what do I owe this unexpected visit?" Kyle asked as he served the drinks himself. Somehow, he suspected this wasn't a meeting he wanted his steward in.

"You rammed it past me," Randall snapped. "Give him the damn thing, O'Connell."

The Senator for Tuatha chuckled.

"Show *some* grace, Randall," she replied—but she took a small jewelry box from inside her suit jacket and dropped it on the table.

"The Senate has signed off on a new promotion list," she told Kyle as he took the box. "Congratulations, Vice Admiral."

The box contained two pins, each with two gold stars, to replace the single star currently on his collar. Slowly, carefully, Kyle examined them, then laid the box back on the desk.

"I've only been a Rear Admiral for six months," he pointed out.

"Sixteen major offensive fleets, Roberts," Blake told him. "Operation Medusa was approved, and the Alliance doesn't *have* sixteen O-9s and O-10s qualified to command a fleet action who aren't trapped behind a desk."

"Medusa is approved?" he asked, leaning back in his chair.

"The Imperator is a big fan of yours," Randall said. "So, it seems, are most of my fellows."

"If we're going to take as big a risk as we need to take, we can't justify doing less than going for the throat," O'Connell told him.

"We promoted a half-dozen new Rear Admirals as well," Blake added, "and the main staff is going over JSOC's operations plan as we speak."

"And JSOC?" Kyle asked.

"Dissolved as of noon today," the CNO told him bluntly. "You've done your job, and we need your collection of overaggressive mavericks on command decks as we launch this damn affair."

He nodded thoughtfully.

"Timing is going to be everything," he noted. "Shifting command structures is going to be a pain, but—"

"But we need our best on deck," Blake finished his thought. "That's not your problem, Admiral. Trust that it's being taken care of."

"Your problem, Roberts, is that you've talked the Alliance into one of the biggest goddamn rolls of the dice in human history," Randall told him. "So, tell me: what happens if you're *wrong*? If this whole mess blows up in our face?"

"Worst-case scenarios?" Kyle smiled. "There were a few in the briefing, but the big one is that Marshal Walkingstick kicks off his final offensive while our fleets are in the Commonwealth. We could destroy the Commonwealth and find ourselves Walkingstick's new empire."

"And you had a plan for that, *right*?" the Senator demanded. "Or were you planning on dragging sixty star systems along with you on your usual headlong charge?"

"Operation Medusa called for a stalking-horse fleet to carry out raids along the frontier, to keep Walkingstick distracted," the newly minted Vice Admiral replied. "We'll need to hold his attention, keep him watching his flanks, without letting him realize that the majority of our fleet is somewhere else."

All of this had been in the briefing, but Randall was clearly angling for something.

"Joseph, if you've something you want the Admiral to say, you may as well *ask* him," Nagarkar said bluntly. The dark-skinned New Bombay Senator looked tired, with bags under his eyes that showed on even his skin.

"After everything he's pulled, you expect me to be comfortable with the 'Stellar Fox's' judgment?" Randall snapped. "We're following his ideas into the dark, and I've never seen this man be anything but an overaggressive glory hog!"

Kyle's smile thinned.

"No, sir. All you've ever seen in me is the man who caught your son committing treason," he told Randall. "You've never judged me on any other standard than that—but the Federation *needs* us to be better men than that.

"Doesn't it?"

It was probably the wrong thing to say. The tension in the room ratcheted from "nervous discussion of the war" to "an Admiral just all but accused a Senator of attempted murder."

But if the Federation—if the entire *Alliance*—was going to be following a plan Kyle had drafted, he and Senator Joseph Randall needed to clear the air.

It was silent for ten seconds as he held Randall's gaze. Twenty. Thirty.

Then the Senator blinked and sighed, the tension draining away as what might have been tears glittered in the corner of his eyes.

"Void take you, Roberts," he snapped. "He's my *son*."

"And he sold us out to the Commonwealth."

Randall was silent again, then nodded.

"He did. Didn't raise him as well as I thought." He shook his head. "Void take you," he echoed, but there was no heat to it. "Will this work, Admiral?"

Kyle glanced over at Blake, who gestured for him to answer.

"Fifty-five / forty-five," he told the Senators. "If Medusa fails, there's only about a one-in-three chance we get enough of the fleets back to hold out afterward.

"Medusa comes with a thirty percent chance of losing the war in the next six months, but doing *nothing* leaves us with a certainty of losing the war in twelve to twenty-four months.

"It's the only option I'd recommend above surrender, sirs, ma'ams," he concluded. "It's a huge risk, but it's a calculated one with an over-fifty-percent chance of winning the war outright."

"I'm not going to pretend I like you, Admiral," Randall told him, levering himself off the wall. "But you're right. I've misjudged your record because of that dislike. Do your damned job. Prove you're worth that piece of gold my fellows gave you."

With that admission, the Senator for Castle calmly walked out of Kyle's office.

"WELL, that was more positive than I was expecting," O'Connell muttered after Randall left. "Put the damn stars on, Admiral Roberts. You and Admiral Blake have work to do."

Shaking his head, Kyle obeyed, replacing his single gold stars with the pairs in the box.

"What do we do now?" he asked.

O'Connell downed her coffee.

"*I* was here to give you the stars," she pointed out. "Nagarkar joined me after Randall attached himself, just in case we needed an extra set of lungs to shout him down. Apparently, we should have just left you to deal with him on your own!"

"The Senator and I disagree on many things, but we serve the same cause," Kyle told her, allowing his normal cheer to return. "When the Federation calls, he and I will both answer in our own ways."

And if that call stopped Randall sending assassins after him, Kyle would take it as a win.

"Which benefits us all," Nagarkar rumbled. "Thank you, Admiral, for your service and your honesty. Good luck with your mission."

The two Senators stepped out, leaving Kyle alone with Admiral Blake.

"And my mission?" he asked her.

"Waving your reputation under Walkingstick's nose," she told him. "We're still sorting out exact strength levels, but you'll be assembling a new Forty-First Fleet for the purposes of your stalking-horse raids. I'll freely warn you that you won't have nearly the strength you'd like: no matter how we harped on the need for an all-out strike, we're still reserving twenty percent of our starship strength for home defense."

"That still leaves us two hundred ships," Kyle concluded. "We could be a lot worse off."

"About the only thing that's certain right now is that you're getting *Gaia* and *Elysium*," Blake told him. "And that's only because they're both in the Castle System and *Elysium* doesn't even have an assigned CO yet."

"Is she even combat-ready?" he asked. DSC-080 *Elysium* was the latest *Sanctuary*-class ship, the newest sister to his old *Avalon*.

"Undergoing space trials as we speak. *Gaia* has been headlining the Home Fleet since she was finished, but, like sending you, sending either of the *Titan*-class battleships is a message outside all numbers."

The Federation had only built two modern battleships before deciding to give up on the type for the foreseeable future. *Kronos* and *Gaia* were the only eighty-million-cubic-meter battleships in existence. There were also six *Sanctuary*-class carriers and four *Conqueror*-class battlecruisers of a similar size—and those twelve ships, the Castle Federation's most modern, were the only eighty-million-cubic-meter ships around. At all.

"You're probably going to end up with a fleet of our best and the Imperium's best," Blake told him, "something that will punch well outside what its numbers might suggest, but we're also going to be sending you right at Walkingstick."

"That's the job, ma'am," Kyle told her. "A half-dozen eighty-million-cubic ships will turn more heads than twice that in thirty-million-cubic ships pulled from the reserve. I can make Walkingstick hunt me if you give me *one* ship, ma'am, but I'd rather a fleet."

"You'll get a fleet. That's why you got the second star," she said. "And it'll be a fleet worth taking into battle; I promise you that."

"We need *sixteen* of those," he admitted. "Logistics are going to suck."

"You gave us the outline. Now it's up to JD-Logistics to make it work," Blake replied. "You have this office until you move spacewards, but we'll make sure the flag deck on *Elysium* is clear for you in a few days.

"I suggest you take some leave first," she continued. "Once we kick this off, all leave is canceled until it's over. And you and your fiancée will want to celebrate."

"I'm still wrapping my brain around the star at all, ma'am."

Blake chuckled.

"You won't be the only one," she told him. "Mira got her first star, though she won't be part of Medusa. She'll be taking command of the gunship flotillas around Castle, one of several officers tasked with the fallback if this strike fails."

It was a job that needed to be done, but a thankless one. The fleets of sublight gunships that guarded the Alliance's core worlds wouldn't stop a vengeful Commonwealth Navy from crushing the Alliance if Medusa failed, but they'd have to try.

And if Medusa succeeded, they'd never see action.

"Lucky her," he murmured. "Who's letting her know?"

"She's meeting with the head of Armada at lunchtime," Blake replied. "Don't let the cat out of the bag before then, or her boss *will* make your life hell."

"I'd prefer to leave that task to our good friend Walkingstick!"

6

Via Somnia System
15:00 August 7, 2737 Earth Standard Meridian Date/Time
DSC-062 *Normandy*

Task Force Midori shut down their Alcubierre-Stetson drives with a quivering tension. Q-com channels with Seventh Fleet had told them that Via Somnia remained in Alliance hands, but Vice Commodore Rokos agreed with his fellows.

Normandy, like the rest of the Task Force, entered Via Somnia with her weapons online and every starfighter manned. If the former Commonwealth fleet base had been retaken, they were as ready to fight their way clear as they could possibly be.

Via Somnia was an uninhabited system, but when Seventh Fleet had taken it away from the Commonwealth, they'd managed to take the massive Navy base mostly intact. What damage had been done had been repaired, and the immense facility continued its orbit of Dreamer, Via Somnia's dead rock of a third world.

Four capital ships orbited with the base, and two more swam

through the outer system on a continuous patrol around Dreamer's Alcubierre-interfering gravity well. An immense battleship loomed over Task Force Midori as they emerged, a fifth again the size of the TF's largest ships.

"Launching CSP," Russell's flight controller chanted, and acceleration slammed the Vice Commodore back into his chair. There was a pause as the officer switched over to a private channel.

"What the *hell* is that?!"

"The sign we're in the right place," the CAG replied with a chuckle. The immense warship was adjusting her course, arcing to come in protectively behind the battered task force like a worried sheep dog. "That's *Kronos*. Nothing else is that big!"

"Well, *Normandy*'s scanners disagree with you," the Lieutenant replied. "I've got another ship at the navy base that's just as big."

Russell checked, and a moment of nostalgia rushed over him as he recognized her.

"That's *Avalon*," he told his officer. "Feels wrong to see her anywhere without the Fox in command."

"So, we're safe?"

"I figure that's Rothenberg's call," Russell replied, "though I'll admit it: I'll question his orders if he sends us after Seventh Fleet!"

"ALL RIGHT, everybody, we can stand down," Vice Admiral the Elector Parth Rothenberg instructed his senior officers a few minutes later. "I've touched base with Vice Admiral Conners"—the Renaissance Trade Factor officer commanding Seventh Fleet—"and we're clear to move in and dock.

"We'll be replenishing all of our supplies from the navy base and replacing our starfighter losses from the defensive squadrons. If you weren't flying Falcons already, well, you're going to be flying Falcons," he concluded dryly.

The Castle Federation had taken the point of the assault and lost several ships taking Via Somnia. So, by a logic that Russell couldn't bring himself to disagree with, it had been the Castle Federation Space

Force that had moved in two starfighter groups to help secure the newly-captured base.

"Once we've docked, we'll rationalize our fighter deployments and make sure our repairs are up to date," Rothenberg concluded. "I haven't been told much, but my understanding is that there's work coming down the pipeline for us."

"Are we going back to Midori?" someone asked.

There was a long silence on the channel, and then Russell felt the Admiral shake his head through the implant link.

"Even I'm not being fully briefed on what's coming," he admitted, "and I've been told I can't share what the Joint Chiefs *have* told me. Unfortunately, it's been made very clear that we're being earmarked for other operations.

"For the moment, Midori is going to remain in Terran hands. I don't like it any more than you do, but I am assured that the President was involved in that decision."

Rothenberg let that hang, waiting for further commentary.

"Set your courses, people," he ordered finally. "And make sure your crews get some rest. After this last week, they'll need it."

FTL was safe. There wasn't even much to *do* while under Alcubierre-Stetson drive, so Russell knew his people were, in one way, quite well rested.

But he knew exactly what Admiral Rothenberg meant. There was safe because the laws of physics said nothing could touch you…and then there was safe because you were surrounded by friends and allies.

Russell knew *he* was going to sleep better once *Normandy* was docked.

ONCE TASK FORCE MIDORI was fully inside the protective umbrella of the Via Somnia fleet base, Russell pulled his carrier space patrol back aboard *Normandy*. His fighter group was better off than many of the others, but he'd still lost a lot of people getting out of Midori.

To his surprise, Captain Herrera was waiting for him on the flight deck as he exited his fighter craft.

"Sir." He saluted crisply.

"With me, CAG," Herrera ordered. He was a short, gaunt man with skin as dark as interstellar space, but he moved with the certainty of a falling avalanche. Russell knew better than to ignore even a seemingly polite request from his boss.

The Captain led the way to Russell's own office, however, and took a seat across from the CAG's desk.

"What a *fucking* week," Herrera exhaled in a single breath. "How are your people holding up?"

"Rough," Russell said after a moment. "SFG-292 got away better than most; we only lost twenty ships."

Putting aside the MSDF's suicide charge, the Alliance had lost a third of TF Midori's starfighters. That *Normandy*'s SFG-292 had only lost ten percent of her fighters meant Russell's people had been lucky.

Just not lucky enough.

"We lost a lot of friends in the other groups," he murmured. "LaCroix and I weren't close, but we'd known each other since the war began." Russell chuckled. "Since back when she tried to seduce the Fox, though he was just Wing Commander Roberts then."

Herrera's responding chuckle was tired.

"Your people always take the brunt of it," he said quietly. "Are they going to be ready for action?"

"How soon?" the CAG asked bluntly. "Tomorrow? Only in desperation. Give me a week and we'll be a bit rusty around the new crews we'll steal from Via Somnia, but we can fight. Give me three, and I'll match my people against the Commonwealth's best."

"Might need to hold you to that," Herrera told him. "If Walkingstick took Midori—"

"Then he's kicking off his endgame," Russell agreed. "Which means I'll be *ecstatic* to get that three weeks before we go toe to toe with the Marshall's best."

"You'll get it," Herrera said grimly. "I won't send you into battle before you're ready. We've lost too many people and too many ships doing that when we had no choice."

"Don't make a promise you might not be able to keep," the CAG replied. "'No choice' happens. It might happen again."

7

Castle System
17:00 August 7, 2737 Earth Standard Meridian Date/Time
New Cardiff and Castle Orbit

"THEY GAVE me a star and all I got was a pile of gunships," Mira Solace grumped, leaning into Kyle's shoulder as the two embraced at the edge of the landing pad. "And what are they giving you, *Vice* Admiral?"

Kyle chuckled.

"At last count, I'm shepherding thirteen capital ships and nine logistics ships," he told her. "My understanding is that I don't get to *keep* them—all I've been promised is *Elysium* and *Gaia*—but that's the flock I'm taking out to Via Somnia."

"Must be nice to be *important*," she said, but she was smiling as she said it.

The flotilla of sixty *Gallant*-class gunships Solace had been given command of might be restricted to the Castle System, but it represented over twice *Gaia*'s firepower and four times her crew.

"I don't know about that," he replied. "They're putting you in charge of a good chunk of *Castle's* defense and sending me off as far as they can! Plus, you get to sleep in your own bed at night!"

The *Gallants* didn't have flag decks. Rear Admiral Mira Solace would lead her command from a buried operations center on the surface, though tradition required she spend as much time aboard her ships as possible regardless.

"A bed that's going to be cold and empty," Mira said. "You be careful, Kyle," she ordered. "I want a living husband-to-be, not a dead hero; are we clear?"

He chuckled again and kissed her, ignoring the collected officers waiting around them as the surface-to-orbit shuttles swept down.

"I have every intention of coming back alive," he told her. "You think a minor obstacle like the Commonwealth's top commander and a hundred or so warships are actually going to put me in *danger*? Have you *met* the Stellar Fox?!"

Mira shook her head.

"I have, actually," she pointed out. "I've also met Kyle Roberts, and my impression is that they're not necessarily the same man. And I want them *both* to come back to me."

"You keep Castle intact and I'll come home to her. And you," he promised.

Behind him, Archie Sterling coughed.

"Admiral, sir? The shuttle is here...and tradition does say you board first."

Kyle sighed and nodded, wrapping Mira in his arms again in a fierce embrace she returned tightly.

"I *will* be back," he assured her. "Through Void, through Hell, through Summerlands or war, I will return to you. I promise you."

She kissed him.

"I know. Now go! You can't keep twenty-two starships waiting while the Admiral makes out with his fiancée!"

He stepped back and grinned at her.

"Why not? Isn't rank supposed to have its privileges?"

"Go!" she ordered, but she was smiling as she said it.

Elysium LOOKED SO MUCH like *Avalon* that it took Kyle a moment to recover his composure. He'd commanded two ships after *Avalon*, but the big *Sanctuary*-class carrier still held a special place in his heart.

His new flagship was her twin. Even knowing she was a different ship, there were no differences Kyle could pick out from the outside. A few sensor arrays or Stetson stabilizer emitters in different places, but nothing identifiable as his shuttle approached the kilometer-and-a-half-long abbreviated arrowhead.

Behind the big carrier hung the equally immense form of one of the only two *Titan*-class battleships in existence. *Gaia* was longer than the carrier, not needing a flattened prow for a landing deck, and bristled with a massive array of firepower.

Past her, none of the other ships assembled into Kyle's convoy were visible as more than tiny white triangles at best. Four more carriers, four battlecruisers, and three strike cruisers filled out the thirteen warships he was taking out.

His understanding was that he would keep *Elysium, Gaia,* and *Carolus Rex,* the three most modern ships in the convoy, while the remainder of the ships would be joining Vice Admiral Rothenberg as the Imperial officer took command of a newly expanded Seventh Fleet.

Kyle may have drafted the plans that were now setting the Alliance's fleets into motion, but he didn't have need to know on the final details. He could *guess* which target Rothenberg was going after, but he hadn't been briefed.

For that matter, if they were following the plan, *Rothenberg* wouldn't have been briefed. Even the Admirals leading the strike fleets wouldn't know their destinations more than eight hours in advance of going FTL.

It would be obvious to the Admirals who would be leading the strikes at the closer switchboard stations that *something* was going on. Some of the fleets would have seven-week flight times. Others would only have three. Flag officers weren't going to miss dozens of starships disappearing and entire fleets going off the grid for an entire month.

"*Elysium* Control has provided landing clearance," the pilot announced. "They've been advised we have Forty-First Fleet Actual aboard and are clearing a priority lane."

Kyle sighed.

"'Forty-First Fleet' currently is officially, what, two ships?" he murmured to Sterling.

"Maybe," his aide-turned-chief-of-staff replied. "But one of those ships is *Elysium*, so Captain Novak wants to put her best foot forward, after all."

"Well, then. I suppose I should prepare to be impressed, shouldn't I?"

"It would be…polite, sir."

THE SHUTTLE SLID to a perfectly calculated halt in the middle of *Elysium*'s massive flight deck. Neat rows of Falcon-type starfighters and Vulture-type bombers lined the walls, tucked away into alcoves that allowed them to be fueled, cleaned and maintained without interfering with landing operations.

Interspaced with those alcoves were the massive hatches covering *Elysium*'s fighter-launch tubes. Twenty-four tubes to a side of the hangar linked to twelve on each of the carrier's four "broadsides". In an emergency, the automated trucks, arms and systems of the flight deck would feed a fighter or bomber into each of those tubes every fifteen seconds.

Assuming she had a flight group in the tubes, *Elysium* could clear her decks in one minute. It would make her deck an extraordinarily dangerous place for a crewmember who wasn't paying attention, but the crews knew their jobs.

To Kyle's knowledge, there hadn't been an accidental fatality during launch operations aboard a Federation carrier during the entire war so far. Injuries were another story entirely, but given the speed with which the systems slung around multi-thousand-ton starfighters, a lack of deaths was impressive enough.

His own attention was unavoidably drawn to the Gods-cursed cheap red carpet *Elysium*'s crew had rolled out, with its flanking double file of Federation Marines in full dress gear. A bosun's pipe trilled, and an amplified voice bellowed over the flight deck:

"Forty-First Fleet, arriving!"

Kyle made his way carefully down the carpet and returned a quick salute from the tall, dark-haired woman waiting at the other end.

"Welcome aboard *Elysium,* Admiral Roberts," Captain Ivana Novak told him. "May I present my XO, Senior Fleet Commander Sung Yi? I believe you've met my CAG as well?"

"Indeed I have," Kyle replied, offering his hand to now *Vice Commodore* Michelle Williams-Alvarez. She'd come a long way from the traumatized officer he'd offered a psych discharge three years before. "It's good to see you, Michelle. The extra circle and the wedding ring suit you."

"It's your fault, you know," the starfighter pilot replied with a smile. She and her new Captain could have been sisters, both of them pale-skinned dark-haired women. "You keep dragging me into situations where I have to be a hero."

"I don't suppose we can hope to be luckier?" Sung Yi asked. The XO seem to almost fade into the background next to his Captain and CAG, a dark-skinned older man with a shaved head and tired eyes. "There's an old saw about how heroes happen."

"When someone screws up," Kyle agreed cheerfully, concealing a concerned look at the XO. With Forty-First Fleet's mission, the last thing he needed was a hesitant XO aboard his flagship.

"Given the war we have to fight, though, sometimes just *surviving* is heroism enough," he continued. "And sometimes, acts of heroism are the only way forward. We have a job to do, after all, Commander Yi."

"We do," Captain Novak agreed instantly. "Chief Campbell! See to the Admiral's staff and their bags. Can I show you to your office, sir?"

"Of course."

THE SPEED with which Kyle had blazed past being a one-star admiral meant that he'd never actually had a flag officer's office aboard a starship before. He'd been in them—as Captain of *Avalon*, he'd been a flag captain himself—but they hadn't actually been *his* space before.

He hadn't realized just how much computing support was available to a flag officer from their desk. Just from this room, his implants could access tactical feeds and strategic information, and set data analysis runs on a dedicated set of hardware and AIs.

The room itself was nothing to sneer at either. He'd spent most of his time in *Avalon*'s admiral's office paying attention to the occupant, but he now realized the room was large enough for small-scale meetings on its own—and had the same kind of holoconferencing gear that they'd used for the JSOC presentation.

From here, he could arrange a virtual meeting with every officer in a fleet without having to actually get out of his chair.

Of course, since it was now *his* office, there were some familiar items.

"Your beer fridge made it up yesterday," Novak told him, gesturing to the machine in the corner. It certainly *had* a beer fridge in it, though it also had a coffee maker, tea maker, and general mixed-drinks facility that was hooked directly into the ship's water lines.

"I don't know if it's stocked," she continued, "but I suspect your steward..."

Kyle had already popped the fridge open and removed a pair of beer bottles, inspecting the labels.

"Took care of that," he concluded for her, sliding a bottle across the desk to her. "New Cardiff's finest microbrewery. Try it."

"I don't drink on duty," she said slowly.

"I won't make you," he said cheerfully, "but I will give you permission."

He dropped into the big chair, sighing in relief as it automatically adjusted to his form. "If you don't want the beer, coffee? Tea? The drink machine can do just about anything."

Novak shook her head at him...but cracked the beer and took a sip as she seated herself.

Kyle smiled and leaned back against the chair.

"All right, Captain. Brief me," he instructed her. "I'm familiar with *Avalon* inside and out—what's different?"

"Not much," Novak told him. "Wartime construction; they didn't want to mess with what worked. My understanding is that there's a new generation of Alliance-standard eighty-five-million-cubic-meter ships coming down the pipeline, but they're building the *Sanctuaries* to the template."

That was Project Armada, not that Kyle could say much. A new generation of battlecruisers, carriers, starfighters and now star bombers.

"If there *is* such a thing," he stressed, "we'd only be laying down keels now. Years before we'd see new ships."

"And that's assuming we're still here," she said grimly. "Hard to read the strategic briefings without seeing that as a problem—not least from how much more restricted they are now than they were two years ago."

"I'll get you cleared for the full versions," Kyle promised. "There's stuff going on I can't brief you on yet, but as my flag captain, you'll need to know exactly where we stand."

"That doesn't sound promising, sir."

"It's ugly, is what it is," he warned her. "Forty-First Fleet, once fully assembled, is going to be seeing what we can do to take the momentum back. If you've any concerns about *Elysium*, your crew, or your starfighters, I need to know. We're only in Castle for twenty-four more hours, Captain."

"That's…a fast move-out," she admitted. "I only came aboard three days ago. Yi ran *Elysium* through her trials, though she passed those with flying colors. We haven't had time to shake out problems yet."

"Shake out what you can," Kyle ordered. "We don't have any more time. We'll have some more in transit to Via Somnia, but…" He shook his head. "From there, it looks like we'll have all of five days to exercise the assembled Forty-First Fleet before we move out."

"Do we get briefed before that?" Novak asked.

"Sure. About twenty-four hours before we move," he told her with a chuckle. "There's a lot of cards in play, Captain, and the Alliance is keeping most of them under wraps.

"That said, speaking of Yi…he's not exactly following my drift,"

Kyle noted. "I don't need people who *want* to be heroes, Captain, but the last thing we need is an XO who's determined *not* to be one."

"He's seen action twice already," Novak said. "Wounded in action at Kematian and decorated for pulling people out of the bridge after it was wrecked."

"Damn. He was at the Massacre?" Kyle asked.

A lot of people had been, but he'd thought he'd known every senior officer of Alliance Battle Group Seventeen. He'd been BG-17's flag captain in that godawful disaster, after all.

"Seconded to the Kematian Navy," Novak confirmed. "He was acting as tactical officer on their flagship and ended up saving the Captain's life—along with about six others—before he took an ugly gut wound from shrapnel."

"So, he understands how men end up heroes," Kyle said. He wasn't going to pretend that anyone who'd served at the Kematian Massacre wasn't going to get a little bit of extra leeway from him.

They'd all watched a world die together, after all.

8

Castle System
22:00 August 7, 2737 Earth Standard Meridian Date/Time
DSC-080 *Elysium*, Castle Orbit

In a perfect world, it wouldn't have taken Michelle Williams-Alvarez six months to get back into a combat command. In that perfect world, however, Vice Commodore Williams-Alvarez wouldn't have been the only person to actually command one of the Alliance's new bomber formations in action.

The success of that command, along with the rest of what then-Captain Roberts had got up to out beyond the Alliance's Rimward borders, had trapped Michelle in a months-long training command as the Alliance churned out its first wave of bomber crews.

After what felt like two or three trillion lectures, classes, and training flights, she was finally back where she belonged: aboard a carrier with a starfighter on the flight deck with her name on it.

The only good part of the stint on a desk was that Nurse-Commander Angela Alvarez had managed to take a month of shore leave on the capital planet in it. Enough time, apparently, for them to turn a shared apartment into an impromptu wedding.

The admittance chime for her office chimed.

"Enter."

To her surprise, it was Sung Yi who slipped into the room, almost furtively, and took an uninvited seat in front of her desk.

Michelle had come aboard the ship alongside Captain Novak and had barely managed to pick up the executive officer's *name,* let alone get to know him.

"Can I help you, Commander?" she asked. She and the Senior Fleet Commander were both O-6s, splitting command authority over the supercarrier's Naval and Space Force crew between them.

"Probably," Yi admitted. "Eternal Stars know that all of this is hitting like a ton of angry bricks. A week ago, I was running space trials on our girl and carefully ignoring the betting pool over who'd end up in command.

"Now we're shipping out in less than a day as part of a Void-cursed *fleet* that's pretending to be a convoy, and nobody seems to know just what our actual mission is going to be," he continued. "You've served with the Fox, right? You were with him at Istanbul and that mess, right?"

"And Tranquility too, if you were wondering," Michelle said slowly. "I wouldn't count on knowing much more than you do about the old man, though, Commander. There's always been a few links in the chain of command between him and me."

"You know more than I do," Yi told her. "Only time I was even in the same system as him, a couple of billion people *died.*"

"Kematian."

"Kematian," he agreed. "No one is going to miss the son of the Void he blew away for that, but...Void knows if any of us were the same afterwards."

"I wasn't there," Michelle said. "But I doubt it. Our counselors are good, but that kind of thing changes you."

Her own trauma had been more personal and extended, but the Navy's doctors had pulled her through it. Pulled her through well enough that she was *married* now, much as the thought terrified her.

"The Fox…some say he's a glory hound. Even a loose cannon," the XO finally admitted. "I mean, Void, he *rammed a battleship*. Made a tactical alliance with a Commonwealth officer. He's…he's something else."

"He's something else, all right," Michelle agreed carefully. "The last damn thing the Commonwealth ever sees coming. He *earned* his rep, Commander Yi—the good and the bad alike. Earned it the only way you end up a hero: by being the last man standing when all your enemies are dead."

"I find being a hero usually involves a bunch of people being stupid," Yi retorted. "Including the poor bastard who rushes in and ends up with the medal."

Michelle laughed.

"That's fair enough, Commander. But I can assure you that Roberts isn't setting out for glory. He's setting out to *win*—which is a different thing entirely, isn't it?"

Yi snorted.

"Fair, I suppose," he echoed. "Thanks, CAG. I…needed to talk to someone who knew him, and it pretty much had to be you."

Anyone junior and he'd have been asking whoever he spoke to to speak ill of a superior. There was always a special case between XO and CAG, though. They needed to be able to be utterly honest.

"If Roberts is dragging us into something secretive, it's something big," Michelle told him. "And he'll need our best…and he'll get it. Because he's the *Stellar Fox*.

"And like I said: the Commonwealth is never going to see him coming."

9

Niagara System
23:00 August 7, 2737 Earth Standard Meridian Date/Time
BB-285 *Saint Michael*

"I HOPE, sir, that you weren't expecting to find anything *useful* here," Vice Admiral Lindsay Tasker said bluntly over the q-com link. "They blew the repair yards, the storage depots, everything. Void, sir, they did a better job wrecking the base than we did when we left Via Somnia."

"That, Admiral Tasker, is because the Alliance realized there was a possibility of *losing* the fleet base," Fleet Admiral James Calvin Walkingstick, Marshal of the Rimward Marches for the Terran Commonwealth, observed acidly. "Something that our own compatriots apparently failed at."

The big bronze-skinned Marshal adjusted his long braid in a practiced gesture that *appeared* random but was actually a calming meditation.

"We don't expect to lose," Tasker agreed. "An idea that both the

Alliance and the League have happily disabused us of, of late. Speaking of Via Somnia…"

James shrugged with a cold smile.

"You could retake it, I suppose, but my intelligence suggests that Midori's defenders retreated there," he pointed out. "We may have ground their Seventh Fleet down to something that doesn't deserve the title anymore, but with Rothenberg's ships and the defenses they moved in, it would be an even fight.

"I hate even fights. Besides, why bother?" He shrugged. "It's not like Via Somnia has anything there other than the fleet base. We advance onwards and cut off its supply chain. They will have to abandon the base eventually as we take systems behind them. It is useless without something to defend, after all."

"Speaking of things other than the fleet base, we're going to need more troops," Tasker told him. "Lieutenant General Pék apparently underestimated the locals' willingness to fight. It…didn't end well."

"How bad?" the Marshal asked levelly. Blago Pék had eight transports' worth of power-armored Marines, each carrying an entire division. The man had an entire Marine Expeditionary Group under his command. He shouldn't need reinforcements.

"He opened his landings with two divisions," Tasker replied. "They…no longer exist, to all intents and purposes. Something like seven thousand dead, half again that wounded."

James concealed a wince. Sixteen thousand–plus casualties was eighty percent losses of two divisions. Tasker was right: those units were functionally gone.

"I'm sure Pék has reported this up his chain of command, but it may not have made its way back down to you," his Admiral continued. "Most of the MEG is tied up securing Midori. I don't think we're going to be breaking any of Pék's troops free for further operations anytime soon—and frankly, I want a new Marine CO!"

Pék, James suspected, was spinning his reports to his own superiors to blame a lack of Navy fire support for his failings. That his fire support was supposed to come from his own transports could easily be obfuscated when Tasker had eighteen capital ships in orbit.

"If I need to dig up another Expeditionary Group, that will delay things," he warned. "Are you capable of proceeding?"

"My *Lexington*s are shuttling new starfighter crews back and forth as we speak," Tasker told him. "Even with the logistics helping out, it'll be another week before I have my wings back up to strength." She shook her head.

"I need more carriers, sir," she admitted. "Eight battleships looked impressive as hell on paper, but we didn't have enough starfighters to blunt their bomber strike. With *Vesuvius* gone, I *really* don't have enough Katanas to go up against anything resembling a comparable Alliance fleet."

"The rest of the *Volcano*s are with Gabor," James pointed out. "And the Alliance hasn't seen him coming yet. I'll see what I can pull free from our other positions, but it'll be *Lexington*s and *Assassin*s."

The only sixty-million-cubic ship he had sitting in his reserve was *Saint Michael,* and while he could send her forward, his superiors would explode if he went with her.

"None of the new ships, huh?"

"Most of them went after the League," James reminded Tasker. "We have what we need, Admiral. I'll have replacement starships and a new MEG out to you within two weeks. After that, well, I'm going to have work for you."

"Only reward for a job well done," Tasker agreed brightly. "Lay it on me, boss."

10

Via Somnia System
08:00 August 19, 2737 Earth Standard Meridian
Date/Time
DSC-062 *Normandy*

"So, uh, did anybody *else* not know we were expecting a battle fleet?" Russell asked quietly over the tactical feed as the Alcubierre-Stetson emergences died down.

"It seems Admiral Rothenberg had enough of a heads-up to make sure that nobody accidentally went over the top when they showed up," Herrera pointed out. "But still. That's an *Imperial* fleet. Even with the Alliance, I always kinda half-figured I'd end up on the wrong side of one of those sooner or later."

The CAG just nodded. He was sitting in his office right now but was linked into a virtual conference of *Normandy*'s senior officers that Herrera had called as soon as the sensors started reporting emergence signatures.

"We've broken it down," Commander Tyrik Vang, *Normandy*'s tactical officer, reported. "Confirmed with the rest of the fleet, too.

"We're looking at sixteen ships but only ten are warships," he continued. "Three *Righteous*-class carriers, three *Defender*-class battle cruisers, two *Majesty*-class strike cruisers and two *Rameses*-class strike cruisers. Eight modern ships, forty- to-fifty-million-cubics, and two older units."

"With *Righteous Fire,* that's half of the Imperium's *Righteous*-class carriers," Herrera noted. "They've got two *Imperator*-class ships that just commissioned—*Sanctuaries* with the serial numbers filed off—but that's still forty percent of Coraline's modern carrier force."

"What the *hell* is going on?" Russell demanded.

"I don't know," the Captain replied. "What I *do* know is that I just got pinged by the Vice Admiral. Captains, CAGs, and XOs to report aboard *Righteous Fire* for what sounds like a fancy meet 'n' greet. Dress uniforms, gentlemen," she concluded with a grin Russell could *feel* through the link.

"This is more capital ships than the Alliance has concentrated since Fourth Fleet hammered the Commonwealth back to the frontier. Something is going down, people, and when it does, *Normandy* will not be found wanting.

"You get me?!"

Righteous Fire turned out to have a massive open space that was easily repurposed as a ballroom. Or, quite possibly, *was* a ballroom that was easily repurposed for other uses.

Russell would have called the latter an extravagant waste of space, but Federation warships all carried an atrium, roughly an acre in size, as "part of the life support system." Warships didn't have a lot of excess space, but despite his own dislike of established nobilities, he couldn't complain about the ballroom.

He *liked* having an atrium on his own ships, after all.

Right now, however, Vice Admiral Rothenberg had gathered the senior officers of twenty-four Alliance capital ships into that room, along with five flag officers—two Imperial and three from different Allied powers—and their staffs.

Rothenberg had taken the time to greet each of the hundred-plus officers as they'd entered and directed them all toward the buffet, where Russell had discovered that, if nothing else, aristocracy could *feed* people.

His wife's pastries were better—but these had been baked this morning. He was sure the rest of the buffet was perfectly fine, but he happily settled in next to the dessert table, watching the swirl of officers.

The party was the first time since the war began that he'd been in a room that wasn't dominated by Federation officers. The Imperium was the Alliance's second-largest military power, but the Federation's stronger economy meant that while they'd have identical active fleets, the Federation had twice as many reserved ships—and had been able to build new ships faster as well.

The Federation hadn't spearheaded every major fleet action of the war—but they had led every formation Russell had served in. With fifteen Coraline capital ships and two flag officers in Via Somnia, however, the Imperials weren't only the largest contingent at the party, they were the majority.

Since it was also their ship, the party was definitely tuned to their taste, which was ever so slightly…*off* to Russell. A Federation party would have had subtle incense, several punch bowls, an entirely self-serve buffet…

With an Imperial party, there were several stewards along the line of the buffet, preparing specific dishes or carving meat, and there was no drinks section at all. There was no incense wafting through the room, but there were uniformed stewards drifting through the crowd, collecting drink orders and using their implants to unerringly deliver them on request.

Or…perhaps even before request, the Vice Commodore realized as one of the stewards materialized at his right arm with a long-stemmed flute.

"Orange juice and sparkling water, Vice Commodore Rokos?" the middle-aged man in a Chief Petty Officer's dress uniform with steward tabs asked politely.

Russell chuckled and shook his head.

"I see the Admiral has files on us all," he noted. The only time he ever drank alcohol on ship was when beer was being handed out as celebration, and that was more for the principle of the thing than anything else.

"More accurately, his head steward," the steward replied as Russell took the drink. "That would, after all, be our job, Vice Commodore." He smiled. "The beef pasties on table three might also be to your taste," he noted. "The Coraline pasty is a solid evolution of the Cornish original, if I say so myself."

Russell laughed again.

"All right, Chief, I'll try those," he promised. "Thank you."

The man inclined his head and drifted away, three more drinks, likely each as uniquely tailored to the intended recipient as Russell's.

"Imperials," Captain Herrera muttered in his other ear. "They know how to make you feel pampered, but I'll be damned if it isn't vaguely creepy at times."

"They can fight," Russell pointed out.

"They can," his Captain agreed. "But some days, I swear we have more in common with the Commonwealth than with many of our allies."

"Except for the whole 'trying to conquer us' business," the CAG agreed.

Herrera laughed. "Fair enough," he conceded. "Looks like our newest Imperial friend is about to speak. Find yourself a seat or a wall, Vice-Com. Looks like it might be time to work."

THE TINY ADMIRAL with Rothenberg tapped a spoon on her wine glass as she stood on the dais at the end of the ballroom. The room's acoustics were impressive—the gentle noise carried through the entire space, over conversations and the sound of eating.

A lot of people had noticed her getting up and turned their attention to her, but the room's design allowed her gesture to gather everyone's attention.

"Officers of the Alliance," she greeted them all. "A toast."

She raised her glass.

"Spacers of the free stars, I give you liberty and the Alliance!"

"Liberty and the Alliance!" the crowd echoed back, the loyalty toast forged in the fires of the first war against the Commonwealth before many of these officers were born.

"For those of you who don't know me," she continued after a moment, "I am Rear Admiral the Elector Yong Ju von Song. I was the passage commander for convoy X-73, the warships and transports that arrived this morning.

"I am charged today to speak for my master, Imperator John Erasmus Michael Albrecht von Coral," she reeled off crisply. "I bear his Writ and, in this, speak with his voice."

She smiled.

"Vice Admiral Rothenberg, stand up, please," she instructed her superior.

Rothenberg rose. The Vice Admiral was darker-skinned than the Asiatic von Song, taller and less graceful than the petite woman currently speaking for his ruler.

"For any who will wonder," von Song continued, "I was dispatched with my master's Writ before the Battle of Midori, but I have confirmed his will with him.

"Parth Rothenberg, it is my honor and privilege to inform you that you are promoted to the rank of Fleet Admiral," she told the tall man, passing him a new set of insignia. "His Majesty sends his congratulations and his certainty of your continued loyal and skilled service."

Rothenberg took the insignia and carefully replaced the two gold stars on each side of his collar with the sets of three von Song had given him.

"He does me too much credit," he said slowly. "My life is the Imperium's."

"And he calls upon you to serve the Imperium," von Song replied. "As he called upon us all. Good luck, old friend."

They traded smiles, but then von Song returned to her seat—and Vice Admiral Conners rose.

"I have my own communications from Alliance Commander," she told Rothenberg and everyone else in the room. "As of this evening, *Fleet Admiral* Rothenberg is now the commanding officer of Seventh Fleet, absorbing both Task Force Midori and convoy X-73's escort into that formation."

She saluted him crisply.

Rothenberg shook his head but returned the salute.

"I relieve you, Vice Admiral Conners," he told the red-headed Trade Factor officer. "Thank you."

"I stand relieved. Or sit, as the case may be," Conners concluded with a grin as she retook her seat.

Still shaking his head, Rothenberg faced the crowd.

"It's not every day you get ambushed like this," he said dryly. "I should have guessed when I was asked to host this little affair.

"It will take us a few days to sort out the exact chain of command and division of ships and authority," he continued with a smile.

"I doubt the Alliance has assembled this large a fleet for decorative purposes, but for the moment, our primary purpose is to protect Via Somnia. Many of these ships are supposed to be somewhere else, which means we hope the Commonwealth will underestimate our defenses here.

"If they do, they're going to get an ugly shock. An even uglier one if they wait a few days."

Russell leaned forward to hear what the Admiral was suggesting, and he doubted he was the only one.

"The Imperium isn't the only one to have sent reinforcements. An entire Alliance battle fleet is on its way as well—under Vice Admiral Roberts. My understanding is that the Fox himself won't be joining Seventh Fleet, which means the Alliance has other work for him."

Rothenberg grinned evilly.

"I won't pretend I wouldn't rather take the offensive myself, but between myself and the Stellar Fox, I don't think Walkingstick's going to enjoy the next stage of his plans!"

11

Via Somnia System
12:00 August 21, 2737 Earth Standard Meridian
Date/Time
DSC-080 *Elysium*

"Emergence in five minutes," Captain Novak informed Kyle over the implant network. "*Elysium* is clean across the board."

"Thank you, Captain," he told her. He turned on his flag deck to level a questioning look at Senior Fleet Commander Sterling. "Archie?"

"All ships report green," his chief of staff replied instantly. "If something has changed since our last update, we've got thirteen capital ships ready to kick whoever's causing trouble all the way back to Earth!"

Kyle smiled.

"That hopefully won't be required. Last I checked, our update from Via Somnia Control is what…two minutes old?"

"Less," Sterling said cheerfully. "We're linked in live. Seventh Fleet is looking big and intimidating."

"Twenty-six capital ships, fifteen of them Imperial?" Kyle shook his head. "They'd better."

Once his own convoy, including Forty-First Fleet arrived, Via Somnia would have almost forty capital ships in one place. The largest force Kyle had ever seen before had been twelve—and the most he'd commanded before this convoy had been four.

"Any concerns on Control's scans?"

"Nothing," Sterling replied. "Not a peep. If we were hoping for the Commonwealth to stick their nose in this wasps' nest, I think they've chosen to decline."

"Shame," Kyle said mildly. "We'll have to make them reconsider that. Do you have a meeting set up with Rothenberg?"

"Nineteen hundred this evening," his chief of staff replied instantly. "His chief of staff said they've got some of the microbrews the Imperator introduced you to when you visited Coral."

The Vice Admiral chuckled.

"Somehow, I'm not surprised von Coral passed that tidbit on," he observed. "What do you think, Archie? Imperial Starburst or no?"

The last battle Kyle had taken *Avalon* into—while part of Seventh Fleet, in fact—had included his rescuing several hundred thousand prisoners of war, many of them Imperial. In exchange, when he'd passed through Coral on his way Rimward, the Imperator had hung their highest award for valor on him.

"Well, unless I miss my read, this is going to be a knock-down-drag-out fight for which ships go to Forty-First Fleet instead of Seventh," Sterling noted. "Reminding the Elector that the Imperium owes you isn't a bad place to start."

Kyle smiled.

"Mostly, I just want his Federation supercarrier and battleship," he observed. "But you're not wrong. I might as well get *some* use out of the Starburst. I keep having to *feed* the thing, after all."

The native coral of the Coraline Imperium's capital planet had a great deal of symbolic meaning to the Imperials, which meant that, among other things, the platinum-and-coral Imperial Starburst was actually *still alive*.

Fortunately for it, the Imperator had given Kyle easy-to-follow instructions for taking care of it. They apparently didn't expect officers to be able to baby their living jewelry, after all.

"I'll have Lionel lay out my dress uniform with decorations, then," he admitted with a sigh. "If we're lucky, this will be the hardest fight of this campaign."

Somehow, Kyle doubted that was going to be the case.

Righteous Fire was only slightly more than half *Elysium*'s size, but there were no shortcomings in her crew. Kyle was met by a perfectly turned-out honor guard of Imperial Marines with Admiral Rothenberg waiting beyond them with his chief of staff and *Righteous Fire*'s commander.

Lord Captain Dietlinde Kistner was a stoutly-built woman with shockingly pale skin and hair, edging almost into full albinism. From her quick, careful, looks around the flight deck as Kyle passed between the honor guard, anyone who embarrassed her in front of the Federation Admiral was going to get an earful.

From the looks of the crew confidently going about their business away from the landed shuttle, that wasn't going to be much of a worry.

Kyle offered Rothenberg his hand as the Imperial closed the distance with a brisk step.

"Welcome aboard *Righteous Fire,* Admiral Roberts."

"Thank you for having me, Admiral Rothenberg," Kyle told him. "I've never been aboard one of your *Righteous*-class ships."

Rothenberg smiled.

"I'm sure Captain Kistner would be happy to give you a tour," he replied. "I know they're no match for your *Sanctuaries,* but not much in the galaxy is."

"You'll have the Armada designs soon enough," Kyle murmured. "The *Istomin*s make even the *Sanctuaries* look slow and lightly armed."

Project Armada had taken the best technology from all of the Alliance powers, resulting in a carrier that was slightly smaller than a *Sanctuary* that carried almost a hundred more starfighters, a third again as many missile launchers, and fewer but heavier positron lances.

The *Istomin*-class supercarrier wasn't quite as well defended as a *Sanctuary*, but with over three hundred starfighters and bombers aboard, if someone was actually close enough to shoot at her, they'd done something wrong!

"Three years," Rothenberg replied, equally softly. "We'll have the new fighters and bombers first, though I don't know if they'll be *that* large an advantage."

"We'll see. I've only seen the specs for our eighth-gen starfighter, not the second-generation bombers," Kyle admitted. "The Reaper is a terrifying piece of hardware. But..." He shrugged. "Months before we've produced enough of them to be worth deploying."

"You go to war with the ships you have, not the ships you'd want," Rothenberg agreed. "Which, as I understand, is what you and I need to discuss."

Kyle smiled brightly and buffed the Imperial Starburst.

"Indeed, Admiral. Shall we?"

ROTHENBERG'S OFFICE showed the signs of a room the occupant had lived in for some time. A picture of an older woman accompanied by three children of ages varying from "junior officer" to "barely not toddler" hung on one wall, the familial resemblance to the Admiral clear in the children.

The only other picture was a painting of the planet Coral from space. The artist had managed to capture the rings of industrial plants and fortifications in a glittering spray of light that turned mechanical necessity into a stark beauty.

The reason for the lack of pictures, however, was that the Imperial Admiral had installed bookshelves in every space he could squeeze them into. They were quality shelves, too, built from a dark real wood Kyle presumed to be native to Coral.

Those shelves were double-stacked with paper books, about forty percent fiction and the rest physics, sociology and military history texts. Kyle was familiar with many of the reference texts, though he'd read them via implant download back when his implant capacity had been greater.

"My hobby," Rothenberg explained, gesturing at the shelves as he took his desk. "I don't have as much implant bandwidth as most, so I find paper easier to intake than a straight datastream."

If the Admiral's implant bandwidth was below average, it was impressive that he'd had a military career at all, let alone risen as high as he had with the reputation he'd earned along the way.

"When I lost my bandwidth, I was carrying a data tablet for months," Kyle replied. "It was easier to read things on a screen than to deal with the limits of my implant. That was mostly an adjustment, though."

A near miss from an antimatter missile had destroyed Kyle's original implant. The damage had scarred portions of his brain, meaning he could no longer link into an implant to nearly the same capacity he'd had before.

Neural Scarification Induced Implant Degradation. NSIID. A plain acronym for a disorder that had taken Kyle out of a starfighter cockpit and put him on the bridge of a starship.

"I've read your file," Rothenberg said. "From everything I saw, you were lucky to live at all!"

"I owe that to Williams. Who is now CAG aboard my flagship, so I think we all did well out of that," Kyle noted with a chuckle.

"The *Alliance* did well out of you living," the Imperial said. "No one is going to say you singlehandedly turned the tide of the war or anything, but you've done well by us."

"I try," the younger man said cheerfully. "And now, it seems, you and I get to arm-wrestle over how many ships I get to try my next stunt with."

Rothenberg laughed.

"Am I cleared to even *know* what your 'next stunt' is?"

"Yes, actually," Kyle told him. "You're just not cleared to know what *you're* doing with the ships I leave you!"

The senior Admiral shook his head, still laughing.

"That is strange, you have to admit."

"My mission kicks off now," Kyle said. "Yours… Well, I can't say more without telling you things that might cost me my commission."

"Fair," Rothenberg allowed. "So, what is your mission, then?"

"To cause bloody havoc along the frontier," Kyle explained. "I need to interrupt Walkingstick's offensive by making the systems along the border scream for help. Most of our offensives so far have been specific and directed, targeting Commonwealth fleet bases or retaking systems we lost.

"This will be neither of those things," he said grimly. "I'm going to bounce from system to system along the frontier, smashing local defense forces and forcing them to evacuate, and shred orbital industry."

There'd be a fine line to walk there. Destroying industry was one thing. Doing so without evacuating people was an atrocity—one even the Commonwealth generally avoided except when their fanatics got stupid.

He had no intention of causing a single civilian casualty he didn't have to. That might mean he'd have to leave some system's industry mostly intact to evade Commonwealth retaliation—but given that his purpose was to pull those ships away from attacking the Alliance, that was fine by him.

"That's overdue," Rothenberg noted. "Damn. They're not going to see it coming, are they?"

"Even in the last war, we fought mostly defensively," Kyle agreed. "No inhabited Commonwealth system has been taken, even temporarily, by an enemy—ever." His smile was cheerful. "I figure we can wreck, oh, somewhere between four and six before Walkingstick catches up."

Some of those systems were critical to Walkingstick's logistics, but only some of them would be. He had enough intelligence to target just the important systems, but he didn't want to be obvious about having it.

"So, you want, what, everything?" the Imperial asked.

Kyle grinned.

"Nah. That would be overkill—and you're going to need them. What can you give me?" he asked.

"I've already been told I won't keep *Avalon* or *Kronos*," Rothenberg replied. "That gives you at least three ships, two supercarriers and a superbattleship. Out of what you brought, what was already marked for Forty-First Fleet?"

"*Elysium, Gaia* and *Carolus Rex*," Kyle reeled off. "That gives me five. I want *Genghis Khan*, Admiral."

"That leaves me with just *Napoleon* for modern ships," the Imperial objected.

"And if I thought you'd give her to me, I'd ask for *Napoleon*," Kyle pointed out. "Instead, I'm open for suggestions. I need a minimum of ten ships, Admiral, and as big and as ugly as I can get."

Rothenberg shook his head, but he was grinning.

"I'm not giving you every modern battlecruiser I've got," he said firmly. "But I do have *Magellan*, and that kind of raiding operation is probably a better use for battleships than whatever I'm doing."

Magellan was a Renaissance Trade Factor battleship, roughly three quarters of the size of the two *Titan*-class ships.

"Three battleships, two battlecruisers, two carriers," Kyle noted. "Not much of a fleet to play matador to Marshal Walkingstick."

"I can't let you go out on this kind of operation without *any* Imperial contribution," Rothenberg told him. "*Righteous Light, Righteous Sword* and *Righteous Voice* would bring you up to your ten, wouldn't they?"

Kyle's grin widened. Three fleet carriers backing up his two supercarriers would make this whole endeavor extraordinarily painful for the Commonwealth.

"That would bring me up to ten indeed," he confirmed. "They're each carrying, what, four of your squadrons of Vultures?"

"Forty bombers apiece," Rothenberg confirmed. "Plus a hundred and twenty Arrow-B types. If that would be acceptable?"

"I don't know what the *Commonwealth* is going to think, but I'll take it," Kyle agreed. "I was expecting more of a fight, to be honest."

The Imperial Admiral laughed.

"Seventh Fleet still has *twenty-nine* starships, Admiral Roberts," he pointed out. "Even slicing off ten for your Forty-First Fleet, I still have one of the largest fleet commands the Alliance has ever assembled."

Kyle nodded. What Rothenberg *didn't* know was that Seventh Fleet was supposed to receive another tranche of reinforcements—at least four ships each from the Star Kingdom of Phoenix and the Renaissance Trade Factor.

Once they arrived, Rothenberg would command the single largest concentration of force the Alliance had ever put together. Which meant that despite Kyle's not having been briefed on the target allocation, he knew *exactly* where Seventh Fleet was going.

"I'll need time to work them up as a unit," he noted. "There won't be any penny-packet deploying this time. We've put together a sledgehammer and I don't want to miss with it."

"No one wants you to," the Imperial replied. "I don't know what your orders are, Admiral Roberts, not in detail. Any assistance Seventh Fleet or Via Somnia can provide, however, we will be glad to give.

"Let me be the first to wish you good luck!"

"I'll take it, but I hope to not need it," Kyle told him. "If I have my way, shock and aggression are all I'll need!"

12

Via Somnia System
12:00 August 22, 2737 Earth Standard Meridian
Date/Time
DSC-062 *Normandy*

"Somebody's trying too hard," Russell murmured, watching the enemy starfighters flare out in front of him.

"Sir?" his gunner, Jan Hu, asked. "I don't get it."

"They know they're working for the Fox, so they're trying to be clever," he concluded. "And they're expecting *us* to try and be clever."

He thought a sequence of commands at the tactical feed, highlighting what he'd picked up. "Their vectors are designed to swing them around us, stopping us from flanking them and opening up a whole bunch of sensor angles to stop us pulling, say, the Spartacus Protocol on them."

"I see..." Hu said slowly.

"But they've spread themselves thin and only about ten percent of them will have lance range on us if we go straight down the middle," the CAG said fiercely. "Which means...

"All units, form on SFG-292-Actual," he snapped over the main net. "I've spotted a hole and I'm taking everybody right into it!"

"Follow Rokos," Ozolinsh immediately confirmed. "I think I see it too. This is risky if they're playing us, Rokos."

Russell checked the vectors.

"I could see *Roberts* doing that," he admitted to his boss. "But these guys...they're *trying* to be clever like they think he'd want, but they didn't think it all the way through. They've committed *hard* to the counter-flank."

"And far too obviously," Ozolinsh agreed. "You've got the shot, Rokos. Let's take it."

The AI running the simulations was smart. *Very* smart. It could tell when the humans had made decisions and committed to a course of action and accelerated the apparent "time" in the simulation. "Minutes" flicked by in seconds as the hundreds of thousands of virtual kilometers blinked away.

"Fighters, form up to shield the Vultures," Ozolinsh ordered, the simulation slowing as he began to adjust his formation. They'd brought exactly the same numbers of fighters as Forty-First Fleet to the exercise, as a test.

Russell also knew that Roberts himself was just an observer, not giving orders or getting involved. Knowing the Admiral, he suspected that Roberts had seen *exactly* how his people had screwed up and was busy biting his tongue.

"Missiles salvoing," Hu announced. "Looks like someone could go for a damn walk out there."

Two thousand-odd starfighters put a lot of missiles into space, but that was still an exaggeration. The missiles weren't Russell's concern, though. He'd leave the defensive ECM and lasers to his engineer.

No, his eyes were on the vectors and ranges for his starfighters' lances. None of the Chevaliers with their heavier weapons were in play today. This was just Falcons and Arrows, both carrying identical deflectors and positron lances.

"And...here we go."

At starfighter engagement velocities, lance range lasted seconds at most. The simulator could draw it out, much as it had accelerated time before, but it wouldn't. The point was to practice as close to reality as possible without wasting time "in flight".

Of the almost nine hundred starfighters in Forty-First Fleet's formation, barely a hundred and fifty were in range as Seventh Fleet's fighters flashed through. None of those ships survived, and they only took forty of Ozolinsh's starfighters with them—and none of the bombers.

"Coming up on Forty-First Fleet," Ozolinsh said calmly. "We're clear of the fighters; let's do this nice and easy. Bombers, salvo torpedoes at one-point-five-million kilometers. Everyone, salvo starfighter missiles at seven hundred thousand klicks.

"We'll hit anything left with lances…"

KYLE WATCHED SILENTLY as Seventh Fleet's fighters swarmed over the icons representing his own fleet. *Genghis Khan* died first. Then *Avalon*. Then *Elysium*. *Carolus Rex* survived the torpedo strike only to fall to the missiles along with all three *Righteous*-class carriers.

The three battleships somehow survived every single torpedo and missile, but over half of Seventh Fleet's starfighters remained when they swarmed over the ships, and five hundred positron lances were too much even for the Federation's mighty superbattleships.

"Well."

He let the single word hang in the silence of his flag deck.

"Well," he repeated, studying the sequence of events in his implant, "it appears that I owe Vice Commodore Rokos some beer. A *lot* of beer." He paused thoughtfully and glanced over at Sterling.

"Archie, how much beer does it to take to make three thousand fighter jocks *stop* bragging?" he asked with a degree of false plaintiveness in his voice.

"I'm not sure your salary stretches to that, sir," his chief of staff told him.

"Damn. Well, then, we're just going to have to do *better* next time, aren't we?" Kyle asked aloud, glancing around his staff. They were all very distinctly busy.

"CAG debrief in one hour," he told them. "And Archie?"

"Sir?"

"Get in touch with Seventh Fleet's canteens. Beer for the fighter jocks is on Forty-First Fleet's tab tonight." He grinned. "Gods know they've earned it, but you're right—I can't pay for it. I also don't have to.

"I have a *budget* for this."

Forty-First Fleet's CAGs were present aboard *Elysium* in person. The CAGs from Seventh Fleet's carriers were present by virtual link. Everyone from the exercise was linked in, as were Admiral Rutherford and both flag officers' staffs.

"Well," Kyle said brightly, "it appears that Commodore Ozolinsh and his people have demonstrated something of what happens when we *epically fuck up*."

His tone was still bright and cheerful, but the emphasis on the last three words had every one of his CAG's recoiling.

Well, every one of them except Michelle Williams-Alvarez, who looked about ready to deliver the same lecture he was going to lay on them. She was his most junior Vice Commodore, however, which meant she wasn't fleet CAG despite being the flagship's CAG…and, he guessed, that his other CAGs weren't giving her comments the weight they might deserve.

"Does anyone want to try and defend themselves before I explain exactly how you managed to accidentally wipe out an entire ten-ship battle fleet?" he continued. "Anyone?"

The fact that his CAGs were all in the room with him meant he was quite certain there wasn't anything on the floor, despite their simultaneous study of it.

"We got fancy and clever," he said after a moment. "Too fancy, too clever."

"…it usually works for you," someone muttered. Kyle carefully didn't note which officer had spoken.

"The trick, people, is to get *exactly* fancy enough," he told them. "Ozolinsh's people hadn't settled on an attack plan yet. They hadn't done anything to suggest their course or their plan, but instead of holding position, we got fancy…and we *committed* to that fancy.

"Isaac Newton is the deadliest son of a bitch in space, and sometimes that's because he says you can't change course on a dime," Kyle continued. "You may have five hundred gees of acceleration, but every second you're pointed in the *wrong* direction is an extra second you have to spend accelerating to get back to the right one.

"So, when you commit first—and do it in a way your enemy can see—you put Sir Newton on *their* side. If you have to commit like that, commit with a hammer they can't stop. Two kilos of aggression can be worth three of sleight of hand."

He grinned.

"The *best* stack, however, is a kilo of both." He lit up a holoprojector. "Now, this is what we all *did*."

The recording played through rapidly, showing an hour-long exercise—that would have been a twelve-hour real-life battle—in roughly a minute.

"Vice Commodore Rokos spotted your mistake and Commodore Ozolinsh rammed a thousand starfighters through it," he told them. "I took the liberty, however, of running a simulated scenario of how you could have *countered* Ozolinsh's maneuver."

A new scenario played out. This time, as Seventh Fleet's fighters began their hard charge toward the gap in the defending fighter's formation, hundreds of ECM drones flashed out from Forty-First Fleet's formation.

In the original scenario, they'd been held for missile defense. In this one, Kyle used them to create a mass of confusion over just where his starfighters were. It *looked* like they were still on their wide course—but in reality, they were using the cover of the drones to close up their formation.

This time, Seventh Fleet's strike ran into a solid wall of missiles and a closed-up starfighter formation. With AIs pretending to be pilots, the resulting fight was even more of a mutual massacre than it probably would be in reality…but far too few fighters made it through to threaten Forty-First Fleet.

"We screwed up," he told his people, stressing the "we" to make sure they realized he was including himself. "We can do better. We *have* to do better—Walkingstick is going to send his best after us, and if we muck up like this in a real fight, the Commonwealth *will* be sending us home in boxes.

"And I don't know about you lot, but I have a kid and a fiancée I'd rather go home to in one piece!"

13

Via Somnia System
08:00 August 28, 2737 Earth Standard Meridian
Date/Time
DSC-080 *Elysium*

"ADMIRAL ON DECK!"

Kyle shook his head at Sterling's booming voice and grinned impishly at his assembled starship Captains and staff as he stepped up to the head of the conference table next to the flag bridge.

There were only five people physically in the room, but even the nine attending virtually were at least making an effort at standing to attention as he waved them all back to their seats.

"At ease, people," he told them. "We officially do not have time for Academy spit and polish today."

He took his own seat and grabbed the cup of coffee a steward had left waiting for him, studying his officers as he took a sip.

It was an eclectic bunch. Six Castle Federation Captains, three Coraline Imperial Lord Captains and one Renaissance Trade Factor Captain for starship commanders, plus the four Federation Senior Fleet Commanders of his staff.

Captain Bai'al of *Magellan* stood out the most. The Trade Factor Captain was one of the most obvious transhumans Kyle had ever met, with visible circuitry across their shaved head and a pair of mechanical tentacles mounted on their shoulders.

Right now, the tentacles were relaxed, hanging down the Captain's torso like silver suspenders over their breasts, but they still marked them as unique even in this crowd.

Novak sat at Kyle's right hand, *Elysium*'s Captain one of the physically present officers.

Captain Elijah Hammond, *Avalon*'s new Captain, sat to his left. Hammond's holographic image could have been Mira Solace's sibling, with the same dark skin and tall, slim build as the Admiral's fiancée.

He seemed *very* aware that he commanded the Admiral's old ship, too.

Both of Kyle's Federation battleship Captains were cut from the same mold, older women with sharp features and pure white hair. Both Captain Edmonda Blue and Captain Lara MacLeod were veterans of the last war with the Commonwealth, junior officers who'd spent the peace calmly accumulating experience and rank.

His battlecruiser Captains, however, were a study in contrast. Captain Augusta Pekkanen of *Carolus Rex* was a squat woman with a short golden braid and a seemingly squashed face, where Captain Simon Tanaka of *Genghis Khan* was an almost eerily skinny and tall man with dark skin and folded eyes who towered easily ten centimeters over his immense Admiral.

The three Imperial Captains were equally varied. Lord Captain Josiane Vass of *Righteous Light* had almost luminescent gold hair that clashed dramatically with her pitch-black skin, where Lord Captain the Elector Maria von Kita of *Righteous Sword* looked like her family had left Japan last month instead of four hundred years earlier, and Lord Captain Pino Mihailović of *Righteous Voice* was as swarthy and dark-haired as his Russian last name suggested.

"We've had a week," Kyle noted. None of the officers he'd been given were weak links. Few of the Alliance's less-capable Captains were in uniform, with the Commonwealth having taken care of many that the Alliance's member fleets hadn't caught in time.

"Does anyone have any immediate concerns?" he asked. "Our mission profile calls for us to move out at midnight ESMDT, but I have a lot of discretion on that if we have a problem."

That was the advantage of his part of Operation Medusa. The deep-strike fleets had to leave at particular times to make sure the final attack went down simultaneously. His own distraction effort was more flexible.

"Our starfighters have improved their coordination dramatically over that week," von Kita noted. "We still have occasional issues with senior officers from the Federation or Imperium requesting support that the other's fighters can't provide." She shook her head. "We should have standardized our fighters as well as our missiles."

"It's being done," Kyle reminded her. "But we have the fighters we have. Have your CAGs focus on that concern, people. I'd suggest virtual exercises in each other's starfighters—have our Falcon pilots fly virtual Arrows and vice versa."

He smiled wickedly.

"In fact, let's make sure that all of our starfighter pilots get at least two or three sim hours in a Vulture bomber. We need them to keep the bombers alive, and having a solid understanding of what a Vulture can and can't do won't hurt."

Nods carried around the room.

"Our starship coordination is still rusty," Bai'al noted in their oddly pitched voice. "The battleships are maneuvering well together, but if we end up in a capital ship action, the battlecruisers need to work with us…and the carriers need to do a better job of hiding behind us."

Tanaka looked like he was about to say something, but Kyle held up a hand to cut him off.

"The cruiser and carrier crews aren't as used to the idea of capital ship actions as the battlewagons' people," he pointed out. "We can drill that in transit—or are we that bad off, Captain?"

Bai'al shook their head.

"No," they replied. "We're just rusty. As you say, we're not used to formation flying with capital ships. Virtual drills for the shiphandlers while in transit should suffice to shake off the rust."

Kyle nodded.

"Anyone else?" he asked. He glanced around, giving them a moment to raise their concerns, then nodded firmly and mentally issued a command to the conference software.

A three-dimensional representation of the frontier between the Alliance and the Commonwealth appeared in the middle of the conference. The Alliance itself was highlighted in blue and Terran space in red—and the occupied systems were blue circled in red.

"This is our area of operations," he said brightly. "As we speak, we have reason to believe that at least one, and more likely two or three, Terran fleets are moving against key targets along the front. Walkingstick is taking his time to set things up, but we are quite certain the hammer is about to drop.

"For reasons I can't get into, we need him to hold off for about eight weeks. Convincing the good Marshal to chase us instead of hammering his way towards our homeworlds is now our job."

He let that sink in, waiting for the inevitable question.

"How?" Tanaka asked softly. "Forty-First Fleet is a powerful formation, yes, but we can't take on Walkingstick's reserves or fortifications at Niagara."

"No, we can't," Kyle agreed. The Niagara System flashed onto the display. Home to the Commonwealth's biggest fleet base on this frontier, it anchored Walkingstick's campaigns and was home to enough defenses to laugh at half a dozen capital ships on their own—and a defensive fleet more powerful than his own.

"But." Four systems near Niagara flashed, bright green carets appearing around them. "Niagara is a relatively lightly inhabited system in its own right and, perhaps most importantly, has never had a large surplus of food.

"The industrial plant that came with the fleet base can do a lot of things, but all it can do for food is recycled protein." A grimace ran around the room and Kyle grinned again. "Exactly. Even the most willing of crews start losing their enthusiasm when they know they're eating protein bars made of their own waste.

"These four systems are key to Niagara's logistics pipeline," he explained. "They provide food, raw materials, replacement small-tech components...the works. The fleet base doesn't *need* them...but without them, their morale and efficiency are going to plummet.

"That said, if we just fly in and level the orbital infrastructure of those systems, they'll know we knew exactly what to hit. They'll know what systems to defend, and they can secure them with, say, a dozen capital ships apiece."

"How much of Walkingstick's force do we need to draw down?" Bai'al asked, sounding curious as they studied the astrographic chart.

"All of it," Kyle told them all.

"To do *that*, we can't be obvious. We need to keep Walkingstick and his people jumping, and we need to hit the good Marshal in the only weak spot the bastard seems to have: his political superiors."

A new flashing caret appeared on the display, locking on to an entirely different system.

"I also want to test this Fleet out against an easy target and send a message to the Commonwealth that while we are playing by the rules of war, we aren't playing by *their* rules anymore," he concluded grimly. "Which brings us to the Aswiri System.

"Twenty-five light-years from here, almost thirty light-years into Commonwealth space." Via Somnia, of course, was already well into Terran space. "Aswiri is a system of almost no importance to anyone. Minimal exportable surpluses, a small Commonwealth Navy refueling facility.

"Defenses at last record were two fighter stations mothering a hundred Scimitar-type fighters apiece and half a dozen gunships. We should be able to secure the system without losses of our own, at which point we will give them forty-eight hours to evacuate all non-residential spaceborne platforms."

Kyle sighed. He did *not* like this part of his mission, even though he'd written the recommendation himself.

"And then we will blow their entire industrial plant to dust bunnies," he told his people, his voice quiet. "We will minimize civilian casualties—to zero, if we can!—and scrupulously adhere not merely to the letter but the spirit of interstellar law.

"This will *not* be Hessian." The system where Kyle had suffered NSIID and where the new war had begun had seen its infrastructure crushed by a retreating Commonwealth fleet…with its civilian work-force still aboard. "I will neither order nor permit atrocities.

"But the destruction of Aswiri's orbital industry will add to the political pressure on Marshal Walkingstick to come after us, and the raid on a minor system will leave them guessing where we're going to hit next.

"Two or three raids of this nature should force him to pull back the lion's share of his fleet to try and intercept us, which is exactly what the Alliance needs. We're playing matador, people, and we need to make sure the bull doesn't gore us."

He grimaced, looking around to test the resolve and understanding of his officers.

"At the end of the day, though," he said quietly, "Forty-First Fleet is expendable so long as we do our job. The Alliance needs Walkingstick watching us. Sooner or later, that means we're going to get hammered. Our job is to minimize the losses we take when that happens.

"I want you to be clear on that and make sure your juniors understand as well," he told them. "We will have objectives and targets for each raid, but absolutely *nothing* we are going after is an all-costs target. I have every intention of abandoning attacks if the defenses are too heavy and of outright flight if a heavy force arrives while we are mid-operation.

"We can't distract Walkingstick if we're dead."

14

Aswiri System
12:00 September 7, 2737 Earth Standard Meridian
Date/Time
Alliance Forty-First Fleet

EMERGENCE BUBBLES GLITTERED in the darkness, the blue flare of Cherenkov radiation bursts lighting up the void around the star Aswiri. Starship after starship emerged from the nothingness, ten capital ships forming a protective dome around three logistics ships.

The first ship out had, of course, been *Elysium,* and Vice Commodore Michelle Williams-Alvarez's starfighter had been in space before half of Forty-First Fleet's capital ships had entered the star system. Her starfighters and bombers mirrored the formation of the fleet, the single wing of Vultures guarded by a moving shield of Falcons.

Her starfighters were out in front, but *Avalon*'s group was only a few thousand kilometers behind her, and the rest of the Fleet's fighters joined up rapidly, the lead wings keeping their acceleration down until the entire massed fist of Alliance ships had assembled.

"Are we seeing any reaction from the locals yet?" Michelle asked her gunner, an aggressively average-appearing man named Ferdi Eklund.

"Our Q-probes are barely a dozen light-seconds ahead of us," he pointed out. "We're still seeing what they were doing two minutes ago."

"And we arrived ten minutes ago now, so…"

Eklund coughed.

"And if they had seen us two minutes ago, they hadn't done anything to suggest it," he told her. "Nobody is doing *anything* in orbit."

She shook her head and dipped into the long-range sensor feed. She wasn't surprised to confirm what Eklund had said, but she'd needed to see it herself.

Six Commonwealth *Scythe*-class gunships, half-million ton mobile missile platforms with…few saving graces. Two *Zion*-class starfighter platforms, each rated for five ten-ship squadrons. A single one of those squadrons flying a standard high guard patrol above the planet Indus.

The Aswiri System definitely had potential. A good-sized asteroid belt. A pair of midsized gas giants. An inhabitable planet. The colonists had been sensible and kept most industry in orbit while slowly expanding the population on the surface.

It wasn't a rich system, but it was clearly self-sustaining and had been carefully laying the groundwork for staying self-sustaining while becoming rich.

Michelle felt a twinge of guilt. Much of that groundwork was in the orbital infrastructure they were here to destroy.

It wasn't much of a twinge of guilt. Spacers and resources from this world fueled the war machine that was grinding down her own people and had smashed half a dozen systems' key orbital infrastructure.

It was war—and turnabout was fair play.

"All right, people, we've got three sets of targets on the board and only one is armed," Vice-Commodore Robert Lakatos's voice echoed over the tactical net. *Avalon*'s CAG was the senior starfighter officer in the fleet, which made him Fleet CAG. Thankfully, he was *usually* willing to listen to advice from his juniors.

"SFG-306, SFG-059," he reeled off, naming the fighter groups from *Carolus Rex* and *Genghis Khan*. Those groups were purely starfighters with no bombers.

"Each of you gets a gas giant's infrastructure," Lakatos told them. "You know the drill: they have forty-eight hours to evacuate all non-residential platforms, then you blow them to hell. They probably have starfighters in place to guard them, but you'll have them outnumbered by far.

"Play it safe. I'd rather none of us were writing letters home when this is over, clear?"

Over a hundred and forty starfighters split off from the main group, two groups of seventy-two heading towards each gas giant and its orbiting cloudscoops.

"Everyone else," he continued. "Form on SFG-012. Williams, you launched first; you get to go first."

She grinned.

"Bombers lead the way, sir," she told him crisply.

"Exactly. The Admiral wants to make this a show. Let's give them one—and get everyone home!"

"STILL NO RESPONSE FROM THE LOCALS?" Kyle asked.

"Nothing," Sterling confirmed.

That was...weird. Intelligence records suggested that Aswiri saw maybe three interstellar transports in a month. Thirteen starships showing up on their sensors should have earned *some* reaction.

But he could see the same thing his chief of staff could. Forty-First Fleet was accelerating toward the planet at two hundred and ten gravities, and their starfighter strikes were zipping along at just over five hundred gravities.

The energy flare from over a thousand antimatter drives was probably visible from the ground, but no one was reacting at all. The gunships remained in orbit. The fighter platforms remained quiet.

"We're in bloody missile range," Sterling complained. "What would they do if we started launching?"

"Take a nap and decide what to do with the missiles in half an hour or so?" Kyle suggested with a chuckle. "Even our missiles have a forty-two-minute flight time; they've got a lot of time to respond to us, but…"

"If *I* had a hundred starfighters and six twenty-year-old gunships to defend a system, I'd be freaking out at even one warship, let alone ten," Captain Novak interjected. "What's the plan, sir?"

"Well, I was expecting them to give me a call by now," he replied. "But someone has to get the ball rolling. We don't really have the time to be subtle, so get me an omnidirectional broadcast."

"On it," Sterling confirmed. "Recording linked to your implant; you have the call."

Kyle smiled broadly, looked into the pickup, and activated the recorder.

"Residents and defenders of the Aswiri System," he greeted them. "I am Vice Admiral Kyle Roberts of the Alliance of Free Stars.

"We could pretend that your handful of defenders were going to make a difference here, but that would be a waste of everyone's time. I am now in possession of your star system. The destruction of the Commonwealth forces here is inevitable, and I strongly recommend their surrender.

"Regardless of whether they choose to fight an impossible battle, *my* clock starts now. You have forty-eight hours to evacuate all space-borne industrial platforms, after which they will be destroyed by long-range lance and missile fire.

"Designated residential stations will be spared, but that designation *will* be validated by close-range inspection by my starfighter wings. You will provide me with that list of designated stations within twenty-four hours or we will make our own list."

He suspected—he *hoped*—that his broad, cheerful grin was unnerving to the civilians watching him.

"I have no desire to inflict unnecessary casualties, but the war has come to this star system, and I will not be leaving this system with your orbital industry intact.

"I will have your list of designated residential stations in twenty-four hours and you will have evacuated all industrial stations in forty-eight," he concluded. "If these instructions are *not* followed, those stations will still be destroyed at that time.

"I request the surrender of your military forces and a clear communication of your intention to cooperate from the system government. Failures of communication at this point will only result in unnecessary death."

He cut the recorder.

"Send it," he ordered. "Let's see if they're going to be sensible or stupid."

"If they don't evacuate the stations…" Sterling half-whispered.

"That's why it was an omnidirectional transmission," Kyle told the junior officer. "Even if the government decides to be stupid, most of the civilians will evacuate themselves."

"And those that don't?"

Kyle grimaced.

"Will haunt my conscience for a very long time," he replied.

"OH, hey, look, someone finally stopped hitting snooze."

Vice Commodore Lakatos probably shouldn't have made his comment on the all-ships channel, but Michelle couldn't blame him. They'd been closing with the planet for over thirty minutes, rapidly approaching the point where they'd start decelerating to make sure they didn't blow past the rock at seven or eight percent of lightspeed, and the locals hadn't even launched the other nine squadrons in the *Zion*s.

"What have we got, Eklund?" she asked, running the data herself.

"I make it six squadrons, all Scimitars," her gunner replied. "One *Zion* launched three squadrons, the other two. They're forming up with the squadron that was already in orbit and the gunships."

Six squadrons. They were Commonwealth squadrons, not Federation, so that was sixty ships, but still…the approaching attack force had more than twice as many *bombers* as the defenders had starfighters in total.

"Any sign they're hiding a Sunday punch somewhere?" she asked. "That's pretty sparse, even for what we were expecting."

"I'd guess the extra squadrons are at the cloudscoops," Eklund told her. "So, the battlecruiser wings will hit them, but…"

"Four squadrons of Scimitars versus seventy Falcons is not a battle I need to watch to know how it will end," Michelle said grimly. Unless the older fighters had been issued new missiles, the Alliance force even had a range advantage on them.

She pinged Lakatos.

"Boss, do we ask them to surrender?" she asked quietly. "Hell, permission to *beg* them to surrender?"

"I'm going to ask," Lakatos replied, but his voice was grim. "But would we, in their place?"

Michelle sighed.

"No. It's a damned waste, though."

"It is," he agreed. "Watch your vectors, Williams. You're in first and I want them gone before they can threaten you. If they surrender, fine. Otherwise…" The sensation of a pained shrug came over the link.

"We'll launch torpedoes at maximum range and blow them to hell," he concluded. "I'll give them the chance to surrender or abandon ship, but I am *not* losing people today. Not against this opposition."

"Understood."

Michelle turned her attention back to her people, tracing all of their vectors and adjusting them, sending the new courses out to her people on the fly. She had almost two hundred Falcons forming the lead wave of the strike, and if every bomber behind them launched, that was going to be a *lot* of torpedoes for her people to stay out of the way of.

"Fleet CAG is on," Eklund murmured, and Michelle picked up the Vice Commodore's broadcast.

"Gunships and starfighters of the Terran Commonwealth, that you are even coming out to meet me suggests that you are either brave or suicidal," he said gently. "You are outgunned, outranged, outnumbered and outmatched.

"Bravery is not enough. Your deaths will change nothing. Surrender or be destroyed."

Seconds ticked by. Minutes. The range was dropping by thousands of kilometers every second, even as the Alliance strike hit turnover and began to deaccelerate.

Michelle checked the numbers. No choices left, but she didn't blame Lakatos for hesitating.

"All bomber squadrons," his voice sounded on the tactical channel heavily. "Select your targets and launch torpedoes. I want a full sweep, people. Every gunship, every starfighter, both defense stations.

"These poor bastards have decided to die for their country. Let's make it happen."

THE CONTINUING SILENCE from the planet and defenders was nerve-wracking. The only good news, such as it was, was that many of the civilian platforms clearly *had* received his message and were starting to evacuate under their own authority.

Even an only moderately prosperous system like Aswiri, however, had *hundreds* of civilian ships and platforms. With the best intentions and hope, it would take someone coordinating affairs to empty them all inside two days.

"Lakatos has opened fire," Sterling murmured. "Torpedoes at just under maximum range." The chief of staff shook his head. "They held some back, but they just threw eight hundred torps at sixty starfighters, six gunships and two defense platforms."

"I can do the math," Kyle agreed. "Hopefully, once they've made us kill a thousand-odd people, they'll find the nerve to actually *talk* to me."

The result of the torpedo salvo was basically inevitable. The defenders didn't have the firepower, the numbers, or the skill to survive Forty-First Fleet's opening salvo, and Kyle stayed iron-faced as the explosions played out.

"Orbit is clear," Sterling reported when it was over. "There's more than a few escape pods out there, though. Some of them decided not to die for nothing."

"Good," Kyle said levelly. "Send out our search-and-rescue craft. Any of them with the brains to ditch before we blew them away deserves a ride to the surface." He paused, considering.

"Pass a course-change order to the Fleet," he told Senior Fleet Commander Zartosht Aurangzeb, his operations officer.

"We will adjust our zero-velocity point to be at least one million kilometers clear of the main orbital zone," he ordered. "We can hit anything we need to from there, and it should help keep them honest."

"Understood," Aurangzeb replied briskly, the darkly tanned man pulling up his own systems as he linked to the Captains.

"Do we have *any* response from the surface?" Kyle asked.

"Negative," Sterling told him. "What do we do?"

"We know where the capital is?"

"Yes, sir. Gubernatorial mansion, even," his chief of staff told him.

"Hit it with a directional radio beam. I want to melt their cursed receivers if they don't listen," Kyle snapped. "One more recording."

He activated the recorders and leaned back in his chair, leveling his hardest glare on the pickup as his implant fed him the information he needed on Governor Soslan Terry.

"Governor Terry," Kyle said grimly into the camera. "Your defenders are dead. My patience is rapidly disintegrating. Every hour —every *minute*—you play games rather than working to evacuate your orbital industry and providing me with the designated safe-zone stations places your citizens at greater and greater risk.

"Enough people have died today for the honor of the flag, but make no mistake: I *will* complete my mission."

Once again, he cut the recording and fired it into space. This time, the radio transmission was a focused pulse, cutting through Indus's atmosphere to bathe Terry's mansion in a wash of coherent radiation.

Radio receivers were getting Kyle's message and burning out. A focused tightbeam from *Elysium*'s main comms array was only an order of magnitude short of a weapons-grade maser.

Kyle waited.

"Incoming transmission!" Sterling snapped. "Relayed via a q-com-enabled satellite, he's trying to hide his location.

"Clever boy," Kyle said. "Play it."

The image of a squat man with dark hair and broad, frog-like features appeared in the screen, Soslan Terry turning a black gaze on his own cameras.

"I don't know who you are or what you're playing at," he snapped. "But this is a Commonwealth world! Run while you still breathe. You can't touch us! We are Terran!"

Kyle waited.

"That's it?" he asked.

"That's it."

"Moron." Kyle considered the frozen image. "How close is that satellite?"

"Not enough for a real-time conversation, but it'll cut about five seconds off the transmission time," Aurangzeb reported.

"Target it. A bit more gently than we hit the mansion," Kyle said. "The governor wants to bluster? Then let's chat."

He activated the recording pickup again, letting his anger fuel the broadest grin he could summon.

"Governor Soslan Terry, what a pleasure to actually be speaking to the man in charge," he greeted Terry. "You seem to be under some misunderstanding of the situation, however.

"The Commonwealth has invaded the worlds of the Alliance of Free Stars. I know that might seem minor to such an important Terran man as yourself, but it does mean that we are at war with the Commonwealth." Even as Kyle maintained his cheery grin, he let his voice get cold.

"Under the rules of war, I am expected to give you forty-eight hours to evacuate your civilian industrial infrastructure. I have done so. While, technically, what you do with that notice is up to you, I have no intention of standing by and allowing you to get your people killed.

"If *you*, Governor, have not begun coordinating the evacuation process in the next twelve hours, I will localize whatever bunker you are hiding in and vaporize it from orbit," Kyle told Terry. "Hopefully, your successor will be more cognizant of the realities of your situation."

His flag bridge was silent as he looked around at his people.

"Send it," he ordered. "And find me the Governor's hole, people. I don't want to kill more people than I have to, but it seems Governor Terry might well volunteer for that list!"

THIS TIME, the response was relatively prompt.

"You're insane," Terry told them without preamble. "You can't do this to a Commonwealth world! I am the elected Governor of a quarter-billion Commonwealth citizens; I will not be intimidated by a two-bit colonial thug with delusions of grandeur.

"No one will be evacuating anything. The Navy will be here shortly and you will see the folly of your actions!"

Kyle considered the message for several long minutes, then sighed.

"Senior Fleet Commander Aurangzeb, can we still trace him if we blow up his relay?"

"Yes, sir," his ops officer said briskly. "Their security sucks. We should have his bunker nailed down in ten, fifteen minutes. Don't need the relay anymore."

"Oh, good," Kyle replied. "Captain Novak?"

"Admiral?"

"Vaporize his communication relay for me."

"Yes, sir," his flag captain said brightly.

A moment later, one of *Elysium*'s massive, megaton-a-second primary positron lances flared to life. A warship's deflectors would have protected it at this range, but the tiny communications satellite had no such defenses. The beam of antimatter that hit it had spread out to be wider than the satellite at impact, utterly annihilating the automated space station.

"Find me that bunker, Commander," Kyle ordered. "And, Captain Novak? Have your engineers fabricate me a deep-penetration special weapons package.

"I don't *like* killing off the Governor's staff, but I have the sinking feeling that if I don't remove this idiot, a whole bunch of other people are going to get killed."

"WE'VE GOT HIM," Sterling told him. "Bunker buried under the mountains to the west of the capital. About a hundred klicks clear of everything, I'm guessing he's got some kind of underground tramway."

"Are we sure it isn't another relay?" Kyle asked.

"It's a larger facility. He *might* be using it as a relay, but there's definitely some kind of bunker there."

"All right." Kyle looked around his flag bridge again, studying his staff.

"Any further word from the Governor?" he asked.

"Nothing," Aurangzeb told him. "No attempt to coordinate an evacuation, no attempt to talk to us. He seems to think if he ignores us, we're going to go away."

"And the uncoordinated evacuation?" Kyle asked.

"Messy," his operations officer replied. "People are moving, but…it isn't pretty. They'll be at least twelve hours behind the deadline."

"I don't suppose anyone else is stepping up?"

"*Something* is going on," Novak told him, the Captain linked into the conversation via their implants. "There's a slow but growing wave of organization, but…whoever is doing it has no authority; it's being assembled on the fly."

"And instead of helping, the local government agencies have been ordered to get in the way," Kyle concluded.

"You have that package for me?"

"Yep. One long-range ground-penetrating bunker buster." Novak shook her head. "Should punch clean through into the bunker and wreck the Governor's day."

Kyle considered the possibility of directly threatening the Governor, but his impression was that wasn't going to help.

"You may fire when ready, Captain," he ordered.

A single white icon appeared in the tactical feed hitting everyone's implants, a weapon closer in size to a new bomber torpedo than a capital-ship missile accelerating away from the carrier at a thousand gravities.

It flashed across the distance to the planet, carefully aligning itself in orbit and then diving straight down. There was a white flash on the feed, and then data began to come in from the Q-probes in orbit.

"Target bunker is gone," Novak confirmed. "Minimal splash damage."

"All right." Kyle shook his head uncomfortably, then sighed. "Get another wide broadcast."

The recorders turned on for hopefully the last time and he looked unhesitatingly into them.

"People of the Aswiri System, your Governor continued to refuse to speak rationally to us or to begin coordinating the ordered evacuation of your orbital platforms.

"We have now destroyed the bunker he was transmitting from. I will, at this point, work with whoever is prepared to organize an orderly evacuation of your space stations.

"The clock is ticking."

15

Aswiri System
20:00 September 9, 2737 Earth Standard Meridian
Date/Time
Alliance Forty-First Fleet

IF HE'D BEEN able to think of a single good reason, Kyle wouldn't have watched. He had no need to watch decades of investment go up in flames—only duty to see his orders carried out.

He stood on *Elysium*'s flag deck with his hands clasped behind his back as fireballs marched their way across the Aswiri System. He'd given them eight extra hours to evacuate and hoped, as hard as he could, that it had been enough.

The cloudscoops were destroyed first, the Q-probes orbiting the gas giants allowing him to watch in real time as his starfighters carefully severed the habitat sections of the stations from the industrial portions. Once the habitats had been boosted into higher orbits, the starfighters went to their real work.

Positron lances flared against the backdrop of the atmosphere of the massive planets below, chopping the immense tanks and refinery plants into flaming pieces. Debris scattered across the atmosphere of the gas giants, and the massive tubes that had hung down from the scoop stations fell.

A massive hydrogen explosion lit up one of the screens, but the starfighter crews had judged the distance well. The habitat sections containing the cloudscoop's crew were thrown about by the explosion but undamaged.

The destruction in Indus orbit was more carefully orchestrated. They could let debris fall into the gas giants. They couldn't let it fall to the surface of the inhabited planet.

Every explosion, every missile strike, every lance beam, had been carefully calculated for hours before the destruction even began. Refinery platforms, orbital factories, assembly platforms, refueling stations…everything in orbit that wasn't purely residential was ripped apart by fire.

Here, the debris was flung into higher orbits. It would form a new temporary ring around Indus. Eventually, the locals—or, more likely, the Commonwealth—would have to clean it up to avoid the navigation hazard.

But none of it fell to the surface, and none of it survived. The Aswiri System would no longer fuel the economy powering the war machine attacking Kyle's home.

They'd done everything in their power to minimize casualties, and he understood the necessity…but it was never something that Kyle Roberts was going to be comfortable watching.

"It's done," Sterling finally said softly at his shoulder. "Recalling the fighters now. Where do we go from here, sir?"

"Our next target," Kyle replied, clearing his throat with a rough cough. "Once the starfighters are aboard, get everyone headed for Alcubierre drive and arrange a virtual conference."

"You could, you know, let people know the plan in advance," his chief of staff pointed out.

Kyle forced his usual chuckle.

"If I do that, Commander Sterling, then I have to admit that half the targets are being picked with a dartboard, and what would *that* do for everyone's confidence in the Stellar Fox?

"Arrange the conference—but make sure everyone is keeping an eye out for trouble. We shouldn't have been here long enough for any of their Navy ships to make it, but let's be ready for it if they do."

EVEN AS HE took his seat in the conference room next to his office and linked into the virtual conference, the tactical feed was running through the back of Kyle's head. There were no threats left in the Aswiri System, but they were entering the earliest time where the Commonwealth Navy could have a response force in position.

"We're done here," he said without preamble as the last captains linked in. "It's a shit job and I don't expect any of us to like it. In truth, any of you that *do* should probably talk to your ship's doctors."

He grinned broadly.

"This is about as bad as our job gets without us committing *actual* atrocities," he noted. "And if anyone under my command does that, you will *wish* the Commonwealth caught you first."

"These kinds of raids are risky for that," Captain Tanaka observed. The battlecruiser commander looked drained—but he was from one of the New Bombay System's cloudscoops. Watching his own fighters dismantle a station almost identical to his home had to have been hard.

"That's why we're keeping the fleet together," Kyle replied. "Most of our first-round targets are sufficiently lightly defended that we could take them with two or three ships—but we need the moral support of the fleet, I think, to make sure we keep our hands clean.

"We did well here," he concluded. "I'm still furious with the Governor, but at least his successors decided to cooperate. Our next target is likely to be smarter…but they're also going to have more of a Navy presence."

"And our next target is?" Bai'al asked dryly.

Kyle smiled.

"The Starkhaven System," he told them, bringing up the astrographic chart of the region. "Fourteen light-years—roughly a week—

away from here. We're bypassing three systems that would be useful targets, but I want to keep Walkingstick and his people guessing.

"Starkhaven is a key supplier of food and raw materials to the Niagara fleet base," he continued. "The first of several systems we are going to hit that are Walkingstick's logistic keystones.

"Of course, since Walkingstick is far from an idiot and knew that, sooner or later, we were going to have to at least attempt an offensive like this, Starkhaven is better defended than most of the systems out this way."

The chart zoomed in on Starkhaven. One inhabited planet, Ferelden, four uninhabited scorched rocks closer in to the massive star, a midsized asteroid belt and a massive super-jovian gas giant.

"Kirkwall is the gas giant and supplies just over twenty percent of the fuel used at the Niagara fleet base," Kyle noted. "There are both civilian and Commonwealth Navy cloudscoops in orbit of Kirkwall, and, at last count, they were protected by eight Terran Commonwealth Starfighter Corps *Zion*-class defense platforms.

"Unlike Aswiri, intelligence is quite certain that Starkhaven's Corps bases have been equipped with both Katanas and Longbows," he continued. "They won't be Walkingstick's best, but they're not back-system militia, either."

"What about the planet?" Captain Hammond asked. "Two separate targets?"

"We're not burning the farms from orbit, if anyone's afraid of that," Kyle told them dryly. "But the transshipment facilities in Ferelden orbit are a major relay point for not only the food and hydrogen from Starkhaven but for spare parts, munitions, and raw materials coming from deeper in the Commonwealth.

"The fixed defenses in Ferelden orbit are lighter than Kirkwall's. Just four *Zion*-class platforms. But…"

He thought a command and the display refocused. The orbiting stations and warehouses of the transhipment facilities were marked in green as they carried on their eternal circles around the planet below. The four fighter bases glittered in crimson.

As did the two battlecruisers orbiting protectively over the entire flock.

"Intelligence puts two *Assassin*-class battlecruisers in Ferelden orbit as of four weeks ago," Kyle told his people. "They're older ships, ones we have quite badly outgunned, but they're probably the biggest threat in the system.

"Since, as Hammond said, we have two targets in the system...I have a plan."

16

Niagara System
09:00 September 10, 2737 Earth Standard Meridian
Date/Time
BB-285 *Saint Michael*

"Sir, Senator Cambridge is requesting to have a q-com call with you sometime this afternoon."

James Walkingstick studied the painting of Earth on his wall for several long seconds.

"Forgive me, Commander, but who is Senator Cambridge?" he finally asked his secretary. "We have one hundred and six Senators at last count and six hundred Assembly Members."

He could access the information from his implant, but Commander Andrea Messere often had useful insight on the people who wanted to talk to him. He didn't get many calls from Senators or Assembly Members—and most of the ones he got were from members of the Committee on Unification.

"Sorry, sir, I…figured you'd know who the Senator for Aswiri was after the last few days."

James winced.

"All right, Andrea, I deserved that," he admitted, then sighed. "Schedule the call. Let's not pretend I'm going to enjoy talking to the good Senator, but it's part of the job."

"He's available immediately if you are, sir," Messere told him. "He seemed to think it was urgent."

The man in charge of over a fifth of the Commonwealth's fleet, tasked with bringing fifty systems into the unification, sighed.

"What's the latest from Aswiri?" he asked.

"The Alliance moved out last night after thoroughly wrecking the local space industry," she reeled off instantly. "We have a three-cruiser task group sixteen hours out, but Rear Admiral Kita never expected to get there before the Alliance left."

"I'd hope not," James agreed. Ami Kita's three strike cruisers were last-generation ships, *Ocean*-class vessels carrying sixty starfighters apiece. Aswiri hadn't been able to give him a decent idea of what the fleet raiding his space looked like beyond "thirteen starships," but even if *half* of those were logistics ships, Kita would have been better off shooting her crews herself than committing them to action.

"But she'll be in position to provide S&R and relief," he continued. "That's useful to know when speaking to the Senator. Let his staff know I'm available."

James Walkingstick shook his head.

"Let's face the music."

SENATOR DORIAN CAMBRIDGE LOOKED, to James Walkingstick anyway, like someone had taken his face and squashed it down by a third. His head was broad and his features heavyset in skin so pale, it could have been carved from ivory.

"Marshal Walkingstick," he greeted James. "I'm glad you could take time out from allowing thugs to rampage over our systems to speak to me."

James smiled thinly.

"Senator Cambridge," he replied. "I am always at the disposal of the members of the Star Chamber of the Commonwealth, though the task of bringing an entire region of space into Unification is a demanding one."

"You are *also* tasked, Marshal, with securing the region behind you," Cambridge said acidly. "A task I must question your commitment to, given the attack on my star system! We cannot simply allow these murderers to have their way!"

"We are at war, Senator," James said carefully. "I know it may seem strange, but not all of our conflicts will be—not all of them can be—fought entirely in enemy space. By engaging in our campaigns of unification, we do open ourselves to attack.

"Vice Admiral Roberts's attack was...unexpected but not unanticipated," he continued. "The Alliance represents one of the largest blocs we have ever attempted to bring into the Commonwealth at once. Unlike many, they have the resources to prosecute offensive operations against us."

"No one has *ever* attacked a Commonwealth system like this!" Cambridge snapped.

"That is unfortunately not true," the Marshal told him. "During the last war against the Alliance, they carried out offensive operations in our territory as well. The Via Somnia System has already fallen in this war."

"Those were *military* targets. Aswiri wasn't even supplying your bases!"

"But Aswiri is a member system of the Commonwealth and a legitimate military target," James said levelly. "I do not wish to sound dismissive, Senator, but the attack on your system was carried out with scrupulous attention to both the accepted laws and traditions of interstellar war."

"That son of a bitch *killed my Governor*!"

"Your Governor, Senator Cambridge, ordered over a thousand TCN and TCSFC personnel to their deaths for no good reason," James snapped back. "He faced a *battle fleet,* Senator. From the moment Roberts emerged from Alcubierre, he controlled the Aswiri System.

"The only way to minimize losses at that point was to cooperate with him. The destruction of Aswiri's defenses and industry was inevitable. The deaths of military and government personnel was not.

"*That*, Senator Cambridge, I fully lay at the feet of your Governor. Admiral Roberts may be our enemy, but he did everything in his power to carry out his mission with minimal loss of life."

"And that's all you're going to say?" Cambridge snarled. "Thousands are dead, billions in infrastructure destroyed, and you're going to defend your enemy?!"

"There are ships already en route for relief operations," James replied. "We will hunt down Admiral Roberts and his fleet, Senator. There will be consequences for what has happened, but the risk of it occurring was always a factor in this operation."

"And my world just swings, does it?" Cambridge asked.

"That is between you and your colleagues in the Senate and Assembly," James told him. "I would strongly recommend a significant package of economic relief and rebuilding assistance myself, but that is entirely out of my scope of authority, Senator.

"Making sure what happened to Aswiri does not happen again is not. And *that*, Senator Cambridge, is now one of my top priorities, I assure you."

If for no other reason than because prosecuting the damned war required more and more political support with every passing week.

THE CALL WITH CAMBRIDGE OVER, James stalked to the wallscreen in his office, switching it to show the view of the world beneath him. The Niagara System had few selling points beyond the big TCN base there. The Navy had seen the fate of Trinity in the last war and carefully separated their fleet bases from major civilian populations.

It wasn't that Trinity had been particularly badly handled when the Alliance had smashed the fleet base there, but the Commonwealth Navy liked to keep the civilian populace well away from its wars. The Committee on Unification's mission had a massive base of support across the Commonwealth, but James Walkingstick was aware of how fragile that support was.

It was easy to intellectually agree that humanity had to be unified. It wasn't a hard leap from there to accepting that Unification was most easily accelerated by forceful annexation. The Unificationists were even willing to accept a certain quota of military personnel coming home in body bags or not at all…

But to see a civilian system come under attack? That could risk the support that drove the core concepts of Unification. Without that support, every aspect of James's mission was in danger. He'd already taken three times as long as planned working against the Alliance, mostly because he'd had too few ships to truly end the fight at any point.

"Messere." He linked to his secretary through his implant. "Get me Tasker and Gabor and…" He paused thoughtfully. "Vasek, I think."

"Yes, sir."

He turned back to his examination of the planet while he waited. Ontario possessed massive waterways and beautiful forests, with the capital of Waterfall named for the most impressive feature of the area, and there were continuing discussions of making it some kind of tourist hotspot.

Interstellar tourism was expensive, though, and the Niagara System was too far away from the core worlds with populations that could afford it. So, it had become a fleet base instead, with the entire local economy driven by the build-up for the campaign against the Alliance.

"I have the Admirals for you, sir," Messere reported.

"Link them in to a virtual conference," James ordered, turning away from the screen and activating the holoprojectors in his office.

"Admirals," he greeted them.

Vice Admiral Lindsay Tasker and Vice Admiral Mihai Gabor were his strong right-hand swords, each commanding a fleet driving into Alliance territory system by system as they attempted to force the Alliance into a major fleet action.

Rear Admiral Johanna Vasek looked uncertain as to why she'd been pulled into this call.

"You've all been briefed on the raid in Aswiri," he said briskly. "Vice Admiral Roberts is once again making himself a giant headache. Tasker, Gabor—I need you to step up the next stages of your offensives.

"The Alliance wants to distract us by hitting in our rear areas. Return the damned favor," he ordered.

"Sir."

"What did you need me for, Marshal?" Vasek asked.

"We're going to have to eat at least one more raid," James said grimly. "I have no idea where the Alliance will strike next, but we need to begin assembling a counter-force. I'm guessing we're facing nine to eleven capital ships, so I want you to begin pulling together a reaction force.

"They're going to have to be second-line units," he continued. "Our *Volcano*s and *Saint*s are all tied up, but we should have enough *Lexington* carriers and *Resolute* battleships for you to assemble a force that can take down Roberts."

Vasek's flagship, at least, was a *Hercules*-class battlecruiser. *Perseus* would be the only modern ship in the Admiral's fleet, though.

"If we're facing eleven modern ships with second-line units, we'll need at least sixteen ships," Vasek pointed out levelly, earning a mental checkmark of approval. Not many were willing to tell the Marshal of the Rimward Marches what they thought he didn't want to hear.

"Preferably eighteen," she continued. "That's not a Rear Admiral's command, sir."

"Scrape together what you can," he told her. "If we need to use even older ships, we need to use them."

And James Walkingstick would be *ecstatic* when the Commonwealth got around to retiring the last of the *Paramount*-class carriers and the rest of their deathtrap contemporaries.

"As for rank, I'm out of damned Vice Admirals who aren't tied up, so consider yourself breveted," he told her. "Roberts is too clever by half, but you *will* catch him.

"And between that and Tasker and Gabor's strikes, we might finally manage to cut the Alliance's numbers down to size for a final attack."

17

Via Somnia System
14:00 September 12, 2737 Earth Standard Meridian
Date/Time
DSC-062 *Normandy*

RUSSELL JOINED Captain Herrera and the XO in the small conference room attached to the Captain's office, wondering just what was going on.

Seventh Fleet had been reinforced again since Admiral Roberts had left, five more ships from the Star Kingdom of Phoenix and four from the Renaissance Trade Factor. That totalled six ships from each of those nations in the Fleet—a quarter of each star nation's naval strength.

Despite that, they'd been under communications lockdown since Forty-First Fleet had moved out. Even as a carrier's CAG, Russell hadn't been allowed to communicate via a live link with anyone.

As soon as he sat down, a virtual conference space took shape around them, linking in to his implants as he found himself in a "room" containing every Captain, XO, and CAG from thirty-eight capital ships, plus Fleet Admiral von Rothenberg and his staff.

"Thank you for making time for this, people," Rothenberg said quietly. "We haven't been as busy as we might like, but we've been damned busy. We're about to get a lot busier, but I've some ugly news to share first."

That got everyone's attention.

"Da Vinci fell last night," the Admiral said bluntly. He continued as if he hadn't announced the beginning of the end of the world. "A twenty-two-ship attack fleet led by no less than ten *Volcano* supercarriers attacked.

"Four Renaissance Trade Factor ships, two Federation ships, and two Imperial ships were destroyed in action, along with approximately thirty-two hundred starfighters from all three nations," he told them. "Total casualties are unknown, but the Commonwealth is now in control of the star system.

"Ground fighting continues as of our last information, but the Commonwealth has now landed ten divisions with orbital fire support. The Alliance Joint Chiefs have had no choice but to declare the system lost for now."

The virtual conference was dead silent. The Renaissance Trade Factor only *had* four star systems, but any of them was richer than three quarters of the systems in the Alliance. If Da Vinci had fallen, the entire tone of the war had just changed.

"What do we do?" Jessica Farrell asked quietly. Captain of the Trade Factor carrier *Portage*, the pale-skinned redhead looked terrified. "My *family* is in Da Vinci!"

"The Joint Chiefs are preparing a counter-operation as we speak," Rothenberg told them. "Given Seventh Fleet's strength, I offered to take us to Da Vinci immediately. We aren't the closest fleet, but we *are* a superior fleet to the one that took Da Vinci and we're only fourteen days away."

He paused, then shook his head.

"I was informed that carrying out our mission was a higher priority," he concluded softly. "As I'm sure everyone here is thinking, I demanded to know just what our mission was."

Russell had certainly been wondering. Just what was Seventh Fleet supposed to be doing that was more important that retaking a major Alliance homeworld?

"That was when Sky Marshal von Stenger decided that we were close enough to launch time to brief me," the Admiral told them. "We kick off our portion of what is being called Operation Medusa in thirty-six hours, people.

"We will be the fifth of the Medusa strike forces to move out and will be coordinating our operations and arrival time with fourteen other such strike forces.

"As I'm sure is no surprise, Seventh Fleet is the largest such strike force, but there is a clear reason for that," Rothenberg concluded, his voice sounding shaky.

"Most of the fleets have a single target, but Seventh Fleet will be hitting three targets in one extremely heavily defended system."

He smiled grimly.

"Officers, in thirty-six hours, Seventh Fleet will move out towards the Sol System."

THE CONFERENCE WAS silent in shocked surprise, and Rothenberg's grim smile remained.

"We are, of course, one hundred and sixty-four light-years from the home system," he noted. "I checked. A direct course will deliver us to Sol in just over twenty-six days. Carrying out our mission and returning will take roughly two months."

Two months. The Joint Chiefs wanted to send their most powerful starship formation deep into enemy territory on a *two-month-long* mission—and that was assuming that Seventh Fleet didn't simply collide with the defenses of the Commonwealth's capital and…cease to exist.

Russell was as shocked as anyone else. Unlike the rest, though, he could see the Stellar Fox's hand in this—rumor had put the new Vice Admiral in charge of a group tasked to plan a war-ending offensive. A strike at Earth itself?

That read like Roberts's handiwork.

"Powerful as Seventh Fleet is," he finally said, the first of the officers to reply, "we don't have the strength to take and hold Sol. We might be able to defeat the local defense, but the Commonwealth will move heaven and Earth—and a hundred or so capital ships!—to take the system back."

"Our mission is not to *hold* the Sol System," Rothenberg replied, his nod to Russell suggesting that was exactly the question he wanted to hear. "The exact details of our targets will remain classified for the moment, but I can tell you that much.

"We are tasked to attack Sol, defeat the mobile defenders, and destroy specific targets before retreating back to Alliance space. All fifteen attacks are being coordinated via q-com to make sure we arrive simultaneously, leaving the Commonwealth unsure where to send their response."

"Sol," someone quipped. "I'm going to guess they'll send it to Sol!"

Rothenberg chuckled.

"I agree. That, people, is why Seventh Fleet has over thirty capital ships," he confirmed. "We are going to go directly to Sol and hammer our heads against the most powerful defenses the Commonwealth has assembled.

"Intelligence suggests those defenses are badly out of date and that the mobile forces to back them up are lighter than we might think, but this will still be no easy mission. The Commonwealth Navy will fight to the last ship, the last starfighter, to defend Earth.

"But we will overcome. We will demonstrate, once and for all, that the Commonwealth cannot wage war across the galaxy without consequences!"

18

Castle System
16:00 September 12, 2737 Earth Standard Meridian
Date/Time
New Cardiff

"Third Squadron, adjust your vector seven-point-three degrees left and go to max accel," Mira ordered. "Close up around *Sunset*. Captain Mason needs your point defenses."

Eight of the *Gallant*s moved as instructed, their more powerful engines wrapping them around the cruiser as the Commonwealth salvo drove home. It was...enough. One of the gunships took a near miss, an antimatter explosion sending the ship reeling away, but the strike cruiser came through intact.

Three more of Mira's squadrons, twenty-four gunships, swept in the trail of the fighter strike launched by the orbital defense platforms. This was Castle, which meant that there were easily a hundred starfighters for each gunship in the strike, but the Terran force was headlined by a dozen *Saint*-class battleships.

Her remaining two squadrons joined *Sunset*, and the other three cruisers left to defend Castle in launching a massive, focused missile salvo. Between the starfighters, the bombers, the gunships and the hundreds of orbiting missile platforms, there were over ten thousand missiles of various capabilities sweeping down on the Commonwealth fleet.

Even *Saint*-class battleships couldn't weather that storm. Anti-matter explosions marched their way across the Commonwealth fleet, and the handful of ships that survived those succumbed when the starfighters swarmed over them.

Mira leaned against the central display projector in her command center and issued a mental command, ending the simulation.

"Well done, people," she told her staff and her gunship captains as the big display returned to reality, showing her eight squadrons of gunships orbiting peacefully along with the terrifyingly small remnant of the Federation Home Fleet.

"Not bad at all, Admiral Solace," her new boss added from *Sunset*'s flag deck. If Fleet Admiral Aeolus Orman had any bitterness at having two thirds of his strength stripped from him for the new offensives and being relegated to the flag deck of an old strike cruiser, it didn't show in his voice.

Orman still commanded Home Fleet, after all. He might have fewer starships now, but he still had all of Mira's gunships and the thousands of starfighters and missile platforms of that command.

"I remain confident," he continued, "that any force the Commonwealth sends to Castle will regret their decision to stick their noses in the meat grinder."

The last force to do so, Mira reflected, had managed to destroy most of a Reserve Flotilla before it could be commissioned. That, however, had predated the deployment of the *Gallants*. Someone could attack the industry around Gawain again, but they wouldn't find the gas giant as easy prey now.

"My confidence, of course," Orman said with an audible smile in his voice, "will only be augmented by further exercises to prove it. This next round is going to be based around a worst-case scenario where ground control is lost.

"My apologies, Mira, but you get system-control responsibility for the next hour or so," he told her on a more private channel. "You've done good work with your gunships. Let's see if they can hold up without you!"

"I hope I am not irreplaceable," she agreed. "After Da Vinci..."

"After Da Vinci, we must be prepared for every possible incident," Orman agreed. "So, let us see how your protégés handle."

"Good luck, sir," Mira told him.

"Shouldn't you be saving the luck for your captains?" he asked.

"I trained them. They don't need it."

AN HOUR LATER, Mira was only somewhat eating those words. Admiral Orman, it seemed, had passed command of the Op Force off to Captain Kelly Mason—and Captain Kelly Mason had spent almost as much time working with Kyle as Mira had.

The ensuing arrival of the same eight-battleship, eight-carrier fleet functionally *in* Castle orbit had resulted in Mira's gunships going head to head with battleships at point-blank range.

Without any coordination from the ground, every single one of them had ended the simulation as debris...along with four Federation cruisers, several thousand starfighters, dozens of defensive platforms —and the entire Commonwealth attack force.

"Well, that would have been...pyrrhic for us," Mira noted as the senior officers reconvened. "Mission accomplished, I suppose, but rebuilding the defenses would take years."

"Fortunately, my experience is that very few Commonwealth officers are students of the Stellar Fox's patented 'ride the needle into the bastards' throats' school of tactics," Orman noted. "*I* certainly wasn't expecting to see sixteen capital ships attempt to reenact his charge at Tranquility."

"You told me to do something unexpected, sir," Captain Mason replied sweetly. "I actually wasn't sure I'd managed that—after all, everyone knows I was at Tranquility."

Orman shook his head.

"How close did you come to losing a ship?" he asked.

"The computers were being nice," Mason said grimly. "Two of the carriers emerged less than five kilometers from each other. A tiny twitch one way or another and they'd have collided.

"There's a *reason* that stunt is usually reserved for insane ship captains, not fleet commanders," she concluded. "I didn't expect the *Gallant*s to be quite so devastating at close range, though. Easy to forget we built them around battleship-grade beams."

"Let's sleep on that," the Admiral told them. "I doubt we're going to have the Commonwealth show up tomorrow, but..." He shrugged. "No one was expecting them at Da Vinci."

"Any word on what the plan is there?" Mira asked.

"Not that I can share," Orman said. "Too many of our ships are tied up in existing operations, but the Trade Factor doesn't have enough ships to retake Da Vinci on their own. It's a giant mess.

"That," he concluded sharply, "does not leave this conference. Clear?"

"Clear."

"Good. Now, what I want you all plotting for the next round of exercises is some way for us to sneak the *Gallant*s right up to whatever battleships the Terrans bring to the party," he told them. "Those big guns are *far* too useful to let go unused!"

At least, having a "command" that she held out of a bunker under New Cardiff meant that Mira Solace and her staff got to go home at night. The apartment felt empty without Kyle in it, however, which occasionally left her considering a dog to have at least one large, warm animal in her home.

Her fiancé probably wouldn't appreciate the comparison, though, she reflected.

She was spared from deciding between cooking for one or ordering in by an implant message from, of all people, Lisa Kerensky—the mother of Kyle's son—asking if she was free for supper.

Mira didn't even waste the time to glance in the refrigerator before responding positively and heading to change.

She doubted Dr. Kerensky would object to her showing up in her day uniform, but if she had the opportunity to wear civvies for once, she was going to take it!

SOMEHOW, Mira wasn't surprised when Kerensky directed her to Daniel Kellers's house. The Member of the Federation Assembly for New Cardiff was the neurosurgeon's boyfriend—and it was quite possible they'd moved in together and no one had told Mira!

Rank had its privileges: among them, Marine bodyguards and access to the Joint Command's transport pool. Mira's pair of armed bodyguards greeted Kellers's armed bodyguards, and the collection of armed individuals promptly did their best to vanish as a hundred and forty centimeters of overexcited preteen swept out of the house to give her a massive hug.

Mira blinked against the unexpected embrace but returned Jacob Kerensky's embrace gently as she looked through the open door to the suburban house. Daniel Kellers and Lisa Kerensky were standing just inside the door, both grinning broadly as Jacob hugged her.

"Good to see you, too," she told the kid dryly, detaching herself and returning a significantly-more-expected embrace from Lisa Kerensky. "I appreciate the invitation," she continued. "Cooking for one is starting to *suck*."

Kellers laughed.

"I'm familiar with the feeling," he said, his face even redder than usual as he tucked Lisa Kerensky's hand behind his heavyset back. "Lisa and Jacob only moved in a few weeks ago, but I'm already dreading my next work trip."

So, they had moved in together—and Kyle's son had gone with them. Mira suspected that *Kyle* had to have known, but their own communications were heavily curtailed by the lockdown throughout the entire Alliance.

"Come in, come in," the MFA insisted. "Lisa wanted you to be the first to know. Well"—he paused thoughtfully—"the third to know, but we already told Mrs. Roberts, and communicating with Admiral Roberts is…difficult."

Mira laughed, delighted by the sheer mundanity of the affair. From that alone, she could guess.

"You may as well stop hiding your hand, then, Lisa," she instructed the neurosurgeon. Lisa promptly smiled and extended her left hand, showing off the simple yet glittering ring.

"Dan asked me to marry him," she said, unnecessarily. "I sent a message to Kyle… Do you know when he'll be able to get back to us?"

She sounded almost worried, which was adorable to the woman Kyle *was* marrying.

"The entire fleet is under communications lockdown," Mira warned her. "I'm not sure when he's getting *my* messages—and some of those are even work-related."

"I'm…briefed on Admiral Roberts's mission," Kellers admitted slowly, earning him questioning looks from both women, "but it remains classified at the highest levels."

"I know," Mira agreed. "I *also* know he wrote the damn op plan that has the entire fleet on lockdown. Whatever he's doing, better him than a lot of people, but I'm still allowed to miss him."

"That we are," Kellers agreed, glancing over at his fiancée. "We want to wait until he's back to get married. That…could be a while, though."

"I know it's weird," Lisa Kerensky admitted, "but after all we've been through, the only people who absolutely *have* to be at my wedding are Kyle, Jacob, and Kyle's mother."

Kellers smiled and kissed her fingers.

"I understand," he confirmed. "I've a few added to that list myself. Come on. I need to check on dinner, and I'm sure Jacob has, oh, only about two and a quarter million questions for you," he finished.

Mira returned the smile, basking in their joy and glad to be accepted. Given how poorly Kyle and Lisa's relationship had gone for much of the past, she was happy to be there.

And her experience suggested that, yes, Jacob the Navy-mad was going to have a few million questions for his Rear Admiral step-mother-to-be.

19

Deep Space
22:00 September 13, 2737 Earth Standard Meridian
Date/Time
Alliance Forty-First Fleet

THE FLIGHT DECK mess was not, in Michelle Williams-Alvarez's experience, usually a particularly subdued place. The one aboard *Elysium* had been a notable exception since leaving Aswiri. Conversations were in quiet murmurs, gazes flickering away from the CAG and other senior officers as they walked through.

She'd let it slide for a few days, but four days of *fighter jocks* being depressed was a bad sign. She might be new to commanding an entire fighter group, but she'd learned from some of the best.

Her Wing Commanders followed her as she walked into the big room, scattering out to the tables as she glanced around the several hundred officers in the room. Only about half of her people were present, but that would be enough for this.

Gazes flicked toward Michelle and then away as she walked up to the mess bar—which should have been doing brisk business this late in the ship's day but was currently abandoned except for the pair of bored-looking ship's stewards.

She nodded to the two young men, gesturing for them to clear away to the sides of the bar, and then hopped up onto the bar and turned to face her people.

She hadn't said a word yet, but the quiet conversations were already fading away as everyone turned their gaze to the Vice Commodore now standing on their bar.

"All right, people," she said briskly. "Four days. Four days you lot have been moping around, pretending to be a bunch of sad sacks instead of starfighter crew.

"Your simulator scores suck. Your efficiency ratings suck." In comparison to before Aswiri, anyway. They were still good pilots, after all. There was only so much slacking they would do. "Which tells me, boys, girls, and the rest of you, that your *morale* sucks.

"And worst of all," she concluded, "I didn't have to kick anyone away to get up on the bar. Now, I could go with the Admiral's idea of a solution for this and crack open a couple of kegs of microbrew beer from back home, but if you lot aren't drinking the beer you *normally* drink, I don't see how that'll help."

The room was now silent and she shook her head.

"So, you've all got your pants in a twist," she told them. "And we're back in action in three days—against *actual* warships this time. Lay it on me, people. What bug crawled up your asses?"

She could guess. Stars, she *knew*. But she also knew that someone had to say it out loud who wasn't her.

The room was silent for several long seconds.

"Ma'am…this don't feel clean," one of the gunners finally said aloud. "My folks live and work on an orbital platform like one of the ones we blew up. We just wrecked a lot of people's livelihoods."

"It wasn't even a fair fight," someone else interjected. "We ran an entire battle fleet into someone's local high guard. Aswiri…they never did anything to us."

"And Da Vinci never did anything to the Commonwealth,"

Michelle reminded them. "Neither did Midori. None of our home systems wanted this war, people. The Commonwealth came to us.

"And they came to us because their own citizens believe that it was the right thing to do. That conquering our worlds and forcing us to kneel to Terra is for our own benefit. It's the citizens of systems like Aswiri that allow the Commonwealth to wage war against us. They vote for Unificationists. They believe in Unification.

"And they are *so certain* that they are in the right that the concept of us bringing the war to them is impossible," Michelle told them quietly. "I don't like it. Nobody does. Void, I guarantee you that Admiral Roberts *hates* it.

"But we need to show the Commonwealth that they can't wage war with impunity. We need to teach them that violence has consequences.

"Most importantly right now, though, we need to get Walkingstick to chase us instead of attacking our homes. We'll do everything in our power to fight a clean war, people. That falls as much on you as it does on the Admiral or Captain Novak or me.

"But we *will* fight that war. You get me?"

"Yes, ma'am."

She smiled grimly at the pathetic response and fell back on drill school.

"I didn't hear you," she bellowed. "Spacers of the Alliance—*do you get me?!"*

"Yes, ma'am!" they bellowed back, and Michelle grinned at them.

"Better," she allowed. "We've a job to do. We're going to do it. And if we do it right, ladies and gentlemen, we get to go home to our families. I have a gorgeous blonde who will be *most* ticked if I do it wrong!"

The chuckle in response was mostly honest, though there were a few awkward silences and gazes. Michelle waited. She knew what was going to come now.

"Do we know when the comms lockdown will be lifted?" one of her pilots asked slowly. "My wife...she's pregnant. Due anytime now. Feels wrong that it could be days afterward before I know."

"Quigley, there are over fifty thousand people in Forty-First Fleet," Michelle told him gently. "Best guess is that there's at least a dozen spacers and officers in the same boat as you, and it *sucks*.

"But right now, that comms lockdown is protecting the lives of hundreds of thousands of your fellow spacers. It's protecting *your* lives, too. If Walkingstick learns our next target in advance, we will walk into one hell of a trap.

"I'll talk to the comms department, though," she promised. "They'll keep an eye out for any messages from your wife for you." She looked around. "That goes for all of you," she added. "If there's something from home that's important, that you need to know about, let us know and we'll make sure it's fast-tracked through the lockdown.

"That does *not*, I'll note, include sports scores for your gambling," Michelle warned them. "Like any privilege, abuse my goodwill and you'll find my help drying up fast.

"But for those of you with legit concerns back home, I'll help where I can. That help, Quigley?"

The young man—almost certainly a first-time father, which couldn't help with his nervousness—nodded, looking somewhat calmer.

"Now, since we seem to have talked out at least some of this, I think it's time for Admiral Roberts's solution," Michelle told them all with a returning grin as the two stewards returned, each pushing a cart with two full-size kegs of expensive beer.

"OUR PEOPLE UNDERSTAND THE MISSION, but I'd be lying if I said it wasn't impacting morale," Bai'al said grimly, their tentacles fluttering around the Captain's head as they poured tea for them.

"It's affecting *everyone*'s morale," Kyle told his Captains. "I was hoping that it would be offset a bit more by the fact that we're finally hitting back at the Commonwealth, but it probably says good things about our people that they don't like it."

Lord Captain von Kita, the senior of Kyle's three Imperial Captains, shook her head.

"We could have found ships whose crews would have enjoyed it," she said grimly. "Hessian's ships. Midori's ships. Others."

Kyle nodded. Enough systems had passed back and forth between the Alliance and Commonwealth over the course of two wars that it wouldn't be hard to find people with a grudge.

"We intentionally didn't," he told von Kita. "The last thing we need is to start adding atrocities to our side of the ledger."

"It's not like there's much galactic opinion left to screw with," Bai'al noted. "With us, the League and the Commonwealth fighting each other..." The tentacles laid down the tea as they shrugged. "That's, what, seventy-some percent of the human race tied up in this war? And the rest is like Antioch or Istanbul. They barely matter."

"Honestly?" Kyle asked. "At this point, we're more worried about opinion *inside* the Commonwealth. If we can appear more reasonable than their Unificationists, we begin to win the moral battle.

"The moral is the physical as three is to one," he quoted. "If we can undermine the willingness of the Commonwealth's population to support the continued expansion of Terran hegemony, we win."

"How do we do *that*?" Novak asked.

"We kick the Commonwealth Navy's ass repeatedly to demonstrate that they can't protect the Commonwealth from the consequences of the wars the Unificationists start. There's a few irons in the fire to demonstrate that point as thoroughly as possible," Kyle said cheerfully.

"*Our* job is to get and hold Walkingstick's attention. Sooner or later, that's going to get us hurt," he warned, "but I look forward to seeing just what the good Marshal thinks is needed to take *us* down."

20

Starkhaven System
14:00 September 16, 2737 Earth Standard Meridian Date/Time
Alliance Forty-First Fleet

"Q-PROBES DEPLOYING," Senior Fleet Commander Zartosht Aurangzeb reported calmly in the moments after *Elysium* tore a hole back into reality. "All ships have emerged on target, no drift."

"Hold the fleet here," Kyle ordered. "Let's see what Starkhaven holds for us, shall we?"

Initial impressions were already coming in, but he waited to let Aurangzeb's staff go through them. What they could see from old light could be both informative and deceptive. Once the q-com-enabled probes arrived closer in to the warships and planets, they could feed him more information.

"So far, it's looking like Intelligence was bang-on on the fixed defenses, at least," Kyle's operation officer told him. "I've got eight *Zion*s orbiting Kirkwall and four over Ferelden. Nothing solid on warships yet. There's a few big energy signatures moving around, could easily be tankers or…"

Aurangzeb trailed off.

"Zartosht?" Kyle asked, linking into the tactical feed.

"We have two *Assassins* in Ferelden orbit as reported…and a trio of *Ocean*-class strike cruisers in Kirkwall orbit."

"Ah," Kyle replied, studying the data feed himself. The ships were separated, vulnerable. Forty-First Fleet had emerged closer to Kirkwall than to Ferelden, but he could still adjust his course to hit either group of defenders on their own.

Of course, the starfighters from the other force would probably arrive while his people were busy mopping up the first one. He'd win—there was no question about that, really—but he could get hurt. He didn't want to lose people and he couldn't spare the time to repair damaged ships.

Studying the system layout, though, there were always options.

"Hold all starfighters aboard," he ordered. "Deploy ECM drones to make it look like we've got a strike formed up around us, and then follow this course."

He laid the course out in the tactical feed by feel as much as thought, relying on the AIs permanently assigned to assist the Admiral to adjust it to work best.

"That course is…asking for trouble, sir," Sterling said quietly.

"Oh, I know," Kyle agreed cheerfully. "And hopefully, the Commonwealth will be *glad* to deliver."

THE ALLIANCE SHIPS couldn't see them, but it was a safe assumption that the defenders had layered the system with passively orbiting Q-probes to keep a careful eye on everything. The Commonwealth forces would have had real-time information on Kyle's fleet as soon as they'd arrived, where it would be an hour or more before his Q-probes were in position to give him the same.

The course he'd set for the fleet looked hesitant, like he'd made a mistake coming out so close to Kirkwall and changed his mind. Ten capital ships—and several hundred ECM drones pretending to be starfighters—shaped their course toward Ferelden.

"The orbital platforms have deployed their starfighters, and they're forming up around the *Assassins*," Aurangzeb said. "They're holding position for the moment, letting us come to them. Designating them Force Alpha."

"Logical, gives the Kirkwall force—Bravo, I suppose—time to catch up with us," Kyle agreed. "What are they up to?"

"All of the starfighters are in space, forming up on the *Oceans*," his ops officer told him. "Looks like the *Zions* had pure wings of Katanas, but the *Oceans* were carrying half and half starfighters and bombers. Ninety Longbows, four hundred and ninety Katanas.

"They're coming after us. Hard. All of them are burning at five hundred gees, leaving the starships behind."

"Reasonable. Those starfighters, added to Force Alpha, are enough to give us a massive headache," Kyle concluded. "Let them commit. Get our probes on both Bravo's fighters and Bravo's ships."

Aurangzeb shook his head.

"They're going to figure you're trying something clever, sir," he pointed out. "I'm sure they've been briefed as to who is leading this fleet."

Kyle grinned.

"Oh, I *know* they think I'm trying something clever," he agreed. "But they don't have a lot of choices. Neither Alpha nor Bravo stands a chance against us in isolation, but combined and backed up by the *Zions*' fighters, they can hurt us, if not stop us.

"So, let them think they have a chance—and see what they do with it!"

"ARE we actually planning on launching starfighters at some point?" Vice Commodore Lakatos asked Kyle bluntly. "Or is this all some shiny game that you're enjoying too much for that?"

Kyle smiled cheerfully at the man over the com.

"Please, Vice Commodore, allow me my fun," he told the

starfighter pilot. "You'll have yours before the day is done, but I'd like to make sure your people are all around to enjoy it."

"I don't *mind* that, but I'm wondering how this is contributing to that," the junior man grumped.

"Watch and learn," Kyle promised. "Watch and learn."

Minutes continued to tick away and he watched Force Bravo's fighters commit to their pursuit of his fleet, with Force Alpha continuing to maneuver to keep between him and Ferelden's orbital industry.

"I don't suppose anyone has hailed us?" he asked.

"Everyone seems to be assuming this is only going to end in fire so far," Sterling told him. "Not a peep of radio; just starfighter launches."

He nodded, analyzing the vectors again. After an hour of accelerating after him, Force Bravo's fighters had traveled almost two light-minutes and built up a velocity over five percent of lightspeed away from Kirkwall.

With Forty-First Fleet accelerating away from them, they'd only closed the original four-light-minute range by one light-minute, with a relative velocity of three percent of light. They'd close to weapons range after he intercepted Force Alpha.

For himself, he'd closed a full light-minute towards Ferelden and would shortly cross the two light-minute line where it would be no longer wise to enter Alcubierre drive.

He smiled.

"Let's give it another ten minutes," he observed calmly. "Then pass this course to the fleet."

Sterling looked at the numbers he'd sent him, then stared at him levelly.

"Has anyone ever told you you're insane?" he asked.

"Yes," Kyle admitted. "Why? Don't you think our navigators are up to it?"

His chief of staff shook his head.

"They'll be up for it," Sterling replied grimly. "Because if any of them *didn't* start practicing this bullshit after they learned you were in command, they haven't been paying attention!"

TEN MINUTES LATER, Force Bravo's starfighters were a long way away from their motherships and base stations. The *Ocean*-class strike cruisers had been denied a role in the fight the moment Forty-First Fleet had turned away from Kirkwall and remained in the gas giant's orbit, sheepdogs above the cloudscoops and defense stations.

Force Alpha was now accelerating out to meet the Alliance, their course clearly carefully calibrated to reduce the engagement time before Bravo's fighters arrived.

It was all a very clever setup, making the best of the Commonwealth's limited resources and taking advantage of Kyle's swing from attacking Kirkwall to moving against the weaker force above Ferelden.

What they'd *missed*, however, was that Kyle's swing had left his fleet moving through space where they could still bring up their Alcubierre-Stetson drives. With less than five minutes to spare before they moved too close to Ferelden to do so, all thirteen Alliance ships brought up their FTL drives and charged for Kirkwall.

The logistics freighters swung wide, their course taking them well clear of the battlespace, where they'd be safe while the warships secured the system.

The warships went straight for the gas giant. For two minutes, they moved through space that was flat enough for A-S drive...and then they hit Kirkwall's gravity.

"Threading the needle", it was called. Riding the thin line between a warp bubble collapsing and dropping the ship back into normal space unexpectedly and the warp bubble *shredding* its contents.

Few people were insane enough to do with one ship, let alone ten.

The very air in *Elysium*'s flag bridge seemed to scream as a thousand tiny gravity vortexes tore through the ship, and the massive warship jerked around her crew as she charged deep into the gas giant's gravity.

The "needle" only lasted two minutes. It felt like two years...and then Forty-First Fleet erupted back into reality, the gravity warp dissolving as the Alliance warships emerged barely a million kilometers from the *Ocean*-class strike cruisers and the defense platforms.

Genghis Khan and *Righteous Sword* had fallen off the needle, the battlecruiser and carrier emerging twelve million kilometers behind the rest of the fleet.

It didn't matter. None of the carriers or cruisers mattered.

What mattered was that Kyle's crazy trick had delivered *Kronos* and *Gaia* to well within the range of their massive, megaton-and-a-half-a-second positron lances.

Even *Magellan*'s one-point-two megaton lances were redundant. Ten seconds after Forty-First Fleet emerged from Alcubierre-Stetson drive, every Commonwealth warship and military installation in Kirkwall orbit was fire and debris.

"Bring us about," Kyle ordered grimly. "Get me a status on Force Alpha and Force Bravo's starfighters."

He smiled thinly.

"And then get me a radio relay."

THE TWO COMMONWEALTH forces were maneuvering to rendezvous, combining all of the starfighters into a single force with the *Assassins* for fire support. With Kyle in control of Kirkwall orbital space, however, they now had to choose if they were going to come to him or let him continue to control the pace of the engagement.

For now, however, it was time to talk.

He leaned casually back in his chair and smiled at the pickup as they started recording.

"Commonwealth forces, this is Vice Admiral Kyle Roberts of the Alliance Forty-First Fleet," he told them. "I won't deny your courage, but I think enough people have already died here today.

"I am going to take the Starkhaven System," he continued. "I would prefer to do so with you as prisoners, but make no mistake, I *will* take this star system.

"I am prepared to discuss the terms of your surrender," he said gently. "I think you will find I am prepared to be quite reasonable."

He sent the message, then turned his attention back to the sensor feed, considering his next moves.

"Think they'll take you up on it?" Sterling asked.

"No," he admitted. "They're going to throw every one of those starfighters at us. The question"—he tapped his fingers on the arm of his chair—"is the battlecruisers."

"The cruisers, sir?"

"If they're smart, they know this is a lost cause," Kyle explained. "Walkingstick himself might order them out of the system. It's not the most…politically expedient decision, but it makes a lot of sense from a pure military perspective."

"Won't change much, will it?" his chief of staff asked.

"Not today," Kyle agreed. "Even if they take their starfighters with them, they can't take the *Zions*' birds or the *Oceans*'. That's still almost eight hundred starfighters and bombers they'd leave behind."

Twelve *Zions* between the two planets. Three strike cruisers. Two battle cruisers. The *Assassins* could only carry sixty starfighters—and there were eight hundred and forty Commonwealth fighters and bombers in the star system.

"So, what do we do?"

"We take the system. Do we have damage reports for *Khan* and *Sword*?"

"We do. Both erred on the side of dropping out rather than taking damage; they're a little fried around the edges but otherwise fine. *Kronos*, on the other hand, rode it too hard," Sterling reported. "She'll be fine in the long run, but her Class One Mass Manipulators are badly misaligned."

"So, she can fight, but she can't run," Kyle concluded. The Class Ones were the largest and most powerful of the mass manipulators that served a thousand different functions aboard a starship. They were the only ones that could generate the miniature black holes necessary to establish an Alcubierre bubble.

If *Kronos*'s Class Ones were misaligned, she wouldn't be able to go FTL until they were fixed.

"Estimated repair time?" he asked.

"Twenty-four hours," Sterling said instantly. "Can't do it while under fire, though."

"Of course not," Kyle allowed. "Fortunately for Captain Blue, I have no intention of leaving this system that quickly.

"Aurangzeb." He turned to the ops officer. "Pass the order to the Fleet: formation Mu, deploy all starfighters.

"No more games, people," he continued to his staff. "We head straight for Ferelden and see how much spine the Terrans have today!"

21

Starkhaven System
17:00 September 16, 2737 Earth Standard Meridian
Date/Time
Alliance Forty-First Fleet

"Go! Go! Go!"

The words echoed in the cramped cockpit of Michelle's starfighter, moments before a moderately grumpy god sat on her chest.

A Falcon's mass manipulators were rated to absorb five hundred times the gravity of Earth. That was, however, with other mass manipulators dedicated to adjusting the mass of both the starfighter and its fuel. There was, as with everything else, an efficiency curve. With every mass manipulator set to counter acceleration, the ship could completely absorb two thousand gravities and reduce the next thousand by ninety-nine percent—and would consume *every* mass manipulator and erg of energy the spacecraft had.

The mass manipulators in the walls of *Elysium*'s launch tubes left absorbing inertia to the starfighters themselves. They spun up to reduce the mass of everything in the center zone by a factor of roughly fifty thousand. Then a series of massive electromagnets charged up and the massive railgun surrounding Michelle fired.

Ten gravities slammed Michelle Williams-Alvarez and the rest of her crews into the back of their chairs, but the launch was over in fractions of a second, allowing her to breathe again.

"Form up, form up," she barked over the tactical net. "Clear the tube launch paths; everyone else is coming out after us!"

Every carrier in Forty-First Fleet had been built around a sixty-second standard launch. In the space of one minute, the Fleet went from ten capital ships maneuvering to match velocities toward Ferelden on their own to having over eleven hundred starfighters and bombers in space around them.

"Defensive formations," Lakatos ordered. "We stick with the fleet for now, hold acceleration to match the capital ships."

Nothing truly stopped a capital ship from pulling the same acceleration as a starfighter. There were several plateaus or "tiers" in the efficiency curve of the mix between mass manipulators and antimatter engines. Starfighters rode Tier Three, around five hundred gravities, where warships usually rode Tier Two, around two hundred gravities.

The difference in fuel efficiency was roughly four orders of magnitude. A starship could accelerate at Tier Three—but it cost them over ninety-nine percent of their delta-V.

It was much cheaper for starfighters to do it—but it also saved fuel when the smaller ships kept pace with their parent vessels.

"We'll see what the Terrans do next," Michelle murmured, studying the formation around her. The Alliance fighters would crush their Commonwealth equivalents, the numbers alone guaranteed that—but eight hundred Katanas would take their toll of Alliance fighters along the way.

FORTY-FIRST FLEET MOVED AWAY from Kirkwall, leaving the wreckage of the first set of defenders they'd clashed with behind them as the

Alliance force headed toward Ferelden. With the starfighters spreading out around them, their engines formed a glittering wall in space.

"Incoming transmission from the planet," Aurangzeb reported. "Looks like the Governor."

"Hopefully, this one is smarter than the last," Kyle said. "Play it."

The woman who appeared on his screen was one of the tiniest adults he'd ever seen. She made it work, somehow, with an outfit that accentuated a clearly adult figure and a hairstyle that stacked her dark red hair up high enough to bring her to perhaps a hundred and fifty centimeters tall.

"I am Miriam Chae-Won," she introduced herself. No title or rank, but Kyle's implant quickly confirmed that she was the Governor of Ferelden, in the middle of her third term.

"It is not within my mandate to order the surrender of the Commonwealth forces in this system," the tiny woman told them. "I am prepared to offer a compromise: we will not intervene with the evacuation or destruction of the military cloudscoops around Kirkwall, and you will withdraw with no further interference.

"If you approach this planet, however, the forces assembled around us will defend my people to their utmost. I can accept what I must, Admiral Roberts, but I also must do my duty."

The message ended and Kyle sighed.

"Well, she's smarter than the last one," he admitted. "Possibly even more stubborn."

He shook his head. He could respect where she was coming from, but it didn't leave him a lot of choice.

"No response," he told Sterling. "Keep the fleet on course. How long until we engage the enemy?"

"A little over two hours to turnover," his chief of staff replied. "We'll enter Ferelden orbit in four hours, seven minutes.

"Assuming they don't come out to meet us, we'll make torpedo range thirty-five minutes before that. Starfighter missile range twenty-five minutes afterwards. Heavy lance range somewhere in between."

"And when the starfighters come to meet us?" Kyle asked.

Sterling shrugged.

"About seventy-five minutes earlier for all of those if they leave the starships behind."

"They'll leave them behind," Kyle concluded. "I bet you a hundred stellars the cruisers are gone by then."

"That would make sense," Sterling agreed. "But when has the Commonwealth ever made decisions based on what makes sense?"

"When Walkingstick was in command. And this whole sector is under Walkingstick's authority."

———

"THERE GO THE CRUISERS," Michelle murmured, watching as the two *Assassins* broke away from the cluster of starfighters.

"What are they doing?" Eklund asked, the gunner looking over the feed. "Looks like they're scooping up fighters as they go..."

"They've been ordered to pull out," the Vice-Commodore told him. "They know they can't hold, so someone with a brain is salvaging what they can." She studied the sensor feed and shook her head.

"And they're not scooping up fighters, Lieutenant," she pointed out. "They're loading up the bombers. All of them. That's...going to be cramped, but it looks like they packed all one hundred and twenty bombers aboard."

That was telling. If nothing else, it meant that Walkingstick was being careful about expending his bombers.

On the other hand, it still left six hundred-plus seventh-generation starfighters coming out to meet Forty-First Fleet. Michelle and her compatriots outnumbered that force almost two to one, but the question wasn't if the Alliance was going to win.

It was how badly they were going to get hurt—and six hundred Katanas could dish out a lot of hurt.

"Commodore Lakatos. Do we pursue the cruisers?" she asked the Fleet CAG. They could, after all, break free from the Fleet and pursue the *Assassins*.

"Negative," Admiral Roberts cut into the channel. "I'm not trading starfighter crews we can't spare for a pair of obsolete battlecruisers. Hold formation.

"We'll take this slow and easy, let them come to us, and whittle them down as they do."

"ANY CLEVER IDEAS, BOSS?" Sterling asked, the older officer watching as the Alliance fleet hurtled towards the defending starfighters.

"Nothing that isn't more likely to get a battleship killed than anything else," Kyle admitted. He could see three different ways to catch the cruisers and a few ways to surprise the fighter strike, but all of them were risky—and his opponents would be watching for something clever now.

"Order to the fleet. Target the *Zions*," he told Aurangzeb. "Long-range missile fire. If we can take those out, it opens up options."

"What kind of options?" his chief of staff asked as the missiles began to flare out. It would take most of an hour for the weapons to reach their targets, but they'd do so well before the real clash between the defenders and Forty-First Fleet began.

"I'm not sure yet," Kyle admitted. They had time, right now, but their options were limited. A few hundred missiles wouldn't make that big a dent in his ammunition stockpiles, but would make certain the platforms in Ferelden orbit didn't contribute to the fight.

"Adjust our course," he ordered after a moment. "Keep us outside the gravity well as long as possible. Let's see what they do."

He smiled as a thought struck him. "Force Bravo's fighters can't have that much fuel left," he noted. "Chasing us hither and fro across the star system. The bombers went aboard the cruisers, but…everyone else is still running on their original fuel load.

"Let's see if we can make them dance."

Minutes ticked away as Forty-First Fleet arced away from the planet, adjusting their orbit away from the enemy, forcing the starfighters to adjust their courses again. And again. And again.

The missiles flashed past the defending starfighters, at a long-enough range that only a handful fell prey to the Commonwealth crews' attempts to defend their home base. Then…

"Somebody did the math," Aurangzeb announced. "The *Zion*s are abandoning. Escape pods and shuttles across the board."

"Can you tell if they're keeping a skeleton crew aboard or stripping them completely?" Kyle asked.

"Not from this range. It won't matter," his ops officer continued. "Skeleton crew will be dead in twenty minutes. They can't stop that salvo."

"Is there anything else in orbit that can service starfighters?" Kyle said.

His staff pored over the scanner data for several minutes, making sure they had the right answer. They had the time, still.

"A few things," Sterling finally told him. "Nothing that can do so in bulk, nothing that can rearm them. Just refuel and resupply life support, maybe twenty birds at a time across the entire orbital infrastructure."

"So, they're in last-stand territory," Kyle said softly, watching as the *Assassins* vanished into Alcubierre drive on the other side of the planet. "They can't win. They have no second chances. They've got one chance to hurt us as much as they can."

"We could summon them to surrender?" Sterling suggested.

"No, Commander, they won't surrender," the Vice Admiral replied. "We wouldn't, and sadly, I have faith in both their courage and their skill."

He sighed.

"No. We've played this game out as far as we can. Everyone knows where we're at. If they were going to surrender, they would have.

"Take us in, gentlemen. Have the capital ships stand by for long-range lance engagement." He grimaced. "We won't hit many of them with the big beams, but every one of them we take out early is one that isn't shooting at our people."

NO STARFIGHTER PILOT was going to turn down going into battle with the big boys in formation, but Michelle had to admit it was a little bit disconcerting. The entire purpose of starfighters, after all, was to go out and mix it up because they were expendable and capital ships weren't.

And when you were firing antimatter warheads and directed positrons, it didn't take *that* much more firepower to kill a capital ship than a starfighter.

Worse, capital-ship weapons systems were designed to target other capital ships. The risk of being accidentally obliterated by your own side was significant.

"Formation CD-5, everyone. Bombers forward," Lakatos ordered, earning an approving nod from *Elysium*'s CAG. "Conical donut 5" was exactly what the full name described – a cone of starfighters and bombers to help protect the starships with a hole at the "tip" for the capital ships to fire through.

It started with capital-ship missiles, the massive weapons larger than even the torpedoes the bombers carried. They blazed through the gap in the formation, charging down the gravity well toward the Commonwealth starfighters.

Six salvos of full-sized Jackhammer VIIs passed through the gap in the fighter formation, over a thousand missiles now leading the way.

"Bombers stand by."

Seconds turned to minutes and the first capital-missile salvos struck home. The Jackhammers were smarter and more capable than any other weapon in the arsenal—and priced to match!—but charging into the teeth of over six hundred starfighters was a worst-case scenario for them.

A thousand missiles killed perhaps a hundred starfighters—but then the bombers launched, a second wave of twelve hundred missiles sweeping toward the enemy.

Those hit at the same time as the battleships and battlecruisers entered range. Their massive positron lances tore through space, lighting up the gap in the Alliance formation as they tore into the Commonwealth fighters. Dozens of starfighters died to the torpedoes. More died to the battleship beams as they cut into space.

Then the rest of the capital ships entered their own range, more and more beams of pure antimatter cutting through the void at the speed of light.

And then, finally, the Terran fighters finally reached their own range. Over half of their number were gone, but three hundred starfighters still salvoed over a thousand missiles back into the Alliance's teeth...and the Alliance starfighters fired *six thousand* in reply.

"Break formation, maneuver independently," Lakatos ordered. "Defensive patterns. They're gone, but they're going to launch twice more before they die. *Don't join them.*"

The starfighters scattered, pulling the incoming missiles after them as their neat conical formation disintegrated into a confusing swarm.

Michelle *rode* that chaos, her mind linked intimately into her fighter's and her subordinates' computers. Random as the whirlwind her starfighters now moved in appeared, she and her people were in full control of it, creating a series of carefully calculated vectors and angles.

No missile was going to come near any of her ships without running through the defenses of at least a dozen of them. The whirling dervish of death and survival cut across space, dodging around the incoming fire and hitting the missiles from a thousand angles.

Three times, the Commonwealth missiles swarmed the Alliance formations. The first was the deadliest, with their motherships still intact to guide them in and provide computer support.

The second and third salvos were on their own.

Michelle breathed a sigh of relief as the last missiles died. None of *Elysium*'s starfighters or bombers had been hit. As she let her attention expand, she could see that the rest of the fighter force hadn't been that lucky.

It wasn't as bad as it could have been. Sixty, maybe seventy starfighters lost. Some of those crews would have ejected before the fighters died, and the logistics ships had the spares to fabricate new starfighters for them.

Most of them were gone forever. Not even a tithe of Forty-First Fleet's fighter strength, but they had no replacement crews till they went home—and that wouldn't be until the mission was done.

The Commonwealth starfighters hadn't been nearly as lucky. There was a reason the Alliance hadn't launched a second salvo—after the torpedoes, the starship missiles and the heavy beams, only three hundred fighters had remained to face the six thousand missiles that had come at them.

"Well done, people," Admiral Roberts's familiar voice echoed over her implants. "Now do me proud and make sure we flag every survival pod the Commonwealth launched. The fight's over. Let's make sure no one dies who doesn't have to."

KYLE STUDIED the sensor feed for several long seconds. Every threat in Starkhaven had been neutralized. Three capital ships and twelve defensive platforms destroyed, along with over six hundred starfighters. Two more capital ships driven from the system, with a hundred bombers aboard.

No capital-ship losses. Not even a scratch on any of his starships. Enough starfighter losses to be painful, but not enough to materially impede the fleet's combat strength. Search-and-rescue shuttles were already swarming the debris from the battlespace—and *Magellan* was on her way back to Kirkwall to pick up the S&R shuttles they'd left there.

Magellan would also bear the responsibility of finishing the job of destroying Kirkwall's infrastructure.

He sighed.

"Do we have a comm channel with Governor Chae-Won?" he asked.

"We have a frequency and a receiver, yes," Sterling told him.

"Get a Q-probe in place for a real-time conversation," Kyle ordered. "Let me know once it's done."

"We already have one in Ferelden orbit," Aurangzeb replied. "Give me sixty seconds and I'll have it lined up."

The Vice Admiral waited patiently until his operations officer gave him a thumbs-up, and then opened the channel.

"Governor Chae-Won, this is Admiral Roberts. Please respond."

It only took a few seconds for the tiny woman to appear on his screen. She looked exhausted, her complex piled hairstyle fraying around the edges. She'd almost certainly been running since his arrival in the system twelve hours ago.

"Admiral," she said flatly. "I allow myself no illusions. We are beaten. What do you want?"

He raised a hand.

"I have neither the soldiers nor the desire to invade or occupy your worlds," he told her. "Nor do I intend to permit Marshal Walkingstick to catch me, Governor Chae-Won.

"I also have no desire to inflict any casualties beyond what is absolutely necessary. My objective here is the destruction of your system's orbital industry. You have forty-eight hours to evacuate all of your civilians to designated residential platforms."

He gave her an intentionally flat smile.

"Understand that we will validate your designation of platforms as residential," he noted. "My intentions are to carry out this destruction as cleanly as possible, but I will not be manipulated or deceived. Do we understand each other?"

Chae-Won bowed her head in silence.

"Governor?" he asked softly.

"I understand," she finally allowed. "You're talking decades of work. Millions of people's livelihoods. How can you be so *damned* casual?"

"Because I was at Kematian, Governor," he told her. "Where a Terran officer bombarded a world. Because I was at Hessian—where the spaceborne industry was destroyed with the workers aboard. Because *my* nation, Governor Chae-Won, did not choose this war.

"There are consequences for what the Commonwealth has chosen to unleash. My own honor requires they be administered…cleanly. But I will see the Commonwealth punished for bringing war to my worlds regardless."

"The evacuations will be carried out as you order," she finally said stiffly. "I do not know if there are any purely residential platforms in Kirkwall orbit at all, though."

"Then you will evacuate to the least industrialized platforms," Kyle noted. "We will be as reasonable as we can, Governor, but our duty remains."

"*Fuck* your duty," she snapped. "We will do as we must."

"As will we all," he told her. "As will we all."

22

Niagara System
08:00 September 19, 2737 Earth Standard Meridian
Date/Time
BB-285 *Saint Michael*

FLEET ADMIRAL JAMES CALVIN WALKINGSTICK, Marshal of the Rimward Marches, chosen champion of the Terran Commonwealth, commander of over a hundred starships and, by any of a dozen measures, among the most powerful human beings alive…stared at the shattered plant pot resting against the wall of his office.

The little plant had been a gift from his staff, a small piece of life from his homeland on Earth to brighten up his working space. It had also been the only thing to hand when the final reports from Starkhaven had come in.

He'd *liked* the potted fern, a memory of a continent he hadn't set foot on in twenty years. But everything else in his office was virtual or built-in. Nothing else had been easily grabbed.

Another star system's industry destroyed. Three capital ships lost—

and the only reason it hadn't been five was because he'd directly ordered Commodore Freeman to withdraw. The man had been perfectly willing to die standing in Starkhaven's defense.

"Sir?" Andrea Messere's voice pierced his thoughts. His secretary was standing at the entrance to his office. "Are…are you all right?"

"I'm fine," James said slowly. "Just a lovely cascade of bad news. Any updates?"

"Roberts and his fleet just entered Alcubierre-Stetson drive," she told him. "Starkhaven is no longer occupied, but our closest force is still four days away."

"And they still need to go play relief." James crossed over to the plant, kneeling down to try and pull together enough dirt around the fern's roots to keep it alive. "Can you get me a new pot, Andrea? I'd like to save the plant if I can."

She didn't say anything aloud, but he saw her nod in the mirror.

"Where's Freeman?" he asked.

"Five days from here," she confirmed. "He'll arrive on the twenty-fourth."

"We'll assign him to Vasek when he gets here," James concluded aloud. "Set up a conference with him and my tactical team. Include me. We need to try and get a handle on what Roberts is doing—Vasek's fleet isn't helping anyone, arriving a week late every time.

"We need to get ahead of the ball with this bastard."

"Of course, sir. I'll set it up." Messere paused and James finally turned to look directly at his attractive blonde aide.

He sighed.

"Drop the damn shoe, Andrea," he ordered. "What is it?"

"Senator Burns has requested a q-com call as soon as possible," she told him. "He didn't sound happy."

James sighed again and nodded.

Senator Michael Burns headed the Committee on Unification. More than any other person, he was responsible for James Walkingstick holding his current command—which made him the closest thing James had to an actual boss.

"Help me clean this up," he said, gesturing at the plant, "then connect him through."

SENATOR MICHAEL BURNS was a heavyset black man with pure white hair, the elected representative of the Alpha Centauri System. His holographic image paced across the floor of James's office—just as Burns was pacing across his actual office in Sol.

"James. Please tell me you have a plan," he said without much in terms of preamble.

James chuckled.

"Hello, old friend," he said dryly. "How's your wife and kids?"

Burns snorted.

"My latest *ex*-wife hasn't spoken to me in three years—which you damn well know," the Senator pointed out. "My kids are busily turning Daddy's millions into their own billions. I see them at Christmas. Most years.

"If you *want* pleasantries, we can do them, but dammit, James, what is this mess?" Burns demanded.

The Marshal shook his head silently. It wasn't like *he* had a wife or kids of his own. The Commonwealth was his life, just as it was for Burns, and the Navy had never left him time for even the Senator's failed marriages.

"'This mess,' as you so eloquently put it, was the inevitable consequence of my not having enough ships to end this damn war a year ago," he said quietly. "Sooner or later, the Alliance was going to launch a real offensive into our own space.

"I'm honestly surprised it took them this long. Their insistence on closing ranks and liberating worlds we took away from them has worked thoroughly in our favor to this point." He shrugged.

"They're being damned careful about it, too," he pointed out. "Hitting systems they know are weak with overwhelming force. I don't think they knew Rear Admiral Ngô was in Starkhaven, so they were expecting to face two capital ships with ten."

"Admiral Ngô's task force certainly didn't change anything!" Burns snapped.

"No. Because Roberts was in command, and while he's no demon, he is certainly a superior tactician," James concluded. "I'd give my right arm to have that man under my command, Senator. I've Admirals who are his peers, but none who are his equals."

The Marshal smiled thinly.

"Except myself, of course," he admitted. "That flair for the dramatic and sense of when to go for the jugular reminds me of my own early commands."

"I don't care if he reminds you of yourself," the Senator told him. "I care about how you plan on stopping him!"

"Carefully," James replied. "He has too powerful a force under his command for me to disperse my fleets in penny packets across every potential target. I have assembled a strike force under Admiral Vasek, but…they need to know where he's going, and I don't know that.

"If you want to light a fire under Intelligence, that would make my life a *lot* easier," he concluded.

"I'll do what I can," Burns promised. "But that's no guarantee, you know that. Not if they've got half a clue on OPSEC—and I'm hearing rumblings out of the intelligence community that a lot of their networks are getting rolled up right now.

"The Da Vinci operation seems to have set them to running."

James smiled grimly.

"Let them run. Michelangelo and Raphael are next up. Tasker and Gabor are ready." He shook his head. "Leonardo will depend on how bad their losses are, but if all goes well, the Renaissance Trade Factor will be out of the war in a month."

"Be careful, James," Burns advised. "I don't want to interfere in your operations, but if Roberts keeps smashing systems with Senatorial representation…the Senate *does* have the authority to give you orders."

"Keep the damned politicians off my back, Michael," James replied fiercely. "The Senate has cut my feet out from underneath me too many times already. All you ever needed to do was give me enough ships and get out of my way!"

"I am one of fifteen on the Committee," Burns reminded him. "One of over a hundred in the Senate and over a thousand in the Star Chamber. I trust you, Admiral. I respect your skills.

"But when the skies above our worlds burn, the Senate must look to protecting our citizens first!"

"WITHOUT SOME KIND OF EVIDENCE, we need more than two data points to know where to send your fleet, sir!"

Commander Seamus Bousaid was a slim, dark-skinned man with flaming red hair tied back in a neat ponytail. He was the most junior man in the call, but the analyst faced Admiral Vasek levelly as he spoke.

"The Starkhaven System is one of Niagara's key supply points, but Aswiri is, well, frankly militarily and industrially valueless," Bousaid continued. "And if Roberts knows our key supply points, he traveled right past the Calibri System to get to Starkhaven—and Calibri is equally important to our logistics situation."

"So, you're saying we need to let this son of a bitch burn out *another* Commonwealth system before we can intercept him?" Vasek asked. The newly breveted Vice Admiral sounded grouchy. James couldn't blame her—taking down the Stellar Fox would guarantee that she'd get to keep the extra star, but every system Roberts raided was a massive black mark on every officer in the Rimward Marches.

"That's not what Commander Bousaid is saying," Commodore Anjali Corna said flatly. The dark-haired Indian woman who led James's tactical analysis team leapt bravely to her subordinate's defense. "He's warning you that we have no guarantees. Any target we give you is little more than a guess.

"That said, we've done some guessing," she concluded dryly. "If you're interested, sirs?"

"Lay it out, Anjali, Seamus," James ordered.

An astrographic chart appeared in the holographic conference, showing the entire sphere of Terran Commonwealth space.

"In theory, there's nothing stopping Roberts from driving even deeper into the Commonwealth," Bousaid noted. "Restricting that are two things: time and his actual objectives.

"Our assessment is that his objective is to cause political chaos and pressure for us to divert from our offensives," he continued. "That means he won't go for any deep strikes but will almost certainly focus his operations in the area of the Commonwealth that's considered part of the Rimward Marches—and hence our area of responsibility."

The chart zoomed in, focusing in on the border between the Commonwealth and the Alliance.

"Depending on how we draw that line, it includes between twelve and nineteen star systems, including Niagara and Via Somnia," Bousaid noted. "Six of those star systems are key to keeping the Niagara fleet base supplied and operational.

"While we've tried to keep which systems are important for that under wraps, it's unlikely that Alliance Intelligence isn't aware of them. That tells me that Roberts is hitting other systems to make us think that he *doesn't* know—but almost certainly does."

"That would fit," James agreed. "It's what I would do."

Corna shook her head.

"My staff and I *guess*"—she stressed the word—"that Roberts is only going to hit our key systems every two or three attacks. That means we can eliminate five systems from our potential targets."

Those five systems flashed green, leaving only twelve potential targets.

"The main question left is whether he's going to make another longer-distance gap between systems or hit something close to Starkhaven," she noted. "I think he's going to make a short jump, probably hitting Presley or Vigil."

Those two systems, the closest to Starkhaven at four and seven light-years away, flashed red.

"I and several of the other analysts think that he's going to make another long jump," Bousaid told the conference. "He's being clever, but he doesn't want to risk being too clever, and making a ten-or-more-light-year jump gives him a lot of options to keep us guessing.

"He hasn't taken any significant losses, but I think his next attack will move him closer to Alliance space, allowing him to return home and rearm and replace starfighters," the analyst concluded.

James put a mental checkmark next to the younger man. Not many officers would offer an alternative analysis to their superior in front of the Marshal of their operating area—and the fact that Corna had clearly encouraged it was a good sign for her as well.

"Would you like to hang odds on particular targets, Commodore, Commander?" he asked.

The two exchanged a glance, then Corna gestured towards her junior.

"Fifty-five / forty-five on a short jump versus a long one," Bousaid said levelly. "All told? I'd say thirty percent chance Presley, twenty percent Vigil, five percent another close-in system. For a long jump… fifteen percent each for the Carnelian or Jinsei No Ai Systems, fifteen percent for another system we haven't considered."

James considered, then shook his head.

"Vasek, you can't get to Presley in time," he noted. "If they're going to Carnelian or Jinsei No Ai, that puts them close to Via Somnia, and they could easily slip another task force off of Seventh Fleet to mouse-trap you."

"You're thinking Vigil, then?" the Vice Admiral asked.

"All of this is guesswork and random estimations," Corna warned. "Vigil makes the most sense if we can't make Presley, but the odds of intercepting Roberts still suck."

"They do," James agreed. "But we'll take them anyway. I want you on your way to Vigil as soon as possible, Admiral. How long?"

Vasek laughed.

"About five minutes after I get out of this conference," the Admiral said dryly. "We pulled everyone aboard and starting prepping to go as soon as we heard Roberts had taken Starkhaven."

23

Deep Space in the Terran Commonwealth
18:00 September 20, 2737 Earth Standard Meridian Date/Time
DSC-062 *Normandy*

In many ways, Russell was surprised that it took a whole week for the first fight to break out in the Space Force mess. A week wasn't an unusual amount of time to spend in FTL, though usually you knew that it wasn't going to be much longer after that.

With another twenty days before Seventh Fleet was going to arrive, the pressure of the isolation and inability to leave the ship was beginning to wear down on the fighter crews. The ship crew itself was busy with the thousand and one tasks necessary to keep even a warship under Alcubierre-Stetson drive safe and functioning.

The starfighter crews had much less to keep them occupied. There were only so many times a day you could double-check the same systems to make sure that nothing had somehow crept into them while they were shut down.

Exercises and training could only take up so much time as well, which left Russell's people with too much time to get into trouble.

He wasn't sure who had started the fight, but by the time he made it into the main mess hall, it had already spread. There were no coherent sides, no alliances, just a group of physically fit men and women taking their cabin fevered frustrations out on each other.

"Seal the doors," he ordered, watching security barriers slam down in response. Now, at least, the trouble was going to be contained.

He stalked into the middle of the chaos. Someone, not paying enough attention, spun out of their most recent fight and took a swing at Russell.

The Vice Commodore caught the fist in his own massive hand and slammed the offending officer to the ground. He probably should have noted who it was, but he understood the nature of what was going on there.

He leapt on top of one of the still-standing tables and looked down on the chaos, shaking his head.

"ATTEN-HUT!" he bellowed, training and muscle allowing his voice to hammer through the noise. Starfighter crew weren't the best-disciplined military personnel, but they'd gone through boot camp like everyone else in the Federation armed forces.

About half of his people tried to snap to attention. The other half kept punching—which left about a third of the officers in the room still standing, looking abashedly up at where Russell was standing above them.

"You bunch of idiots," Russell said conversationally. "Do any of you even know what started this?"

An ashamed silence answered him.

"Right. Apparently, we need to up the tempo of the exercises to make sure you all don't have enough energy to cause this kind of bull-shit," he continued. "You are *soldiers of the Federation*. What's your excuse?"

His people remained silent and he shook his head.

"The stewards are *not* cleaning up this mess," he told them. "Chief Lomond!"

The head steward for the mess—a Navy Chief Petty Officer—materialized next to the table Russell was standing on.

"Sir?" he asked politely.

"I'm turning control of the security system over to you," Russell explained. "None of these fine officers of the Castle Federation Space Force leave until the mess hall is clean to your satisfaction."

He smiled.

"Whether or not you want to give them any *tools* for that cleaning is entirely up to you!"

LATER, in Captain Herrera's breakout room, Russell found it significantly harder to find the humor in the situation.

"My people are feeling it the worst," he noted to Herrera and the XO, Melanie Craven. "But everybody aboard is starting to get itchy. Long flights are hell on morale."

"We haven't even accelerated up to our maximum pseudovelocity yet," Craven pointed out. "That's ten days." She shook her head. "And another ten to slow down at the other end. We only spend six days at full speed, though that's a terrifying realization."

"I don't remember the last time I was aboard a ship that even reached ten light-years a day," Captain Herrera admitted. "I'm not sure I ever have been."

"I have," Russell admitted. That mission was classified still, but he wondered if the super-long jump involved in *Chameleon*'s raid on Tau Ceti had been practice for this. "There's nothing worse about it. Hell, there's nothing about any FTL velocity that really bothers us.

"It's just the isolation. Comms lockdown means all we get is recorded messages. No live chats with friends and family. Nothing." Russell shook his head.

"It's hard on the crew," he noted. "Add being locked inside an invulnerable bubble offset from reality? My little brawl isn't going to be the last issue we have. And, well…there is only so much work we can have our people do."

"You underestimate my imagination," Craven said dryly. "A tool I suspect I may not have given enough rein just yet."

"We have twenty more days," Russell replied. "After which we take our crew into battle against the most fortified star system in human space. We can't let them spend that time getting into fights and trouble."

"We also can't take them into that battle exhausted," Herrera said. "We need them rested and ready for the fight of their lives."

"They won't be that if we let them cause chaos for three weeks," Craven said. "I think we need to link up with the other ships. Build some fleet-wide exercises. Work everyone like dogs until…mmm…D-day minus two?"

"And then give them two days to relax after we've worn them down?" the Captain asked. He nodded thoughtfully. "We'll want to touch base with the Admiral, but you're right. That's probably our best shot."

Russell shook his head.

"It's all we've got," he agreed. "So, we'll make it work. But I think we also need to make sure our people understand the stakes.

"I've read the full brief, but we need to tell our people more of what they're getting into. They need to *know* this one is for all the marbles."

"We're not cleared to share that much information," Herrera objected.

"So, talk to the Admiral," Russell suggested, "and *get* us cleared. Our people have been strapped into giant steel coffins for a week, with three more weeks ahead of them, and then one great mothering battle.

"They need to know why. We need to tell them enough that they know that the entire fate of the Alliance is riding on how this mission goes.

"If they don't know that, we're just going to have more trouble. If they *do* know that, I think we'll have them behind us all the way."

Herrera sighed.

"I'll talk to Admiral Rothenberg," he promised. "I doubt you're the only one thinking that way, CAG. We're asking people to do a hell of a thing—especially the Trade Factor crews with family in Da Vinci.

"You're right. They *have* to know what they're part of."

24

Presley System
05:00 September 23, 2737 Earth Standard Meridian
Date/Time
Alliance Forty-First Fleet

"Welcome to the Presley System," Sterling intoned as the starships flashed back into reality. "Home to the planet Ambrose, known for its tropical paradise of constant rain and wind, complete lack of holiday appeal, tidal power, and fish."

"You've visited, I take it?" Kyle said dryly as his implant feeds updated him on the star system. Ambrose was a *very* wet world, over ninety percent water with a scattering of large island chains that supported a quarter-billion or so humans.

The rest of the planet's eight hundred million people lived underwater, in domes that protected them from the vicious elements of Ambrose's surface but were reputably quite comfortable and well appointed. From those domes, Ambrose's population had access to some extraordinarily rich deposits of transuranics as well as the strange and wonderful wildlife of an ocean that had spent four billion years above those transuranics.

Other than that one wet-but-habitable world, Presley was a whirling mess of a star system. It didn't have asteroid belts so much as the entire system had a mobile rock infestation. Ambrose's large moon protected the world from most of the potential problems, but there was a reason most of the planet's life was underwater.

A single undersized gas giant, Anderson, orbited outside the swarm of rocks that probably had been several rocky inner worlds before some kind of planetary scale catastrophe had occurred. A single lonely cloudscoop in its orbit provided fuel to the orbital platforms tucked under the protective cloak of Ambrose's moon.

Those platforms, however, made the Presley System one of the more important in this region of space. Mass manipulators were required for starships to function at all—they played games with the mass of both fuel and ship to allow for efficient acceleration, played other games to create gravity fields, and did a thousand other minor chores essential to modern technology—and that was before getting into the big ones required for Alcubierre-Stetson drives.

Mass manipulators were built around carefully calibrated coils of exotic matter. That exotic matter was a massive endeavor to produce—and the factories that did so had a voracious appetite for exactly the transuranics that were so common on Ambrose's ocean floor.

The chaotic swarm of meteors and asteroids that filled the inner system made Presley an unwise place to put shipyards or even large exotic-matter coil production facilities, so Presley didn't build starship coils or starships. There was no *military* production here, and Presley didn't fuel the Niagara fleet base at all.

The facilities in Presley, however, produced something like three percent of the exotic-matter coils used in civilian industries in the Commonwealth.

"I never visited the surface," Sterling admitted. "I came through here as part of a merchant venture about fifteen years back, buying exotic-matter coils for civilian industry."

He shrugged.

"They were cheap and high-quality, so we imported them. Made sure none of them went to military applications," he noted with a grin, then shook his head as the smile faded.

"Feels weird to come back here like this."

"It should," Kyle told him. "In any case, this meteor cloud is making me nervous. It's not a threat…but it'll make it far too easy for the locals to hide from us. Anything out there in terms of starships?"

"Negative," Aurangzeb replied. "I'm picking up six *Zion*s in orbit, but that's it."

"That's it? That can't be right," the Admiral replied. "This system should have a lot more than that. A *lot* more."

"They *had* more," Sterling added. "When I was here, they had at least twenty defensive platforms. Not *Zion*s, older platforms, but still…"

"Get the CSP up," Kyle ordered. "And everyone keep your eyes open. Something stinks and I don't think it's the fish."

"There was a mutiny," Commander Aysel Vasilev said softly. Kyle's dark-haired and petite intelligence officer rarely spoke any other way. "About twenty-two months ago. The orbital defense platforms went rogue, seizing control of their systems and declaring a new, independent republic.

"The local populace went along quickly enough that the Commonwealth thinks it was all prearranged. It didn't save anyone—not with Walkingstick and the Niagara fleet base barely a week's travel away," she concluded.

"The entire orbital defense matrix was destroyed and a Pacification Corps was deployed." Vasilev shivered. "Communications out of the system have been badly restricted, and our own agents were swept up in the pacification."

"So, we assumed that Presley's defenses had been completely replaced," Kyle concluded. Assumptions were risky things, but at least this time, Intelligence had erred on the side of caution. "Do we know anything about the current situation on Ambrose?"

"Very little. We've managed to get our hands on the Pacification Corps reports, but—"

"But those are a garbled mess of bullshit because even the Commonwealth would have to prosecute if half of what those bastards did became public knowledge," he finished for her.

"The good news is that we can handle eight *Zions*," he told his staff and captains. "The bad news is that if they're run by PC crews, they are *not* going to surrender."

The Pacification Corps was staffed with fanatics and psychopaths. Officially, they didn't exist, simply being regular Marine Corps units with some organic Navy support. In practice, they were the counterargument to revolution: brute squads sent in to restore order by any means necessary.

Most of those means were illegal by Commonwealth law, something the Senate turned a blind eye to and was careful to make sure nobody else found out about.

Since those means were *also* illegal by interstellar law, the Pacification Corps weren't known for surrendering to outside forces, either.

"We will engage the platforms at maximum range with missiles," Kyle concluded. "I'm not certain we want to get involved in the situation on the surface, but we can carry out our mission without doing so."

"Most likely, the Corps has secured control of the underwater cities by threatening to breach the domes," Vasilev half-whispered. "Any attempt on our part to assist will only make things worse."

"I intend to operate on the assumption that Presley is a Commonwealth system," Kyle told his people. "We will complete our mission and withdraw. The destruction of the *Zions* and our continued distraction efforts should keep the Commonwealth response to any further events on Ambrose delayed and understrength.

"Intentionally trying to make contact with the locals puts them at a risk we cannot provide any reasonable return for," he admitted. "We could potentially take Ambrose with their assistance...but we can't stay. So, it would do them no good whatsoever."

"It would probably make things worse," Vasilev pointed out. "Presley is too far into Commonwealth territory for the Alliance to be able to protect them. Any attempt to liberate the system will end poorly for them."

"So, we won't," Kyle said. "We move in as planned; we move out as planned.

"No complications."

RELOADED and rearmed before leaving Starkhaven, Forty-First Fleet's warships adjusted their courses, each ship changing her alignment to line up the largest number of missile launchers with the defensive platforms. It would change the final arrival time of the missiles by only fractions of a second, but those fractions of a second could make all the difference to the survival of the missile that destroyed a target.

Almost one hundred and eighty missiles flashed away, flying toward a mere eight targets.

Targets that didn't react.

"Shouldn't they be doing *something*?" Sterling asked. "I mean… without their starfighters, they don't have the missile defense to survive that salvo."

"They should have already launched," Kyle realized aloud. "We've been in-system for thirty minutes. They can't have missed us."

It was an over forty-minute flight time for the missiles, but still… the defensive platforms should have reacted by now.

"Is there *any* sign that they know we're here?" the Admiral asked.

"None," his chief of staff replied after a few moments. "They don't even have fighters in space. It's like they didn't see us arrive, let alone launch missiles."

"That's impossible. What are they playing at?" Kyle replied. "Get our fighters into space," he ordered. "I can't help feeling we're walking into a trap."

Elysium trembled underneath him as her launch tubes came to life, firing starfighters into space with abandon. Hundreds of the tiny ships took up formation around his fleet, a shield against a hidden enemy Kyle couldn't help but suspect was there somewhere.

The Presley System was one of the few where someone *could* hide, after all.

But...nothing. There was no reaction.

The Alliance fleet spent forty minutes on high alert, watching their missiles flash across the two light-minutes between them and Ambrose...and then watching them slam home. Eight starfighter launch platforms died in massive balls of fire that would be visible from the surface, without even a twitch to suggest they'd seen their death coming.

"Sir," Vasilev interjected in her soft voice. "We're being contacted from the surface—it's via the Commonwealth Q-probe network, but it's one of our covert operations authentication codes."

Kyle sighed. "No complications" was starting to look like a pipe dream.

"Put them through."

An icon of a holographic swimming dolphin appeared in front of him and a calm voice greeted him.

"Alliance commander, this is...Green Dolphin, let's call me. I speak for Open Ocean, the organization dedicated to the freedom of Ambrose and the Presley System.

"I received this authentication code from a Coraline Imperium Intelligence agent who is unfortunately now dead. The Pacification Corps killed him, along with every other rebel and intelligence operative they could catch...and a few thousand innocents they threw in for good measure."

That was consistent with what little the Alliance knew of the Corps' operations. "Break a few eggs to make an omelet" summed up their methodology.

"As you may have guessed by now, we have taken control of the planetary scanner sensor and its communications." The dolphin laughed in a way that Kyle was relatively sure the real animal physically couldn't.

"If they'd thought to use their *own* sensors, they'd have seen you coming, but they decided to rely on the Q-probe net entirely," Green Dolphin concluded.

"So far, the surface forces only know that the *Zion*s are gone. We are moving in to secure the planetary command center as I speak, but any assistance you can provide could make all of the difference."

"Do we have a live channel?" Kyle asked.

"We have a return frequency, yes," Vasilev confirmed. "Your orders, sir?"

Kyle sighed.

"*Complications*," he cursed. "Link me through."

THE GREEN FLOATING dolphin icon returned a moment later.

"This is Vice Admiral Kyle Roberts," Kyle introduced himself. "And while I understand, please realize I am less than enthused to be talking to a virtual projection."

"Believe me, Admiral Roberts, there is nothing I would love more than to meet you in person," Green Dolphin replied. "You have quite the reputation in Commonwealth space. I hope our little contribution to your arrival here was appreciated."

"It was," Kyle said cautiously. "Understand that my mission here is a counter-industry raid, not a liberation. I am neither authorized nor equipped to help win your revolution."

"I didn't expect you to be," Dolphin told him. "But we couldn't pass up this opportunity. Right now, the only armed spaceships in the system belong to you. We *believe* we have neutralized the bombs on our domes, which means we only need your assistance neutralizing the Pacification Corps positions on the surface."

"I don't have a ground-landing force," Kyle warned the rebel. "And only limited safe ground-bombardment capability."

One of his bomber squadrons would suffice to render a planet uninhabitable, but there was nothing any of his starfighters could do for ground bombardment. His capital ships had a small supply of special kinetic munitions like the one he'd used to take out Aswiri's Governor. They could fabricate more—there were few simpler systems in their inventory—but their base load was only a few dozen rounds.

"We managed to preserve most of the equipment we acquired in the last uprising," Dolphin explained. "We have people and guns and will shortly control the planetary command center.

"If you can provide us with armored Marines and orbital bombardment to deal with major Corps positions, we can secure the islands in three or four days. Five at most."

"I'm not sure I can stay that long," Kyle warned. "My mission is on a strict timeline...and I cannot leave your orbital industry intact either way."

There was a long pause.

"We built it once," Dolphin said grimly. "Then we built it again after the Commonwealth destroyed it. We can build it a third time.

"We know we are too far away for the Alliance to protect us," he continued. "Our plan is to withdraw our entire population to the domes and demolish the surface spaceports.

"The underwater domes are highly resilient to orbital bombardment and a nightmare to try and take with ground troops. Once everyone is below water, Ambrose will be far too expensive for the Commonwealth to try and retake."

"That's leaves you hiding underwater for a long time," Kyle noted.

"Most of us have already lived under the ocean. The rest will learn. Given the choice between never seeing the sky and being shot by the Pacification Corps, we know our course."

Kyle waited, considering.

"Please, Admiral Roberts," the dolphin finally said. "Please help us. I know we're still asking a lot, but with your help, we can be free. Without it...we may have just got a whole lot of people killed for nothing."

Vice Admiral Kyle Roberts sighed. When you put it like that...

"We'll be in orbit in a few hours," he promised. "If you'll help us coordinate the evacuation of the orbital platforms to the underwater domes as well, we will help you secure your planet.

"But we must then withdraw."

"I know. Thank you."

25

Niagara System
15:00 September 23, 2737 Earth Standard Meridian
Date/Time
BB-285 *Saint Michael*

About the only good news out of the mess was that it appeared that James's analysis department had their heads on straight.

"Do we have *any* fucking clue what crawled up Brigadier Morrison's ass that caused him to ignore a goddamn *battle fleet*?" the Marshal of the Rimward Marches snarled at the virtual conference. "Anyone? *Anything*?"

"General Coelho isn't responding to any attempts at communication," Corna said grimly. "What intelligence I've been able to dig out from secondary sources suggests that the entire planetary communication net has been compromised—and that Thirty-Fifth Corps' planetary command center has been taken by rebels."

James Walkingstick grunted. He was reasonably sure he knew exactly what 35th Corps' job on Ambrose had been, but even *he* wasn't entirely certain the rumored "Pacification Corps" existed. Certainly, 35th Corps had been sent to Ambrose to secure it against a second revolt, which was suggestive to anyone who believed those rumors.

"Which means that Morrison is dead," James concluded. "Blown to bits with his defense platforms. And Coelho is either dead or captured."

Which meant dead. Whether 35th Corps was guilty of the crimes James suspected or not, there was no way the commander of the occupying garrison would have survived capture.

"And Ambrose is in open revolt," Corna confirmed. "We have no contact with any organized formations on the planet, but what I'm getting from Intelligence sources is that the rebels came out of the woodwork with weapons acquired from the garrison they wiped out in the first uprising.

"They don't have the gear to deal with any of the hardpoints—so I have *no* idea how they took the planetary command center!—but they have the numbers and the gear that it probably won't take more than twenty-four hours to push Thirty-Fifth Corps back into their secured positions."

"And with an Alliance Fleet in orbit, those secured positions won't hold long," Vasek pointed out, the shaven-headed Admiral linked in via q-com. "I have to wonder if all of this wasn't a ploy to get us looking somewhere else while they took control of Ambrose."

"Unlikely," James replied. "His raids made us putting together something like your task force inevitable, Johanna. If they'd just moved in and punched out the Presley System's defenders with the help of the rebels, they'd have had weeks to make sure we couldn't take the system.

"No, this is the rebels taking advantage of a golden opportunity," the Marshal concluded grimly, yanking on his braid. "And they've handed us a glorious trap. What's your ETA to Vigil, Admiral Vasek?"

"Thirty-six more hours," she said instantly.

"And from there, four light-years and four days to Presley," Corna pointed out. "If the rebels convince Roberts to help them, he'll probably still be there."

"Five and a half days," James considered aloud. "Not sure I'd be willing to stay that long in his place. He knows the risks of letting us catch him."

Vasek cleared her throat.

"I have...discussed the situation with several key navigation officers aboard my fleet," she told them. "Presley is sufficiently close to our vector to Vigil that they believe they can adjust our course and get us there without slowing down.

"Our current pseudovelocity is one-point-five light-years per day. They estimate it will take twelve hours of *extremely* careful adjustments to get us on course, and three and a half days to get to Presley.

"Four days, total. From now."

James winced.

"That is...phenomenally dangerous, Admiral," he pointed out. You couldn't see anything from inside an Alcubierre-Stetson bubble. Nothing outside it could see you, either. Your course was set before you left, based on up-to-date information on your destination relayed through q-com networks and massive interpolating calculations.

Changing course in midflight was based on the worst kind of dead reckoning—and could result in you overshooting and trying to emerge from warped space inside a star. The risks were high, but the rewards...

Vasek had eighteen ships. None were as large or as powerful as Roberts's ships, but they carried modern fighters, bombers and missiles. They could take the raiding fleet.

"It is," Vasek agreed levelly. "But my people think they can do it, and stopping this bastard before he blasts any more systems' industry to pieces is worth the risk."

James sighed, studying the chart on his wall, then nodded slowly.

"I won't order it, Admiral," he said levelly. "And *you* won't, either. If you don't get all of your Captains and navigators to sign off on it, it's a no-go. Understood?"

"Understood," she replied, her voice equally level.

"But if they do...kill that son of a bitch for me, Admiral Vasek!"

26

Presley System
12:00 September 24, 2737 Earth Standard Meridian
Date/Time
Alliance Forty-First Fleet

KYLE WATCHED with hard eyes as the explosions stomped their way along the foot of the mountain range. The Terran Commonwealth Marines' 35th Corps' Third Division had dug themselves in along the base of Ambrose's only mountain range, a set of stony spires that split Golden, the largest island on the planet, in half.

Of the five divisions on the planet, Third had made the most of a name for itself among the locals. As soon as the revolt had started, Third Division's units had executed a clearly preplanned maneuver, abandoning their barracks and prisons in favor of prebuilt heavy fortifications in the mountains.

Footage from the militias that had broken into those empty facilities had eliminated Kyle's last vestiges of hesitation. It had been over a year since the revolt—but there were fresh bodies hanging from the gallows in the barracks' courtyards and prison entryways.

Even the rebels didn't have any estimates of how many people the Pacification Corps had killed. Certainly, the Alliance ground troops who'd broken into 35th Corps' bases hadn't found any records of their executions.

Third Division had known they couldn't hold the cities and towns, not against an enraged populace out for blood. They had, however, thought they would be the ones with orbital fire support. If the rebels had been forced to attack the fortifications along the Golden Mountains' base, they would have died in their thousands.

Even with power armor, any assault would have been a massacre—and with the *Zion*s in orbit to provide fire support, the Division would have been almost untouchable.

Instead, however, *Forty-First Fleet* held the orbitals, and kinetic rounds marched along the line of fortifications, collapsing caverns and shattering bunkers. Over ninety percent of Kyle's bombardment munitions had been allocated to this strike.

His logistics ships were already capturing convenient asteroids to turn into more. It was going to be a long few days.

"Bombardment complete," Captain Novak reported. "If there's a single intact facility down there, our scanners can't pick it up."

"Have Major Konstantin's Marines sweep it with assault shuttles at low altitude," Kyle ordered. Jane Konstantin was the commander of *Elysium*'s Marine battalion, and the woman with the misfortune of being the senior ground force officer in Forty-First Fleet.

There'd been no plans for landing in the operation, after all.

"Understood," Novak confirmed. "What's the next stage?"

"From our discussions with Open Ocean, we get Golden clear of hostiles and then start island-hopping," Kyle replied. "A good third of the populace is on Golden, so that will give them a head start on evacuating them to the domes."

His flag captain shook her head.

"Do they have enough *space* in the domes for another couple hundred million people?" she asked.

"I have no idea," he admitted. "If nothing else, they have the tools to build more domes, but..." Kyle sighed. "Given how harsh the fighting has been down there, I understand why they think the Commonwealth won't want to pay the cost to take them back!"

Because of the breaching charges mounted on the domes' exteriors, only two of the Pacification Corps Divisions had been in the underwater domes. Twenty thousand soldiers, against half a billion *very* angry people.

About half of them had promptly surrendered. The troops in the domes had been the least...actively vicious of the occupying force. They'd had a big-enough stick backing them up that they hadn't needed to be.

"*Eternal Void*," Aurangzeb suddenly cursed, the operations officer's voice echoing across the flag deck.

"What is it?" Kyle demanded.

Aurangzeb was silent and white-faced, but he flipped what he was seeing to Kyle's implant feed.

A spike of energy under the oceans. A thermonuclear charge, Kyle recognized half-absently, smothered by over a kilometer of water.

He closed his eyes. It didn't stop the implant feed, but it at least made him feel better.

"Which..." He coughed to clear his throat.

"Which one?" he asked.

"New Carpathia," Aurangzeb finally responded. "The Terran's 35-4-3 Brigade was holding out but their positions were being overrun. They apparently got around the lockout on the charges."

"Or had another nuke in their stockpile," Kyle said quietly. "How many?"

"Six million people, give or take," his ops officer said. "It depends on whether any of the internal systems held. With a nuke against the exterior of the dome, though..."

"Almost certainly not," the Admiral confirmed. "Record *everything*," he snarled. "Every piece of footage from their Gods-accursed barracks and prisons. Every scrap of data on that bomb. We'll dump everything we find into the interstellar data feeds.

"Let the Commonwealth pretend the Pacification Corps is only slanderous rumors *then*."

It took another full day to fully secure Golden, running out Kyle's original forty-eight-hour planned stay. They'd evacuated most of the orbital platform's population to Golden itself, turning Ambrose's largest island into a massive transit depot.

Shuttles landed from the space stations, off-loaded their cargos of confused and often-terrified civilians, and then returned to orbit as surprisingly organized collections of ragtag militia in green armbands corralled them, guiding them toward the fleets of submersibles that would take them to safety.

"We're running out of time, Dolphin," Kyle warned their contact. So far as he could tell, the colored Dolphins were the senior dozen or so members of Open Ocean, the survivors of the men and women who'd coordinated the original uprising. The organization and preparedness of Ambrose's revolution were down to them—and they were being *very* careful that not even the mostly friendly Admiral in orbit was going to know who they were.

"Forty-First Fleet needs to be on our way," he told Green Dolphin. "Our ops plan called for us to spend a maximum of sixty hours here."

"We've still got an entire division and a half of Pacification Corps troops dug in across the planet," Dolphin replied. "We *need* your help still. At least a hundred million people still need to be evacuated."

"And are we going to pay with six million lives for every day this continues?" Kyle asked gently.

The dolphin icon shivered.

"I pray not," he said. "Give me another three days, Admiral, *please*. Give us three of your support, and I'll have hidden everyone underwater. We've secured the domes, removed the remaining charges. There should be no more mass murders."

"And what happens when you have eight hundred million people crammed into domes meant for five hundred?" Kyle said. "I don't know how much help I can be."

"That's been handled," the rebel spokesperson told him. "There are domes the Commonwealth doesn't know about—and expansions we've kept hidden. We have the space and we have the life support for everyone.

"All we need is to get the damn Commonwealth troops out of the way—and we won't get that done fast enough without your help, Admiral Roberts."

Kyle exhaled a long sigh, then nodded.

"Seventy-two more hours," he told Dolphin. "There's only a pair of ships at Vigil, anything else will need at least four more days, even if they left as soon as we arrived here. But after that, we need to be gone.

"I sympathize with Open Ocean's cause, but I can't fight an open fleet battle for you."

"I understand that, Admiral. We thank you for your aid."

"You'd better," Kyle said with an only semi-forced grin. "Now, Mr. Dolphin, where do you need my Marines next?"

"It's a risk," Sterling pointed out. "A big one. We don't know for sure where all of Walkingstick's ships are—if he'd moved a smaller force into this region for a nodal defense, they could be a lot closer than we're expecting."

"Vigil is closest," Kyle replied. "They're four days away with two *Paramount*-class carriers. Nobody is going to send two *Paramount*s against this fleet, people."

"But they might have reinforced Vigil. We don't know," Vasilev admitted. "The communication lockdown is working against us now. We've sent a bunch of agents dark for their own protection, and Command can't send us up-to-date intelligence for what we've got."

"We have to take the risk," Kyle told them with a sigh. "Eight hundred million people. These sons of bitches blew up *six million* innocents to try and stop this rebellion. We're not even sure how many died in the uprising or in the Pacification Corps' occupation.

"We can't guarantee their safety, but they had a plan for that." He shook his head. "We can give them five days, people. We can't give them any more than that—by hour one-twenty, we will be on our way out."

"It's costing us Marines," Aurangzeb pointed out grimly. "We've lost over two hundred so far. We're throwing maybe two brigades' worth of Marines against entire divisions in dug-in positions."

"Our fabricators are keeping up with the need for bombardment projectiles so far," Kyle replied. "We'll keep hammering the bastards from orbit. Our people are the stiffening to the rebels."

"Which means they're the tip of the spear," his ops officer told him. "We'll lose more, Admiral."

"And if we asked them to volunteer, do you think a single one of our Marines would refuse?" Kyle demanded. "Would any of our people?"

Aurangzeb sighed.

"No, sir."

"We're in this war to protect our own people, yes," Kyle reminded his staff. "But…we can't turn away from people in need of help. Not and stay true to ourselves. Not and stay true to our honor.

"That said, you're right that there's a risk. It's entirely possible that there are ships closer than we think, and we need to be ready for that possibility."

A broad grin spread across his face.

"I have some thoughts," he concluded. "I suggest we get the rest of the Captains and CAGs in on this. We might be caught by surprise, but I refuse to be caught unprepared!"

27

Presley System
16:00 September 27, 2737 Earth Standard Meridian
Date/Time
Alliance Forty-First Fleet

"Pandora Isle is secure," Major Konstantin reported, her voice drained. "No prisoners. No…"

She sighed.

"Nothing left," she admitted. "Where do they *find* these motherfuckers? Entire towns leveled by artillery. My people can't even count the dead. We evaced maybe twenty thousand people, and there might be another twenty thousand in the towns we haven't reached or in hiding. This island was supposed to have eighty thousand people, sir."

Kyle winced. The rumors and horror stories about the Commonwealth's Pacification Corps were paling in comparison to the reality his people were now encountering—but no one had *ever* successfully taken a planet away from them before!

Everything combined totaled far less than the one destructive moment when they'd blown New Carpathia's dome, but so much of the killing had been so much more...personal.

"How are your people holding up?" he asked.

"So far, so good," Konstantin told him. "But..."

"But?"

"I strongly recommend that these troops are *not* deployed against Commonwealth forces again until they've spent time in counseling. All of them. including me," she admitted. "After this...*Voidshit,* I can't guarantee we wouldn't do something we'd regret."

"Understood, Major," Kyle replied. "A thousand times over."

His father had been a Marine in the last war and had ended up one of exactly seven suicides from post-traumatic stress disorder in the Federation afterward. Modern counseling was good—but you had to get it before it could help.

"I'll make sure it happens," he promised. It was probably going to require a major interruption in the ops plan to take the Marines back to Alliance space and find new ones...but he owed it to his people.

And if *this* mess wasn't going to distract the Commonwealth, nothing was.

"How much longer?" he asked.

"Pandora was the last significant Corps presence," Konstantin told him. "There are still major groupings of civilians for the locals to evacuate, but all that's left are scattered companies and platoons now.

"We'll coordinate with Open Ocean, but we should have the last of the Corps swept up inside thirty-six hours."

"You don't have thirty-six hours," Kyle warned her. "We need to be on our way in twenty-four. Less, preferably."

She sighed and nodded.

"We can clean up the major forces by then," she promised. "We're past the point where orbital bombardment is going to help, anyway. The locals can deal with the last few platoons if we make sure there's no power armor left on this damned rock."

"They'll have to," he said grimly. "The clock is ticking."

"Sir!" Aurangzeb's voice interrupted his conversation. "Alcubierre emergences! Multiple Alcubierre emergences."

Kyle's smile twisted.

"It seems, Major, that the clock has run out. Deal with the Pacification Corps. This mess is *my* problem."

VICE ADMIRAL KYLE ROBERTS turned his attention back to the feed in time for space itself to explode in front of his fleet, a ball of fire the size of the *planet* behind him lighting up a temporary new sun in the Presley System barely a light minute from Ambrose.

"What the hell was *that*?" Sterling demanded.

Kyle winced as the data on the explosion ran through his feed, and traded a look with his flag captain.

"You tell him," he ordered Captain Novak.

"That, Senior Fleet Commander, is why threading the needle is the last resort of the deranged and the desperate," she said gently. "And why you don't change course in a warped-space bubble. Someone overshot, hit the needle, and fell off on the wrong side of caution."

It had started as the regular pulse of Cherenkov radiation…and then had turned into the energy release of an entire ten-million-ton-plus warship converting itself to energy. Along with its crew.

"Eternal Stars," Aurangzeb breathed. "That…that…"

"Was a starship," Kyle finished for him. "And it's one we're not going to have to fight, unlike their friends. What do we have, Ops?"

Senior Fleet Commander Zartosht Aurangzeb shook himself, focusing on his duty to put away the terror of what he'd just seen.

"Commonwealth warships," he stated the obvious. "I've got seventeen ships…left, I suppose. Mostly reading in the thirty- to fifty-million-cubic range, but I think there may be a couple of twenty-five-million-cubic-meter ships out there."

"Nail down the details," Kyle ordered. "So no *Saint*s, no *Volcano*s, but there's a Gods-accursed difference in threat level between seventeen *Resolute*-class battleships or seventeen *Lexington*-class carriers with a proper ratio of bombers."

"We're working on it," Aurangzeb promised.

Kyle left them to it, focusing on the feed and linking in with his Captains.

"All right, people, it looks like we ran out the clock," he said grimly. "We've got eight thousand Marines on the surface, so we aren't running. That means we have to fight, and Walkingstick has sent a fleet with the hulls and starfighters to give us a run for our money.

"One of the poor bastards overshot, and that may have taken the odds from *screwed* to *even*, so let's not waste it. Formation Alpha-One. Let's head out to meet them, people."

"What about the starfighters?" Bai'al asked.

Kyle smiled.

"They have their own job."

"WILL the radiation be damaging on the surface?" Green Dolphin asked, the voice behind the holographic icon clearly concerned.

"No," Kyle told him. "Anything with a planetary-scale electromagnetic field or a military-grade electromagnetic deflector will be fine."

The electromagnetic deflectors on his starships and starfighters, after all, were intended to deflect focused beams of charged antimatter. Even a solar mega-flare or the self-annihilation of an Alcubierre-drive starship paled in comparison to that threat.

"That's...good, I suppose," the representative of the organization that was now, basically, Ambrose's government replied. "What about non-military ships?"

Kyle winced.

"Let's just say it's a damned good thing we'd evacuated your orbital platforms," he said quietly. "And, well...I'm probably not going to bother blowing them up now."

Once the radiation wave swept over the exotic-matter refineries, coil-growth facilities and other advanced, high-tech manufacturing facilities in Ambrose orbit, none of their sensitive electronics and systems were going to be functional.

Most likely, even their *airlocks* were going to be fused shut. Actually destroying the space stations would be almost pointless now. While it would be cheaper to restore the facilities than to build new space stations, it would take almost as long as building new manufacturing facilities.

That part of his mission was apparently complete. Now, however…

"We didn't expect the Commonwealth to respond so quickly," Dolphin said quietly. "The numbers don't look good. I'm sorry."

Kyle snorted. He'd known from the beginning that Open Ocean's revolt was effectively, though unintentionally, a trap for his fleet. He'd tried to evade it by setting a time limit, but he'd guessed wrong.

"It isn't as bad as the numbers look," he told the civilian. "My ships are bigger and more advanced than theirs, though the fighter balance isn't as heavily in my favor as I'd like.

"No, this fight had to happen sooner or later, Dolphin. This way, I at least get to set the terms of engagement, *plus* they blew up one of their own ships getting to me."

"Is there any way we can assist?"

"Finish your evacuations and help my Marines get ready to move out," Kyle told him. "This part is mine."

"Then I shall get out of your hair, Admiral. Good luck."

ECM DRONES FLARED out around Kyle's fleet, concealing starships and starfighters alike from the incoming enemy. His formation shook out with calm practice—with three star-system invasions under their belt, his crews were comfortable with themselves and their Admiral now.

He'd organized his fleet into a rough cube, with a five-ship "wall" of battleships and battlecruisers forming the front face of the cube, and a second five-ship "wall" of carriers bringing up the rear. A hundred Falcon starfighters formed a protective screen in front of the battle wagons, helping keep Presley's ever-present rocks from interfering with the formation.

"We have a count," Aurangzeb told him over the tactical feed. "Better than it could have been, but we still might be in trouble."

Kyle nodded wordlessly, trusting the implant link to carry the intent to his subordinate.

"Three battleships. All *Resolute*-class," his ops officer started.

"Older battlewagons, but still heavy hitters. No starfighters, but big lances and lots of missiles. Three strike cruisers, all *Ocean*-class. Nothing special about them, sixty fighters, a dozen launchers, bugger-all for offensive lances.

"Six carriers. Four are *Lexington*s, but two are *Paramount*s. That's the good news. They've got starfighters and bombers, but none of those six have missiles or lances worth mentioning.

"Four battlecruisers, including the joker in the deck," Aurangzeb concluded. "One *Hercules*-class battlecruiser, presumably the flagship. Rest are *Assassin*s."

Kyle nodded again, then smiled viciously.

"I'm almost insulted," he said aloud, making sure his voice was carried over the bridge and fleet link as well. "We spend a month poking holes in the Commonwealth's vulnerable spots, and this is all Walkingstick has to send us? His second string of ships he wouldn't trust in a real fight?"

The truth was a bit more complex, and he knew his people knew it…but there was a solid core of confidence to his intentionally boisterous enthusiasm. Seventeen second-rate ships were a real threat to his fleet, but one they could almost certainly defeat.

The problem, of course, was the Commonwealth commander was almost certainly running the same calculation and coming up with a different answer. The cold calculus of war suggested one of them was getting their inputs wrong, but there was only one way to find out.

"Forty-First Fleet will move to engage the enemy," Kyle told his crews.

28

Presley System
18:00 September 27, 2737 Earth Standard Meridian
Date/Time
Alliance Forty-First Fleet

Twenty-seven Alcubierre-Stetson drive capital ships maneuvered toward each other through Presley's debris-filled voids. Few systems in the human sphere could assemble that many warships. Even the Sol System's immense economy could fund only a handful of warships without bankrupting itself.

Fleets of this scale took multi-stellar nation-states, not a single system. Whatever happened here today, Kyle was grimly certain Presley was about to see more than its annual economic output destroyed.

"They're playing it cautious so far," Captain Novak noted. "Starfighters moved forward about two million kilometers and are holding position there."

She paused.

"Missile launch," she reported calmly. "One-seven-zero inbound." She shook her head.

"New birds too, Admiral. Ten-fifty gees."

"Understood." Kyle studied the screen for a moment, then smiled again. "Let's return the favor. Senior Fleet Commander Aurangzeb!"

"Sir!" his ops officer responded crisply.

"All ships are to target the *Hercules* and launch missiles," Kyle ordered. They'd have a better chance of taking out, say, the *Paramount*s, but with the carriers' starfighters already in space, the old ships' real role in this fight was already over.

More missile icons speckled the display. The range was still nearly two light-minutes, well out of range of any other weapon system in either fleet's arsenal. The capital ship missiles could make the distance, though each salvo was the cost of an entire starfighter squadron.

"Are we limiting salvos, sir?" Novak asked. With the price tag of starship missiles, there were only so many of the weapons aboard the fleet.

"No," he told her, then linked in the rest of the Captains. "Empty the magazines, Captains. I have no intention of holding back anything in our first real fleet action.

"We'll pull back to Via Somnia after this to rearm and replenish our stocks. For now, let's give our new friends everything we've got."

Acknowledgements came back over the link, and a second salvo blazed out. Most of his ships carried a hundred missiles per launcher with a cycle time of a bit under a minute. By the time the first salvos arrived, he'd have thirty-five more salvos in space following them.

They'd be *through* the Commonwealth fleet before they could actually empty their magazines. His people knew what he meant, though.

Most fleet actions were decided by starfighters, and this one would be no different—but if he wanted the enemy to think he was courting a true ship-to-ship action, he had to play the game.

DESPITE THE PHENOMENAL acceleration and speed of missiles and starships, space combat still took time. Lots of it. From the moment the missiles first launched to their reaching the range of the starfighter screen in front of each fleet was over thirty minutes.

Those Falcons and Arrows dedicated for missile defense swarmed around the incoming missiles, lasers and positron lances flashing desperately. The capital ships behind them had been watching the missiles coming for half an hour themselves, and their own lasers and defensive positron lances opened up as well.

None of the missiles made it through. But the second salvo had been launched with that touch more velocity and that touch less far to go. The gap between their arrival was less than the gap between their launch times.

Each salvo came closer than the one before it, the line of explosions marching closer to his fleet.

Their own salvos weren't even getting as close as the Commonwealth's. The attackers' fighter screen was far denser, with over eight hundred starfighters formed into a solid defensive screen in front of the Terran fleet. It was costing them starfighters, but it was stopping every one of the Alliance missiles.

And the Alliance's own defense was costing them starfighters as well. Kyle watched the icons flash red and disappear off his feeds with a forced level expression.

He'd once been in a starfighter that had been too close to a *successfully* stopped missile. He'd lived, but his crew hadn't—and he'd been grounded forever.

"Are we at Point Turkey yet?" he asked quietly.

"Negative," Sterling replied. "Another three minutes and counting."

So far, none of the enemy fire had reached his fleet—but he could only lose so many starfighters from his limited screen before that changed…

"TURKEY in one hundred fifty seconds. Williams-Alvarez, you're closest. Call the shot."

Lakatos's voice echoed in Michelle's implant as she rechecked the positions of her fighters.

"SFG-012 ready for Turkey," she told him. "Ready to call the shot."

The hundred and ninety-two starfighters under her command continued to drift through one of the denser sections of Presley's spread-out asteroid belts. SFG-012 was spread out across about half a million kilometers, each starfighter and bomber locked onto a hunk of rock big enough to conceal the eight-thousand-ton spacecraft.

The main use of those hunks of rock and ice was as heat sinks. Every erg of waste energy being produced by eight hundred Falcons, Vultures and Arrows was being dumped into Presley's asteroids. With their drives down, their sensors deactivated and their heat dumped into natural objects big enough to absorb it, Forty-First Fleet's fighter force was functionally invisible.

They were also spread out across an arc some ten million kilometers wide. They'd been positioned based on the theory that any fleet had to be coming from Niagara, but that still left them with a lot of space to cover.

Michelle checked.

Her entire fighter group, bombers and starfighters alike, was going to be in range. Of the rest...well, most of the bombers would be in range for the torpedoes.

Everyone else was going to have to close the range. The sucker punch was on her.

"That *Hercules* is getting pounded by radiation, even if none of the fleet's missiles have hit her yet," she observed to her people. "Vrubel, one squadron only against the *Hercules*. Then the *Resolute*s, then the closer *Assassin*s. One squadron each."

As she spoke, Wing Commander Dusana Vrubel updated the targeting parameters for her bomber wing, forwarding the data back to Michelle. Eight bombers on each of the battleships and the modern battlecruiser.

That left one battlecruiser, the strike cruisers and the carriers unengaged.

"Alpha Wing, you're with me on the last *Assassin*. Bravo Wing, Charlie Wing, Delta Wing: each of you takes a strike cruiser."

"What about the carriers, ma'am?"

"This bunch of obsolete trash doesn't even have missile launchers," Michelle replied, keeping her voice as dismissive as possible. "Take out the escorts and they'll know the game is up!"

Seconds ticked by as she waited for a response.

"Turkey in thirty seconds," Lakatos told her quietly. "The call is yours, Vice Commodore. Everyone else will close in your wake."

"Understood," she replied levelly, checking the time and the position of the Commonwealth fleet hurtling toward her little section of space. If they hadn't been using q-coms, the entire conversation would have risked their stealth—the lead formation of Terran starfighters was already past them!

"Turkey Shoot in fifteen seconds," she declared over the all-ships channel. "Let's go bag us some starships!"

"POINT TURKEY" was a moving target, the point in space and time where the Commonwealth warships were in range of the most Alliance starfighters. The computers aboard the starfighter force were constantly recalculating it, factoring in the boot-up time of the fighter's engines, the initiation cycle for the launch systems, and every other variable they'd been told to look for.

The final call, however, always belonged to a human. The computers and AIs supporting Michelle allowed her to slow her apparent time, letting tenths of a second drip by like glaciers, watching for the exact moment to strike.

The fifteen seconds she'd announced passed. Then fifteen and a half seconds. Then sixteen…

"Turkey! Turkey! Turkey! Break and attack!" Michelle barked over the tactical network.

She suited actions to words as well, triggering her Falcon's engines and tearing the agile starfighter from the lump of ice and metal she'd attached it to. The asteroid came apart under the heat of her engines, with a couple of millisecond-long preprogrammed pulses from her positron lance helping clear the way.

Her target was the *Assassin*-class battlecruiser currently a hundred thousand kilometers away but flashing past her at eight thousand kilometers a second. The *Paramount*-carrier *twenty* thousand kilometers away hadn't been in her plans.

The carrier was old and obsolete. She had no business in a front-line battle, but her defensive positron lances were fully functional... and age left her with at least some crew who'd served on her for over a decade.

Even as Michelle's missiles blasted free of her fighter's hull toward the approaching *Assassin*, the *Paramount*'s lances were already flaring to life. Two of her bombers died before they could launch. Another trio of Falcons died just after launching.

Old as the ship was, she was in the wrong place at the wrong time and proving *far* too dangerous.

But she was also in lance range of the *starfighters*, and Michelle sent a wordless command to her flight crews as she took her own fighter forward in a spiraling charge, her Falcon's positron lance flaring to life again as she closed with the old starship.

Others followed her—and the *Paramount* class's major flaw was a complete lack of armor. She pre-dated the multilayered ablative ceramic armor that modern warships carried to stand off beams of pure antimatter, and post-dated the sandwiched neutronium armor that pre–positron lance warships had carried.

The fifty-kiloton-a-second beams sliced through with horrifying ease, sending pieces of the carrier spinning off into space.

Torpedoes and starfighter missiles were exploding all around Michelle, her second salvo flashing out at the same battlecruiser as before as she brought her Falcon up to its full acceleration, burning *past* the Commonwealth fleet.

One of the *Resolute*s lurched across her path. The battleship had taken at least one torpedo hit, but her size and armor meant she was still in the fight, her defensive lances reaping a vicious harvest of Michelle's subordinates and friends.

She triggered her positron lance again, slashing the beam of pure antimatter across the entire length of the Terran battleship. It lurched again, losing atmosphere and weapons from her blow—and then a salvo of Starfire missile flashed in from the other starfighters. A cascade of explosions obliterated the battleship.

And then she was through, spinning her fighter in space to unleash a final salvo of missiles after the surviving starships—no longer charging Forty-First Fleet so much as fleeing the starfighters that had ravaged their ranks.

Somehow, despite everything, the *Hercules* had survived. Of the cruisers and battleships, though, she was the only survivor—and only one *Paramount* and two *Lexingtons* still accompanied her.

Thirteen Commonwealth capital ships had died in under a minute, and Michelle allowed herself a moment of vicious celebration.

Then she looked at the Alliance's losses.

KYLE STOOD on his flag deck and tried to continue to appear calm as the numbers rolled in. The Commonwealth fleet had been functionally destroyed, but their starfighters remained in play, hurtling toward his fleet at over five percent of lightspeed.

They were leaving the battered trio of capital ships behind and accelerating at their full speed now. Eleven hundred bombers and starfighters, and all he had was the two hundred he'd kept behind for missile defense.

He'd lost over a third of the starfighters at Point Turkey. Heavier losses than he'd hoped for—but in exchange for an even more significant victory than he'd hoped for. But the five hundred starfighters and bombers from that strike were now well behind the Terrans and opening the distance at a combined seven hundred gravities.

His cube formation continued forward as he tried to calculate some way to turn the odds, now hugely in his favor, into a battle that wouldn't result in lost capital ships on his side.

"Sterling, get me a broad-radio transmission at the Commonwealth," he finally ordered. He couldn't see a way to fight the Commonwealth without taking further losses, but he'd already shattered their morale. It was possible…

"Forces of the Terran Commonwealth." He focused his gaze on the pickup. "You know who I am."

That was egotistical. It was entirely possible that there were pilots and officers over there who didn't know his reputation or only knew it by the name of "the Stellar Fox." Anyone who didn't recognize him would be quickly informed by their implants, however.

No one would have been sent to this front without a database of Alliance senior officers, after all.

"This is no longer a battle you can survive."

His missiles were continuing to pound the remaining three capital ships. Even with the fighter screen, that wasn't a barrage a crippled battlecruiser and two old carriers could survive for long.

"I will freely admit that you can still hurt my fleet," he told them. "Perhaps even enough that the Commonwealth would claim this as a victory. But your capital ships will not survive. The planet behind me is hostile to you.

"Even if you were to destroy my fleet, you would all die before relief could arrive. Your *only* hope of survival is to negotiate with me. If you surrender, I will arrange for you to be rescued and delivered to a safe prison camp on the surface of Ambrose, where the Commonwealth can negotiate your retrieval with the new local government."

It would delay him, but not enough for another fleet of this scale to reach Presley—and if he could end this fight now, that would be worth it.

"You have"—he checked the time in his implant—"fifteen minutes from your receipt of this message to make a decision. Any starfighter safety pod that is ejected will be regarded as having accepted my offer, regardless of the status of the rest of the fleet."

He smiled grimly.

"Enough people have died today. Don't make me kill the rest of you."

KYLE WASN'T REALLY SURPRISED that no one took him up on it. By the time his deadline expired, all three capital ships were floating debris, but the starfighters continued on their determined course.

"There are days I wish the Commonwealth military had the moral courage equivalent to their leadership," he said dryly. "Keep the missiles flying. If you *can* pick out the bombers, well, you know what to do."

"Four minutes until they're in torpedo range," Aurangzeb told him calmly. "Gunners are vectoring missiles as best they can, but we're still looking at a thousand fighters in space when they reach range. No idea how many bombers."

Both the Katanas and the Longbows had powerful ECM systems. Telling the difference at this range was all but impossible, and any Q-probe that got close enough to have a chance was also close enough to be detected and destroyed.

"Move the carriers forward into the wall," he ordered. "We'll want every lance and laser emitter synced together when those torpedoes arrive."

The "wall" of warships spread out as the second layer of the cube adjusted their course, filling in newly opening gaps between the battle-cruisers and battleships. Defensive lances and lasers continued to flicker through space, picking off the last orphaned missiles from the Commonwealth starships.

"Torpedo range," Sterling reported.

It was almost unnecessary as the tactical feeds lit up with hundreds of the midsized missiles. Not as capable as all-up capital-ship missiles with their hour-long flight times, but still smarter and longer-ranged than the lighter missiles their starfighter brethren carried.

"We got some of the bombers, at least," Kyle noted. Like his Vultures, the Longbow design carried four torpedoes. "Only" seven hundred and fifty appeared on his feed, which meant they'd probably killed at least thirty or forty bombers.

"Starfighter screen is moving forward to intercept," Aurangzeb replied. "Estimate starfighter missile launch as the torpedoes reach us. Gunther is requesting permission to use her Starfires in counter-torpedo mode."

Flight Colonel Xun Gunther was *Righteous Sword*'s CAG, the senior officer of the starfighters that had been held to screen the fleet.

"One salvo," Kyle confirmed instantly. "He's to hold the remainder of his missiles for the starfighters themselves. His Arrows are our best chance of clearing a safe zone for the fleet."

The Arrows' lances were very short-ranged compared to their Terran equivalents—but only the bombers matched their missile output.

Seconds ticked into minutes, and the defender starfighters fired, salvoing over a thousand missiles into the teeth of the torpedo salvo.

The starfighters followed their missiles in a moment later, the front wave of the missiles disintegrating into a chaos of explosions and lance fire—and then the capital ships' defenses opened up as well, ten modern ships layering over a thousand light positron lances and four times that many laser projectors into the mess.

It only took one hit from any of the defensive systems to stop a torpedo—but it only took a handful of torpedoes to destroy a capital ship.

And with over seven hundred of them inbound, they could only stop so many.

"*Kronos* is hit!" Sterling barked. "So are *Carolus Rex* and *Magellan*."

Flashing red bands encased the battlecruiser and two battleships on Kyle's feed. There wasn't even enough information to estimate their damage, but all three ships were still around—and even *Carolus Rex* could take a hit better than, say, the Imperial *Righteous*-class ships.

"Starfighter missiles launching, ours and theirs," Aurangzeb reported. "We have a thousand heading their way; they have…"

Kyle could see the numbers. There were still over seven hundred Commonwealth starfighters and bombers coming his way—and they'd responded to Gunther's thousand-missile salvo with *three* thousand.

"Hold defensive formations," he ordered calmly. "Stand by to receive enemy fire."

For the first time in his entire career, Kyle watched the missile storm sweep down on a fleet and realized that his part in the fight was already over. Forty-First Fleet's Admiral had arranged formations, split his fighters and given the orders that had annihilated the enemy starships.

Now, however, it came down to his starfighter crews and starship captains, and everything the Admiral could do had been done.

He stood on his flag deck and watched the fire come. The same defensive layering that they'd unleashed on the torpedoes blazed over the incoming starfighter missiles, and while the starfighter missiles were more numerous, they were also stupider and less maneuverable, the price of their far lesser size.

Thousands of missiles slammed into the defensive perimeter—and thousands died. Defending starfighters were caught in the explosions, careening out of formation, and Kyle concealed a wince as more of his people died.

They stopped the first salvo. Somehow. The Terran starfighters were less lucky. With all of their own weapons launched, their biggest threat had been deployed—but hundreds died as Lakatos's missiles struck home.

The second salvo was it for the Commonwealth ships. Their numbers reduced, their formations ravaged, the last Alliance missiles shattered what was left, leaving the Terran fighters scattering away from Forty-First Fleet, many of them triggering safety pods to make it clear their involvement in this fight was over.

The Alliance had won.

But there still six thousand missiles bearing down on Kyle's fleet. He carefully took his seat, his hands digging into the arms of his chair as he fought the utter helplessness of this stage of command.

More starfighters died. With their launching starfighters dead, the missiles were dumber now. They stopped...almost all of them.

Elysium lurched, a damage report flicking into Kyle's mind instantly. A single Javelin starfighter missile had broken through everything and collided with the starship's lower port broadside. A third of the starship's launchers and heavy lances were down, possibly destroyed—but the deck to retrieve her starfighters was intact.

Righteous Light was less lucky. The Imperial carrier was still with them, but she was reeling, spewing atmosphere from two direct hits that had nearly crippled her...and then the third and last Terran salvo arrived.

The Imperial carrier was hit at least three more times. Not even the battleships that desperately tried to shield her could have survived that fire, and *Righteous Light* simply...disappeared.

None of Forty-First Fleet's ships survived untouched, but the shattered remnants of the Commonwealth fighter strike flashed through without firing their positron lances, most of the ships already abandoned and others flashing surrender signals on all their transmitters.

Righteous Light was the only loss, but that was bad enough. There had been forty-six hundred people aboard that carrier.

As Kyle started to receive damage and casualty reports from the rest of the fleet, he knew that was only the beginning.

29

Niagara System
02:00 September 28, 2737 Earth Standard Meridian
Date/Time
BB-285 *Saint Michael*

Senator Michael Burns's expression was flat. The poker face of an experienced politician just handed a complete and utter shock.

"Destroyed?" he repeated, his voice level.

"Destroyed," James Walkingstick confirmed. His own control over how much emotion made it into his voice and face was ironclad. He might be a soldier, but to end up as one of the Commonwealth's Marshals, he'd been a politician, too.

Hell, he'd built a damn cult of personality in both the Navy and Congress to get this far. James Walkingstick had no illusions about what he'd done to get there, or what he was prepared to do to go further.

Marshal was the most directly personally powerful position the Commonwealth offered, but it was also simply one more step. The

Committee on Unification was the final target, but to get there, he had to win a war of conquest and get elected to the Senate.

He could do the latter.

The former was starting to give him a headache.

"There were survivors," he noted after a moment's silence, "But Rear Admiral Vasek wasn't one of them. She died with her flagship. The rest of her fleet died with her." James shook his head. "The Fox mousetrapped them and ambushed her fleet with bombers at point-blank range.

"Our starfighters hit his fleet hard, and he'll have to withdraw for repairs now, but..."

"You know what the Senate's response is going to be," Burns told him. "Three systems raided? A Commonwealth fleet not merely defeated but *destroyed*? A world in open revolt?"

"Finishing this war requires pressing the offensive," James replied firmly.

"That doesn't matter right now," the Senator snapped. "You *must* end this Stellar Fox's depredations. Whatever plans or offensives you had ready to trigger, your priority must be stopping these raids."

James stared at the Senator stonily.

"Am I or am I not the Marshal of the Rimward Marches?" he demanded. "I was promised I would not be interfered with."

There'd been enough delays and issues with his reinforcements, but for Burns to actually order him to recall his fleets...

"That was before this damn war took two years when it was supposed to take two *months*," the Senator snapped. "You are the Marshal, but if you do not act to defend the systems under your protection, you won't be the Marshal for very long!"

That managed to shock James to silence. He had not realized that his position was so precarious.

Burns shook his head.

"I have faith in your skill, Admiral," he told James. "But others are starting to waver. We were promised a quick victory—one that has turned into a two-front war with the only powers in the galaxy even close to our weight class."

"We will overcome," James insisted.

"I know," Burns agreed. "But the Senate is nervous, and watching Roberts rampage along the frontier like this… Deal with him, Marshal."

"He'll retreat to Via Somnia next," the Commonwealth Admiral concluded. "He'll replace his starfighters, do what repairs on his ships he can within whatever timeline he's working on. With their Seventh Fleet at Via Somnia as well… I'd need both Tasker's and Gabor's fleets to take them down."

"But that would turn the war, wouldn't it?" Burns asked. "If you smashed that many of their capital ships in one shot."

"At the risk of giving up any chance of winning the war for at least three or four years," James said quietly. "After losing Vasek's fleet, if I lose Tasker's and Gabor's ships, I won't have the capacity to carry out *any* major offensives without further reinforcement."

That would be over sixty capital ships gone.

Burns chuckled grimly.

"James…if you lose three damned fleets in as many weeks, you won't need to worry about how much capacity for offensives you have."

JAMES WALKINGSTICK ALLOWED himself ten whole minutes to breathe and calm himself before he started the next conference call. Everything to this point had proceeded along lines of possibility he'd at least allowed for.

Well, everything except the war with the League. He hadn't expected that, and it had thrown a major wrench in his plans, but he'd adjusted his expectations and moved forward. He'd thought he had the Senate and their reactions dialed in, but this new threat via Burns—a man who *was* his ally, in most senses—warned him he was on shakier ground than he'd guessed.

But he'd deal. He'd always deal. That was the job.

"Andrea, get me Tasker and Gabor," he ordered his secretary. "Priority One."

According his mental schedule, Tasker was mere hours away from entering Alcubierre drive on her way to Michelangelo. Since Gabor was already in Renaissance Trade Factor space, he had less distance to go and needed to be present in Da Vinci to keep the system under Commonwealth control.

Priority One meant *drop everything*. And if Tasker was already accelerating away from Midori, he needed that level of priority!

The two Admirals appeared quickly enough. At least someone still respected his authority.

"Sir, what's going on?" Tasker demanded immediately. "I'm less than ninety minutes from entering warped space. I was going over plans with my people."

"This is a full abort," he said bluntly. "Our political masters have decided to override our operational planning for internal reasons."

"An abort?" Gabor asked. "I'm guessing we're going somewhere else?"

"You're both returning to Niagara *now*," James told them. "Get your fleet moving, Admiral Gabor.

"From here, we're going to work out our best guess of where our dear Admiral Roberts is, and then we're going to take sixty or so warships out to meet him," the Marshal said grimly. "Our political masters have made it clear that raiding our territory cannot be tolerated, so we're going to blow the 'Stellar Fox' to furry stardust.

"Hopefully, we'll pin another fleet or two down at the same time. If we can remove the Alliance's forward concentrations, having our entire force in one place opens up additional possibilities."

He didn't *want* to assemble a hammer and drive for the Alliance core systems. There wasn't going to be much of said hammer left by the time he was done—but if the Senate was getting twitchy, then he was unfortunately going to have to trade his people's lives for speed of victory.

Unification was inevitable—but if didn't happen soon, someone other than James Walkingstick would reap the benefits.

30

Presley System
06:00 September 28, 2737 Earth Standard Meridian
Date/Time
Alliance Forty-First Fleet

KYLE HADN'T SLEPT since the battle, his time consumed by the thousand and one tasks required to get Forty-First Fleet ready to move again. The last of the Marines had finally reported aboard. Search-and-rescue shuttles had swept the debris of both *Righteous Light* and the Commonwealth fleet.

They'd delivered just over fifteen thousand prisoners to what had been a residential district of Ambrose's capital city and was now a prisoner of war camp, secured by Open Ocean militia and attached to the only spaceport the locals had left intact.

That was a significant number...until you realized that seventeen warships and their associated starfighters carried over *eighty* thousand people.

It wasn't the worst losses the Commonwealth had suffered in a single battle even in this war...but it was probably the most one-sided victory the Alliance had won in the last two years.

That didn't make the five thousand-odd dead from Kyle's fleet any easier to swallow, but it was true nonetheless.

"All of our small craft and starfighters are reporting less than an hour to report aboard," Sterling told him. "What's our next step, sir?"

"I'll talk to the locals," Kyle replied. "But once everyone is aboard, we need to get moving immediately. Our course is for Via Somnia."

"We need a lot of work, sir," his chief of staff warned him.

"And Via Somnia won't be able to do it all," Kyle agreed. "But they'll be able to do enough. The time line is the problem."

"Time line, sir?"

"Our next attack has to go in by October eighth," the Admiral replied. "We need to make certain that Walkingstick's attention and his fleets are oriented towards Commonwealth space when Medusa goes down."

Sterling shivered.

"Yeah, I can see how it could be a problem if one of his fleets is already on its way when that happens," he replied.

Sterling was one of the few people on Kyle's bridge who knew the full details of Medusa, but he'd been part of JSOC.

"Get the orders passed to get the fleet moving," Kyle told him. "I'll be in my office, talking to the dolphins."

His chief of staff chuckled.

"Enjoy, sir."

To Kyle's surprise, however, the image that appeared on his screen when he opened the link to Open Ocean *wasn't* a holographic dolphin. Instead, it was a startlingly gorgeous woman with pale skin and raven hair, wearing a brilliant smile and a dark green business suit.

"Admiral Roberts," she greeted him in a smooth voice. "I'm Lisa Excelsior, the designated head of the caretaker government that's taking over for Open Ocean." She winked. "I was also Green Dolphin."

Kyle chuckled.

"Funny, I thought Green Dolphin was a man," he pointed out.

She giggled in response.

"All of the Dolphins used male voices," she replied. "Only four of us were actually men, but it helped keep our identities secret." The giggle faded into seriousness.

"It wasn't enough after the first uprising failed," she said sadly. "My husband was killed. I only survived because I officially 'died in a car accident' shortly after his capture. The Pacification Corps figured it was suicide to avoid capture and let it go."

Kyle shivered.

"And what now, Ms. Excelsior?" he asked.

"We caretake the government," she replied. "I have a press conference in about an hour where I'll lay out our promises. Basically, we keep everyone safe, and we have free elections in six months in which none of the caretaker government will stand."

She grimaced.

"Keeping everyone safe is going to be the hard part, but you've already done more for us than we ever expected from anyone. Thank you, Admiral."

He shook his head.

"You were almost a trap that destroyed my fleet," he pointed out. "But I'm glad we were able to help."

"The Commonwealth has lost one fleet in Presley now," Excelsior said. "I hope we'll be able to trade the prisoners you're leaving with us for a degree of peace.

"And what happens with your fleet now?"

"We're moving out immediately," he told her. "Falling back to Alliance space to rearm before resuming our attacks. I'm sorry, Ms. Excelsior, but there's nothing more we can do for Ambrose."

"You've already done more than we could hope," she repeated. "Thank you, Admiral Roberts. Without your arrival and intervention, this couldn't have happened…and I'm not sure how many more would have died before the Pacification Corps decided we were 'secure' again."

"Good luck, then, Madame President," he told her.

She smiled again and nodded.

"And to you, Admiral Roberts. No matter what happens from here, remember this: we remember you. And we owe you.

"Thank you for everything."

Michelle Williams-Alvarez looked at the calmly worded memo on the screen, signed by both surviving Imperial Flight Colonels and all of the remaining Federation Wing Commanders.

Lakatos had been senior to her, but he hadn't survived Turkey Shoot. Technically, both Flight Colonels were senior to her, but that was what the memo was about.

They were officially yielding to her authority, making the senior Federation officer the official Fleet CAG.

She shook her head, studying the numbers. They'd lost almost half of their starfighters now. If she was Fleet CAG, she only had six hundred ships left, roughly one third each Arrows, Falcons, and Vultures.

The bombers had taken relatively light losses throughout everything. The Federation Falcons from the two *Sanctuaries* and the *Conquerors* had borne the worst of the losses. *Elysium* had half of her fighters left, but *Avalon* was down to a single forty-eight-ship wing—and the two *Conquerors* didn't muster much more between them.

The *Righteous*es probably didn't feel as empty as the Federation ships, but that was only because they'd lost a carrier along with over a third of their starfighter strength. She wasn't sure how many starfighters were at Via Somnia after Seventh Fleet had left, but she doubted it would be enough to replace her losses.

"Ma'am, Flight Colonel Gunther is on the q-com asking for you," Eklund interrupted her thoughts. Her gunner wasn't supposed to be acting as her secretary—but her *actual* secretary's girlfriend had died in the Battle of Presley.

Allowances had to be made.

"Put him through."

Flight Colonel Xun Gunther was a stereotypical resident of the Coraline Imperium's homeworld, with the stocky build of the planet's

German colonists and the dark skin and slanted eyes of its Chinese colonists.

"Vice Commodore," he greeted her, saluting.

"You've got, what, two years in rank on me?" she replied. "Can the salutes, Gunther. What's the deal?"

He grimaced.

"The memo doesn't give much reason, does it?" he asked.

"No. Though I see the Admiral already signed off," she told him. "Not that fleet commanders tend to argue when the starfighter crews say that someone is going to be Fleet CAG."

"It's a simple tradition, Commodore Williams-Alvarez," Gunther replied. "You're the O-6 with the largest fighter contingent. You're the Fleet CAG. When you and Lakatos both commanded *Sanctuary* fighter groups, it went to his seniority.

"Now it goes to you." He shrugged. "That you are also the CAG aboard the flagship and have served with the Admiral helps. He trusts you."

"Roberts doesn't mistrust a lot of people," Michelle pointed out. "Usually, you have to literally have tried to kill him to get that distinction."

Gunther chuckled.

"My understanding is that it takes less than that," he replied dryly. "There are *stories* in the Imperial Navy about his first joint operation with our people. The phrase 'discipline your dogs or I will make you put them down' stuck in our institutional memory for some reason."

Michelle blinked.

"I…hadn't heard that story," she admitted.

"Believe me, *every* Imperial fighter commander has," he replied. "One glory hound screwing up in front of our allies was enough, trust me."

"So, that makes me CAG?"

He shook his head.

"No. That you command *Elysium*'s fighters makes you Fleet CAG. You haven't done anything that would cause you lose you our trust, either. We'll follow you, Williams-Alvarez. And we'll follow the Fox."

"Be careful with that one," she warned. "He's led more than one fleet into the fire."

"I know." Gunther shook his head. "But he led one of them into the cauldron to save a quarter million mostly Imperial POWs. No, Vice-Commodore, the Imperial Navy will follow Kyle Roberts wherever he leads.

"Our honor demands it."

31

Via Somnia System
06:00 October 3, 2737 Earth Standard Meridian
Date/Time
Alliance Forty-First Fleet

To the casual observer—and hopefully to the inevitable stealthed Commonwealth sensor platforms—the Via Somnia System buzzed with life. Starships orbited the fleet base like watchful sentinels and starfighters swarmed the space above it.

To an Alliance officer, able to read the encrypted IFFs and ping q-com beacons as their ship approached, the truth was quite different.

Seventh Fleet and Admiral Rothenberg's thirty-plus capital ships were long gone. A pair of old Star Kingdom of Phoenix *Fearless*-class battlecruisers remained, mothering the thousands of ECM drones that flitted around Via Somnia to give off the impression that the fleet remained.

The starfighters, at least, were real. A hundred Templars and a hundred Falcons flew high guard over the fleet base. A quick consult with his implant, however, told Kyle the truth there: that was *all* of the Phoenix Templars in the system and half of the Falcons. Many were being flown by backup crews lacking the skill or implant bandwidth capacity to actually take the fighters into combat.

Via Somnia *looked* like an impenetrable fortress against any foe, with fleets and battle stations and starfighters to guard her flanks. In truth, however, the fleets were ghosts, the battle stations were undermanned, and the starfighters were stretching themselves thin to give the impression of more strength than they actually possessed.

"Who's in command now?" he asked Sterling.

"Captain Laureline Hardy, sir," his chief of staff replied. "Royal Phoenix Navy."

Kyle nodded.

"Can you get me a q-com channel?"

"Already linking in."

The Admiral gave his staff an approving nod, then turned his attention to the communication feed "knocking" on his neural implants.

"Captain Hardy, this is Admiral Roberts," he greeted the tall and somewhat chubby blonde who appeared in his mental vision.

"Admiral Roberts. We've been expecting you," she confirmed. "From the report on your damages, though, I'm not sure how much help we're going to be. We've got repair slips open for your ships, but we don't actually have *crews* for the fleet base's repair systems."

"We'll do what we can with our own people," Kyle told her. "We don't have much choice—we need to be on our way again in thirty-six hours."

Hardy whistled silently.

"I don't know how much you'll be able to do with that," she admitted. "I don't pretend to be briefed on the timelines, sir, so I'm not going to argue. But that'll give you maybe twenty-four hours in the slips. That's barely enough to—"

"—to close the major holes in the hulls," Kyle finished for her. "Hopefully, that's all we'll need. I'll need to steal every starfighter you can spare, though."

The Star Kingdom officer shook her head at him.

"I don't suppose *I can't spare any* is an acceptable answer?" she replied. "I only have three hundred starfighters, Admiral. And keeping even two hundred in space to look like we've got more is hurting my people."

"I'm down almost half my fighter strength, Captain," Kyle admitted sadly. "I don't plan on actually picking a fight when I head out next, but I need to at least *look* like I'm going to."

He was relatively certain his true mission had been accomplished, but he needed to keep the Commonwealth's gaze riveted on him. That meant he had to make at least one more attack.

It didn't need to *succeed*. It just needed to happen.

MICHELLE CAREFULLY BURIED her discomfort as she looked around the virtual "conference room." The two Imperial Flight Colonels were senior to her but had conceded command of Forty-First Fleet's fighters to her. The senior Wing Commanders now in charge of the fighters from *Avalon*, *Genghis Khan* and *Carolus Rex* were all junior to her, though, and she had exactly three days' seniority over Vice Commodore Kimi Wirt, the commander of the Federation detachment there in Via Somnia.

"You'll understand, Vice Commodore Williams-Alvarez, that I'm… unenthused with these orders," Wirt finally said as she finished reviewing her instructions from Roberts. "We already stripped the cupboard here at Via Somnia bare to fill Task Force Midori's losses when they moved out as Seventh Fleet.

"Via Somnia *should* have a full Commodore or even a Rear Admiral commanding a flotilla of a thousand starfighters or more," she concluded. "Instead, we have me, four wings of Falcons, one wing of Vultures and two battlecruisers' worth of Phoenix Templars.

"Three hundred and thirty-six starfighters," she concluded unnecessarily. "If we stripped Via Somnia bare, we couldn't replace your losses, and then Via Somnia would be basically defenseless!"

"I'm not certain of Admiral Roberts plans," Michelle admitted, "but I suspect we're taking *Unstoppable* and *Defiant* with us. If this operation works out, holding Via Somnia won't be nearly as difficult—and if it fails, whether we hold Via Somnia won't matter."

Everyone else in the room winced at her frankness.

"We're going for checkmate, people," she reminded them. "I doubt that's a shock to anyone, but if you hadn't realized it, let's make it clear: we've hung the entire survival of the Alliance on a black swan play. *Our* job is to keep the Commonwealth looking at the Stellar Fox while the sucker punch swings.

"So, yes, I am aware that I'm asking you to strip Via Somnia bare," she told Wirt. "I've already spoken to JD-Personnel, and *your* transfer orders, Vice Commodore Wirt, are being processed as we speak. You're moving aboard *Avalon* to take command of SFG-001.

"And we are taking *all* of the starfighters," she continued grimly. "I suspect we'll leave one of the freighters as an evac ship, because I doubt that Roberts is going to expect the defense platforms to hold on their own."

Wirt was silent for several seconds.

"I guess we should have figured that when Admiral Rothenberg left the system with thirty-eight capital ships," she admitted. "That's the largest force the Alliance has ever deployed as one unit. For all of the marbles, eh?"

"For everything," Michelle agreed. "That's classified, but since the entire damn Alliance is under coms lockdown, it's not like you're telling anyone.

"Let your subordinates know the immediate plan," she continued. "We need every fighter aboard Seventh Fleet by oh six hundred hours tomorrow. Last plan I heard is that we're going to be back in FTL by twelve hundred hours."

Around her, *Elysium* had barely made it into her repair slip, the supercarrier's crew already suiting up and swarming over her hull.

They'd have twenty-four hours to do as much good as they could and load the starfighters aboard. Then…then they went back to war.

"I know this is a harsh turnaround and we're barely going to have time to exercise our new wings and groups before we go straight into action with the Commonwealth, but needs must when the Void drives," she told them. "We know what we need to do. Let's make it happen."

CAPTAIN HARDY and her fellow Star Kingdom of Phoenix officer, Captain Delilah Sutherland, looked more than a little shocked and discomfited by their inclusion in Kyle's briefing for Forty-First Fleet. With all nine of the original ships in repair slips, he'd corralled all of his Captains into an in-person meeting aboard the fleet base.

"We are abandoning Via Somnia," he told them without preamble. "I'm officially commandeering both of your cruisers and all of the base's starfighters.

"We've used up enough munitions and supplies to empty one of my logistics ships, so we'll use *Sunlight of Richmond* to evacuate the defensive platforms. We'll leave an AI to continue running the ECM systems to try and fool the Commonwealth as long as possible, but once we've completed what repairs we can, we are leaving the fleet base empty."

"What happens when the Commonwealth comes back?" Hardy demanded.

"The AI destroys the base," Kyle said flatly. "We're honestly not getting that much use out of it—we seized it to remove a threat to our spinward flank. We don't have much need for its facilities, and we need the ships, fighters, and people we've deployed to defend it.

"Let the Commonwealth have the system back if they want it. There won't be anything of value left here for them."

"So, when do we move?" Novak asked. "All of our ships need a lot of work."

"Twelve hundred hours tomorrow," he said levelly. "We are five light-years—just over four days—from the Leopold System.

"Leopold is one of the key systems for Niagara's logistics support. I expect Walkingstick to have reinforced it heavily, and I intend to arrive on the ninth and threaten it, keeping his attention focused on us."

He glanced around the room, waiting to see if anyone picked up on his careful phrasing.

"Threaten it, sir?" Bai'al finally asked, the Trade Factor officer looking amused.

"We will arrive at roughly fourteen hundred hours on October eighth," Kyle told them. "Our job, more than anything else, is to make sure that Walkingstick dispatches no offensives into Alliance space before October tenth.

"In no way, shape or form does that objective require us to actually *take* the Leopold System, and given the state of our fleet, I have no intention of even trying," he continued. "My plan is to drag our coats in front of the defenders, draw them into a missile-and-starfighter duel, and allow them to 'chase us off.'

"My goal is to be in the Leopold System for twenty-four to thirty-six hours, and to be gone before the Operation Medusa assault kick-off," he concluded.

"We need Walkingstick looking over his shoulder, not sending his fleets at our homeworlds, when the ax finally drops."

"What happens then?" Hardy asked. "I haven't been briefed…"

"And you won't be," Kyle admitted. "Not until it happens. Then, well… At that point, either the war will be over…or this fleet will be all that stands between James Calvin Walkingstick and conquest of the Alliance.

"I will *not* risk Forty-First Fleet to sustain the distraction at this point. We need to attack somewhere Walkingstick is looking—but we do not need to press that attack hard enough to take losses."

Kyle smiled.

"Victory this week, people, rests in the hands of others."

32

Niagara System
14:00 October 5, 2737 Earth Standard Meridian
Date/Time
BB-285 *Saint Michael*

The entire Niagara System buzzed with activity as the twenty-two capital ships of Vice Admiral Gabor's Twenty-Fifth Fleet jockeyed with the existing nineteen ships of Walkingstick's reserve, officially Thirty-Eighth Fleet.

The forty-one capital ships represented a third of the strength he'd had two weeks before, the Marshal reflected. With the loss of Vasek's seventeen ships, they were now, well, forty percent of his command.

Tasker had another twenty on their way. That would bring Niagara up over sixty warships, every ship he'd been given that wasn't tied up in defensive commitments that the Marshal of the Rimward Marches couldn't help but feel shouldn't have fallen under his jurisdiction.

He'd been tasked to conquer sixty-five star systems. Expecting him to protect the twenty Commonwealth stars closest to his enemy was...aggravating.

James would admit, at least in the privacy of his own mind, that he hadn't cared when they'd included that in his assignment. He hadn't expected the war to last this long—he'd had plans and allowances for the possibility, of course, but they'd been low-probability items.

First, the Alliance had frustrated his early campaigns. Then, just as he'd finished grinding them down so he'd be able to take them with his expected reinforcements, the war with the League had broken out and his reinforcements had evaporated.

He didn't buy that as coincidence. It was far more likely, in his opinion, that that whole mess had been an Alliance covert operation—but no one had any proof of that.

Not that it would have mattered. Not anymore. As soon as the punitive expedition had been launched, *that* war had been unavoidable too.

"Sir, Commodore Corna is requesting some of your time this afternoon," Andrea Messere told him. "I think the analysis department may have a...well, a guess as to Robert's next step."

James smiled.

"I have my own guesses, but we need to make a decision." He thought for a moment.

"Get Corna, Bousaid, Gabor and Tasker in a conference in thirty minutes," he ordered. "And tell Captain Tarr that he should make certain *Saint Michael* is ready for action in all respects."

Captain Bohumil Tarr was James's flag captain, an unflappable veteran of a dozen annexations.

"You're taking command yourself, sir?" Messere asked.

Good subordinates were a treasure, James reflected. Clever subordinates were worth their weight in gold.

"Yes," he confirmed. "If our political masters are going to insist I take down Admiral Roberts, then I am going to make damned certain it's done right."

ONCE AGAIN, Commodore Corna and Commander Bousaid found themselves facing a wall of stars as James assembled his senior officers for the planning meeting.

Tasker was still half a day out, attending via q-com. Everyone else was present in person. It was a small meeting: the two analysis officers, James, Admiral Gabor and Commander Messere.

"All right, Commodore," James told Corna. "You weren't far off last time. What's your guess this time?"

She shook her head.

"There's a lot of factors in play," she admitted. "We've confirmed that he fell back to Via Somnia after clashing with Vasek's fleet, but our stealth platforms in Via Somnia have gone dead."

"Dead?" he asked. "I thought they were supposed to survive anything."

"They're not supposed to survive Alliance starfighters firing positron lances into them," she said grimly. "Someone had clearly spent the last few months nailing down the location of every drone we had in the system. They got a clean sweep, roughly thirty hours after Roberts arrived."

"So, there's something in Via Somnia they want to hide," Gabor replied. "Should we be heading there?"

"No," James replied instantly. "If we combined all three fleets, we'd be able to take their Forty-First and Seventh Fleets, but Roberts won't have stayed—and if they've blown our surveillance platforms, they've almost certainly sent their Seventh Fleet somewhere as well."

The Marshal shook his head.

"We're in the endgame, people," he said grimly. "We need to punch out this damn Forty-First Fleet and then head right back to the Trade Factor and finish what we started there. Our political masters want it very clear that attacking our systems will not be tolerated."

The hypocrisy wasn't lost on James, but it wasn't a surprise. Few of the Unificationists really understood what "waging war to unify humanity" really meant. The Commonwealth was too used to being invulnerable.

"But that means we need to *catch* our dear Fox. That's where you come in, Commodore Corna." He gestured to his chief analyst.

"Much of what we discussed last time around him moving back to Via Somnia applies now in reverse," she told them. "The Carnelian or Jinsei No Ai Systems are the closest systems to Via Somnia that are lightly defended.

"The Leopold System is about as close but already has Rear Admiral Hopper's battle group there. Three *Assassin*s and a *Lexington* aren't going to slow Roberts down much, but so far, he's avoided heavier defenses."

"Leopold is also one of our key logistics centers," James pointed out. "We've basically taken over the local zero-point-cell industry to supply our needs. If he destroys Leopold's orbital industry, we're in actual trouble logistically."

"So far, he's only hit one of those systems," Bousaid pointed out. "I think the odds are that if he knows them…well, he's probably trying to keep us guessing. I'd expect him to hit one more non-key system first."

"It depends on how much Admiral Roberts and his superiors want our attention," the Marshal replied. "You're right, he wants to keep us guessing—but he also has to actually undermine our war effort, and he hasn't done much of that yet."

"What about Vasek's fleet?" Tasker asked.

James shook his head.

"That wasn't part of his plan. The rebels held him up and allowed Vasek to catch him. No, he wants to make a splash, weaken us."

The Marshal smiled grimly.

"How far are we from those systems?" he asked, running the numbers in his head.

"Between four and five days," Gabor said instantly. "Roberts will need to repair his ships. The yards at Via Somnia can take care of his damage, but it will take them time. We've plenty of time to move into place."

"Roberts is too aggressive for that," James disagreed. "He'll do the minimum amount of repairs, replenish his starfighters from Seventh Fleet and head straight back out. If he does it right, he'll smash the next system with just his starfighters, keeping his starships out of the way."

"We can't let him do that," Tasker objected.

"And we won't," James agreed. "But we need to cover all of our bases still. Gabor—I need you to split your fleet in three. You'll take one detachment to Carnelian. You'll pick a subordinate to take another to Jinsei No Ai.

"The third will join my Thirty-Eighth Fleet and we will head directly to Leopold."

"What about my ships?" Tasker asked.

"You'll follow us to Leopold," James told her. "Seven ships, with the local defenses, should at least force Roberts to hesitate at Carnelian or Jinsei No Ai. I expect him at Leopold, however, and I want the forces to *crush* him.

"Utterly."

33

Deep space, en route to Leopold System
15:00 October 7, 2737 Earth Standard Meridian
Date/Time
Alliance Forty-First Fleet

"YOU KNOW that I have no idea where you are," Mira's recorded message told Kyle. "But I know you, which tells me that you're in about the largest amount of trouble you can possibly find."

The tall Rear Admiral he was engaged to shook her head at him with a bright smile.

"Hopefully, you're unleashing it on the Commonwealth and not suffering from it, love. Be careful.

"For myself, well, I'm learning some degree of appreciation for these gunships I've ended up in command of," she continued. "I'm not sure I wouldn't have rather had the same stellar investment in starfighters, but they can certainly pull their weight."

That was about all she could say about her own work, though, so the recording paused for a moment as she considered.

"Your friend Mason has grown into command well, too," she noted. "I even got to meet the baby!"

Kyle smiled. Mason's lover, his old friend Michael Stanford, had died in the Battle of Huī Xing, but he'd left sperm samples behind, just in case. He hadn't met their child himself, but he was glad to know the little girl existed.

And if having a four-month-old baby, even if he had been carried to term *ex utero*, was why Captain Kelly Mason and the strike cruiser *Sunset* had remained in Home Fleet when most of the Navy had charged off on Operation Medusa…well, Kyle hadn't asked and couldn't bring himself to mind.

"Don't worry," Mira continued, "I'm only coming over *somewhat* maternal from the adorable baby. What Mason's doing is brave and romantic and I bloody well *refuse* to try and raise a kid without you; am I clear, Admiral Roberts?"

He laughed. That was a more pointed comment directed at him than it would have been at most—given that he hadn't met his son with Lisa Kerensky until the boy was ten years old—but her intent was clear.

"I'm pretty sure Rear Admirals can't give Vice Admirals orders, but I'm also pretty sure everyone will forgive me for this one," she noted. "Come home, Kyle. Kick the Commonwealth's ass, and then come home to me so we can plan a future."

Her smile was sadder than it had been before, and she reached out to touch the camera pickup.

"We both know the risks," she admitted. "And I'd rather be with you, flinging defiance in Walkingstick's teeth. But we got the orders we got, and we carry out the missions we have.

"I love you, Kyle. I'll see you when this is all over."

WITH LESS THAN two days before what Kyle hoped would be Forty-First Fleet's final battle, *Elysium*'s corridors were quiet. His flagship's crew were either on duty or in their quarters, recording messages to loved ones or listening to responses.

He found himself in the atrium that was at the center of every Castle Federation warship, an oasis of greenery and life in the midst of the steel and function of a starship. Given the religious preferences of the Federation's populace, most of the ship's shrines and chapels were either attached to the atrium or inside it.

His own Reformation Wicca was in a perennial duel with Christianity for second-largest religion on Castle, though it was a more distinct third place in the Federation as a whole. The Stellar Spiritualists were the majority in his home country, but his own faith was large enough that there was a small circular clearing hidden away in the atrium around a plain stone altar with two candles.

Both candles were lit and he wasn't alone in the clearing. None of the dozen or so officers and enlisted in the space took any official notice of the Admiral as he joined them in quiet meditation amongst the trees.

Nine warships. Eight hundred starfighters and bombers. Forty thousand lives.

That rested on his shoulders, without question or abatement.

But everything else his plans had set into motion weighed down on him as well. Fifteen fleets. A million spacers and starfighter crew.

If Operation Medusa failed, the Alliance was doomed—and while the blame could be spread around, the final architect of Medusa had been Kyle Roberts.

He wanted to go home to Mira and have a future with her, and yet…he wasn't sure that he could embrace a future where the Federation fell and he lived.

MICHELLE WILLIAMS-ALVAREZ BLEW a kiss at the camera pickup recording her message to her wife.

"I love you, Angela Alvarez-Williams," she told the surgeon she'd married. "I'll see you soon!"

That was optimistic, but it was a hope that she, like everyone else in the Alliance navies, clung to. Angela Alvarez-Williams was a senior doctor aboard a hospital ship, accompanying one of the fleets unleashed on the offensive everyone knew was happening and almost no one seemed to know the details of.

There were only two hospital ships in the Alliance, both retrofitted last-generation Federation battleships. Angela and her crew had served so well with the first one, a second battleship had been refitted to match.

Like every other ship now, though, their locations were classified. No one in the Alliance knew where their uniformed loved ones were anymore. That couldn't last forever, but it sucked for everyone. Most spacers were used to being able to talk to their families live at least once a week or so.

Only recorded messages for weeks was starting to grind on Michelle and her people.

"Ma'am?"

"Come in," she told her second in command, Wing Commander Evelyn Lin.

Lin was a tiny, slim woman of clear Old Earth Chinese extraction, with dark hair, skin and eyes. She perched on the chair across from Michelle as much as sat down, and met her boss's gaze levelly.

"There's not much left we can do in twenty-four hours," she said without much preamble. "Maybe get everyone drunk and laid."

"That is outside the scope of our official duties," Michelle pointed out. "Plus, you're not allowed to sleep with your subordinates."

Lin shrugged. "I'm sure I could arrange 'cross-service integration activities' if I chatted up Lieutenant-Major Nazarian," she replied.

Lieutenant-Major Liam Nazarian was Lin's equivalent in *Elysium*'s Marines—and the Wing Commander's on-again, off-again lover, if rumor was correct.

"There are activities that, if they *were* being arranged, you can't tell the CAG about," Michelle pointed out dryly. "Where are we, Evelyn?"

"You want to take this lot into battle? We're fucked, and not in a way anyone's going to enjoy," Lin said flatly. "We're running short an entire wing and have the lowest ratio of replacements in the fleet…and I wouldn't want to put us in the line of fire for another week."

"You figure the rest of the fleet's worse." It wasn't a question. Of course, Lin figured *Elysium*'s fighter group was in the best shape.

"No one's *pure* cannon fodder," the Wing Commander said after a moment's thought. "But none of us are where I'd like to be. We're running up against real defenses in Leopold; they're going to be ready for us.

"And we're not ready for them."

"We have to be," Michelle said quietly. "We go to war when we have to with the crews we have, not when we'd like to with the crews we wish we had. How bad is it, Evelyn?"

Lin winced and sighed.

"The raw material is solid, and we had a decent matrix to drop them into," she admitted. "And most of the rest of the fleet we slotted entire squadrons into, but the two new Phoenix cruisers are the only ones with intact fighter groups.

"Everyone else is either flying with a new wing, a new squadron leader, or a new wing leader. No one is going to screw up…but we're going to lose a lot more people than we should."

Michelle nodded with her own sigh.

"We don't have a choice, Evelyn. The timeline is what it is."

"Why?" Lin asked. "I haven't been briefed on any of this shit. We're sending our people into the fire before they're ready and I don't even know why!"

Michelle considered for a moment, then shrugged.

"I don't know everything," she admitted. "What I *do* know is that the entire offensive that's been launched is scheduled to hit home on the ninth. We need Walkingstick watching his back, not attacking us when it does.

"So, the timing is the most important part of this. We have to go out."

Lin chuckled bitterly.

"You were never high guard, were you, Vice Commodore?"

"No," Michelle admitted. High guard were local planetary patrols, starfighters and boarding shuttles permanently dedicated to policing the orbits of inhabited worlds—the spaceborne equivalent of a coast guard.

"If you had been, you'd know the other half of that statement," Lin, who *had* been a high guard squadron leader before the war, said.

"Which is?"

"We have to go out. We don't have to come back."

34

Leopold System
08:00 October 9, 2737 Earth Standard Meridian
Date/Time
Alliance Forty-First Fleet

If Forty-First Fleet had been trying to be sneaky, the Shrews would have provided a brilliant opportunity. Leopold's seventh and eight planets, Harriet and Margaret, were gas giants to put Sol's Jupiter and Saturn to shame.

Hiding the Alcubierre emergences of an entire fleet behind them would have taken some doing, but it might have actually been possible. Most system's planets didn't allow for that level of stealth.

Of course, the Shrews had a shared name because they shared an orbit, and they were currently on the far side of the Leopold System from Katrina, the habitable fourth planet. Since Katrina and Henriette, the uninhabitable but resource-rich third planet, were the focus of Leopold's population and industry, they were also the focus of Kyle's attack.

Eleven warships burst into reality, Q-probes firing away in the moment they emerged and scanners reaching out to find the enemies that they knew were there.

"Starfighters deploying," Sterling reported. "Passive scanner take coming in now."

Leopold should have both a fleet and significant fixed defenses. There were no surprises in the passive take. The data was two minutes old, though as the Q-probes got closer to the planet, the data would get fresher.

"Looks like bang on what Intelligence suggested," Aurangzeb reported. "I've got three cruisers, a carrier, about twenty defensive platforms—only half appear to be fighter bases.

"One hundred Katanas on patrol. That number will start ramping up quickly. Best guess is about seven hundred and fifty fighters with heavy missile support."

Kyle nodded, watching the data signatures continue to populate his feed as Aurangzeb's team identified the various civilian orbit platforms as well. Leopold was the most heavily industrialized of the systems they'd moved against so far, with significant home-built defenses. Many of the fighters that they were picking up would be high guard ships, more used to being police officers than combatants.

Underestimating them could be deadly. Those pilots were fighting for their homes, their families.

"Let's go with Course Delta-3," he told Sterling. "Keep us on the far side of Katrina from Henriette, and watch our distance and vector from space we can jump from."

Everything was exactly as he'd expected. It was a light-enough defense force that he could take them if he pushed, and a heavy-enough defense force that his enemies wouldn't question him choosing to withdraw rather than take heavy losses.

If everything in Leopold was exactly what he needed…why did the hair on the back of his neck want to climb his skull?

"All fighters, form up, form up," Michelle barked. "Falcons and

Templars: primary defensive formation Epsilon-Three, two million klicks in front of the fleet. Arrows, secondary defensive formation Alpha-One; stick to the cap-ships like glue.

"Acknowledge!"

Acknowledgements flickered back from her subordinates as hundreds of starfighters leapt to her orders. It was a heady feeling—and a terrifying one. If they got the plan wrong, if they had the wrong formation or the wrong division of fighters, or if there was something they'd missed…

Two hundred Arrows formed up around Forty-First Fleet behind her, and she led four hundred Falcons and a hundred Templars forward, accelerating over twice as fast as the fleet as they opened the distance.

"Enemy starfighters deploying," Eklund reported. "Numbers match up with three *Assassins*, a *Lexington*, and twelve *Zion*s. Eight hundred Katanas, fifty Longbows."

He paused.

"What about our bombers, ma'am?"

"The Admiral is hanging on to them. Just in case," she told him. "The plan isn't actually to take the system today, Ferdi. We're just here to make them look."

Eklund snorted.

"Eight hundred and fifty starfighters and three battlecruisers are definitely *looking*, boss," he pointed out.

He was right. The three *Assassin*s had formed up into a triangle formation, with the starfighters filling in the gaps to form a massive spearhead thrusting directly toward Forty-First Fleet.

It was a moving wall of antimatter fire, closing with the Alliance at two hundred gravities. As capital-ship missiles launched and ECM flared to life, that wall became a solid shield of radiation and jamming. There weren't going to be many long-range hits today.

"Fleet is opening fire with missiles," Eklund told her. "What do we do?"

"Hold course and plan," she said calmly. "We'll swing around Katrina, draw their forces out and chop of chunks of them as we swing by."

"We could totally take them," her gunner objected.

"Probably," Michelle agreed. "But the Admiral doesn't want to lose more people than he has to over a system the Alliance doesn't want or need.

"So, we go by the plan."

"Do we have any Q-probes in position to look up dear Admiral Hopper's skirt?" Kyle asked conversationally. "I don't like the way our Terran friend is blocking our view of a nice, shiny chunk of space."

"We've accounted for all of his ships and starfighters," Aurangzeb pointed out. "What could he be hiding?"

"Ships we *don't know about*," Kyle replied. "We've seen everything we knew about, but I expected Leopold to be reinforced. While we're at it, get me a probe hooked around Henriette. We haven't seen the dark side of that rock yet, and my paranoia is *itchy*."

His chief of staff and operations officer both chuckled at his joke—but they also got to work.

The Q-probes were launched in waves: a first wave that blasted through the system at the same thousand gravities as a missile, then turned around and came back; three more waves that did much the same thing at lower accelerations; and a final wave of probes that slowed themselves into stealth position across the star system, providing a live view of a battlespace that would, at a minimum, be two light-minutes across.

His staff went to work on the third wave, adjusting the courses of some Q-probes and accelerating others, wrapping them around towards Kyle's blind spots.

"Sending probes B-18 through B-22 on a suicide run into the fleet," Aurangzeb reported after a minute. "Give me five minutes and I'll know what Hopper has under his skirt. Three of the C-wave probes are looping Henriette. That'll be fifteen minutes."

"First missile impacts in twenty-five minutes. They'll have torpedo range on our forward fighter formation in thirty-three."

Kyle nodded his understanding, watching the drama continue to unfold. They'd thrown over a thousand missiles at Task Force Leopold so far, and he considered that expenditure for a moment.

"Hold the missile fire after ten salvos," he ordered. "Two thousand missiles have a better than fifty-fifty chance of clearing those battle-cruisers out of the fight, and I'd like to hang on to our other ninety salvos.

"Just in case."

"Understood. Passing the order," Aurangzeb replied. "What about the bombers?"

They still had a hundred and sixty bombers tucked away aboard his four carriers, loaded into the launch tubes and ready to go.

"Keep them on standby," he ordered. "Something doesn't feel right..."

"*Son of the darkest Void*!" Sterling suddenly cursed, the officer staring into space at a data feed only he could see. "Probe B-20 made it through their defenses. *They've got six more starships in that formation*."

"Ah," Kyle said levelly. "Yes, that *will* be a problem, won't it?"

"HOW DID WE MISS AN ENTIRE *FLEET*?" Aurangzeb demanded, the operations officer turning to glare at the closest members of his analysis team.

"Blame no one," Kyle snapped. "But yes, I would like to know the answer to that as well."

The ops officer turned an apologetic glance on Kyle, then stepped out of the core of the flag deck to confer with his team. As they spoke, both audibly and through their dedicated implant channel, Kyle turned his own attention to the oncoming Commonwealth fleet.

They clearly realized that the drone had revealed their secret before its death. The game was up—and so was their deception. Nine starships now spread out, with another sixty starfighters blazing away from the two immense, modern, sixty-million-cubic-meter warships at the center of the formation.

"Two *Hercules*es. Four *Resolute*s. Three *Assassins*," Sterling said quietly from Kyle's right elbow. "Plus the *Lexington* that's still hanging back to reinforce the orbital platforms. We're a more modern fleet, but they're almost as big."

"We could probably take them," Kyle replied, watching the angles, studying the numbers. "Focus missile fire on the *Hercules*es, swing our course out to force them to engage with starfighters only at first, then swing back in and send our battlecruisers and battleships in.

"I'd back two *Titan*s against four *Resolute*s any day of the week. But…" He shrugged. "We'd lose three quarters or more of our fighters and probably at least two of the battlecruisers. This system isn't worth it."

His chief of staff chuckled.

"And you're tempted anyway."

"I didn't earn my reputation by turning away from a fight," Kyle admitted. "There's some truth to those who call me a glory hound… but this isn't a fight we need to have today.

"Aurangzeb!" The ops officer turned back to him. "Do we have an answer?"

"They were hiding in the defense platforms," the Senior Fleet Commander replied. "We're not entirely sure how, but they'd disguised them as much smaller immobile platforms. They waited until Hopper had his arrowhead formation up to cover their engines and then came after us."

"Clever," Kyle allowed. "Almost something I would do." He shook his head.

"Not clever enough," he concluded. "This looks far too much like a fair fight to me. Fleet orders! Course Zulu-Seven. Get us out of here!"

BB-285 *Saint Michael*

"They're running."

"Of course they are," James Walkingstick agreed. It had been too long since he'd stood on the flag deck of a ship of war as she went into action. "Roberts isn't going to fight a fair fight. Hell, I'm not even sure the arrogant bastard planned on fighting anyone here."

The Marshal smiled at his operations officer, Commodore Clarette MacGinnis.

"Of course, he came here anyway, and that's the last mistake he got to make," he said quietly. "Update Tasker on his new vector and then pass the order to TF Thirty-Eight-Two.

"Initiate Mouse Trap Bravo."

They hadn't managed to localize the Q-probes vectoring to peek behind Henriette, but they'd got enough blips to be sure the probes were on their way. That Roberts hadn't already turned to run—or chosen a different course—told Walkingstick he hadn't seen TF 38.2 yet.

Now, mighty engines came to life and launch tubes flared as the second jaw to his trap swung into motion. Four *Volcano*es and four *Lexingtons* put a thousand starfighters and four hundred bombers into space.

Two *Hercules*es added another sixty starfighters, a tiny but important portion of the trap, though he'd use their missile launchers more.

Saint Michael, Saint Lawrence, Saint Columbus and *Santa Maria* came to life at the heart of the fleet, four of the Commonwealth's most modern battleships—and every *Saint* under Walkingstick's command outside of Tasker's fleet—now charging at Vice Admiral Roberts.

"He can run," James declared as his flagship lurched into the action. "But if he was going to hide, he'd have come in elsewhere. And he only has so many options left, people—and we're ready for them all!"

35

Leopold System
08:45 October 9, 2737 Earth Standard Meridian
Date/Time
Alliance Forty-First Fleet

"Oh, Starless Void."

Aurangzeb's oath echoed through the renewed silence in *Elysium*'s flag bridge as the second Commonwealth fleet emerged from behind Leopold's fifth planet. A thousand-plus starfighters led the way, screaming on an intercept vector for Forty-First Fleet at five hundred gravities.

"Run the numbers," Kyle ordered. "Will they intercept us before we reach the A-S safe zone?"

He suspected he already knew the answer. If there were that many *Saint*s over there, there were only two people who could be in command…and he would bet stellars to peanuts that it was Walking-stick himself.

It seemed they'd achieved the objective of *get the Marshal's attention*, all right.

"The starships will not make lance range before we can warp space," his operations officer concluded after a few moments. "They are already in missile range. Both forces are launching."

"Of course they are," Kyle allowed. "The fighters, Aurangzeb?"

"They'll reach us if we don't change course," his ops officer confirmed.

Kyle sighed, running numbers in his implants and throwing them up on the main holographic display.

"All right. Let's assume that this actually is Hopper but reinforced," he began, highlighting the first fleet. "Mostly battleships and local starfighters. Call them Bogey Alpha. We can take them, but it will hurt."

A dark red cone lit up the projection. Two larger cones surrounded it, one covering almost the entire inner system.

"This is their interception zone. We can break free of it, avoid a lance or starfighter missile engagement with them, relatively easily. They'll hit us with missiles almost no matter what we do, and a lot of our potential course changes put us in range of bomber torpedoes."

He added a second cone, dark orange and then lighter shades of orange.

"Bogey Bravo," he concluded. "My guess is Walkingstick is in command himself. Modern battleships, modern carriers, bad news all around. We can't evade their missiles, but we can evade their starfighters...but only by accepting torpedo strikes from both fleets."

A blue cone materialized on the screen.

"This is our maneuver zone," he concluded. A small, dark blue, irregular shape appeared in the center of the cone. "This course, a modified version of Zulu-Eleven, will avoid starfighter missile range and lance range of both fleets and fighter forces.

"We'll take their missile fire for just over an hour and we'll take the full brunt of both fighter forces' torpedo fire, but we'll avoid both a dogfight and a true ship-to-ship engagement."

Kyle shook his head.

"They left us an opening," he murmured. "Why?"

"We were about to identify their location anyway," Sterling pointed out. "They had to know we were about to maneuver to evade them anyway, a few more minutes..."

"That's not right," Kyle replied. "A few more minutes wouldn't have changed anything. They needed another thousand kilometers a second of velocity. They could have used Henriette and the Shrews to hide their drive signatures, built up that velocity with only a minimal chance of being seen."

"We don't have a lot of choice, sir," his chief of staff said. "If we do anything else, we go headlong into one of their fleets."

"And if we let them herd us, do you want to bet how that ends?" the Admiral asked. Logic said to punch through the gap, take whatever Walkingstick was planning because it couldn't be worse than what he *knew* was coming.

His *instincts*, however...those had made him the Stellar Fox.

"Course is Bravo-Six, unmodified," he snapped. "Full reverse, take us right back along our original path."

"Sir...if we do that..."

"Bogey Alpha *will* engage us," Kyle confirmed. "We'll go right down their throats, starfighters and battleships first. Launch the bombers and prepare for close engagement."

"Sir..."

"That gap, Commander Sterling, is a trap," Kyle told them. "And I will take the fleet I *know* I can fight over the trap Walkingstick clearly thinks can beat us any day!

"Execute your orders!"

MICHELLE LISTENED to the new orders and forced herself to stay calm. She needed to not merely appear calm to the crew aboard her own starfighter but radiate calm through the neural implant network. Most of the emotional side channels were shut down in combat anyway, but some "context" always snuck through.

"Bombers are launching."

"All starfighters, all starfighters, all bombers, all bombers," she recited, overriding the communication network to make sure everyone could hear her.

"We've got a new plan down from the Old Man," she told them. "Our old friend Walkingstick is over there in Bogey Bravo. He thinks he's clever. Well, he is clever—we all know that."

It was a grim truth they all had to live with, that the man tasked to conquer their home nations was one of the best strategists the Commonwealth had produced in a generation. Michelle's own estimation was that only the war with the League had robbed him of enough reinforcements to smash the Alliance a year or more earlier.

"But clever as the good Marshal is, he's up against the Stellar Fox today, and the Fox smells a trap! The Terrans have left us a nice hole to slip through, not entirely safe, no—not that obvious.

"But the hole is there and we could escape through it…except it's a trap," she concluded dryly. "So, the boss says we turn the trap on them, and *that*, ladies, gentlemen and the *rest* of you, falls where it always falls: on the starfighters."

She knew her people. Some of them had flown with the Fox before this latest campaign. All of them knew who he was, what he had done. If Admiral Roberts said there was a trap, they'd believe him. If *she* said she believed Admiral Roberts, they'd believe her.

"All wings, all squadrons, converge into Epsilon-One formation and maintain position at two-fifty thousand kilometers ahead of the fleet," she continued. "We're going to be playing anti-missile shield pretty quickly here, but shortly after that, well…

"We have some Terran battleships to kill."

———

Missile fire resumed as Forty-First Fleet turned in space, hundreds of the massive smart weapons blazing into space at Bogey Alpha. The entire plan now hinged on punching through Alpha as hard and fast as possible.

Williams-Alvarez was already moving her starfighters and bombers where he wanted them, without his even needing to give specific orders. Competent subordinates were a treasure. As he watched, the battleships and battlecruisers shifted their formations, moving forward to form a seven-ship shield in front of the four carriers.

Their defenses and heavy lances would decide this battle. They'd either smash their way through Bogey Alpha and exit the system unharmed, or Bogey Alpha would pin them in place while the currently unseen Bogey Charlie maneuvered to trap them.

Charlie was presumably still in Alcubierre drive, which gave them almost infinite options of where to arrive—but once he destroyed Bogey Alpha, *he* had a lot more options to maneuver.

Eleven ships against nine. His were more modern. He knew in his bones that Bogey Alpha was doomed.

The only question was whether what was left of his fleet after killing them would be able to escape the next jaw of the trap.

THE ARRIVAL of the first missile salvos from Bogey Alpha marked the true beginning of the battle. Launched before any of the Commonwealth's tricks had been unveiled, they were a mere forty missiles per salvo. They weren't harmless, but they were the smallest threat currently on the battlespace.

They collided with Williams-Alvarez's fighters and died, their fireballs lighting up the darkness of the Leopold System as the fleets danced.

The same salvos from Forty-First Fleet were less badly calibrated to the strength of their target, but they'd been fired at an enemy Kyle had believed was weaker. They were split into three groups of sixty-six, each targeting one of the *Assassins*.

Faced with three older ships, it had made sense. Faced with nine ships, two of them top-of-the-line modern units, it was a recipe for wasted ammunition. There was only limited capacity to update missile targeting via Q-probes, so the first three salvos went in unchanged.

And died. A few starfighters went with them—more than the Terran missiles had achieved against Williams-Alvarez's squadrons—but not many.

The fourth salvo was different. All one hundred and ninety-eight missiles lunged at a single target. With the older battlecruisers still in front from being used as a shield for the other ships' drive signatures, they were the easiest target.

The fourth salvo took out the first one. The fifth took out the second. By the time the sixth salvo reached Bogey Alpha, however, the third *Assassin* had withdrawn into formation with the other capital ships. The massed fire of six capital ships saved her from that salvo.

The remaining four salvos of the first push focused on the closest *Hercules*, hammering almost eight hundred missiles at a single ship. Fire lit up the Terran formation, shredding missiles and starfighters alike, but the Alliance only needed to get lucky a handful of times.

They only got lucky once.

The battlecruiser reeled, her fire slackening as half of her missile launchers vaporized in a blast of antimatter, but she dropped herself back on course, continuing to lunge after Forty-First Fleet with her sister ships.

The two fleets had matched acceleration now. While Kyle's velocity toward Katrina was dropping at two hundred and twenty gravities, Bogey Alpha was continuing to close with him at roughly one percent of lightspeed.

It would take him three hours to escape the system, and he'd reach zero range with Bogey Alpha in just under ninety minutes.

The gap in missile fire let Bogey Alpha breathe, but it wouldn't last. Soon, both sides would be under fire by hundreds of missiles again—and this was just foreplay.

The real battle would begin when the starfighters clashed.

Kyle sighed.

"Orders to Williams-Alvarez," he told Sterling quietly. "The fighter group will advance and engage the enemy."

He'd been a fighter pilot before and he hated it, but the reality was that starfighters existed to die so starships didn't have to. Duty required him to spend Williams's people to save as many of his starships as possible.

He still didn't know where Bogey Charlie was going to come out, after all.

BB-285 *Saint Michael*

"He's reversed vector entirely," MacGinnis reported. "They're going to drop right down TF Thirty-Eight–One's throat. That's…odd."

"No, it's smart," James replied. "He knows he can take Hopper. He's guessed that we had a hammer ready to drop in the gap we'd left him. Smart fucker."

"Hopper is going to get mangled," MacGinnis said quietly. "What do we do?"

"Continue laying on the missile fire as hard as we can and maneuver to cut off his options," the Marshal replied, flipping a course from his implant into *Saint Michael*'s systems. "This course will remove a good third of his possible courses. We probably won't be able to engage him except with missiles, but that's not the point."

His operations officer threw the courses and probability cones up in the flag deck's big holodisplay.

"Sixty minutes after he crashes through Thirty-Eight-One, he can go FTL," she concluded. "We can't catch him. Our missiles might take a ship or two, but it's all down to Hopper…and he doesn't have the firepower."

"No, he doesn't," James agreed. "But Admiral Tasker *does*—and she can still adjust her emergence."

He opened the q-com channel to *Saint Brigit*.

"Lindsey, I'm sending you a new emergence locus," he told her. "I don't expect you to hit it perfectly, but the closer you get, the more *fucked* the Stellar Fox is.

"We'll see," she replied. "We're less than ten minutes from emergence; there's only so much we can do!"

"Do what you can," James ordered. "Let's finish the job."

36

Leopold System
09:15 October 9, 2737 Earth Standard Meridian
Date/Time
Alliance Forty-First Fleet

FORTY-FIRST FLEET'S fighter force was dramatically understrength, but Michelle still had eight hundred starfighters and a hundred and fifty bombers. The Commonwealth fighter force outnumbered her, with just as many bombers, but she trusted her people's skill over that of the local high guard.

"Bombers, hold your torpedoes for the capital ships," she ordered. "Use your Starfires with the rest of us. We're going to punch a hole for you—launch torps *after* we've cleared the fighters with the missiles."

The Gemblade torpedoes would range on the capital ships before the two starfighter forces charging toward each other could use their shorter-ranged missiles on each other.

With Forty-First Fleet accelerating *away* from the closing starfighters, however, Michelle's people would have a chance to gut the Commonwealth fighters and bombers before they could launch.

A stern chase was a long chase—but her fighters were now charging straight at the enemy. The Commonwealth fighters had waited until she'd begun her charge to come out to meet her, but the space between the two fleets was about to light up with fire.

"Twenty-eight minutes to missile range," Eklund told her. "They're just under forty from torp range of Forty-First Fleet. No luck pulling the bombers out of the mix so far."

Hiding bombers as starfighters was such a basic use of ECM that Michelle would have been surprised if they *could* identify them now. Bombers didn't have weaker defenses than the starfighters around them, but they were a much bigger threat to the capital ships the starfighters needed to take them home.

"Massed salvos as soon as we hit range," Michelle ordered. "Save one salvo for the capital ships, but throw every other missile we've got right at the starfighters. Like I said, let's punch a hole, people."

KYLE'S FOCUS was on the fighter strike, even the continuing three-way missile engagement a secondary priority in his mind as he watched Williams-Alvarez and her people charge forward. His implant, linked into *Elysium*'s computers, gave him a series of timelines and countdowns.

The whole thing was going to be rough on his starfighters. It was going to be rougher on the Commonwealth in the long run, but he was grimly certain he was going to lose more of his people than he'd like.

Of course, even *one* was more than he'd like.

"Alcubierre emergence!" Aurangzeb suddenly barked. "Multiple emergences, dropping vectors on the feeds now."

Kyle's focus changed instantly, refocusing the tactical feed running through his implant as he rose from his command chair to study the main display.

"What have we got?" he asked.

"Looks like the fleet that hit Midori, plus some replacements and reinforcements," his operations officer told him. "Five *Saint*s. Three *Hercules*es. Three *Volcano*s. Four *Lexingtons*. Four *Ocean*s and two *Resolute*s."

Seven battleships and an equal number each of carriers and cruisers. Twenty-one warships.

"Emergence locus?"

"About halfway between where we would have been warping space if we'd gone down the gap and our current target," Aurangzeb reported. "This was their ambush and they tried to redirect it."

But they hadn't done it well enough. If Kyle didn't change his course at all, the Commonwealth fleet's fighters would catch him but the capital ships wouldn't.

But...

"Adjust fleet course twenty-six degrees clockwise along the ecliptic plane and seven degrees up," Kyle ordered softly. The course change would bring them closer to Bogey Bravo, but not *quite* close enough for torpedo range...and would remove them from Bogey Charlie's range entirely.

They were still going to have to fight Alpha, but Charlie's emergence had been *just* wrong enough to save them.

"I've got starfighter and missile launches from Bogey Charlie," Sterling reported. "Course change...will keep us out of starfighter and bomber range.

"We're going to start eating missiles from them in forty minutes, shortly after our bombers hit Bogey Alpha. Any change to targeting orders, sir?"

Kyle shook his head. His hundred and ninety-eight launchers were enough to be a threat to any single fleet facing him, but splitting his fire would waste his missiles.

"Maintain focus on Bogey Alpha," he ordered. "We'll punch them out and run for home. Keep your eyes on the bouncing ball, people.

"We've got to live through Bravo and Charlie's missiles, but we cannot afford to be distracted by them."

Missiles flashed past Michelle's people in both directions and she shivered at the sight of them. Her people were doing what they could, but their relative velocity to the Terran weapons was too high for them to eliminate more than a tenth of the missiles the Commonwealth was flinging at Forty-First Fleet.

So far, the fleet was holding their own, dodging and destroying the salvos as they came crashing down, but that could only last so long. Outnumbered six to one, there was no way they could survive an extended missile engagement.

Which meant it was up to Michelle and her people to reduce those odds.

"We're in torpedo range," Eklund told her.

"Everyone, hold your fire," she barked. "If we launch through the starfighters, we'll lose too many of the torps. We need every hit we can get—our job is to plow the road for the fleet!"

The reminder was unneeded. Her bombers stayed silent, holding their fire as they closed. Four more minutes.

Then three more minutes. Then two.

And then it was time.

"All fighters, fire at will!"

Her Falcon-C command starfighter trembled as her four missile launchers fired, cycled to the next missile in their magazines, and fired again.

She held her last salvo—only three missiles instead of four on the command starfighter—and watched as her enemies unleashed their own firestorm.

The Alliance force had fewer fighters, but while her Templars had fewer launchers than the Terran Katanas, her Arrows had more. The Commonwealth launched four thousand missiles at her—and she sent thirty-four hundred back.

The Terrans weren't holding missiles for a capital-ship strike, though. They sent three salvos of starfighter missiles at her people, and she only sent two back at them.

Twelve thousand missiles versus seven thousand. Somehow, she was grimly certain this wasn't going to be a good day for her people—but they needed to hold together.

"Protect the bombers," she ordered. "At all costs."

That order was going to kill her people. She knew it. Her starfighters would have to sacrifice themselves to cover the bombers from the incoming missiles—but the bombers were her best chance at killing the battleships closing with her people's only way home.

Being the starfighter strike commander sucked.

WATCHING the starfighter clash was the worst part of being a fleet commander. Kyle had been in those tiny ships in those deadly, terrifying moments, and he knew what he'd sent his people into.

But he was safe. Far behind the conflict, as thousands of missiles hammered down on the fleets of tiny ships like crashing tsunamis.

The cascades of antimatter explosions made it hard to see what was going on from the outside, even with the sensor feeds from the starfighters and the Q-probes accompanying them.

"Torpedo launch!" Sterling announced. "...Damn. They must have launched just before the missiles reached them."

Kyle nodded silently.

That was the best of the bad options. The bombers might still die, but their torpedoes wouldn't have to pass through as many starfighters as before to reach the capital ships.

He hated to interfere in the middle of the battle, but he watched the losses stack up and came to a decision.

"Orders to Williams-Alvarez," he said quietly. "She is to expend all of her missiles on the starfighters and fall back on the fleet. The torps will clear the way and the battlewagons will finish it. Her people's part in this is almost over."

MICHELLE'S FALCON writhed in the valley of fire and death. Dozens—hundreds!—of antimatter explosions pockmarked the space around her ships as she received the new orders.

They might not be the most tactically efficient order, but she couldn't help but feel relief as she was told *not* to spend her people's lives for the smallest of benefits. She was already losing people left and right, the starfighters burning like fireflies as they covered the bombers' launch, clearing the way for the torpedoes that might, just *might*, save the fleet behind them.

"Launch all remaining missiles and reverse acceleration," she snapped, passing on the order. "Kill these bastards and fall back to the carriers. The big guns are coming in to finish the job!"

The last gasp of her force blasted into space, barely two thousand missiles instead of the three thousand–plus from before. She'd lost a third of her ships in the first exchange—but the Terrans had come off even worse.

If the exchange rate continued, the lance duel that was rapidly growing on them was going to be well in her favor.

She forced herself to stony-faced calm as the reports continued to trickle in of shattered ships and lost lives. About twenty percent of those wrecked ships had launched their escape pods, blasting their crews clear before they were destroyed.

Those "lucky" crews would be Commonwealth prisoners. There was no way that the Alliance fleet could retrieve most of the escape pods. Some might be close enough to be scooped up by daring S&R ships as the fleet passed by, but almost all of them would be left behind.

The second wave crashed down on her people and she focused on survival, twisting her Falcon through the incoming fire and letting Eklund line their lasers and positron lance up on the missiles.

Every missile she killed was one that couldn't touch her or her people. Somehow, *somehow*, she danced through the second salvo alive.

And the third.

Two thousand starfighters and bombers had fired twenty missiles at each other, and barely five hundred from *both* sides survived to reach lance range.

Before Michelle could say anything, give any orders, the remaining Templars—forty-six Phoenix ships—suddenly shifted their acceleration, charging into the teeth of the closing Terran force.

The Templars were the only ships in her force to match the Katanas for lance range. Their shift in course bought them precious seconds before the Terrans reacted—precious seconds in which they shattered the forward squadrons of the Commonwealth force.

"After the Templars!" Michelle barked. "Down their throats with everything we've got—we punch these bastards out and we get to go home!"

In the back of her mind, she was watching the torpedoes hammer home into the Commonwealth fleet—but her own focus was on her lance and her engines, dodging around enemy fire as she unleashed havoc on them in turn.

She survived.

Only one hundred and eighty-two of her starfighters came through with her.

EVEN AS PART of Kyle mourned the fighter crews he'd lost, the rest of him—the cold-blooded bastard who'd earned an Admiral's stars on the backs of more bodies than he could count—was focused on the torpedo strike.

Nine hundred torpedoes paled in comparison to the thousands of weapons that had just lit up space in a cataclysm of fire around the starfighters, but it was four times as many missiles as each of the earlier salvos his fleet had flung at Bogey Alpha.

Less capable missiles, true, but still more capable than the starfighter missiles that had been spent in their thousands to open a path. All nine hundred torpedoes made it past the Commonwealth fighters, swarming forward like an avenging storm.

The seven surviving capital ships spread out to better defend themselves, lasers and defensive positron lances alike lighting up space as they tore massive gaps in the formation of incoming weapons.

Kyle watched the attack hit, his entire flag deck silent around him. Torpedoes died in the hundreds—but there were hundreds of them *to* die.

The damaged *Hercules* went first, followed almost instantly by the last *Assassin*. The remaining torpedoes flung themselves at the four battleships at the core of Bogey Alpha, their suicidal brains driven by one determined mission: destroy themselves and take the enemy with them.

Two *Resolute*s staggered under the fire. One lunged forward to rejoin her companions. The other spun helplessly off toward Leopold, her engines shattered by the hits. Most of her crew had likely survived, but she was out of the fight.

She was probably the lucky one, Kyle reflected. His own battlecruisers and battleships were adjusting their formations, dropping behind the carriers to make sure their escortees were protected. He'd have opened the range even farther, but that would have left both subformations vulnerable to missiles.

His *Titan*s and *Conqueror*s outranged the *Resolute*s. Everyone knew how this battle was going to end now, but the *Resolute*s charged forward anyway, their missile launchers hurling death at Kyle's fleet as they tried to close to the range of their own one-megaton-a-second beams.

They never made it. The two fleets crossed an invisible line in space, where intelligence suggested that the modern Federation ships' one-point-five megaton positron lances would overwhelm the older battleships' retrofitted electromagnetic deflectors.

The first beams missed and Kyle inhaled sharply.

"They've upgraded again," he murmured. "That's at least ten percent stronger than we anticipated."

"Fully modern screens," Aurangzeb agreed. "Should have guessed that was part of why Walkingstick held back his fleet." The ops officer shook his head and flashed a predatory grin. "Won't save them, though."

The three ships danced in the fire, but four of the Alliance vessels had the range—and the Terran ships didn't. A hundred massive positron lances flayed the space around the Commonwealth battleships, and even the best maneuvering and twisting would only save them for so long.

The damaged *Resolute* misstepped first, colliding with six lancebeams from *Genghis Khan*. The battlecruiser's beams only connected for a quarter-second at most, but it was enough. Six hammerblows of pure focused antimatter smashed into and through the old battleship.

She reeled for a half second after the impact, then detonated as her antimatter containment failed.

A second battleship seemed to just...stop in space as she collided with *Kronos*'s fire. Even with *Elysium*'s computer support, Kyle couldn't tell how many of the superbattleship's thirty-six massive beams hit the *Resolute*.

There wasn't enough left of the enemy battleship to judge.

One last ship remained. Either lucky or cursed, she dodged everything again and again—managing to survive the full light-second to enter *Magellan*'s reduced range.

Her luck could only last so long, and her captain and gunners knew it. There was no way to score reliable hits at this range, but her megaton-a-second lances spoke anyway. Fire flashed across space, flung aside by the massive powerful electromagnetic fields wrapped around the Alliance ships.

One lucky beam hit *Avalon*. The supercarrier lurched and Kyle's heart leapt into his throat as his old ship struggled, but she swung around the damage. His data feed showed she'd lost lances and missile launchers, but she was still moving.

She could still make FTL.

Another series of beams slammed into *Kronos*. The massive battleship was among the most heavily armored modern ships in existence, and massive panels of ablative armor detonated under the blows. Antimatter met matter and converted it into energy—but the ablative armor kept the explosion away from her hull.

Beams vaporized and launchers were lost, but like *Avalon,* the big battleship was still flying.

The *Resolute*'s luck ran out at the same time as the latest salvo of missiles came smashing down on her. Without her sisters to defend her, it would have taken more luck than she had to stop all two hundred missiles.

The last of Bogey Alpha's starships died in an immense fireball as missiles swarmed over her, and Kyle breathed a sigh of relief.

With Bogey Alpha gone, his fleet was clear out of Katrina's gravity well to where they could warp space and escape.

And then the first synchronized salvo from Bogey Bravo and Bogey Charlie smashed over his fleet. *Elysium* jumped like a startled puppy as her own ablative armor tried to deflect the missiles making their final charge against her.

It failed.

37

Leopold System
10:00 October 9, 2737 Earth Standard Meridian
Date/Time
Alliance Forty-First Fleet

THE LIGHTS FLICKERED BACK on after a few seconds, the implant network coming back moments later as the emergency power redirect ended. Sensors and the tactical feed took a few seconds longer, but the rough automated damage report was in Kyle's head by the time they came live.

It wasn't good.

Three separate missiles had hit *Elysium,* each carrying a one-gigaton antimatter warhead and roughly the equivalent in kinetic energy. Like *Kronos,* the supercarrier had massive armor and defenses, the ablatives only the first layer of countermeasures to attack, but six gigatons of force was more than they could take.

The rest of the fleet was continuing to accelerate away from Katrina at two hundred and twenty gravities. *Elysium* wasn't accelerating at all, her engines offline as she reeled from the damage.

As Kyle watched, the rest of the fleet began to reduce acceleration and he shook his head.

"Do we have coms?" he barked at Sterling.

"Yes, sir!"

Kyle didn't acknowledge his chief of staff's response, instead diving right into the mental network with the rest of the ships…and blinking as it told him he didn't have a q-com link.

"Sterling? The computer doesn't agree with you!"

His chief of staff swallowed, eyes glazing as he went through his implant, and then met his gaze.

"The q-com array is *gone,* sir," he said quietly. "We still have the backup radio and laser connections."

"Thanks."

Kyle linked into those.

"This is Roberts," he said calmly. "All ships will resume maximum acceleration. All starfighters will proceed to *Avalon* and the battlecruisers. *Nobody* lands on *Elysium* until we have a final damage assessment."

He paused.

"If *Elysium* cannot keep up with the fleet, the fleet will leave without her. That order is non-discretionary."

"We can't just leave you behind," Bai'al's voice arrived via radio seconds later. "We can't just abandon a supercarrier!"

"We can lose one supercarrier better than the entire fleet," Kyle replied. "My orders stand."

He turned his attention back to his flagship as *some* of her engines flickered to life.

"Captain Novak? What's our status?"

"Not…great," *Elysium*'s Captain told him. "FTL coms are down. Most of the engines are down. We can only pull about fifty gravities."

Kyle nodded. That was unfortunate, but they might still be able to pull the ship out. She'd be under fire for a long time, though…

"That's not the worst of it, sir," she said grimly. "The reason we can only pull fifty gees is that the Class Ones are down."

He winced.

"All of them?"

"Right now, all of them," she confirmed. "Engineering is digging into if we can get any back up, but at this moment, sir, there is no way that *Elysium* can go FTL."

He studied the vectors. Shuttles could pull five hundred gravities, but the fleet was drawing away at two hundred and twenty, and while he'd trust the Commonwealth not to *intentionally* shoot down evacuation ships, there were enough missiles flying…

"Sound the evacuation order," he told her. "Everyone who can make it to a shuttle in under five minutes gets off this ship."

"Yes, sir."

Even as the message rang out across the ship, he could *feel* her hesitance over the link.

"Sir, that doesn't include the flag deck. You're at least…"

"Seven minutes, running and using the lifts, from the flight deck," he confirmed cheerfully. "*Elysium* is a fine ship, Captain. Whatever happens, I think we're both going down with her."

KYLE REMAINED STANDING, letting the chaos and activity of his flagship wash over him as her crew fled.

"Turn us about," he heard Novak bark. "Let's cover the shuttles."

He didn't hear the response, but the grim humor of her next comment suggested what it had been.

"If we cover them with our hull, we're still covering them. We get those people out of here!"

None of their communications were real-time. The data feeds from the rest of the fleet and the approaching starfighters were already starting to be distorted by relativity. There were a thousand aspects of space travel that the q-coms allowed them to ignore, but the spike of fire that had shredded *Elysium*'s FTL communications had killed all of that.

"Sir, I have the report from Engineering," Novak said quietly through his implants. It was a private channel, just the two of them. She wasn't even speaking aloud on the bridge.

That was a bad sign.

"How bad?"

"Three of the Class Ones are gone," she told him. "We might be able to get two of the others online, get ourselves back up to a hundred gees or so, but we aren't going to be able to warp space."

"I understand."

He stared at the holodisplay. All of his options had shrunk down.

"Turn us around, Captain Novak," he ordered quietly. "We'll use *Elysium* to break their missile salvos, cover the rest of the fleet's retreat."

"Sir, the fleet *can* slow down, wait for a shuttle…"

"Negative, Captain," he cut her off. "Every minute they delay is another missile salvo they have to stop. I will *not* put my people at risk for myself; am I clear?

"No," he concluded softly. "We'll cover the retreat. We'll ram this ship right down Walkingstick's throat, and the old bastard can *choke* on it."

The channel was silent.

"Yes, sir."

Obedient to his orders, *Elysium* turned at bay. Behind her, the other ten ships of Forty-First Fleet fled toward flatter space, space where they could engage their FTL drives and flee the Leopold System.

Starfighters and bombers streamed past her. *Avalon* alone could carry all of the survivors of the fighter strike, Kyle reflected. Williams-Alvarez, at least, would survive. They'd made it this far—he'd trade his life for the pilots who'd survived the strike that had saved his fleet.

"Sons of bitches," Sterling snapped. There was no real heat in his curse, just resignation.

"Commander?"

"They've switched their missile targeting," Sterling explained. "The missiles salvos are trying to bypass us and go after the rest of the fleet." He paused. "To give them credit, that course change *also* minimizes the chance they'll hit our evacuation shuttles."

"I'll give Walkingstick that much credit, yes," Kyle agreed. "Can we still intercept them?"

"That's a question for Novak's crew, and I don't want to interrupt them," his chief of staff admitted. "It'll be long-range, but I don't see a reason not to try!"

"What about missiles? Can we return fire?"

Aurangzeb laughed bitterly as Kyle directed the question his way.

"Six launchers, sir," he said flatly. "We're not getting through *anyone's* defenses with six launchers."

"Release them to Novak's control," Kyle ordered. The entire fleet's missile launchers had been linked to fire on fleet orders, focusing the missiles on a minimum number of targets. "She can use them for missile defense."

Using all-up Jackhammers as counter-missiles was expensive but, well, he couldn't use them for much else now.

Moments after the bridge regained control of the launchers, missiles began to flash out. He didn't need to check their orders to know they were being sent out as counter-missiles. Even as he watched, *Elysium* adjusted her course, the big, crippled carrier charging into the heart of the missile fire from Bogey Bravo.

Bogey Charlie's fire wouldn't come anywhere near her, but she could gut Bravo's salvos if they chose to ignore her.

And ignore her they did. Missiles slipped past—a single ship couldn't stop those massed hundreds—but far fewer than would have hit *Elysium* if the salvo had been aimed at her. For five minutes, the big supercarrier was wreathed in explosions.

Ten minutes.

Fifteen.

Some missiles made it through everything, but *Kronos* and *Gaia* were trailing the rest of the fleet now, "dragging their skirts" to lure the missiles to them. Both superbattleships took hits, but they *could*.

"*Gaia* has lost a Class One," Sterling murmured. "Thank the Stars for redundancies."

Not every fleet gave their ships an extra Class One manipulator.

The Federation had never stopped...and that had just saved one of their most modern battleships.

"There they go," Aurangzeb added. "They're clear."

Cherenkov radiation flickered across *Elysium*'s scanners, and Kyle looked at the tactical feeds.

The big supercarrier was alone in Leopold now, facing almost fifty Commonwealth warships.

"There are, what, fifteen hundred missiles still out there?" he asked conversationally.

"At least," Aurangzeb confirmed. "We're...well, we're fucked, sir."

"I know." Kyle shook his head.

"Captain Novak?"

"Sir?" his flag captain responded, her voice tired. She knew what order he was going to give.

"Samson Protocols, if you please. Make sure everyone gets to a pod." He smiled grimly, making sure his determination crossed the channel.

"That *includes* you. We got everyone clear; now we need to make sure the Commonwealth doesn't get a *Sanctuary* to dissect—and you *will* not go down with her at this point, understood?"

"Yes, sir."

BB-285 *Saint Michael*

HUNDREDS OF MISSILES swept across the Leopold System, obedient to James Calvin Walkingstick's command. Already, they were all changing their courses, giving up their hopeless chase of the now-vanished Alliance fleet and hurtling toward the remaining *Sanctuary*-class carrier.

"I wonder," James said aloud, considering. "Roberts always was a carrier man."

"Sir?" MacGinnis asked.

"Two Federation carriers. Two Imperial carriers. I make the odds fifty-fifty that the Stellar Fox is on that ship," James said conversationally.

"Then he is about to cease to be a problem," his ops officer said with satisfaction, then looked surprised as James shook his head.

"If he's aboard that ship, he's already ceased to be a problem," he pointed out gently. "And whoever is aboard that ship, they put themselves into a position where they were going to give their lives to protect the rest of their people.

"Besides, they'll scuttle her before they let us capture her...but if we hold off the missile fire, they can evacuate in an orderly fashion before they do so."

Part of him wanted to grind Roberts's face in this defeat, incomplete as it had been. The rest of him knew the crew over there deserved more respect—and while James Walkingstick would admit, in private at least, that he was a Unificationist fanatic, he wasn't a mass murderer.

Not when he'd already won.

"Order all missiles into holding pattern and send a transmission to that ship," he ordered firmly. "We are prepared to accept their surrender."

"And if they fire on us, sir?"

James smiled thinly.

"They won't be that stupid, Commodore," he replied. "But if they do, vaporize that carrier."

38

Castle System
15:00 October 9, 2737 Earth Standard Meridian
Date/Time
New Cardiff

DR. LISA KERENSKY gestured with one hand, rotating the holographic model of a human brain floating in the middle of her office. The holographic model of a *very specific* human brain, whose owner was sitting on the other side of the projection from her, looking at her with hope in his eyes.

"If you look here, Mr. Solokov, you'll note that this set of serotonin receptors is glowing orange," she told her patient. "That means they're absorbing neurotransmitters with less efficiency than normal. They're not entirely outside of the regular range, but it's quite low.

"Now, *normally*, the brain compensates for this on its own," she continued. "But take a look at this."

She highlighted a blue line that ran right through the receptors in question and down into Wesley Solokov's amygdala.

"That is one of the data trunks for your neural implant. It's not supposed to have anything to do with neurotransmitters, but it has a clean, smooth polymer surface. The excess neurotransmitters are following that surface down into your amygdala, which is triggering your anxiety attacks."

She smiled gently at him.

"In most cases, your implant would detect the neurotransmitter imbalance and automatically adjust, but because the balances look correct on the surface, the implant thinks everything is fine—even while the implant itself is part of the problem."

"Can you fix it?" Solokov asked softly. "That sounds…complicated."

"That's why your local hospital couldn't identify it," Lisa told him. Most cases of anxiety and panic attacks could be dealt with by ordering the implant to adjust for the neurotransmitter imbalance. It could take days to identify the exact imbalance—the implant would automatically deal with the most common issues—but once the instructions had been given, the implant could fix most cases in under seventy-two hours.

In Solokov's case, the neurotransmitter levels all looked normal. They were just moving in a way they weren't supposed to because of overlaid random factors.

"But they sent you to me," she continued with a smile. Even after Kyle Roberts had disappeared out of her life, leaving her with a baby and a high school education, he'd continued to pay a maximum amount of child support—and his mother had taken Lisa and Jacob in.

His distant help had seemed too little at the time, but it had helped her get galaxy-class training and skills—and hence this office.

"We could try having your implant do a target adjustment of your neurotransmitter levels," she noted. "That would be the extent of what your local hospital could do if they'd identified this, but that's attacking the symptom, not the source.

"What I'd like to do is a two-fold solution," she continued. "We can use a nanotech treatment to adjust the receptors to regular efficiency and mo—"

The door to her office swung open and she looked up in surprise.

None of the staff at New Cardiff Central Hospital would interrupt her when she was meeting with a patient. She had her implant com and schedule set to DO NOT DISTURB.

"Dr. Kerensky," the young man in blue scrubs in the door said apologetically. "I'm sorry for interrupting, but main reception just called. There's an Admiral at the front desk asking for you—she says it's urgent."

An Admiral? But Kyle was on duty…

"She?" Lisa asked. "Did Reception give you a name?"

The young nurse coughed.

"I think Sana is being terrified by stars, Doctor," he admitted. "Tall black woman? Rear Admiral?"

Solace. What was Jacob's stepmother-to-be doing here?

"Mr. Solokov, I think I need to speak with this caller," Lisa said slowly. "A family matter. If you'll excuse me?"

"It's fine, Dr. Kerensky," he promised. "I'll talk to your staff and schedule the appointment. We'll proceed as you suggest."

With a distracted nod, Lisa left her office, barely avoiding breaking into a run.

There was *no* good reason why Kyle Roberts's fiancée would be in her hospital.

AS LISA ENTERED the main reception area for New Cardiff Central, she released the do-not-disturb on her implant. A single text message from her own fiancé flashed to the top of the priority list.

Cancel your next meeting. I'm on my way. Dan.

She'd spent ten years becoming the best neurosurgeon on the planet. One of the skills Lisa had needed to learn was the ability to look a patient she couldn't save in the face and be calm. She'd had trouble with it, but she could present a façade now.

It took every scrap of that hard-won skill to remain even outwardly calm as she saw Mira Solace. The Rear Admiral had always been fully composed and utterly put-together when Lisa had met her.

Now the tall black woman was leaning against a pillar next to the reception desk, waiting for Lisa like a puppet with her strings cut. Her eyes were red as she turned to see Lisa, and she tried to force a smile—and failed.

Lisa didn't even remember crossing the hall, wrapping the older woman in her embrace.

"What happened?" she demanded.

"I can't give you details," Solace gasped out, her voice gravelly with shed and unshed tears. "But...*Elysium* was lost. Kyle was aboard."

Lisa was leaning against the pillar herself. For ten years, she hadn't cared what happened to Kyle Roberts—she thought, at least—but they'd carefully danced a friendship back together the last few years, when the war gave them time.

But...*gone*? He couldn't be gone!

"Dr. Kerensky?" Sana Macar asked quietly, the darkly tanned receptionist looking worried. "Can I...help?"

Lisa swallowed, forcing her façade back up as she delicately turned to the staff member.

"Sana, dear, can you contact my staff and have them cancel the rest of my appointments for today?" she asked quietly. "I..." She swallowed. "I need to go tell my son his father is dead."

DANIEL'S ARRIVAL was preceded by a pair of Assembly Security Force officers in black suits. Technically, Lisa was sure, they should have declared the area secure or some similar official term that meant there were no assassins waiting to leap out at New Cardiff's MFA.

Instead, Daniel Kellers was barely two steps behind the guards, the chubby man wrapping both women in a warm embrace.

"I figured I'd find you here, Mira," he told Solace. "How much do you know?"

"Standard MIA next-of-kin message," she admitted. "But knowing what he was doing..."

"I know more," the Member of the Federation Assembly said quietly. "Not in public. Are you both free?"

"Yeah," Lisa said quickly. "We need to tell Jacob."

"Agreed. But we also need to be sure we tell Jacob the *right* thing." Daniel looked grim. "Someone—I can't say who—has already leaked this to the media. My car is right outside. Let's go."

Lisa took a moment to check in her implant that her appointments had been canceled—she did have responsibilities, after all—then followed her fiancé out.

"Did you bring a car, Admiral?" Daniel asked politely.

"Marine aircar," Solace confirmed, gesturing up. "Already linked to the pilot. They'll fly overwatch."

Lisa followed Solace's gesture and saw the black vehicle hovering above the hospital, using one of the building's towers to hide its presence from a casual glance. Her understanding was that the Marine vehicles weren't armed, but from the way the vehicle was positioned, she suspected that wouldn't save anyone who decided to mess with Mira Solace today.

"Good," Daniel replied. "My car is armored. If someone tries something stupid, they won't get to regret it for very long."

He led the way into the black government car, the two suited guards piling themselves into the front seat as the vehicle moved away from the hospital. Whatever instruction Daniel had given the driver had been by implant, and he sealed a privacy barrier to leave the three of them alone.

"Everyone is going to be leaping on the 'Kyle Roberts is dead' bandwagon pretty damned quickly," he said grimly. "Whoever leaked it to the media didn't really fudge the facts, but they kept enough details of the affair under wraps to satisfy Navy classification and let the reporters draw their own conclusion."

"So, he's *not* dead?" Lisa demanded.

"We don't know he's dead," Daniel corrected. "Forty-First Fleet got neatly mousetrapped by a mind-bogglingly overwhelming force. Admiral Roberts managed to extract most of his fleet, but several vessels were badly damaged.

"Including," he sighed heavily, "*Elysium*. What information I have is that *Elysium* wasn't capable of keeping up with the fleet or warping space, so Admiral Roberts ordered the fleet to leave them behind.

"Her q-coms were damaged, so our last report is from shortly after Forty-First Fleet warped out," he concluded. "The Q-probes left behind weren't going to be of any use to *Elysium*, so the self-destruct codes were sent to keep them out of Commonwealth hands."

The MFA shook his head and took Lisa's hand.

"As of our last information, *Elysium* was intact but facing an incoming salvo of approximately seventeen hundred capital-ship missiles," he told them. "It is entirely possible that Admiral Roberts and Captain Novak abandoned ship before her destruction, but we have no guarantees.

"So, *Elysium* is missing in action along with all crew aboard her at that time. They got thirty percent of her crew out by shuttle, but there were still over three thousand people on that ship."

"So, Kyle might be alive?" Lisa asked. "...What do we tell Jacob?"

"Just that," he replied. "We can't tell him everything I just told you. Chunks of that are classified. But we need to make sure *he* knows that Kyle is only *possibly* dead.

"Because the media is sure as hell going to spin it as 'definitely dead'."

Lisa rubbed her eyes, brushing away tears that were trying to fall.

"Typical Kyle," she half-whispered. "Can't even *die* in a way that lets us be sure what's going on!"

39

Deep space, en route to Sol System
18:00 October 9, 2737 Earth Standard Meridian
Date/Time
DSC-062 *Normandy*

RUSSELL CLOSED the latest message from his wife—almost certainly the last he'd see before this entire mess exploded in Seventh Fleet's face. One of the several silver linings he could find in this insanely extended mission was that, one way or another, once it was over, he could go home to her.

For now, however, delayed messages run through the coms lockdown were all they could exchange. He'd want to record one for her before they arrived in Sol, but he only had an hour before the final meeting of the major officers.

Tomorrow was going to be a long day.

His door buzzed.

"Enter," he told the air, allowing Captain Herrera to step into his office.

"How's it going, CAG?" *Normandy*'s commander asked.

"We are twelve hours away from the most insane stunt pulled in the history of warfare," Russell pointed out. "It's a little late to be checking in for doubts."

Herrera chuckled.

"If you didn't have doubts, I'd suggest you to talk to the ship's doctor," he pointed out. "We are attacking *Sol*, Vice Commodore."

"Believe me, I know," Russell replied. "Do we know the status of the rest of the Medusa strike forces?"

Herrera nodded.

"I believe the Admiral will be filling everyone in, but there are channels," he confirmed. "Everyone else is in position, ready for emergence at the appointed minute. Fifteen simultaneous strikes across over a hundred and twenty light-years.

"What lunatic came up with this?"

Russell laughed softly.

"The Fox. Who else?" he told his Captain. "They gave Roberts the job of designing a strategy to win the war, and this is what he came up with."

"If it works, it will be something new in the galaxy," Herrera said. "I don't even know what the consequences will be."

"I suspect we'll find the Commonwealth is more fragile than we think," the CAG said. "There's too many people in there who want out, who were independent before a fleet showed up and told them they weren't.

"Without the ability to coordinate their government and their Navy…I think they're fucked."

"And I'm guessing that's what Roberts thought, too," the Captain agreed. "Damn."

"What?"

"He won't see it," Herrera said quietly. "With the lockdown, it's mostly under wraps, but *Elysium* was reported lost this morning. Admiral Roberts is MIA, presumed dead."

"Damn," Russell echoed. "This one's for absent friends, then, isn't it?"

Herrera shook his head.

"No, CAG. We'll avenge Roberts while we're at it, but this one is for everybody. The Alliance never wanted this war. None of us did."

"The Commonwealth did," Russell agreed. "And now we get to show them why they shouldn't have."

It seemed that Admiral Rothenberg, like many of the crew and officers aboard the thirty-eight starships under his command, had grown sick of a view of steel walls and speed-shifted stars. The virtual conference software used to allow the Captains, XOs and CAGs of almost forty starships each traveling in their own inviolate bubbles of warped space didn't *need* to show a plain military conference room.

It usually did, because that was easier to make certain everyone was comfortable. After twenty-five days under Alcubierre-Stetson drive, however, the Admiral had clearly decided on something different.

The hundred and thirty officers who commanded the warships and sub-groups of Alliance Seventh Fleet found themselves taking seats in a stone amphitheater built on the top of a sandy beach. The glittering blue of a warmly lit ocean glittered behind the dais Admiral Rothenberg stood on.

If the air was too perfectly controlled, the sun too perfectly positioned, and the acoustics too good for the place to be real, well, some sacrifices had to be made.

"This seemed appropriate," the Admiral told his people, gesturing at the vista around them. "This is the refurbished amphitheater on the island of Cyprus—on Earth.

"Tomorrow is probably the closest any of us will ever come to the homeworld, and we'd all rather we came for different reasons and in a different time," he continued sadly. "But we have our mission, and the nations we are sworn to defend have called on us.

"Please, be seated."

Like the rest of the gathered officers, Russell was already sitting in his own office, but the virtual presentation had taken over his senses.

The stone was warm as he sat, a false sun warming a place that didn't actually exist.

"We've all gone over this roughly, what, a million times?" Rothenberg asked to a responding chuckle. "I ask you to be patient with me as we do it one last time. Twelve hours, people, until we fight one of the largest space fleet actions in human history."

He gestured and a projection of the Sol System appeared above the amphitheater, spinning in the air as the officers looked over their target.

"We have three individual targets, and the intent is to hit all three at once," the Admiral noted. "The first target is here, hidden in the upper atmosphere of Uranus." Sol's third, oft-forgotten gas giant flickered in the display.

"This q-com switchboard station isn't officially acknowledged and is the Commonwealth's emergency continuity-of-government system. Only warships and system governments have entangled-particle blocks from this switchboard, and they don't even know they have them.

"It exists to counter the exact type of attack we are about to launch," Rothenberg concluded. "It is also, like the rest of Uranus, only lightly defended."

As the projection zoomed in on the gas giant, Russell reflected that *lightly defended* was a relative term. There were dozens of fortresses orbiting Uranus to defend the gas-extraction industries and civilian populations.

The problem—for the Commonwealth!—was that all but a tiny handful of those fortresses predated the first Commonwealth-Alliance war.

"There are forty-four defensive stations," the Admiral continued. "Four are *Zions*. Our understanding is that they are currently equipped with Scimitar-type fighters, but it is not unreasonable to assume they have been supplied with Katanas and Longbows.

"The other forty stations have been lightly retrofitted, but their primary weapons systems are obsolete. Their only true threat is the four hundred or so missile launchers they have between them."

As the stations were highlighted, four ships appeared in the display at the minimum distance from Uranus.

"We will open our attack at T-minus ten minutes with *Summerlands, Portage, Invictus,* and *Horatio,* constituting Task Force Seven-Three under Rear Admiral Annegret Novacek, arriving at Uranus."

Two modern carriers, a modern battleship and a modern battle cruiser. TF 7.3 was half-Imperial, but the CO was a Trade Factor Admiral aboard *Portage.*

"It should not be necessary for Admiral Novacek's people to destroy most of the fortifications," Rothenberg noted, "but their Falcons, Arrows and Vultures should be able to handle the fortresses if needed."

The Trade Factor hadn't had a seventh-generation starfighter design ready when the war started, so they'd bought the Federation's. There were several reasons the Falcon was the most numerous starfighter in the Alliance's inventory now.

"The Uranus portion of this operation is primarily predicated on surprise: the Commonwealth doesn't think anyone knows that switchboard station exists. We are hoping for Seven-Three's attack to draw enemy forces out of position, but ten minutes isn't enough for any detachments to move out to Uranus and engage them."

The asteroid belt now flashed.

"The second target of this operation, for Task Force Seven-Two, is the Ceres Military Complex," he continued. "Ceres is the primary off-planet military headquarters for the Terran Commonwealth, and is protected as such. While the defenses include a significant number of refitted old fortresses with mass drivers, the asteroid itself has been equipped with bays and launch tubes for approximately one thousand starfighters."

The rotating form of the planetoid anchor for the spaceborne complex now filled the sky above the virtual amphitheater, its defending fortress glittering stars around the massive metalwork that covered the planetoid's surface.

"Ceres is *not* Seven-Two's target," Rothenberg stated. "That honor goes to this station." A tall, spindle-like platform orbiting amidst the fortresses flashed and became the focus of the hologram.

"That is Terran Commonwealth Navy Communication Relay Alpha-One," he explained. "One of two dedicated military q-com switchboard platforms. The destruction of Alpha-One will dramatically reduce communication bandwidth for all military craft and stations in the TCN, and render a not-insignificant portion of their Q-probes completely noncommunicative.

"Of course, to attack Alpha-One, we will have to fight Ceres's defenses. Those fighter bases and fortresses are a serious threat, and we have reason to believe that the Commonwealth's first *Ambrosia*-class super-battleships have been assigned to defend Ceres."

Russell winced. He wasn't the only one. The fact that the Castle Federation had been the only people to break the sixty-five-million-cubic-meter mark for Stetson stabilizers had given the Alliance a solid advantage in the war. It didn't cost that much more to build an eighty-million-cubic-meter starship than a sixty-million-cubic-meter one, but the bigger ship was a more powerful combatant in every sense.

If the *Ambrosia*s were actually rolling out…

"The good news is that *Ambrosia* and *Manna* appear to be the only eighty-million-cubic ships the Commonwealth has built, and both of them are at Ceres," Rothenberg reminded them. "They also have no starfighters aboard, and while I'm planning based on Ceres being fully loaded out with Katanas and Longbows, those bays might also still be filled with Scimitars.

"That said, we can't take any chances," he said grimly. "I'm sending our entire Trade Factor and Star Kingdom detachments, under Vice Admiral Lux Salvail, against Ceres. That's three *Magellan*-class battleships, two *Traveler*-class carriers, two *Vigilance*-class and two *Fearless* battlecruisers and two *Indomitable*-class carriers."

Three modern battleships, four modern carriers, two modern battlecruisers and two older battlecruisers. It was a powerful force, but…

"I also intend to detach all four of our *Last Stand*-class battlecruisers, as well as *Righteous Voice* and *Righteous Star*, under Admiral Salvail's command," Rothenberg noted. "Regardless of what types Ceres's thousand starfighters are, Admiral Salvail will have them outnumbered and outgunned.

"There will be at least two other starships at Ceres, and we don't know who they are," he admitted. "It will fall to Salvail to make certain that Relay Alpha-One is destroyed."

The hologram shifted again, to the only place left for it to go and the place that utterly terrified Russell to be attacking.

"Our third target is the crown jewel of Operation Medusa, the linchpin of the Commonwealth's communication network, and contains the very first q-com switchboard ever constructed," Rothenberg said calmly.

"The Central Nexus is fourteen kilometers long, two kilometers wide, and contains an estimated seven-point-six-*trillion* entangled particles. It is entirely unfortified but has been placed in orbit directly between Earth and her moon, well inside the protective enclosure of the homeworld's defenses.

"Like most of the Sol System's security, that enclosure is badly out of date. A modernization program was commenced a year ago but has suffered delays and problems all along." He paused. "We do not know with one hundred percent certainty how much of Terra Fortress Command has been updated to modern weapon systems.

"We estimate that at least forty platforms have been replaced with *Zions*, basing a total of two thousand starfighters, and that at least forty more have been upgraded with positron lances and modern missile launchers. The other eighty platforms will have the ability to launch modern missiles, but their mass drivers are not a serious threat.

"In addition to the one hundred and sixty fortresses of the TFC, a minimum of ten capital ships are kept in orbit of Earth at all times. Currently, we believe this force consists of two *Saints*, four *Hercules*es and two *Volcano*es, plus two older vessels.

"We will be meeting them with our largest force: Task Force Seven-One, under my direct command from *Righteous Fire*."

The network of fortresses and defending starships glowed crimson above Russell's head.

"Seven-One will consist of seventeen Imperial and Federation warships, led by two *Invictus*-class battleships and ten Imperial and Federation carriers."

Rothenberg looked up at the hologram above his head.

"We have a limited ability to redeploy ships once we're in the system," he admitted. "If anyone sees problems, now is the time to raise them."

Russell wished he could see better answers. Attacking *Earth* seemed crazy enough. Doing it with just seventeen warships?

Well, it had to be enough. They couldn't magically conjure up more now.

40

Leopold System
19:00 October 9, 2737 Earth Standard Meridian Date/Time
BB-285 *Saint Michael*

There was a loud *thud* as the escape pod slammed onto the deck of the shuttle bay of whatever ship Kyle and his staff had been brought aboard. The "sensors" on the pod were a joke that didn't deserve the name, though he was reasonably certain they'd been brought aboard a *Saint*-class battleship in Bogey Bravo.

Given that they'd passed a carrier and, indeed, at least one more battleship on the way in, Kyle was quite certain they'd been brought to Walkingstick's flagship. The Commonwealth knew who they'd caught.

With a soft hissing sound, the hatch to the escape pod slid open. All he could see outside was the plain metal of a starship's interior. It could be anything.

"If you have any weapons, leave them inside the pod," a voice barked. "Any resistance will be met with all necessary force."

Kyle leveled a firm glare on the four Marines standing closest to the exit.

"You heard them," he said quietly. "Disarm. *Completely*."

He waited for the troopers to lay aside their sidearms and carbines, following suit with his own almost-never-used Navy-issue pistol. Once everyone had laid aside their standard weapons, he turned his gaze back on the Marines.

"And the rest, people," he told them. "We're prisoners of war now. We play by their rules. Leave them in here."

The Marines looked mutinous…but another dozen knives, concealable pistols and one-shot anti-armor penetrators joined the pile of weapons. As he continued to look levelly at them, the pile increased in size by another half-dozen.

"All right," he conceded. "I think we know who's waiting for us, people. My turn to go first."

He walked across the pod, squeezing past Marines and his flag staff to the door, and stepped out onto the metal deck of the first Commonwealth warship he'd ever set foot on.

He'd worked with a Commonwealth officer out at Antioch, but every time they'd met in person, it had been aboard Kyle's ship. He'd never been in a Terran ship before, and he was somewhat surprised by how much it was identical to a Federation or Imperial ship.

There were Commonwealth Marines standing right outside the exit, waiting for him.

"Hold right there," the same speaker, a harsh-looking woman with Lieutenant's insignia, snapped at him. "Corporal, search him!"

"That won't be necessary," a voice with a cultured Terran accent cut through the orders, and Kyle looked up to meet the gaze of the Marshal of the Rimward Marches.

James Calvin Walkingstick was a big man, matching Kyle's own towering two meters in height. He wasn't as broad across the shoulders or as muscular, and his hair was dark and tied into long braids instead of Kyle's short-cropped bright red.

"It's their job, Admiral Walkingstick," Kyle said quietly. "After all, many would think trading their lives for yours was worth it." He nodded to the Marine who'd stopped at the Marshal's bark. "Carry on, Corporal."

Walkingstick smirked, but allowed Kyle's voluntary sacrifice. The Marines quickly patted him down, finding nothing, then waved him through.

"Welcome aboard *Saint Michael,* Admiral Roberts," Walkingstick told him. "I'd hoped that we'd get a chance to meet, rather than simply blowing each other to pieces along the way."

"I appreciate your willingness to allow us to evacuate," Kyle replied, bowing his head slightly as he heard his people exit the pod behind him, each undergoing the search in turn. Every second of this false courtesy grated on him, but Walkingstick hadn't had to spare his people's lives.

"There is a point, Admiral Roberts, where further conflict becomes a mere massacre," the Terran Admiral said. "Other men have crossed that line and paid the price for it. I will not become them."

Somehow, Kyle was quite certain that Walkingstick wouldn't hesitate to bomb worlds if he thought it would meet his objectives. Kyle couldn't say much, though. He was the man who'd drafted Operation Dragon, after all, grateful as he was that it hadn't been executed.

"We have confirmed pickup of all of your escape pods from both *Elysium* and your starfighters," Walkingstick continued. "We're still working on a proper headcount or list, but your wounded are being taken care of.

"We have no reason not to be civilized about this, after all."

Kyle smiled bitterly.

"Evidence suggests, Admiral Walkingstick, that we have different standards for *civilized*."

The Marshal chuckled.

"That, my dear Stellar Fox, is always a matter of perspective and discussion, isn't it?"

He stepped back, gesturing for the Marines to escort Kyle.

"I've arranged quarters for yourself and your senior staff, separate from the rest of the prisoners," Walkingstick told Kyle frankly. "We will speak at more length shortly."

"I doubt you'll find I know anything of use," Kyle told him. More accurately, his implant would probably lobotomize him before he could reveal anything of use.

The Terran Admiral made a throwaway gesture.

"I have no interest in what you know, Admiral," he admitted. "The end of your Alliance is coming. But I am intrigued, I must admit, by the man who has caused me so much trouble."

JAMES WALKINGSTICK LINKED his office to the ships surrounding him and let a victorious smile spread over his face as Tasker and Gabor appeared in his office. The projection was entirely in his head, there wasn't even a hologram of the two officers there, but it looked real enough.

"Where are we at?" he asked briskly.

"My fleet wasn't even scratched," Tasker told him. "We shot off about fifteen percent of our missile magazines, but we're otherwise ready for combat."

"Hopper's reinforcements were from my fleet," Gabor pointed out. "Losing those ships hurt. The rest of my ships are still scattered around the region. Should I be recalling them here to or to Niagara?"

"Thirty-Eighth Fleet has shot off over *seventy* percent of their magazines," James told his subordinates. "Leopold has some missiles and I have ammunition colliers in the system, but we're probably better off withdrawing to Niagara to rearm our ships.

"I'm absorbing both of your fleets into Thirty-Eighth," he continued. "You'll continue to command your existing formations as Task Forces Thirty-Eight-Two and Thirty-Eight-Three, but we'll move on from Niagara as a single force."

Any disappointment at losing independent command was invisible as the two officers leaned forward to hear his plan.

"Where are we going?" Tasker asked.

"What's left of Forty-First Fleet remains an extremely powerful force," James told them. "We only actually took out Roberts's flagship, after all."

"In trade for Hopper's entire fleet," Gabor added bitterly.

"Indeed. A poor trade on the surface," James allowed. "Except that we *crushed* their fighters and damaged most of their ships.

"We will return to Niagara, rearm and reconsolidate our forces. I've issued orders for most of our defensive formations to send half of their units to Niagara as well—if we can eliminate their Forty-First and Seventh Fleets in one strike, the Alliance has nothing left to carry out offensives with."

"With how they've reinforced Seventh Fleet..." Tasker trailed off.

"There will be *fifty* capital ships in Via Somnia once Roberts's survivors arrive," James said. "Fifty. The Alliance can't lose fifty ships and sustain any significant offensive action, not without stripping their home-system defenses to the bone.

"I don't intend to give them the time," he told his subordinates. "It will take us a week or so to consolidate our forces at Niagara, and then I intend to move on Via Somnia with seventy-eight capital ships."

That would leave most of the frontier lightly defended, but the Senate's insistence that he pull Tasker and Gabor back to deal with Roberts, combined with the Alliance's concentration of force at Via Somnia, gave him a chance to end the damn war.

"We will smash their fleet at Via Somnia and then move on to complete our operations against the Renaissance Trade Factor," he laid out. "From there, we will reassess, but I expect to move against either Castle or Coraline."

With the RTF and either the Federation or the Imperium out of the war, he was quite certain he could convince the rest of the Alliance to surrender.

"They have gathered the strength to make a serious attack on us but, in doing so, have given us a glorious target," James Calvin Walkingstick assured his Admirals.

"The time has come. We will end this war."

James had made certain that the quarters put aside for Admiral Roberts and his senior staff were better than the brig. They were junior officers' quarters, smaller than the O-6s and above they'd kept out of the cells would be used to, but they were at least actual quarters.

If the new morning saw Marines outside each door in the hallway and power-armored fire teams at either end to make sure any escape attempt ended quickly, well, James had to take precautions.

He stepped up to the door of Admiral Roberts's quarters and traded nods with the Marine guard before hitting the admittance button.

"Admiral Roberts?" he said. "This is Marshal Walkingstick. May we speak?"

The door clicked open in response, and James stepped into the room.

The Federation Admiral laid aside a datapad as the Marshal entered, looking up at his captor. The prisoners quite distinctly did *not* have access to *Saint Michael*'s datanet via their implants. Even the datapad was linked to a specifically restricted library, pretty much purely light entertainment to keep prisoners from going crazy.

"I'd say welcome to my abode, but I have no illusions about which of us owns this room," Roberts said cheerfully, a surprisingly broad grin on the prisoner's face. "It's your ship, your room, Gods, even your chairs.

"So, you may as well sit down."

James did, using amusement to cover his surprise at Roberts's reaction.

"You seem to take captivity well," he said dryly.

"Given the alternative is fire and ash, I'll take it," the Castle-born man told him. "I must repeat what I said earlier, though. You won't learn much of use from me."

"Implant security protocols being what they are, I have no intention of even trying," James told him. Roberts almost certainly knew many things of value to the Commonwealth's campaign—he would know what Seven Fleet's exact strength at Via Somnia was. He'd probably even know why the surveillance platforms had been destroyed—potentially even how they'd been localized.

The stealthed Q-probes were, after all, supposed to be nearly invisible.

But he'd never give up that information voluntarily, and his implant would probably kill him before he surrendered that information under torture or chemical interrogation. Walkingstick's implant would, in the other man's shoes.

"If you'd care to share any exact details of Via Somnia's defenses or what forces have been sent to reinforce the Trade Factor, I won't complain," he continued, "but I have a certain degree of faith in the Alliance's security protocols.

"And I prefer you *alive*."

Roberts chuckled.

"So do I," he admitted. "Though I'm guessing I might regret that. Are we resurrecting the old Roman triumph? Parading me in chains through the streets of Terra?"

James echoed the chuckle.

"That would take a while. Terra has a *lot* of streets. You are roughly correct in your role, though," he admitted. "You are a trophy, and a shiny one at that. When this is over, we'll probably try and convince you to put on a Commonwealth uniform."

His prisoner winced.

"Gods, you bastards would, wouldn't you?" He shook his head. "Forgive me, Marshal, but I don't expect this to end in a way that has you making generous offers!"

James smiled thinly.

"I doubt the Alliance would have fought as long and as hard as they have if you thought differently," he admitted. "A lot of blood has been shed that perhaps didn't need to be, for a war that will end much the same as if you'd surrendered."

"And we clearly still think differently," Roberts pointed out with that same broad grin. "We'll fight you kicking and screaming the whole way. You know that."

"I am afraid of that," James admitted. "But with both your fleet and Seventh Fleet at Via Somnia, you have finally given me a target worth unleashing the full might I have been given upon. With the defeat of those fleets, the Alliance will fall."

Something in Roberts's expression twisted, the grin not faltering but…smirking? The Federation Admiral was *smirking* at him?

"You will see," James said calmly, even as he began to wonder if he could scout Via Somnia before he could arrive. If the Stellar Fox was smirking at him, there was something he didn't know.

"We will all see," Roberts replied. "Whatever comes to pass, we will all see."

Before James could respond, his implant suddenly pinged with an emergency alert.

"What is it?" he demanded, careful not to vocalize aloud.

"Strategic Omega Alert," MacGinnis said flatly over the neural network. "Sol is under attack. So is Tau Ceti. A dozen other systems; we're still identifying where and what."

James couldn't help himself, he turned an accusing glare on Roberts.

"Ah," the Federation Admiral replied. "It has begun, I see."

"What have you *done*?"

"Unleashed armageddon."

41

Sol System
07:00 October 10, 2737 Earth Standard Meridian
Date/Time
DSC-062 *Normandy*

Normandy flashed into the Sol System with an unusual degree of discomfort for her passengers. Russell closed his eyes for a moment, accessing his implant's functions to control the sudden unexpected wave of nausea that swept over him.

That had been a *long* trip, and they'd clearly pushed the emergence by accident. Instead of emerging two light-minutes from Earth, trailing behind the planet's orbit and on the far side of the moon, they'd emerged a "mere" thirty million kilometers from the homeworld.

Six million kilometers wasn't much in the scheme of a voyage of a hundred and sixty light-years, but it was enough to make for a spectacularly rough emergence.

"Launch! Launch! Launch!" he barked as he regained control of his body. A dozen gravities slammed through the gravity field compensating for his acceleration, and his six-thousand-ton starfighter was flung into space.

He wasn't alone. *Normandy* alone launched forty-eight starfighters in her first wave. A second wave followed fifteen seconds later, then a third, and then a fourth that was entirely bombers.

Sixty seconds after TF 7.1 arrived in-system, two thousand starfighters and bombers were forming up around the phalanx of capital ships and heading toward humanity's homeworld.

Russell didn't doubt that Terra Fortress Command and their accompanying warship fleet had known about their arrival the instant it happened. For that matter, he was quite certain they'd known about TF 7.3's ten-minute-past arrival at Uranus the moment it had happened.

"All right, people, keep your eyes peeled," he told his squadrons. "If we're lucky, the Terrans are out of position, moving to deal with what they must think is a spoiling raid."

His smile was predatory.

"If we can fight the warships and Fortress Command separately, I will officially call us the luckiest sons of bitches alive," Commodore Ozolinsh told the senior officers. "And...it's looking quite possible."

The data feed from the capital ships' passive sensors take and the first waves of Q-probes began to filter into Russell's implant.

The Navy had reacted exactly as hoped, though their forces were lighter than anticipated. Four *Hercules* battlecruisers and two *Volcano* carriers had clearly been charging away from Earth at two hundred-plus gravities for almost ten minutes.

They were a million kilometers closer to TF 7.1 than the fortresses. They *could* turn around and fall back, but that would probably look bad.

And stupid as it sounded, Russell could understand that there was no way anyone on those ships or starfighters was going to risk looking cowardly here, above Earth, under the eyes of the Star Chamber itself.

"They are adjusting course to intercept us," Hu noted. "They're going full scramble on their fighters, and the fortresses are launching their ready squadrons."

Hundreds of new icons speckled the feed, many dancing through the chaotic mess of Earth's busy orbitals. The Navy ships alone threw out five hundred-plus starfighters, presumably including some bombers.

The fortress in orbit launched about the same, fewer than Russell was expecting. On the other hand…

"Well, there goes Intelligence's happy daydream," he said aloud on the command channel. "Those *Zions* just put six hundred Katanas in the air from their ready squadrons alone."

"At least that's only thirty *Zions*," Ozolinsh replied. "Two squadrons each. TFC might be weaker than expected, even if they have modern starfighters."

The Commodore's evil smile carried perfectly over the implant network.

"In any case, until they have their non-ready squadrons up, the numbers are on our side.

"Let's teach them how to dance!"

DESPITE THE ALLIANCE commander's enthusiasm, the Commonwealth starfighters were much less willing to charge forward. The starfighters launched by the Navy ships stuck with them, while the fortress fighters remained with their fortresses for almost ten full minutes.

At that point, however, the *Zions* launched their other three squadrons, and all fifteen hundred starfighters swarmed out to meet them.

"Did we interrupt the regularly scheduled nap or something?" Russell asked dryly. "Ten minutes from unconscious to launched. My squadrons would never hear the end of it!"

"There's a lot of ECM out there," Vice Commodore Emilija Santiago, of the carrier *Trafalgar*, said. "But is anyone else getting the feeling they're playing games with signatures?"

"Probably hiding bombers," Russell replied. "It's what we're doing." He checked the timing. "Speaking of bombers, they've screwed up royally. Our bombers will launch before their starfighters range on us."

"We'll lose some torps if we do that," Ozolinsh said. "But...five hundred bombers versus six ships? We can spend them.

"All bomber squadrons, launch at maximum range," he continued, turning Commodores' debate into general orders. "Spread your fire evenly across the capital ships. Let's punch these bastards out and leave the fortresses for the big boys."

Two thousand-plus starfighters were accelerating out now, and Russell quickly reviewed the sensor data, feeding it into Hu's targeting parameters.

"Santiago's right," he said. "There's something weird with their ECM. Emilija, did you get a clearer look?"

"Redirected one of *Trafalgar*'s Q-probes into the middle of them," she said with satisfaction. "We'll have a view in a few moments... What the—"

"Vice Commodore?" Ozolinsh asked.

"There's no bombers in the lead formation," she told them. "Not a one. Just Katanas."

"If the carriers don't have bombers..." The Commodore trailed off. "I'm going to set up a mass hard pulse on that second wave. I wonder..."

Seventeen ships doing general radar and lidar sweeps were enough to provide a lot of information on any ship within a hundred million kilometers.

Seventeen ships, two thousand-plus starfighters, and several dozen sacrificial Q-probes washing directed and carefully sequenced radar pulses over a specific area made it damn hard to hide anything. If the fighter formation had been made of Falcons or Arrows, they'd have been able to conceal a lot.

If it had *actually* been made of Katanas, they probably would have been able to hide bombers.

What they *couldn't* do was conceal that over a thousand of the fifteen hundred starfighters the *Zion* defense platforms had launched in their second wave were Scimitars, not Katanas. The Scimitar was a capable sixth-generation fighter, a worthy opponent to starfighters of its own era.

It was just that "its own era" had been ten years before.

"So, no bombers, and half of them are Scimitars," Santiago concluded. "Told you they were playing games with the signatures."

"Yes, yes, you did," Ozolinsh conceded instantly. "It doesn't change much…other than the certainty that these poor bastards are doomed."

There was a long pause on the command channel, then Russell sighed and shook his head.

"They might be outclassed, boss, but that's *Earth* behind them," he pointed out. "They'll fight harder than we've ever seen before."

THE COMMONWEALTH SHIPS opened fire with missiles as their starfighters finally began to maneuver, the six warships flinging over a hundred missiles at the Alliance task force every forty or so seconds.

Russell watched the missiles fly toward and past the starfighter flotilla, clear orders coming down from Admiral Rothenberg that the starfighters were to avoid the missiles unless actively threatened. There was no point risking starfighters when the fleet's defenses were more than capable of handling the incoming missiles.

The Alliance warships held their own fire, waiting for the starfighters to clear the path. The six warships and two thousand fighters were an obstacle, not an objective—and firing through them would risk the Alliance hitting something they didn't intend to.

There was a *lot* of potential collateral damage in Earth orbit. Centuries-old construction guidelines restricted the orbitals into two perpendicular rings, one around the equator and one over the planet's poles

The rings were densest around the orbital elevator linked to the anchor station where the Commonwealth Star Chamber met. The second densest point was anchored by a newer orbital elevator near Papua New Guinea. If the Alliance was here to wreck Earth's orbital infrastructure, those two elevators and their counterweight stations would be key targets.

Instead, they spent thirty minutes closing the gap with the defending fleet, watching the range drop as the Vultures and Falcons alike prepared their devastating weapon loads.

Thirty-seven minutes after the Alliance fighters had launched, the bombers crossed an arbitrary line in space, some eleven-point-six-million kilometers from the defenders, and fired. Over two thousand Gemblade torpedoes flared to life, leaving the launching bombers behind as they accelerated away at a thousand and fifty gravities.

The starfighters were closer than the capital ships, but the Alliance strike wasn't going to waste torpedoes on starfighters. They had their lighter Starfire missiles for that—and while those had the same Tier Four acceleration as the torpedoes, they had a quarter of the Gemblades' ten-minute flight time.

They fired six minutes later, moments before the torpedoes penetrated the Terran formation. Eleven thousand starfighter missiles blazed clear of the Falcons, Arrows and Vultures of the Alliance formation.

Eight thousand more leapt clear of the Katanas and Scimitars swarming toward them, and then the Terran fighters charged after the Alliance torpedoes.

"Hold your remaining Starfires," Ozolinsh ordered. "We may need a second salvo… We may need to finish this with lances, but there's still over a hundred and fifty battle stations in orbit of Earth, and we'll still want those missiles!"

The Terrans clearly didn't expect to survive long enough to launch their missiles at the capital ships. Three full salvoes blazed into space before the first exchange reached them. The older Scimitars still carried another salvo, just in case they lived long enough, but twenty-four thousand missiles were going to be enough of a headache for the attackers.

"Spread the formation, give them holes to get lost in," Russell ordered his own people. "ECM to maximum. Let's dazzle the buggers—they aren't *that* clever!"

Pulses of jamming swept out from the Alliance flotilla in waves, some sections making themselves larger targets, others making themselves near-invisible behind walls of static—and then switching places.

The Terran starfighters took their toll on the Gemblades, blasting over half of the Alliance torpedoes out of space…but their success cost them their focus when the starfighter missiles targeted on them arrived. Two thousand-plus starfighters, half of them obsolete, collided with eleven thousand of the best missiles the Alliance had ever built.

There were no survivors.

Russell had expected the strike to be decisive and crippling. He hadn't expected it to be a *massacre*.

The first wave of missiles swarming their own ranks was no less deadly, however. The Alliance pilots and gunners weren't distracted by stopping torpedoes, and they had the full electronic warfare capabilities of two thousand seventh-generation starfighters and bombers to protect them.

They couldn't stop them all. Emilija Santiago died in a silent fireball. Three other CAGs died with her—and over three hundred starfighters and bombers went with them.

The following salvos were less coordinated without their motherships. More vulnerable to the siren songs of countermeasures and jamming that lashed them as they crossed through space. They took lesser tolls on Russell's comrades…but when the dust settled, a full quarter of the Alliance fighter force was gone.

And then it was the Commonwealth warships' turn. A thousand torpedoes crashed down on a mere six ships, their own seekers and jammers far more capable than the lighter missiles the starfighters had used on each other.

Dozens of missiles died as the warships' defenses flared to life. Hundreds of missiles.

For a moment, Russell thought the defenses might actually manage to stand off the torpedo salvo…but numbers and statistics were a cruel mistress.

Both *Volcano*es disappeared under hammerblows of fire. Three of the *Hercules*es followed them, and the fourth spun off course, her engines gone and most of her weapons systems offline.

Russell thought they could ignore her—and then a moment later, the crippled warship flared again on his scanners, launching a ten-missile salvo directly at the starfighters.

"They've got courage," Ozolinsh said softly. "And this is their heart. Their home. *Earth*."

The Fleet CAG paused.

"Take them out," he ordered, his voice sad. "A hundred Starfires as we pass should do it."

THE BATTLECRUISER'S death was almost an afterthought, a passing salvo from the half-dozen closest squadrons. It felt strange that the destruction of a capital ship, the deaths of five thousand or so spacers and crew, would pass with so little comment.

But that was the nature of the day.

"TFC is maneuvering their fortresses around the planet to face us," Rothenberg announced. "We are beginning missile bombardment of the identified platforms. Commodore Ozolinsh, there could still be warships in Earth orbit, and the moon is between us and the Central Nexus.

"I want your starfighters to make a transit between Earth and Luna and engage the Nexus." He paused. "It is not particularly well defended, but if they're paying attention, I would expect those last four warships to be in position to guard her.

"There are also high guard corvettes somewhere in Earth orbit. They're not warships, but I have every expectation that they will attempt to engage you. They may only be high guard...but this *is* Earth."

Missile icons were now appearing on Russell's feed as the Imperial and Federation warships behind him began to trade fire with the fortresses. The good news was that there had been fewer fighter platforms than expected.

The bad news was that there appeared to be even more modern missile launchers over there than they'd expected—and that whoever was in charge of Terra Fortress Command understood perfectly well that her mass drivers were no threat to the capital ships.

So, they were using them to lay a hailstorm of high-velocity metal in the path of the Alliance starfighters.

"One last note, everyone," Rothenberg added as he was about to sign off. "We have confirmation from Rear Admiral Novacek—the

Uranus q-com switchboard has been destroyed. TF Seven-Three has achieved their objectives and is withdrawing from Sol."

One down. Two to go.

"TF Seven-Two has engaged the Ceres defense fleet. *Ambrosia* has been destroyed, as have three *Resolute*-class battleships. *Manna* is attempting to force a lance duel with *Leif Ericson* and her sisters." The Imperial Admiral chuckled.

"It's not going well for her."

The *Ambrosia*-class superbattleship might outgun any one of the three *Magellan*-class battleships headlining TF 7.2, but at three-to-one odds, *plus* eight battlecruisers backing up the *Magellan*s…

"Admiral Salvail reports that he expects to reduce the enemy starship and starfighter strength in next twenty minutes and engage Relay Alpha-One inside forty minutes. Everything is going according to plan."

Even *Russell* knew that was asking for trouble…but it also seemed to be true. Sol's defenses were turning out to be even weaker than expected.

This was the home system of humanity, the capital of the Commonwealth. There had to be another shoe coming.

42

Sol System
08:00 October 10, 2737 Earth Standard Meridian
Date/Time
Task Force Seven-One

"THAT...THAT'S A *LOT* OF MISSILES," Hu said softly.

Eighty of Terra Fortress Command's battle stations had relocated to this side of Earth, and each of them appeared to mount twenty modern capital-ship missile launchers. The only time Russell had seen that many missiles in one place before, they'd literally dumped them in space to allow for mass salvoes.

"Can the fleet handle that?" the gunner asked.

Russell shook his head.

"That's not our problem," he admitted. "That's the Admiral's problem. Our job is to cut through a gap that's barely two hundred thousand kilometers wide at five percent of the speed of light and successfully turn a multi-kilometer space station into vapor."

"Right. We got the easy job," Hu agreed.

The Vice Commodore shook his head and chuckled. It would be almost ten more minutes before the starfighters reached the limit of the moon's orbit. With the chaos in Earth orbit and Fortress Command's quite successful objections to the Alliance's Q-probes, they still had no idea what was going on around the Central Nexus.

He doubted it was going to be good news. At fifteen thousand kilometers a second, they would cross the moon's orbit, dive past the Central Nexus and flash through Earth's defenses over the course of about thirty seconds.

They were going to be an important thirty seconds.

"Do we have any visual on what's behind the moon?" he asked.

"Negative," Ozolinsh replied. "We've got Q-probes trying to swing around, but we're only going to have maybe two minutes' warning before we run right into it."

"Is it too late to consider a career change?" one of the other CAGs quipped. "I'm thinking…farmer. Farmer sounds great. Nobody shoots at farmers."

"Last chance to do that was before we left Via Somnia," Ozolinsh told them with a chuckle. "Time to fly or die, people.

"Hold on."

The minutes blurred past as the fleet engaged the fortresses. Task Force Seven-One was only throwing two hundred missiles back in answer to each sixteen-hundred missile salvo. They were closing the range—intel suggested most of the stations didn't have positron lances, which meant lance range would allow the Alliance to carry the day.

They certainly weren't having much luck with missiles. As Russell watched the situation, the *Heroic*-class strike cruiser *Jessica Anderson* took three capital-ship missiles from the second salvo, the only Federation cruiser in TF 7.1 disappearing in a flash of fire.

Along with all five thousand or so of her crew.

An Imperial *Guardian*-class carrier joined her, the task force's defenses withering under the hammer of Fortress Command's fire. They'd be exchanging missiles for over thirty minutes before the battleships reached their range, unless the fortresses had amazingly weak electromagnetic deflectors.

Given the amount of mass-driver fire the starfighters were dodging, it was possible.

But it wasn't likely.

"Eyeballs on the light side of the moon in twenty seconds," Hu told him. "Bets on whether we're going to die here, sir?"

"I don't make stupid bets," Russell replied, his attention now riveted on the data feed from the Q-probes sweeping ahead of the starfighter force. "I have to assume we're going to live."

The assumption took a blow a moment later.

The Central Nexus was exactly where it was supposed to be. Massive, foundational to the Commonwealth's communication network, almost defenseless beyond sheer size.

Carefully positioning themselves between the Nexus and the oncoming fighter strike were two *Saint*-class battleships and over a hundred *Hamilton*-class high guard corvettes.

"Well," Russell said quietly. "That's going to be a headache."

THE HIGH GUARD vessels barely even qualified as sublight gunships, hundred-thousand ton ships more purposed for boarding and search-and-rescue than combat. The *Hamilton*-class ships didn't even mount missiles.

They did, however, mount hundred-kiloton-a-second positron lances perfectly capable of shredding starfighters and missile defense lasers that could gut the missile salvo.

And the *Saints*, of course, could do the same all on their own.

"What do we do?" Hu asked.

"Our job," Russell replied.

"Sir?" he addressed Ozolinsh. "Recommend we split our forces—we're not going to get missiles past the corvettes and *Saints* to hit the station. I suggest the Arrows and Vultures focus their fire on the *Saints* while the Falcons go for the Nexus itself."

The Federation fighters would have to go *through* the high guard to get to the Central Nexus, but that was going to happen anyway. The

Falcons had heavier lances than the Arrows—and the bombers didn't *have* positron lances.

There was a long pause.

"Agreed," Ozolinsh said. "I'll pass the orders. Your group's in front, Rokos."

"We'll take the tip of the spear," Russell confirmed. "We'll see you on the other side."

The orders got passed and the formation began to shift slightly—and then the Commodore opened a private channel.

"I know I don't need to say this, Rokos, but everything else going on here is a distraction now," he said very, very quietly. "Seven-Two has the Ceres defense force on the run, Relay Alpha-One will be gone in moments. Most of the other strikes are already done." He swallowed. "Losses have been brutal, Rokos, and it's all down to this.

"If the Central Nexus survives, it's all been for nothing. Seven-One will keep Fortress Command tied up, but even that's just cover for us now."

Russell heard the next words before they even came out.

"The Nexus is an all-costs target, Vice Commodore Rokos. No matter what happens, that station has to be destroyed."

"I know," Russell replied. "We'll make it happen, Commodore."

"I know," Ozolinsh replied. "But you're at the front. I had to say it."

THE DEFENDERS DIDN'T HAVE MUCH GOING for them in terms of velocity. Someone on the other side had first held back the battleships—likely in case the Alliance was using the attack on Uranus as a distraction—and then guessed TF 7.1's actual target after TF 7.3 blew the secret switchboard station in the gas giant to pieces.

They'd then put the two battleships and the entirety of the Terran High Guard into the relatively tiny volume of space that the Alliance fighter strike *had* to pass through. There was no way around them. No clever maneuvers that weren't contraindicated by the velocity they were arriving with.

"Wanna bet the lady in charge over there is High Guard?" Hu

muttered. "Forcing us to fly right through them? That's an orbital officer's thinking right there."

"And in this case, it's the right thinking," Russell agreed. It was damn brave of them, too. They'd set up the optimal circumstances to throw a glorified police force in front of a starfighter strike, but those were customs officers and search-and-rescue crews.

His own duty meant he was going to have to blow a giant hole in their formation and vaporize the station they were trying to defend, but he still had to salute their courage.

"Seventy seconds to the lunar horizon," Hu reported a moment later. "Any clever ideas, boss?"

"Only the one we're already on," the Vice Commodore told him. "Throw every damn missile we've got at the High Guard and punch through to use our lances on the Nexus."

He was carefully ignoring the continuing missile duel between TF 7.1 and Terra Fortress Command. Those fortresses would massacre the starfighters if they turned that missile fire on Russell and his comrades, but TF 7.1 was quite definitely *losing* that duel.

For the first time in Russell Rokos's experience, starships were dying to buy starfighters time.

"We won't even have time for a second missile launch," Hu warned.

"I know."

Seconds ticked away. The moon came closer and their course curved. The planetoid's gravity was nothing compared to the starfighters' acceleration, but they had to cut the fine line between Luna and Earth's rings of orbital industry.

"All missiles prepped and targeted," Hu murmured. "Twenty seconds to the horizon."

Half of what would follow would be decided by computers, but the whole point of having a human with a high-interface bandwidth in a starfighter was to add the randomness of the other half. Russell sank into the deepest symbiosis with his ship's computers, becoming the agile starfighter.

Ten seconds. No one needed to speak aloud anymore. The Q-probes were whipping around the horizon ahead of them and dying in their dozens, TF 7.1 spending tens of millions of stellars of equipment every second to make sure the starfighters had the targeting data they needed.

Horizon.

Glittering stars appeared in front of Russell's eyes as he saw through the Falcon's far more capable senses. The two largest ones were the *Saint*s. Somebody else's problem, with hundreds of missiles ear-marked for each of them.

His problem was right in front of him, the solid and unwavering echelons of the *Hamilton*-class corvettes. Each of them was a dozen or more times the size of his starfighter, lacking her missiles but with positron lances that put hers to shame.

Their job might be customs inspections and search-and-rescue, but they weren't going to let him hit their world without a fight. They'd been watching his people come through their own Q-probes, and beams of positrons lit up Earth's sky as the Battle of Sol's final desperate act unfolded.

The Alliance missiles were in space before the first lance beams struck home. Starfighters died around Russell as he danced his own starfighter through the deadly pattern that wove around him. Missiles crossed the mere tens of thousands of kilometers between him and his enemy in moments, hundred-thousand ton corvettes vanishing in the blink of an eye.

His friends and subordinates died around him, but Russell plunged through the High Guard formation, dancing around the lances as he lined up on the Central Nexus. His missiles hadn't reloaded yet—their cycle time short but not short enough for this close of a range!

The only weapon he could use was his positron lance, and he lit up the space station with a beam of pure antimatter. Dozens of other beams joined his, slashing into the immense bulk of the switchboard station.

Vaporized metal and atmosphere blasted into space, short-lived spurts of fire bulging out from the station and dying as their oxygen supply ran out. The station endured. It was *huge*; even dozens of fifty-kiloton-a-second lances were barely scratching the surface.

Then his starfighter lurched, pain searing through him as "his" engines were destroyed by a glancing hit from one of the High Guard ships pursuing him. Linked into his neural implants, entire conversations passed by in seconds.

"We've lost three quarters of the engines and half the mass manipulators," his engineer barked. "No repair. We can't adjust course… maybe fifty gees of accel."

"We're not getting out of this at fifty gees of accel," Hu replied. "What do we do?"

Denial. Fear. Regret.

Decision.

All of it passed through Russell's mind in fractions of a second.

"We finish the job. The missiles can't launch yet, but we can arm the warheads, right?"

"Yes, sir." The pause before Hu spoke would never have registered on any other scale.

"Do it." Russell's own pause was just as infinitesimal. "It's been an honor, gentlemen."

"Oh, go fuck yourself," Hu snapped back. "I told you we wouldn't live through—"

Their world ended in the fire of multiple antimatter explosions.

So did the Central Nexus.

43

Leopold System
16:00 October 10, 2737 Earth Standard Meridian
Date/Time
BB-285 *Saint Michael*

"WHAT DO WE *DO*?" Lindsay Tasker asked softly.

The gap between her question and Mihai Gabor's response wasn't long, exactly. The three flagships were floating roughly fifty thousand kilometers apart, so the delay in two-way transmission was only a third of a second.

James Walkingstick and his officers, however, were twenty-eighth-century military officers. Their neural implants were capable of allowing them to consciously process time millisecond by millisecond if needed. It wasn't a feature that was healthy to use on a regular basis, but their implants gave them a *precise* sense of time.

With a q-com, the communication delay between Tasker, Gabor, and James would have been nearly imperceptible even to them.

Without it…

"I say we take this damn fleet and shove it down the Alliance's throat," Gabor snapped. "They've got to have sent every damned warship they had into our space to pull this off. Their home systems have to be defenseless."

James raised a hand.

"We cannot make our decisions based on emotions or revenge at this point," he told his senior subordinates quietly. "We have no updates. No information. We know *nothing* of what is happening in the core of the Commonwealth.

"And perhaps more importantly, we know nothing of what is happening on the fringes of the Commonwealth," he noted. "There are worlds that were brought into unity recently enough that they will see this as weakness. As an opportunity.

"We have no command-and-control loop. No ability to acquire intelligence. Admirals, we don't even have real-time sensor data *in this system*. If we make war on the Alliance now, we will face an enemy who has all of those things."

He shook his head.

"What information we *have* suggests that Home Fleet and Terra Fortress Command are either shattered or just plain gone. Tau Ceti Sector Command *is* gone; every ship was debris by the time the Alliance fired on the q-com station.

"Most systems are somewhere in between. The Alliance just did to the Commonwealth what we were planning to do to them at Via Somnia: the Commonwealth no longer has the ship strength to reasonably support offensive action."

Tasker looked tired.

"So, what, do we take our fleets back to Sol? Help hold the Commonwealth together from the center?"

James shook his head again. From Gabor's expression, he knew what his Marshal was thinking, even if Tasker hadn't caught up.

"I am a Marshal of the Commonwealth, Lindsay," he told her. "I have a very clear and distinct area of responsibility—and if I *leave* that area without direct authorization from the Senate, I am legally deserting my post."

He chuckled.

"And if I were to bring a fleet with me to Sol, my commission would make that treason, regardless of my intent," he admitted. "My own personal Rubicon. What I give up for the Marshal's mace, Admiral Tasker, is my general authority over the Commonwealth Navy.

"I have absolute authority in the Rimward Marches…and am legally forbidden to command Commonwealth forces outside the Marches."

"We can't just let the Commonwealth burn!" she objected.

"No, we can't," he agreed. "However, it seems that all of our plans and schemes to thwart this exact kind of attack failed. We need to consider what the final orders we sent to our people were."

"Gather at Niagara," Gabor replied, after that slight but all-too-noticeable delay. "All of our secondary forces were heading there."

"And that is where the Senate will expect to find us as well, if they do have new orders for us," James reminded them. "For now, we will return to Niagara."

"What *were* our plans for this kind of attack?" Tasker asked. "My people have checked. Every entangled-particle block in the fleet is dead, spewing garbage radiation data if they're receiving anything at all."

"The Uranus facility was our emergency continuity-of-government facility," the Marshal replied. "Officially, it didn't exist, and only current or former designated flagships even had entangled blocks for it.

"But the Alliance knew where it was. It was the first one they took out," he noted grimly.

"We only had one secret facility?" Gabor asked.

James chuckled.

"We were supposed to have three. One in Sol, one in Tau Ceti and one in Sirius."

"There's nothing *in* Sirius," Gabor objected.

"That was the point." James's chuckle turned bitter. "The program was canceled after the Uranus platform because we discovered the Federation was building eighty-million-cubic warships. The budget was put into building the *Ambrosia*s.

"Not that those seemed to help."

The destruction of both superbattleships in the defense of Ceres was one of the confirmed losses from the Battle of Sol.

"We fall back to Niagara and get our prisoners off our warships," he continued. Niagara had proper POW facilities in orbit, thankfully. "There's too many people with potential access to them while they're aboard our ships."

"You don't trust our people?" Gabor demanded.

"Our prisoners wear the same uniforms as the people who just attacked *Sol*, Mihai," James said flatly. "Some people are not going to be thinking rationally. We have obligations to our POWs, and we *will* see them respected."

Even if, in the back of his head, James Walkingstick suspected that Kyle Roberts had more than a little to do with the chaos that had just been unleashed upon the galaxy.

KYLE WAS AMUSED that the man with quite literally life-or-death authority over him still asked permission to enter the tiny quarters they'd locked him in. Unless he missed his guess, the room they'd put him was normally shared by two Lieutenants or similarly larval officers, but they'd scooped out a bed in favor of a couch when they'd decided to put an Admiral in there.

Even as a prisoner of war, rank had its privileges. They didn't, he expected, actually extend to refusing Walkingstick entry to his quarters —but at least the Marshal asked.

"Well?" Walkingstick demanded as the door closed behind him, looking at Kyle like he wanted to ask a longer question.

Or, potentially, like the Terran officer wanted to strangle him with his bare hands. Given what it sounded like the events of the last twelve or so hours had entailed, that was also quite possible.

"*Well* what?" he asked.

"Don't you want to know how your Alliance's grand offensive, the plan I can see your fingerprints all over, went off?" Walkingstick asked.

Kyle sighed and leaned back in the couch, gesturing around him.

"Marshal, I have a datapad that is linked to an entertainment library that has nothing less than ten years old in it, and four walls that make for a somewhat comfortable prison," he pointed out. "At this point, unless an Alliance fleet has arrived and forced you to surrender, the result of the war isn't going to change my fate."

He did want to know. But he also…didn't. If Medusa had failed, he had doomed his nation and her allies to the dustbin of history.

The Terran officer chuckled bitterly.

"That hasn't happened. So far as I know, but since I no longer have real-time sensor data…" He shrugged.

"Your people did it," Walkingstick concluded. "You may have singlehandedly wrecked the largest human civilization in history, Admiral Roberts. The entire Commonwealth q-com network is down. Do you have any idea of how many people this will kill?"

"The Commonwealth requires all of their systems to be self-sufficient in food and basic industry," Kyle replied, pushing down a momentary desire to gloat. "I think your civilization will survive just fine."

"You saw what happened in Presley," the Marshal told him. "A dozen systems will go up in flames now. Maybe two dozen. Ships will mutiny; the Commonwealth will tear itself apart.

"Millions are going to die, Admiral Roberts. You can argue everything you destroyed was a legitimate military target, but the blood of those innocents is on your people's hands."

"And whose hands is the blood of the Kematians on?" Kyle asked. He'd watched a Terran battleship sear that world with antimatter fire. He'd hunted the ship responsible down and destroyed it, and he'd admit the Captain had gone rogue, but without Walkingstick's war…

"Ours," Walkingstick admitted without flinching. "Mine, even. It shouldn't have happened, Admiral Roberts. Unification, bringing all of humanity together, is how we *stop* things like that.

"And now…now you've set more of those flames in motion."

"You give me a bit too much credit," Kyle replied. He'd drafted Medusa, but he'd been one of over thirty officers in the Joint Strategic Options Command. And hundreds of thousands of spacers, starfighter crew and officers had carried out the mission.

"Speed, aggression and shock used as psychological weapons?" Walkingstick said drily. "I can see the mind behind Tranquility and Hui Xing in this strike, Admiral. Other hands may have carried it out, but I know the fingerprints of the architect."

The Terran shook his head.

"You remind me of myself, though with a poorer luck in birthplaces, I suppose," he told Kyle.

"What do you expect?" Kyle told him. "I quite like where I was born, Marshal, but *someone* wrote 'A Treatise on Aggression and Calculated Risk as Psychological Warfare in Modern Carrier Combat' as a Military Strategy Theory thesis… and it wasn't me."

Walkingstick stared at him for a long, long moment.

"That should never have left the Commonwealth," he said.

"Apparently, it ended up in the Castle Federation's Academy library," Kyle replied. "If I remind you of yourself, Marshal, it's because I read your damn book."

They glared at each other for several moments, then Walkingstick sighed and shook his head.

"You realize that I can no longer trust my people to take proper care of yours," he admitted. "We are returning to the Niagara System, where I will be turning your people over to a civilian prison authority. I believe I can rely on their restraint more than my own people's."

He sighed.

"If nothing else, they have a smaller proportion of people actually *from* Sol," he noted. "Attacking the home system has made your Alliance no friends, Admiral."

"You came for our homes," Kyle told him fiercely. "You came for our independence, our freedom, our right to live as we chose. You burned our worlds and killed our brothers and sisters, and *you* tell *me* that we have ourselves no friends?

"Every drop of blood shed in this war and whatever consequences this unleashes come back not only to the Commonwealth but to the man who set this in motion," he snapped, watching Walkingstick recoil in surprise.

"*Your* choice, Walkingstick. *Your* war. You want to blame us for it? Look in a Gods-cursed mirror."

For a seemingly eternal moment, their gazes locked again, and then Walkingstick inclined his head in a single sharp nod—and turned sharply on his heel, leaving Kyle alone in his cell.

His Operation Medusa had succeeded. The tide of the war changing.

If only he knew what the price was going to be for himself.

44

Castle System
15:00 October 12, 2737 Earth Standard Meridian
Date/Time
New Cardiff

ALL THAT MIRA SOLACE really wanted to do was take Jacob and Lisa Kerensky, along with Daniel Kellers, and bury them all in a bubble of soft blankets and armored Marines a million kilometers from anything from importance or weight.

Since Rear Admiral Mira Solace had a job to do, however, she was in a small briefing room deep beneath Castle Federation Joint Command as Fleet Admiral Meredith Blake personally briefed the flag officers actively in charge of Castle's defense on the events of the last few days.

"All of you are aware that we have spent the last six weeks under an unprecedented communications lockdown," Blake told them. "That lockdown lifts at zero hundred hours tomorrow. By that point, all of the Medusa strike fleets will have returned to FTL and be on their way home.

"Most of those fleets have already withdrawn. What's left of Seventh Fleet, for example, held undisputed possession of the Sol System for less than two hours before they got the hell out of Dodge."

The mutters around the table were soft, but the words *Sol System* were repeated too much to not be audible.

"Yes, Admirals, you heard me correctly," Blake noted with a smile. "Some of you have heard the name Operation Medusa. Few of you in this room were aware of more than fringe elements of it, but I can now brief you on what it involved.

"We just threw fifteen major fleets totalling over two hundred warships deep into Commonwealth space to attack the key foundations of their communications network. We succeeded."

The briefing room was silent as that sank in.

"Succeeded how?" Mira asked.

"As of approximately nine hundred hours on October tenth, the Terran Commonwealth no longer possesses *any* functioning q-com switchboard stations," Blake explained. "Their faster-than-light communication network has been destroyed.

"Along the way, a number of key systems—including the Sol System—at least temporarily fell to our fleets, though most of our attacks were more on the order of raids."

The Federation's Chief of Naval Operations shook her head.

"The Battle of Sol *should* have remained a raid, but it became necessary for the entire fleet to deploy against Terra Fortress Command to extract a portion of Admiral Rothenberg's forces. As of our last update from Sol, TFC and the Commonwealth Home Fleet have been completely destroyed."

She shrugged delicately.

"We have reason to believe that a minimum of twenty other capital ships are now headed to Sol and fully support Admiral Rothenberg's decision to withdraw as soon as possible rather than remain to facilitate, say, cease-fire negotiations."

An astrographic chart filled the room.

"All fifteen strike fleets are being directed to the Via Somnia fleet base, where they will rendezvous with Forty-First Fleet," Blake noted. "Given the damage and losses all of these fleets—including Forty-First —have taken, Alliance Joint Command is hesitant to commit to further offensive action.

"If nothing else, it will be six weeks before all of the fleets have returned, and damage may force additional ships to be abandoned en route."

"How many did we lose?" another Admiral asked.

Blake sighed.

"Including the loss of *Elysium*—as Admiral Roberts's endeavors along the frontier were a related operation—we have confirmed the loss of sixty-eight Alliance capital ships."

The room was now very quiet.

"None of our major allies escaped unscathed, and many of the smaller powers committed everything they could spare…and lost it.

"In exchange, however, we may have destroyed the Commonwealth," Blake pointed out. "We have confirmed the destruction of ninety-six Commonwealth starships, at least five *hundred* Commonwealth defensive platforms, and approximately twenty thousand starfighters.

"Reports are vague, especially in situations where subordinate task forces were badly damaged or destroyed, but we may be looking at as many as fifteen to twenty additional Commonwealth starships destroyed, and possibly as many as forty sufficiently damaged as to be incapable of offensive operations."

Mira joined the rest of the table in inhaling sharply. That was…crippling. The Alliance losses were crushing, a brutal loss that would take years to recover from, but the Commonwealth Navy had just been *gutted*.

"While this may seem like the perfect time to launch a new offensive, I must note that we *know* Walkingstick has accumulated a striking force of sixty-plus capital ships," Blake continued grimly. "Admiral Roberts bought us that knowledge at the highest possible price.

"There are too few ships currently in Alliance space for us to prepare a counter-operation. It will be three weeks before the first Medusa fleets return home. Six before the last ones do."

She paused.

"We expect to hear from the Commonwealth Star Chamber in approximately four to five weeks. At that point, whether or not the war will continue will be a political decision.

"Until then, however, we must act on the assumption that Walkingstick may resume his offensives at any time. He lacks many of the tools we rely on in combat these days, but we would be fools to write him off," Blake said grimly.

"We have every reason to believe this war may be soon be over, but until it is, we must all stand ready to defend our homes!"

NORMALLY, Mira was driven around by Marines or used an override on the usual transit-car network to get around. Today, however, she walked from the towers of the Joint Command to her apartment. Being a flag officer of the Castle Federation Space Navy, that meant that at least two Marines had to walk with her.

They hung back, though, letting her wander silently through the crowds in Castle's second-largest city. The people around her didn't have the news she'd had. That Operation Medusa had even occurred, let alone been a complete success, was still restricted to the military.

That their hero, her fiancé, was dead had been leaked. If the story of the war was impacting the lives of the people around her, that was the one they knew. There were still newsreels feeding what little footage had been given; someone was advertising a plan to do a documentary on the life of the Stellar Fox…

It was all the tasteless garbage she would expect around a hero who'd lived large and died in defeat…except they hadn't even held a funeral, because no one was even certain that Kyle was dead.

And explaining that to a twelve-year-old had been one of the worst tasks Mira Solace had ever taken on.

It sounded like they'd won the war, but no one could be sure yet. There were still shadows and possibilities that could bring everything down in chaos, but Mira Solace had now read the classified psychological profile that had underwritten Operation Medusa.

Without the q-com network, the Commonwealth couldn't prosecute a war. They might not even be able to hold together as a nation.

And if the largest human civilization in history came down in flames and apocalypse after killing her lover, Mira Solace couldn't bring herself to cry for them.

45

Via Somnia System
14:00 October 13, 2737 Earth Standard Meridian
Date/Time
Alliance Forty-First Fleet

It was a strange sensation to be back aboard *Avalon* for Michelle. It was an even *stranger* sensation to be, without question, *Avalon*'s acting CAG.

Every Castle Federation Space Force officer senior to her was dead, though, so that didn't leave them many options. Hell, she was the only CFSF Vice Commodore left, Wirt having died in the Leopold System along with so many others.

Michelle wasn't even sure how or why she was still alive—but she was. With their losses, most of their starfighters fit on *Avalon*. Enough had landed on the battlecruisers and the Imperial ships that the big carrier's flight deck seemed empty. Unfilled.

If Flight Control felt strange as she watched the countdown to emergence click down on her implant, it wasn't because the room was different. *Avalon* and *Elysium* shared a lot of structure and design, and the primary flight control center looked identical.

But the crew was completely different. *Her* flight controllers had died with *Elysium* and Admiral Roberts.

"Emergence in sixty seconds," someone reported aloud. "Combat Space Patrol ready to go."

Via Somnia should be safe. They still had links to the systems there via q-com—and the crew had been briefed on Operation Medusa this morning.

Their sacrifices had held Walkingstick's attention for long enough for the Alliance to sucker-punch the Commonwealth. It was *worth* it; Michelle knew that.

Didn't make the empty bunks in flight country hurt less. Didn't make the fact that she'd lost a *carrier* hurt less.

It sure as Void didn't make losing the *Admiral* hurt less.

"Emergence!"

Avalon's acting CAG had no business on the CSP. Neither did the fleet CAG. That left Michelle in the flight control center, watching sixty of her people go into space without her.

In theory, Via Somnia was safe. In practice, they'd stripped it as bare as they could without it being obvious, but there still, thankfully, didn't appear to be any Commonwealth ships here.

Hopefully, there was enough equipment left for Forty-First Fleet's desperately needed repairs.

For the second time in barely more than a week, the starships of Forty-First Fleet tucked themselves into the repair yards at Via Somnia. There were no yard workers to help them out this time, though. The repairs would have to be done by the crews themselves.

Gathering aboard *Avalon* with the other CAGs and Captains, Michelle wondered what the news was going to be. No one was even sure who was supposed to be in command of Forty-First Fleet at the moment. Everything was in question.

Elijah Hammond, *Avalon*'s Captain, was standing at the head of the room with Lord Captain the Elector Maria von Kita of the *Righteous Sword*, however, so that was somewhat suggestive.

"Everyone have a seat," Hammond ordered. "I believe now is as good a time as any to pull us all together in person and go over what our plans for the next four weeks are.

Four weeks? That sounded quite specific.

"Lord Captain von Kita and I, as the senior Captains, have been in discussion with Alliance Joint Command as to what we are going to do from here on out," he continued. "Lord Captain von Kita is senior to myself, so I have officially yielded command to her."

"*Avalon* remains our largest and most powerful unit, however," von Kita continued as Hammond stepped aside, "so Captain Hammond will continue to act as my second-in-command until I am relieved.

"And we have confirmed with Joint Command that I *will* be relieved," she noted. "What we were briefed on today that has not yet been made public knowledge, even in the fleet, is that the Medusa fleets will be falling back on Via Somnia.

"All four of the Federation's *Myth and Truth*-class mobile shipyards are on their way here, as well as an unspecified—but likely large!—number of freighters and transports carrying supplies, parts, starfighters and replacement personnel.

"The first fleets will be returning in about nineteen days. Seventh Fleet under Admiral Rothenberg is expected on November tenth. At that point"—von Kita smiled predatorily—"we expect to have consolidated approximately one hundred capital ships in the Via Somnia System to be repaired and rearmed.

"We hope to have our own vessels fully functional by the time Admiral Rothenberg arrives," she noted. "My understanding is that Seventh Fleet took severe damage and may not have a significant number of combat-capable units.

"Other fleets will be following, however, and while the exact execution date is going to be left to Admiral Rothenberg's discretion, the information Captain Hammond and I have received from Joint Command is that, barring a Commonwealth surrender, the Niagara System will fall before December.

"One way or another, people, Command intends to make sure that James Walkingstick does *not* threaten our worlds again!"

46

Niagara System
18:00 November 8, 2737 Earth Standard Meridian
Date/Time
Ontario Orbit

"WHAT IN *VOID* IS THAT?"

James Calvin Walkingstick chuckled at the disconcerted tone of his flag staff sensor tech's voice.

"That, Specialist, is an Alcubierre-Stetson drive courier ship," he explained, studying the strange, bulging ship on the display. His neural feed was time-stamping the data, informing him that the Cherenkov radiation pulse of the ship's emergence was over two minutes old.

The courier's commander had taken no risks with his emergence. Given that he must have left Sol within two days of the destruction of the q-com network and come directly here, that made sense to James. If the message was important enough for that rush, it was important enough to spend the extra hour or so of sublight transit time to not risk having the courier vaporized.

To an eye used to the massive, kilometer-plus lengths and solid hulls of modern A-S drive warships and freighters, the courier was strange. The four Class One mass manipulators that powered her Alcubierre drive made up roughly eighty percent of her volume, massive bulging spheres attached to a central hull barely large enough to keep the Class Ones from just being welded together.

The only part of the ship that remotely rivaled the mass manipulators for size was the engine pods at the rear of the ship. Antimatter engines were already blazing to life, accelerating toward Ontario and the Niagara Fleet Base at five hundred gravities.

Tier Three acceleration on a starship. The strange ship had been built to get where it needed to go in a hurry—and had, until a month before, been utterly obsolete.

"We *have* courier ships?" MacGinnis asked, leaning over her tech's shoulder. "I figured we were going to be using freighters for messages for the foreseeable future."

"That's going to be most of it," James agreed. "We have four. They're intended for delivering physical delegations in speed and comfort, not carrying all of the dictates and messages of an interstellar government."

"And they sent one to us," his operations officer said softly. "Well, it's nice to know we're still important, right, boss?"

"Ask me that again in"—James checked his sensor feed—"two hours after I've reviewed their messages."

This had to have been the first courier to have left Sol. That…probably wasn't a good sign.

THE COURIER WAITED until they were within one light-minute of the fleet base to start sending the complicated electronic challenge-and-response necessary for James to be able to access the confidential messages.

With most of a minute of delay on every transmission, it took over thirty minutes to process the challenges and allow James to open up the official mail.

The very first, urgent, "Marshal's Eyes Only" message was from the Committee on Unification. It was a recorded video and he linked it directly to his implants.

The video put him standing in front of the long table the Committee used for their meetings, and something in how they were looking at the pickup suggested the feeling like he was on trial was not unintentional.

"Admiral Walkingstick," the man closest to the camera—*not*, James noted, Michael Burns, the Committee's acknowledged unofficial leader—greeted him. The speaker was the Senator for Tau Ceti, a chubby albino man named Giorgio Mhasalkar.

"By now, we presume you have realized that the Commonwealth quantum communication network is down. We know, with certainty, that every station in the Sol System has been destroyed—including the supposedly secret continuity-of-government facility at Uranus.

"We have sufficient information prior to the destruction of facilities in other star systems to be quite certain what happened," Mhasalkar concluded. "A series of deep strikes by the so-called Alliance of Free Stars was launched with the specific intent of destroying our communications capability."

He paused, glancing at the other Senators and Assembly Members around him.

"They have succeeded," he said bluntly. "The courier carrying this message also carries a delegation empowered by the Star Chamber to negotiate with the Alliance. We intend to offer a cease-fire in place, returning control of all occupied Alliance systems and recognizing their de facto control of the Via Somnia and Presley Systems.

"That will be used as a starting point for a permanent peace treaty. Your efforts to annex the Rimward Marches, Marshal Walkingstick, are now at an end. You have failed us."

Arguably, they were cutting any chance of victory out from under his feet. James wouldn't exactly call this situation a failure on *his* part, after all. If they'd done what he'd suggested, the Alliance would have been crushed a year or more earlier.

"A similar delegation has been sent to the Stellar League," Mhasalkar noted. "Until we have secured the unity of our own systems, we cannot afford continued external threats and conflicts. We will be forced to negotiate, to make recompense.

"We are being forced to humiliate ourselves," the Senator said bluntly, "but the Star Chamber recognizes that we cannot save the Commonwealth from the consequences of your war with the Alliance without turning our focus inwards."

Your war. Not *our war*. Roberts's words about where the Alliance put the blame were suddenly echoing with chilling weight in the back of James's mind.

He wondered what the delegation the Star Chamber had sent would do if the Alliance asked for one Marshal Walkingstick's head—hopefully figuratively, but he wouldn't put *literally* past the Imperator of the Coraline Imperium—as a condition of permanent peace.

"This will no longer be your concern," Mhasalkar told him. "You are to return to Sol aboard your flagship immediately to surrender your Marshal's mace. Since the Rimward Marches were the origin of this attack, we will need to debrief you on this enemy.

"We may need to pull back for now, but, believe me, Admiral Walkingstick, there will be consequences for this!"

The message ended and James opened his eyes to study his flag deck again. He'd need to go over what information they'd provided. If nothing else, the courier's sensors would tell him how the Battle of Sol had gone after the Central Nexus had been destroyed.

His guess was "not well", though the fact that the Senate was in a position to be sending delegations meant it couldn't have gone as badly as he feared.

The Alliance, after all, was apparently not dictating surrender terms from Earth orbit. They were still *well* short of his worst-case scenario!

THE REAL SURPRISE came when the courier ship reached orbit, and a short-range transmission from the captain asked James to come aboard in person.

He'd been wondering why the courier ship, designed to drop into a system, launch a data pulse, and be on its way to the next as soon as it got a responding pulse, had come all the way into Ontario orbit.

Apparently, it had been to speak with him.

A shuttle delivered him to the nameless courier ship, where a pair of Marines were waiting for him to escort him deeper into its plushly appointed VIP section.

"What is this about, Sergeant?" he asked the senior Marine quietly.

"I honestly don't know, sir," the blonde Sergeant replied quickly, her gaze refusing to meet his. "The Ambassador wanted to speak to you in person. I don't know why."

James grunted. The Marine clearly knew something—and was under strict orders to say nothing. So far, no one had even told him who the Ambassador *was*.

Somehow, he wasn't surprised to be escorted into a palatial sitting area and find himself facing the calmly seated form of Hope Burns. The wife of the Senator for Alpha Centauri was one of the Commonwealth's leading diplomats.

The perfectly composed black woman might be twenty years her husband's junior, but most people who knew them both suspected that she'd pursued and courted the older man to have a Senatorial trophy husband, rather than the other way around.

James was close enough friends with Michael Burns to know that wasn't far from the truth, but also that the pair were actually sickeningly in love—in private, at least. It would never do for two of the most powerful figures in the Commonwealth's government to hold hands where rivals might see them.

The Marines shut the door behind him and Burns rose to wrap James in a tight hug.

"It's good to see you," she whispered. "It's been a hellish few weeks."

He returned the embrace and stepped back to study her. If Hope Burns had had a bad few weeks, it didn't show. But then, he suspected his own appearance didn't reflect the last month either.

"I have the formal notice of my order to return to Earth," he said quietly. "How bad is it?"

"Bad," she said flatly. "While I have several tiers of specific offers that Foreign Affairs top people went through as a ground, my authority is functionally unlimited."

Unlimited. That was a bad word when applied to the woman sent to negotiate peace.

"No one wanted to use the word *surrender*," she noted. "But the level of plenipotentiary authority I have been given made it clear that if the Alliance will accept no less, I'm authorized to negotiate a conditional surrender."

"Or an unconditional one," James concluded.

"Or an unconditional one," she agreed. "If that's the only way to get the Alliance to stop shooting at us while we sort out the wreckage from their destruction of our communications."

She sighed.

"Unification is inevitable," she murmured. "But...damned if they haven't managed to produce the one roadblock that's going to slow it down a *lot*. It'll be years before we have even a basic network back up. Decades before we return to what we had."

"Less, surely, if we focus on it," James replied.

"Perhaps. But we are *crippled*, James. Crippled. The Commonwealth may not survive the next few years—systems that secede will be able to buy q-com blocks from the League or the Alliance's members, but no one will sell them to us."

He winced.

"That bad?"

"Officially, everyone is happy to be Unified, so *of course* they'll stick with the Commonwealth," Burns said dryly. "In practice, well, Michael and I have always kept a solid finger on the pulse of the truth of the Commonwealth.

"By December, at least one system will have seceded. By February, at least one multi-stellar unit. We won't even *learn* about the secessions until it's too late to do anything. Coordinating forces to end these secessions will be...difficult."

"But doable," he pointed out. "We have enough older warships to use as couriers to move the more recent vessels around to put out fires. We *can* hold the Commonwealth together."

"And who would command the forces that would do this?" she asked. "Which Admiral would you trust with the knife at the Commonwealth's throat?"

He blinked. She was right. The civil war to come would require large forces operating with minimal command and control. They would need officers they could trust completely.

"I have several suggestions," he said levelly. "Officers whose loyalty I would trust completely."

Burns chuckled softly.

"You aren't being recalled to ask for your advice, James," she told him. "They told you, what, you're being recalled for debriefing?"

"Exactly," he confirmed, wondering what she was talking about.

"Michael figured they wouldn't have the gumption to tell you the truth. He couldn't tell me what they *did* say, though."

"The truth?"

"You're being recalled to face a trial before the Senate for grand treason," Hope Burns told him quietly. "And the Senate has already made up their mind. If you go home, James Calvin Walkingstick, they will kill you."

JAMES FOUND HIMSELF NOTING, vaguely, the details of how palatially the room Hope Burns had met him in was furnished. Most starships had plain metal floors and walls, maybe with a rug in people's quarters. This room was carpeted and the walls had been carefully painted with a mural of one of Earth's beaches.

The furniture, including the chair he was sitting in, was luxuriously comfortable and the room was being kept noticeably warmer than the rest of the ship. The courier ship crew did their best, it seemed, to pamper the VIPs they carried.

All of that was a distraction from what she'd just told him.

"Kill me?" he finally asked. "That's…extreme. Why?"

"Because they need to blame someone," Burns said. "Because they can't blame the Star Chamber for voting for this war, so they'll blame you for 'dragging' the Commonwealth into it. They'll claim that if you were actually loyal and competent, the war would have been over years ago.

"They'll blame you for starting the war, they'll blame you for not finishing the war, and they'll blame you for 'allowing' the Alliance to launch strikes into Commonwealth space," she concluded.

"It's all…Voidstuff," she noted. "But they don't care. You're going to be scapegoated for the Alliance's attacks on us, found publicly guilty of treason, and executed."

James shivered.

"Even putting aside the fact that I'd rather not be shot, that's a really bad idea," he said. "They'll undermine the loyalty of every flag officer. If we face execution for losing…"

"Then the entire military structure that we need to hold the Commonwealth together will start fracturing," she agreed. "I wouldn't be sitting here telling you this if I *agreed* with them, James. Letting them execute you could destroy the Commonwealth.

"You have to run, James. Send in your mace and resignation and disappear."

"I don't run," he told her. "I never have. I never will."

"It's the only choice you have left, James," she said. "If you go home, they'll execute you. There's no escaping that. If you defy their orders and stay here in command of your fleet, you'll end up accelerating the disintegration of the Commonwealth.

"You'd end up with your own pocket empire, but I *know* you, James Walkingstick. You are a loyal son of Terra."

"For which, it appears my superiors now wish to kill me," he replied.

"Yes," she said steadily. "The Star Chamber has betrayed you, James. But they are *not* the Commonwealth. The best way you can serve now is to disappear. Walk away before they end you."

There was nothing to say, really. James spent a minute staring at the wall in silence. Burns didn't say anything, just waiting.

"Damn it," he finally said. "I appreciate the warning, Hope. But… in some ways, I'd rather have not known until it was too late!"

47

Niagara System
09:00 November 9, 2737 Earth Standard Meridian
Date/Time
Ontario Orbit

IT WAS A SMALL MEETING ROOM. A quiet space aboard a battleship which had few such spaces. Large enough for the dozen or so people James had summoned aboard *Saint Michael* for this council.

Lindsey Tasker and Mihai Gabor had barely met each other before, but the stresses of the last few months allowed them to embrace as old friends. It had been a hell of a war, and that the courier was carrying an ambassador to Alliance space to end it was as much a relief as anything else.

Even to James, he had to admit.

Commodore MacGinnis and Commander Messere were also in the room. The last occupant was a woman that James had rarely met in person, even as he sliced up her command to send her troops all over the galaxy.

General Pearle Krizman of the Commonwealth Marine Corps looked like she'd stepped out of a recruiting poster, even in this informal meeting. She was one of the most heavily muscled people James had ever met, even her Marine dress uniform clearly having been modified to allow for her bulk.

If there were any spare grams of fat on the six-foot-tall woman, forty years of Marine physical training hadn't found them, and if Krizman was perhaps less attractive to most men than other women, she could not care less.

Not least, to James's knowledge, because she was happily married to an accountant on Earth who took fantastic care of their three children.

The three-star General commanded the two Marine Deployment Groups assigned to his command. Each contained three Marine Expeditionary Groups for a total of twenty-four divisions per MDC and almost half a million Marines per the TOE.

The truth was, most of her divisions were understrength or had been chopped up to a thousand different purposes, sent out by battalion or regiments instead of division—and one of her subordinates had managed to get the last intact MEG shattered in the assault on Midori.

Nonetheless, there were plenty of Marines to hand in Niagara to load aboard the fifteen assault transports they still had.

If one James Calvin Walkingstick decided to do something…spectacular.

"People, you're here because there are things I need to explain in person," he told them all. "No encrypted coms. No recordings. No virtual meetings. What we are about to discuss is…"

He sighed.

"What we are about to discuss is arguably treason," he repeated, finishing the sentence this time.

The five officers in the room were silent, all of them waiting for him to continue.

"I have been advised—by sources that I trust *completely*—that my recall to Terra is not for a debriefing," he said slowly. "The Star

Chamber intends to put me on trial for treason—and they've already decided on the verdict and the punishment.

"When I return to Terra, I am to be arrested, put to a kangaroo court, and shot."

He let that hang in the room for a few seconds of silence.

"What has been recommended to me is that I disappear," he admitted. "I…do not see a reasonable alternative.

"My intention is to take *Saint Michael* back into Commonwealth space, leave a letter of resignation and my mace aboard her, and leave at a location somewhere between here and there," he confessed. "I will *not* use this fleet to set up a private empire, even if you would follow me, but I cannot blithely stick my head into the noose for the Commonwealth, either."

The shocked silence continued. His officers traded concerned looks, thoughtful glances, a million pieces of nonverbal communication, but no one spoke.

Then General Krizman rose to her feet.

"*Fuck* that garbage, sir," she told him. "My Marines will follow your orders to the end. No matter where you send us. If they want to hang you, they're going to go through *us*."

"General, I cannot—"

"No," Tasker cut him off. "*We* will not permit this. We will not allow you to be executed or to disappear into obscurity. You are our *Marshal*."

"If you go back to Terra, you're going back with all of us," Gabor concluded. "Together."

"If I arrive in Sol with eighty capital ships and a dozen-plus Marine transports, that *is* treason," James pointed out. He was touched. He was horrified. Stunned that his people would even offer this.

And he was so, *so* tempted.

"If the Star Chamber is prepared to execute you, they are prepared to doom the Commonwealth," Messere, the most junior person in the room, said quietly. "Even if you go into hiding, someone else will be blamed. They will break the contracts and oaths that hold us together, no matter what.

"If you do not challenge them, they will destroy all that we are sworn to defend. What else can we do?"

The question hung in the air, and everyone in the room turned their gazes on James.

"So be it, then," he said softly. "Prepare the fleet to move out. It seems we have a message to deliver to the Star Chamber.

"We *will* save the Commonwealth. With or without them!"

THE CIVILIAN PRISON platform that Kyle and his people had been delivered to was significantly more comfortable than he'd been expecting. It had the same security features as the military POW platforms he'd once sent his Marines to liberate—dual hull structure with a vacuum "moat", automated security, armed garrisons—but the fixtures in the internal prison area were much more comfortable.

The main "prison yard" area of the station even had trees. While there was no space specifically set aside for Wiccans, there were enough of Kyle's coreligionists among the several thousand Alliance prisoners that a small copse had been unofficially designated.

He was sitting cross-legged in that copse in the plain gray jumpsuit they all wore now, meditating on a portable electric light—there were no candles inside the prison segment, so he made do as best he could—when he was interrupted by one of the Marines who'd volunteered as "the Admiral's bodyguard."

Kyle didn't think he needed a guard there, but it made that dozen men and women feel useful—and he could tell already that feeling use*less* was going to be quite common in there.

"Sir, one of the guards is asking for you," she told him. "Apparently, the Marshal wants to speak to you."

The prison was structured so that it *could* be run with tight control, prisoners secured in cells when not specifically allowed out, armed guards everywhere…or it could be run more openly, with the prisoners mostly moving around of their own accord but the accesses across the vacuum moat heavily guarded.

For POWs, they appeared to have chosen the latter.

"All right," he told the Marine, carefully rising to his feet. "I suppose I should go see what our captor wants."

HE WAS ESCORTED through the accessway into the outer station. None of the personnel he could see were Marines. Everyone was Niagara System Judicial Wardens, trained specialist prison officers.

The Wardens had some trouble adjusting to guarding POWs instead of criminals, but in the main, the NSJW's people had taken the task on with aplomb.

It was a surprise, however, to realize that *Walkingstick* was out of uniform. Every time they'd encountered before, the Marshal had been wearing full uniform with his insignia and working decorations.

This time, Walkingstick wore a simple black shipsuit with no insignia. It wasn't like insignia were necessary—there probably wasn't a living soul for a hundred light-years who wouldn't recognize him instantly—but it was unusual.

"Have a seat, Admiral," he instructed, then glanced up at the Wardens.

"Leave us, ladies," he ordered. "And turn off the recorders."

"Of course."

The guards withdrew.

"This is the last time we will meet, Admiral Roberts," Walkingstick said quietly. "That's not a threat," he continued instantly as Kyle began to pull away from him. "It's a statement of fact.

"Your freedom will be gained shortly," he continued. "An ambassador for the Commonwealth is already heading to Alliance space to negotiate a cease-fire and, hopefully, a peace treaty. There is no question in anyone's mind that the prompt and efficient return of all of our POWS as well as all occupied systems will be the minimum offer we can make."

"Most likely, yes," Kyle said carefully.

"That will be arranged between your government, the ambassador, and the NSJWs," Walkingstick continued. "I am leaving."

"So soon?" So late? In Walkingstick's place, Kyle would have had his fleet in Sol already, pledging his undying allegiance to the central government and doing everything he could to keep the Commonwealth together.

But then, Kyle freely admitted he didn't understand Terran politics.

"The choice is no longer mine," the Marshal told him. "It falls to me now to convince my own government that the Commonwealth must be saved. Either they will see the light and save it…or I will find a way to save my nation without them."

Kyle hid his wince. What Walkingstick was saying was quite close to what he'd been thinking, but suggested that the Commonwealth government might not be willing to believe the other man's pledges of loyalty.

He definitely didn't understand Terran politics.

"So, now what?" he asked.

"You and your people will remain here," Walkingstick told him. "Once the ambassador has arranged for your release, presumably the Alliance will send someone to collect you."

The Marshal shrugged.

"I have done all within my power to guarantee your safety and return," he half-whispered. "I owe you that in exchange for justice for Kematian."

"There are those who believe there has not been true justice for Kematian," Kyle replied.

Walkingstick nodded.

"Oh, I know. You told me that yourself," he reminded the Federation officer with a forced smile. "But I have a duty now. So do you."

The Marshal extended his hand.

"I could hate you for what you planned and your people inflicted on my nation," he said softly, the hand hanging unwavering in the air. "But the reverse is also true. We have done our duty. We shall see where it leads us both."

Kyle hesitated for a few more seconds, then shook Walkingstick's hand.

"I won't wish you good luck," he told the other man. "But…I understand."

"That, Admiral Roberts, is all men like us can do for each other."

48

Niagara System
06:00 November 14, 2737 Earth Standard Meridian
Date/Time
Alliance Seventh Fleet

Avalon BLAZED out of the Cherenkov radiation of her Alcubierre-Stetson emergence flash with every sensor online, Q-probes flashing from her probe bays and her first cycle of fighter launchers coming alive.

Vice Commodore Michelle Williams-Alvarez led her people into space, wave after wave of brand-new Reaper-type starfighters. Project Armada's first product had hit mass production just in time for the freighters carrying ships out to Via Somnia to be packed full of the new ships.

The new bombers hadn't arrived yet, but the newly repaired and refitted Seventh Fleet had been entirely reequipped with the eighth-generation starfighters. As a hundred starships flickered out of Alcubierre drive around *Avalon,* hundreds and then thousands of the tiny parasites flared out around them.

Between Forty-First and the Medusa fleets, two hundred and fifteen ships had been sent into Commonwealth space. Only a hundred had been fit for combat when Admiral Rothenberg had decided to move out immediately...but with the Reapers, that should be enough.

"Ma'am?" Eklund said slowly. "There's no fleet here."

She paused, studying the tactical feed.

One hundred Alliance carriers, battleships and cruisers had emerged from Alcubierre. A second wave of twenty assault transports and another four capital ships would arrive in about twelve hours.

And they were the only starships in the system. The immense fleet anchorage in orbit of Ontario was empty, though its fortresses and repair yards continued to glitter with electromagnetic radiation.

"Defenses are intact," Eklund continued. "I'm reading dozens of fortresses and fighter platforms around the fleet base and the planet, but no warships at all. None of the Marine transports that should be here.

"Nothing."

Michelle found herself chuckling at the ridiculousness of it all. They'd brought a fleet that could crush the eighty starships they knew Walkingstick had—and his fleet was gone. Completely.

"Well," she said after a moment, "*that* was unexpected. What about the defenses?"

"They're limited to lightspeed sensors," Eklund pointed out. "They won't know about our arrival for another forty seconds, and we won't see their reaction for a couple of minutes after that."

He smiled darkly.

"Best guess is that they have about three thousand Katanas and Longbows," he noted. "They're doomed."

"I wonder if they're prepared to accept the inevitable for once?" Michelle asked. "I'd rather not be in both the first and last battles of the damned war!"

KYLE WAS AWOKEN by the sound of an argument right outside the door to the slightly nicer cell that his people had insisted become his quarters.

"If you do not stand aside, I will have the Wardens stun you," an authoritative female voice barked. "I understand what you feel your responsibilities are, but I do not have time for this game!"

Since they were only issued the one style and type of garment, dressing had become entirely second nature after two weeks. By the time the speaker had finished threatening his bodyguards, Kyle was dressed and flinging open the door to his cell.

"What is going on?" he asked calmly.

A quartet of Wardens and two youthful men in carefully tailored black suits were standing off with the two Marines outside his door. Those two women might have been unarmed, but they certainly looked prepared to throw down with the Wardens and the...security detail?

The ninth person outside his door had probably been the speaker. She was a tall woman with a wide face that looked used to smiling and long dark hair, clad in a suit tailored almost identically to her security detail.

"I need to speak to you," she barked at Kyle. "Your guards' enthusiasm is commendable, but we have very little time if we are to avoid bloodshed!"

Kyle smiled cheerfully.

"I find myself suddenly extremely willing to hear you out, ma'am," he told her. "Your office or mine?"

His feeble attempt at humor at least calmed his guards and earned him an appreciative nod from the Wardens.

"No bloodshed here," she told him. "Come with me, Admiral Roberts."

He shrugged at his guards and fell in behind her. The assorted security guards fell in behind them like the tail of a pair of comets as she led the way.

"I am Premier Jessica Nkele," the dark-haired woman told him as they walked. "The elected representative of the people of Niagara. I answer, of course, to the Star Chamber of the Commonwealth."

"I am surprised to see a system executive in my, ah, lack of office," Kyle replied. "What do you need?"

"I need you to talk your people out of blowing my orbitals to hell," she said flatly. "There's an entire fleet heading towards my planet, and while I may not be a military woman, I can run the math between a hundred warships and thirty-six fortresses in my head."

"Ah." The Alliance was here, then. That was good news—but he could see Nkele's concern. "You realize, of course, that we *are* still at war?"

"The ambassador was sent to negotiate a peace treaty," she pointed out. "I am prepared to offer Niagara's...parole, I think is the term?

"We won't fight you and won't participate in any future war against you. But your fleet will pick you up and leave. No fighting. No death."

Kyle nodded slowly.

"Yeah. I can do that, Premier Nkele."

NKELE LED him across the vacuum moat and into a small office, then linked him into the station's implant network.

"You should be able to send a message from here, yes?" she asked. "I assume you'll want privacy?"

"If you would be so kind," he agreed.

To his surprise, Nkele gestured for her guards to leave and exited the room with them. There was just him and his two self-assigned Marine bodyguards.

"You may as well be seated, troopers," he told them. "Without q-coms, this could take a while."

He fully accessed the station's systems. Nkele was being true to her word—not only did he have communications access, he also had full access to the station's sensors. He could see the massive armada bearing down on Ontario.

He didn't feel particularly bad for the planet that had spent the last few years hosting the people determined to conquer his home nation, but…the war was over. He didn't have it in him to let people die just because that news hadn't made its way around yet.

Vice Admiral Kyle Roberts sighed and turned on the pickup.

"Alliance Fleet, this is Kyle Roberts," he greeted them. "I assume I have been declared missing, presumed dead, but as you can see, I was taken prisoner by the Commonwealth.

"I have attached my level-one authentication sequences to this message. This channel is not secure enough for standard interrogations for level-two and higher authentications. My understanding is that the locals will happily deliver me to a vessel of your choice for those authentications.

"The Niagara System government does not want a battle today," he continued. "Walkingstick has returned to Sol to deal with internal Commonwealth business—and there is an ambassador on their way to Alliance space to negotiate the end of the war.

"Which means that I don't believe *we* want a battle today. The Premier has offered to release all Alliance POWs and offer the parole of the Niagara System."

He smirked.

"For obvious reasons, I do not regard myself as empowered to negotiate on the Alliance's behalf, but…I think her offer is genuine.

"And speaking merely for my own personal desire to no longer be a prisoner of war, I strongly recommend we take it."

49

Castle System
12:00 November 26, 2737 Earth Standard Meridian
Date/Time
Castle Orbit

IT WAS FITTING to Kyle that he returned to Castle at the end of the war aboard *Avalon*. The big ship had been his first real command after the loss of her namesake, his first *acting* command. He was a passenger on her this time, but it was still the only ship he would have wanted to come home in.

The big carrier had docked with Merlin Orbital Four, giving him momentary flashbacks to returning from the Battle of Tranquility with the crippled old *Avalon*. He and his trio of guards—the Marines from the POW camp hadn't given up the duty yet, and he'd used a little bit of the influence his stars gave him to get them a permanent assignment—were almost lost in the crowds as they boarded the station.

Six capital ships of the Castle Federation Space Navy had docked within minutes of each other, half of the dozen ships escorting liberated prisoners from Niagara home. The six military stations were going to see a massive amount of traffic over the next few weeks, too.

The news had been confirmed earlier that morning: Ambassador Hope Burns and the leadership of the Alliance had extended the initial cease-fire into a ten-year armistice to allow for careful negotiation of a longer-term peace treaty.

The war was over. So far as the civilians could tell, the Alliance had won.

Kyle had read the terms of the armistice agreement. The Alliance *had* won. Commonwealth forces would be withdrawn from all occupied Alliance systems. The independence of Presley was recognized. Via Somnia was officially a joint Castle Federation–Coraline Imperium protectorate.

It was all over.

And he was struggling through the crowds, trying to find a specific set of faces. There were too many people there, and even his stars and Marines only bought him so much space. Mira was *supposed* to be there, but he couldn't find her.

"Admiral!" a familiar female voice bellowed over the crowd. "Hey, people! Make way for the damned Fox!"

He turned to see Kelly Mason, in full Navy Captain's uniform, sending a quartet of uniformed Marines forward to intercept him. A fifth uniformed Marine stood next to her, holding a tiny blond baby.

The crowd heard Mason's words and for the first time actually turned to look at Kyle. The result was impressive. A corridor opened between him and the Captain, the crowds suddenly all focused on him.

It was frankly embarrassing, but he put on his biggest grin and walked toward his old XO.

"Captain Mason," he greeted her. "Congratulations on the promotion."

"Thank you," she replied. "We've been trying to keep people's kids *out* of the scrum," she continued, glancing around at the chaos around them, "with only mixed success.

"That said, your ex is engaged to an MFA, *your* fiancée is a bloody Admiral in her own right and *you* are the Stellar Fox." Mason grinned.

"I used that collection of gravitas to take over a private meeting room and stuffed your family in there."

"Thank you," he breathed. "You are, as always, a lifesaver."

Mason shook her head.

"Consider it repayment for *not* asking for me as your flag captain," she told him. "I had *Sunset* ready to go to war with you, but I won't pretend I wasn't glad to be able to stay home with Mike here."

Kyle smiled at the chubby little boy. From this distance, he could see both Michael Stanford and Kelly Mason in him.

"Meeting room, then?" he asked quietly.

"Follow me."

KYLE WAS AT MOST three centimeters inside the room when a bundle of hyperactive teenager collided with him, Jacob Kerensky burying his face in his father's midsection in a moment of relief.

"Wasn't sure," his son whispered. "Mom and Mira and Dan all said nobody *knew*, but the news kept saying you were definitely dead!"

Kyle grimaced.

"I'm not dead," he promised Jacob. He shook his head sadly, considering the officers and spacers who *wouldn't* be coming home. "I'm not dead, Jacob," he repeated, hugging the boy.

He looked over his son's head at the three adults waiting in the room. They were all standing back to let Jacob hug his father, but then Lisa slipped forward and put a hand on Jacob's shoulder.

"You do have to share him, you know," she told her son with a laugh. Her embrace was much quicker—but with Mira barely steps behind her, that speed was as meaningful as Jacob's refusal to let go.

Lisa stepped aside, leaving Kyle facing Mira. Everyone else in the room was as unimportant they could be as he met her eyes.

"Hi," he said lamely.

"Hi yourself," she told him. "You, *Admiral*, are in a lot of trouble. You promised me you'd come home."

He gestured wordlessly around him.

"I know what the odds were of you surviving when you stayed

behind," Mira reminded him. "If you die on me, Admiral Kyle Roberts, I will kill you."

Kyle laughed and shook his head at her.

"The feeling is mutual, Admiral Solace."

Then she was in his arms, her lips pressing against his...and everything was right in the universe.

50

Sol System
12:00 December 4, 2737 Earth Standard Meridian
Date/Time
Earth

SKYLINK ONE WAS the first space elevator humanity had ever built, one of the two that linked the carefully allocated rings of Earth's orbital industry to the ground. Its base was an immense floating platform, with several huge buoyancy tanks.

When the Commonwealth had been formed, one of those tanks had been turned into the Star Chamber of the Interstellar Congress of the Terran Commonwealth, with no concern for expense. Massive floor-to-ceiling windows opened out onto the Atlantic Ocean, and hundreds of chairs were laid out for the Senators and Congresspeople who ran the Commonwealth.

Immense banners hung from the walls, bearing the image of each member world of the Commonwealth. Some of those banners were obsolete now, James Walkingstick noted as he entered the room.

They wouldn't even know which ones for a while. Days, weeks. It would be months before even the crude solution of carrying messages aboard Alcubierre-drive couriers, freighters and warships reached any level of true organization and usefulness.

For now, these people ran the Commonwealth. They might not have contact with their homeworlds, but they had the authority to give the fleet orders, to send out couriers with orders for officers of the Commonwealth Navy to report back to Earth for their "justice."

The room was deathly silent as he walked along the aisle toward the front stage. It was rare for a room of over seven hundred politicians to be that quiet. It was probably due to the battalion of Marines surrounding the room, combat rifles leveled on the people who *thought* they controlled the Commonwealth.

They hadn't even given him a chance to talk. The moment his fleet had arrived in Sol, they'd ordered Home Fleet into action. Pulled together from scraps, Home Fleet's twenty-two ships had stood no chance against his fleet…and had declined to obey those orders.

Those ships were now part of *his* fleet. The command center at Ceres had acknowledged his authority. The Commonwealth Navy would now follow his orders, not those of the politicians in this room.

That was a terrifying thought, but it was where he was now.

General Krizman walked to his left and two steps behind, Tasker to his right, an equal distance behind. Four Marines followed, and over a thousand more filled the chamber, enforcing the silence.

Michael Burns, the head of the Committee on Unification, and a frail-looking woman with pale skin and hair—Speaker Janet Lane, the leader of the Congress and generally accepted second-most powerful person in the Commonwealth.

With the President a complete nonentity, the *actual* most powerful person was arguably Michael Burns.

Or had been. Now…now even James wasn't sure who was in charge, but he walked up to face those two politicians in silence.

"When I warned you, I expected you to run," Burns said quietly, ignoring Lane's surprised glare. "Bringing your fleet was treason, a Rubicon of unparalleled proportions."

James winced.

"If you were prepared to execute me, you were prepared to destroy the Navy out of paranoia," he said quietly. The acoustics of the Chamber meant everyone could hear the entire conversation. "You left me few choices."

"So, you chose treason?" Lane demanded.

"I chose my oath," James replied. "To protect and serve the *Commonwealth*. Not the Congress. Not the Committee. Not the Senate or the Assembly. The Commonwealth.

"With the network gone, we must hold together our nation with duct tape and blood until we have restored it. This is not the time to turn on each other! But you turned on me."

The silence continued. No one spoke as James met the two politicians' gazes.

Then Burns stepped forward, ignoring the weapons that snapped up to point at him.

"You know how this ends now, James," the old man said firmly. "From the moment you left Niagara with a *fleet*, you knew how this had to end. You set your feet upon an ancient path that can only end here. Can only end in one way. If you would save the Commonwealth, then do it," the Senator ordered. "You leave us only one choice."

Burns knelt, his words booming out across the Star Chamber with unexpected force.

"Ave, Imperator Terrae!"

ABOUT THE AUTHOR

Glynn Stewart is the author of *Starship's Mage,* a bestselling science fiction and fantasy series where faster-than-light travel is possible–but only because of magic. His other works include science fiction series *Duchy of Terra, Castle Federation* and *Vigilante,* as well as the urban fantasy series *ONSET* and *Changeling Blood.*

Writing managed to liberate Glynn from a bleak future as an accountant. With his personality and hope for a high-tech future intact, he lives in Kitchener, Ontario with his wife, their cats, and an unstoppable writing habit.

facebook.com/glynnstewartauthor

twitter.com/glynnstewart

OTHER BOOKS BY GLYNN STEWART

For release announcements join the mailing list or visit GlynnStewart.com

Castle Federation

Space Carrier Avalon

Stellar Fox

Battle Group Avalon

Q-Ship Chameleon

Rimward Stars

Operation Medusa

Duchy of Terra

The Terran Privateer

Duchess of Terra

Terra and Imperium

Vigilante (With Terry Mixon)

Heart of Vengeance

Oath of Vengeance

Bound by Stars

Bound by Law

Bound by Honor (upcoming)

Starship's Mage

Starship's Mage

Hand of Mars

Voice of Mars

Alien Arcana

Judgment of Mars

Starship's Mage: UnArcana Rebellions

UnArcana Stars (upcoming)

Starship's Mage: Red Falcon

Interstellar Mage

Mage-Provocateur

Agents of Mars (upcoming)

Exile

Ashen Stars

Exile (upcoming)

ONSET

ONSET: To Serve and Protect

ONSET: My Enemy's Enemy

ONSET: Blood of the Innocent

ONSET: Stay of Execution

Changeling Blood

Changeling's Fealty

Hunter's Oath

Noble's Honor (upcoming)

Fantasy Stand Alone Novels

Children of Prophecy

City in the Sky

CPSIA information can be obtained
at www.ICGtesting.com
Printed in the USA
LVHW020432131118
596826LV00006B/214/P